THE LIVING DEAD

Brant crept silently down the hallway and paused in front of the first lighted door. His sweating palm was twisting the knob when he heard a footstep on the stairs behind him. He whirled, gripping the butcher knife hard, and moved toward the stairs just as three shots rang out and bullets ripped through the hollow wooden door behind him.

Brant threw the door open and saw Josh Lunger crouched beside his parents' bed frantically dropping spent shells from the .22. A box of live rounds sat on the floor beside him.

"You can't win!" Josh cried. "They'll get you tonight and you'll be converted! You'll be sorry you hit me when Seth finds out!"

"What will Seth do, Josh?" Brant asked.

"He'll punish you! He'll let you die and stay dead if you don't do what he says . . ."

<u>BOOK YOUR PLACE ON OUR WEBSITE</u> <u>AND MAKE THE</u> <u>READING CONNECTION!</u>

We've created a customized website just for our very special readers, where you can get the inside scoop on everything that's going on with Zebra, Pinnacle and Kensington books.

When you come online, you'll have the exciting opportunity to:

- View covers of upcoming books

- Read sample chapters

- Learn about our future publishing schedule (listed by publication month *and author*)

- Find out when your favorite authors will be visiting a city near you

- Search for and order backlist books from our online catalog

- Check out author bios and background information

- Send e-mail to your favorite authors

- Meet the Kensington staff online

- Join us in weekly chats with authors, readers and other guests

- Get writing guidelines

- AND MUCH MORE!

Visit our website at
http://www.kensingtonbooks.com

RISEN

J. KNIGHT

PINNACLE BOOKS
Kensington Publishing Corp.
http://www.kensingtonbooks.com

To my beautiful and loving wife
Julie
And to my parents
Alice and E. A. Strnad

Special thanks to
Stuart Bernstein

PROLOGUE

The murdered man's body floated near the bottom of the Cooves County Reservoir.

A twelve-foot length of rusted chain pinned his arms to his sides, bound his wrists, ran down between his legs and looped twice around his ankles. From there it plunged straight down another four feet where the last link clung to a metal pole sunk ten inches into a ragged block of concrete.

The few hairs on his nearly-bald head waved like seaweed on currents stirred up by lazy catfish. Mud swirled around his face. Turtles nibbled his fingertips.

The murdered man woke. His eyes flashed open, alive with comprehension and fear. He strained to free his arms, kicked and wiggled and squirmed. His body thrashed convulsively.

He wrenched at the chains around his ankles and wrists. He twisted his body one way and the other, fighting the impulse to scream. Panic rose in his throat.

When he could hold it no longer, the murdered man's breath exploded from his mouth. His terrified eyes followed the ascent of bubbles as they fled to the surface. His lungs drew in fish-soiled water. He gagged. His heaving chest pumped water with great spasmodic gulps.

He pulled at the chain, testing for the one weak link that would let his body follow his breath to freedom. The metal post rocked like a child's lead-bottomed toy, but the concrete block refused to budge from the lake floor. The chains held fast.

Bubbles exploded on the surface of the lake, shattering the sliver of crescent moon reflected on the surface. The water boiled for long moments. Ripples chased each other toward the shore.

Below, the murdered man's body went limp, its drama spent. It undulated in the dying eddies of his struggle. Mud began the tedious process of settling around the concrete block while agitated fish resumed their rounds.

Above, the last bubble broke on the surface. The ripples died, the moon assembled its scattered parts, and the water lay smooth as a sheet.

DAY ONE, FRIDAY

ONE

From his desk at the *Cooves County Times*, Brant Kettering could keep tabs on most of downtown Anderson.

The tiny office was one of two dozen store fronts located along Main Street. There was a hardware store, a movie house that charged two dollars a seat and was open only on Friday and Saturday nights, an insurance office, a grocery, the Sheriff's office . . . the usual assortment of Mom and Pop businesses that had served Anderson for the past fifty years. The only concession to modern times was the video rental store that had been opened by the owner of the movie house whose philosophy was, if television was going to drive him out of business, he'd as soon drive himself.

Parking was head-in and meterless. The streets were wide and lined with mature oaks. The tiny park that made up the town square boasted eight park benches, four trash cans, and a civil war cannon set in place by the local Optimists.

The cannon was aimed directly at Brant's head, a fact that seemed especially profound every Friday around noon when he knew he should have this week's *Cooves County Times* written and laid out on the Mac. Sloan Malone, the local printer, needed the layouts before lunch if Brant wanted his papers for Saturday distribution. The only way Brant could get a reasonable price on five thousand copies was if Sloan piggybacked Brant's print run with three other regional weeklies. Missing the deadline meant losing money on this

week's edition rather than more or less breaking even after
paying himself a modest salary as reporter, editor, photog-
rapher, typesetter, manager of distribution and executive in
charge of advertising sales.

Brant sat and stared at eight empty column inches on
the computer screen. He toyed with the idea of a humor-
ous piece concerning the Optimists' cannon. What was so
optimistic about setting a cannon in the middle of the town
square? Wasn't that, in fact, a decidedly pessimistic act?
From whom were the Optimists expecting an attack, the
Rotarians?

Experience had taught him, however, that satire did not
play well in Cooves County. Such a piece would surely in-
flame both the Optimists and the Rotarians, and the *Times'*
paltry subscription list could hardly take a hit of that mag-
nitude. After a few tentative opening sentences his finger
mashed the "delete" button.

He'd planned to spend a few inches introducing the new
preacher, Reverend Talbot Small, who'd joined the Anderson community two weeks before. But he'd put off the
interview because preachers made him uncomfortable.
They always wanted to know when they'd see Brant in
church and Brant would stand there digging his finger in
his ear while searching for a polite substitute for "when
Hell freezes over." By now, word of mouth had spread
whatever tales were worth telling about Reverend Small,
which was typical of Anderson. What mere newspaperman
could hope to keep up with the network of busy tongues
that fueled the local rumor mill?

The tension was making itself felt in Brant's neck. He
swiveled his head a few times, then he reached for the telephone to call his stringer at Anderson High School, a senior
student named Tom Culler. The school secretary answered.

"Sorry, Brant. Tom's a no-show today," she said.

"Sick?"

"Friday Flu. The usual gang's absent. Tom, Darren Coombs, Buzzy Hayes, Kent Fredericks. And the Ganger boy, of course."

Brant frowned. Tom had been a top student and a decent reporter. He'd written a column during his junior year, "My Town," that featured probing portraits of Anderson's notable citizens and their ancestors. Probing turned out to be even less popular than satire in Anderson. When Tom's research linked the current mayor's great-grandfather to deliberate attempts to spread smallpox among the local natives back in the 1850s, Brant had had to pull the plug on "My Town" or face the wrath of the entire Anderson political machine, such as it was. In a town this size, you either got along or you got out. Brant hadn't come to Anderson to make waves and "My Town," though cleverly written, was making new enemies for the paper with every edition.

He'd regretted that decision ever since. Yanking Tom's column was all the proof Tom needed that the entire adult world, and especially that of Anderson, was composed of crooks and hypocrites. Brant, an outsider, had been young Tom's lifeline out of cynicism, and Brant had cast him adrift.

In place of his final "My Town" column, Tom had submitted a poem by Emily Dickinson that began, "It fell so low in my regard/I heard it hit the ground." Brant printed the poem despite a prudent policy against verse of any kind. Since then he'd been flooded with unsolicited doggerel praising babies, pigs, springtime, summer, fall, winter and grandmother's old gnarled hands. As penance for what he'd done to Tom, Brant forced himself to read every one before rejecting it.

Tom's contributions to the *Cooves County Times*, which previously had included items on the new low-fat menu at the school cafeteria and the alarming rise in restroom vandalism, ceased abruptly. Brant was calling Tom now out of sheer desperation. Learning that Tom was hanging with the likes of the Ganger boy awakened a new guilt and Brant hung up the phone feeling like a hundred-seventy-five pounds of horse manure.

And he still had eight column inches to fill.

Bleakly he dialed the number for the parsonage and offered his belated welcome to the Reverend Small.

Brant finished modeming his layouts to Sloan Malone and locked up the office behind him. His neck was as tight as a piano wire after the Reverend Small interview. Of course the Reverend had asked when he'd see Brant in church.

"I'm not much of a church-goer," he'd mumbled, meaning, "If you ask me, the church has been responsible for more misery in the form of guilt, shame, and outright bloody warfare than it could make up for with a thousand years of hospital visits and youth volleyball nights, so don't expect to see my hands passing around the collection plate this Sunday or any other."

Brant was swiveling his head and concentrating on the crunching, popping noises from his neck when he stepped into the path of the local mortician, an exuberant and smiling man named, inappropriately, Jedediah Grimm.

Brant was in his late thirties and Grimm was easily ten years his senior, but Grimm's vigor put Brant to shame. Grimm's barrel chest produced a loud, full voice that would have been at home behind Reverend Small's pulpit. Brant couldn't imagine Grimm speaking in the hushed tones of a mortician comforting the bereaved and, since Brant had no family within a five hundred mile radius, he didn't expect to see Jedediah Grimm at work until Brant's own interment, at which point he'd hardly be in any position to observe anything.

"Whoa!" Grimm said as if reining in a team of Clydesdales. His brawny hands caught Brant in the chest and

Brant felt immediately puny and foolish. "That neck again?" Grimm asked.

"Nothing a potion of lime juice and tequila wouldn't cure."

"All it wants is a twist," Grimm offered. "Let me give it a try."

He spun Brant around but Brant ducked skillfully before Grimm could lay hold of his head.

"No offense, but I never take medical advice from a mortician," Brant said.

"Maybe you should have Doc Milford take a look at it. He'll tell you it only wants a twist."

"Maybe I will."

The two men waved their good-byes as Brant headed across Main Street toward Ma's Diner.

The bell on the door announced his arrival. The sole waitress, Peg Culler, turned and gave him a smile. "Hi, stranger," she said. It was their personal joke, a reference to Brant's lack of tenure in Anderson.

Peg remembered their first meeting clearly. She'd told him to sit anywhere and she'd be right with him. He'd said, "Great, but who's going to bring us our food?" Peg was busy juggling four lunch specials and two boats of gravy on the side and didn't realize for a couple of minutes that she'd just been flirted with, however clumsily, by an attractive out-of-towner. By the time it dawned on her, Brant was sitting at the counter and had already helped himself to a menu. He looked up sheepishly as she approached.

"Sorry about the wisecrack," he said.

"Oh, no. It was funny."

"You didn't laugh."

"Well, not funny exactly, but. . . . " Words failed her.

"Droll? Witty? Clever? You can lie and say 'yes' at any time."

Peg laughed genuinely. The stranger had smiled an easy smile and asked what was good.

"The chicken fried steaks come frozen, so they're safe. There's not much damage you can do to mashed potatoes. The gravy's not bad . . . it's Heinz . . . and the green beans are straight from the can."

"I take it Ma's cooking isn't exactly Cordon Bleu."

"If that's French for 'edible,' I'd say no," Peg said. The stranger's eyes were a lovely chestnut brown.

"Recommend the meat loaf?" he asked.

"Were you going to eat it or poison a gopher?"

"I'll take the chicken fry."

Peg had spent the next thirty minutes in a state of grace. Her feet stopped burning and she lost that persistent ache in the small of her back. Even the lousy twenty-five cent tip at table number one didn't bother her.

And for thirty minutes she didn't think about Annie.

Eight months ago:

Rodney Culler chipped at the ice on the Ford's windshield with the corner of his ice scraper. The snow was no big deal, just a two-inch layer of fluff you could brush off in a moment. But the ice beneath the snow was a quarter inch thick, and breaking it out was a pain in the ass.

Inside the car, the defroster exhaled air only slightly warmer than that outside, which was two degrees Fahrenheit. With the wind chill, it was cold enough to freeze the nipples off a mastodon.

Normally Rod would've just started the car and let it run with the heater on for twenty minutes if that's what it took to loosen the ice without all this damn chipping, but he was late getting Annie back to Peg's and she'd give him hell for making her worry. He could call and let her know they'd be late, but then he'd have to talk to her and he was still too pissed off about the divorce to want to do that.

Annie waited impatiently inside the front door. All bundled up in her down parka and wool muffler and snow boots she looked like a stuffed doll, arms practically perpendicular, legs all but immobile. Rod didn't know why Peg made her wear all that crap, like she was going on a damn polar expedition or something, when all she had to do was dash from the front door to the car, then from the car to Peg's. He'd said as much when he'd picked Annie up, and Peg had stubbornly kept adding layers to Annie's outfit.

"What if the car breaks down and she has to walk?" Peg had asked.

"Jesus, Peg, I just live in Isaac. It's thirty fucking miles, not halfway across the Arctic continent."

"You never know. It pays to be prepared."

"Whatever." In the end it was easier to just give in. That was his problem with Peg. He'd always just given in. It made him feel like a pussy just thinking about it. Maybe if he'd slapped her around a little. . . .

Ah, the hell with it.

Chip chip chip. The heater was starting to loosen the ice from underneath. A big chunk broke away, clearing a space big enough to see through. Good enough. Rodney Culler beckoned to his daughter to come on. She did, and of course she left the door open.

"She's only five." Rod could hear Peg's voice in his head as he ran carefully up the frozen walk to close the front door.

"Old enough to know how to close a damn door," he muttered.

Annie had stopped halfway down the walk, waiting for him to catch up.

"What're you waiting for?" he said, giving her a nudge. "Come on. We're late." He ushered her into the car and slammed the door, hurried around and jumped in behind the steering wheel, thinking that he should get some thermal underwear, he was freezing his goddamn nuts off.

He'd moved out of their house in Anderson before the

divorce, as soon as Peg informed him, after seventeen years of marriage, that "it wasn't working out." Rental housing was at a premium since work began on the nuke plant and hundreds of construction workers had moved into the area. He'd been lucky to find a spare bedroom to rent in Isaac, upstairs in the house of an elderly widow. It had been her husband's "snoring room" where he'd been banished for the last twenty-two years of their marriage. The husband had died of pneumonia, which Rod could well believe considering the gale force wind that whipped through the room on these winter nights.

The highway to Anderson was black and slick in spots. The county did a pretty good job of keeping it clear of snow, but now and again Rod would hit an icy patch that spun his wheels for an instant. No big deal, but it made him long for the 4x4 he'd had his eye on before the divorce.

Annie sat silently beside him. She stared out the window at the piles of snow heaped along the roadside by the plows. They were dirty and ugly now with exhaust. Beyond them stretched pure country black.

She seemed to be handling the divorce well, but with a kid this young, who knew what was going on in her head? At Annie's age it was all pony-this and dolly-that. Rod couldn't relate to any of it and, truthfully, would've been happier with another son.

Tom had turned out good, at least so far. The trouble he'd gotten into was minor. God knows Rod was no angel himself at that age, and he'd turned out okay. At least, in his own opinion he had. Peg obviously disagreed.

These thoughts and more were churning around inside Rod's head as he closed on the bridge that spanned the drainage canal. It looked dry and clear and Rod hit it at sixty.

Sheet ice was a fucker, that's for sure. You don't see it, it just sits there invisible on the road, waiting for you, and the instant your wheels hit it you know you're fucked.

Annie's eyes went wide as the Ford lost traction and the rear end slid around and Rod was suddenly cursing as he spun the wheel and pumped the useless brakes. Annie clutched the arm rest and stuck her feet out to brace herself against the dashboard as the car spun around like a carnival ride. The bridge railing flew past the front window and she looked briefly down the road they'd just traveled as the car continued spinning and flying and then there was the railing again and she had to shut her eyes to keep from getting sick.

Rod spun the wheel one way and then the other. It was as if the whole mechanism had come loose and he flashed on spinning the steering wheel of the kiddie cars at the amusement park when he was small and how frustrating it was that it didn't make any damn difference what he did, the cars just kept circling. He felt small again and just as helpless as the Ford spun around once more, spinning and hurtling unchecked across the ice. Annie was screaming and Rod couldn't remember if he'd made her buckle up.

Suddenly the bridge railing shot toward them and there was the impact of metal on metal and a post broke and the car was in the air and Annie was screaming and there was a loud crunch and a shattering of glass and the next thing he knew he was opening his eyes and it was quiet and Annie wasn't moving and something in his chest felt really, really fucked.

And God help him, his last thought as darkness closed in was that Peg was going to kill him.

Peg saw Brant heading toward the diner from the newspaper office. She stole a peppermint from the basket by the cash register and popped it into her mouth. She looked away so that she could turn and smile at him when the bell on the door announced his arrival.

"Hi, stranger," she said. "What'll it be?"

"Something to rot my gut and make me forget my troubles," Brant replied.

"One lunch special, coming up. Cuppa decaf?"

"If that's the best you can do."

Brant gazed at Peg while she poured the coffee. She was pretty enough, getting a little full in the hips but that was okay. His own figure would never land him a role in a Hanes commercial. Peg was bright and made him laugh, which wasn't that easy these days. All in all, he'd be quite delighted to spend his declining years—and he hoped to have seventy or eighty of them—with this woman.

"Hey, when are we going out again?" he asked. "How about Saturday? We'll drive out to Junction City, take in a movie. . . . "

"Can't. I'll be—"

Brant finished her sentence with her: "—at the hospital."

She smiled at him. Any man in his right mind would've quit asking her out after hearing the same refusal so many times, but not Brant. Not yet. The day would come, though. She wouldn't notice it at first, but then, in the middle of filling a sugar dispenser or washing her hair, she'd realize that Brant hadn't asked her out in a long time, and she'd have to acknowledge that some invisible marker had been passed in her and Brant's lives, and that the days of courtship were over.

She'd gone out with him once, while the giddy feeling was still in her head and the butterflies fluttered in her stomach, and it had gone well. She sensed a kind heart behind his cynicism and a strength of character that needed only true adversity to bring out. Unfortunately Brant had never been tested, only aggravated, worn down like a pair of shoes. So he ended up in Anderson, where life didn't walk so fast because there wasn't much of anyplace to go.

She'd only realized all this later, as she'd gotten to know him better a few minutes at a time. Her son Tom had seemed mightily impressed by Brant for awhile, but then there was that trouble over the "My Town" column and Brant's stock bottomed out in Tom's eyes. It was all or nothing with Tom, as with most teenagers.

Peg was willing to accept Brant's apparent lack of ambition, especially in Anderson where ambitions ran along the lines of big fish and bumper crops and where pulling a weekly newspaper out of thin air was something of a miracle. And she felt confident that, in a time of crisis, he'd rise to the occasion and get them through.

But Peg's crisis point was in the past. Her husband was dead, her daughter in a coma, on life support. All that was left was getting through the daily grind of battles with hospital staff and insurance companies and the slow erosion of hope, and she wasn't sure that Brant was up to that particular task.

Besides, it made her feel guilty to be out and having fun with a man while her daughter lay in a stark hospital room, oxygen being pumped into her lungs, nutrition dripped into her veins from a tube. Could Annie hear? Did she think? Did she know when Peg was there and when she wasn't? On the chance that she did, it was Peg's duty to be there. Every day, every hour she could spare.

So she and Brant carried on in a kind of Möbius strip of flirtation that went nowhere but back around to where it began. Outwardly he seemed to accept this pattern as well as she did, but Peg knew that it would wear thin in time. He'd stop making eyes at her and then it would be just friendship between them. Maybe he'd find a younger woman and they'd move away, and that would be that. Sad and bittersweet.

"How is Annie?" Brant asked.

"The same."

In the kitchen, a crusty Asian man named Ma plopped the hamburger and a scoop of cold french fries on a plate, set the plate on the warming shelf and called to Peg through the service window.

"Order up!" Ma said.

Peg gave Brant a smile as she turned away.

As he watched Peg deliver the hamburger, Brant ruminated on how much he'd like to feel his hands on her buttocks, which he imagined as cool and white and smooth as silk. Then he considered what beasts men were, himself in particular.

Brant was digging a fork suspiciously through his chopped sirloin, thinking he'd just felt something in his mouth that was shaped oddly like an insect leg, when the shift occurred. So he didn't notice.

Peg was wiping the crumbs and water rings off the booth in the corner when it happened, and she didn't notice, either.

Doc Milford was checking Annie Culler's feeding tube and Deputy Haws was sleeping late to prepare for the night shift and the five boys who'd gypped school were passing a joint around and pooling their money for a twelve-pack when it happened, and none of them noticed.

In fact, no one in the entire town of Anderson noticed.

But there were artifacts:

Ants in a colony out by the reservoir began to feast on their eggs.

A flock of crows descended on a mockingbird and pecked it until nothing recognizable remained.

Merle Tippert's stubborn old dog that everyone said was too mean to die lay its chin on its paws and quietly gave up the ghost.

A young boy on his first hunt found the courage to pull the head off a wounded quail, something his father didn't think he could do.

And Madge Duffy, her face still swollen from last night's

blows, put a kitchen knife to the neck of her sleeping husband and sliced his neck from ear to ear.

Artifacts.

Ripples.

Seth had begun.

TWO

The sun was going down as Franz Klempner drove his old John Deere back to the house. A jaunty mutt named "Elmer" ran barking alongside.

When Elmer was still living with city folk, confined to a two-bedroom apartment, he had expressed his exuberant personality by devouring anything he could get his jaws around. He began with the sofa cushions. Once those were reduced to shreds he attacked the sofa itself. Soon it looked like a showroom display of innerspring construction. He also munched on remote controls, compact discs, table legs, books, shoes, rugs, fireplace logs, laundry from the hamper, and one afternoon he swallowed the owners' prized cassette of jazz tunes recorded from old 78s that hadn't survived the last move. It may have been while they were unspooling magnetic tape through Elmer's rear orifice that the owners decided Elmer might be better off as a farm dog.

They made a midnight run to the country and adopted Elmer out to the wild, confident that his natural instincts would provide for him.

Several days later Franz Klempner found the half-starved dog lying in his field, too weak to stand. He carried Elmer to the house and fed him beef broth and kippers until the dog dropped off to sleep. When Elmer awoke, it was on an old horse blanket in a warm corner of Franz' kitchen. He'd slept there every night since.

Franz was no less kind to his demented wife, Irma. Both Irma and Franz were in their mid-sixties. They'd been married for forty-seven years. Irma had been insane, to some degree, for most of those years.

It was hard to pinpoint exactly when Irma Louise Pritchett, now Irma Klempner, had gone around the bend mentally. She'd been raised since the age of five by an aunt and uncle in nearby Isaac after her parents died under mysterious circumstances. Maybe those circumstances were buried deep in her brain, and maybe the memory had dug itself loose over time, burrowing up into Irma's conscious mind like a tapeworm that ate away a little more gray matter with each passing year.

By high school she was considered eccentric, which may have been what young Franz found so attractive. Strange, haunted women were a scarce commodity in Cooves County and Franz was hungry for a little adventure. He might have joined the Navy or bummed around the world or gone off to work on the pipeline in Alaska, but instead he married Irma. They exchanged vows in the Methodist church in Anderson.

Certainly by his second or third wedding anniversary, Franz must have suspected that something in Irma's head wasn't wired quite right. For one thing, she'd stopped talking. Not all at once, but gradually, as if her supply of words were running short and finally gave out altogether, a kind of verbal menopause that was complete by the time Irma hit twenty-two.

She had nightmares of a shapeless black thing that threatened to swallow her, nightmares from which she would awaken soaking wet with sweat. She was given to long periods of sitting motionlessly in a corner of the bedroom, her eyes fixed on the door. She became ever more careless about her appearance. By the age of thirty-five, she no longer bathed unless Franz took her by the hand and guided her to the tub, though once she was hip deep in soapy water she was quite able to wash, dry, and dress herself.

It was as if certain relays in her brain had become corroded and undependable. Sometimes she would simply stop and stand in one place until Franz found her and started her going again.

Other times she would scream. For no reason that Franz could discern, she would let out such a bloodcurdling howl of terror that he could hear it even over the chugging of the tractor. He'd race to the house to find her wedged into the cupboard or hiding under the bed or cowering in the fireplace, grimy with soot.

And yet, much of the time she functioned, if not well, at least tolerably. Her housekeeping was not the worst in town. She cooked all the meals. She tended a garden. She canned beets and rhubarb and peaches and tomatoes. She liked to rock in front of the fireplace while Franz read to her from the Bible.

Franz knew plenty of couples whose marriages were less gratifying.

Franz tromped into the mud porch, pounding the dirt from his boots and slapping it from his clothes. Elmer the dog bounded in behind him and made straight for the kitchen. Irma's careless attitude toward spills was a godsend to Elmer, who considered the floor his twenty-four hour, self-serve deli.

Franz announced his arrival. His nose warned him that this was a bad cooking day. (He'd disconnected the smoke alarms years ago, never mind what the fire department said.) He washed up and sat down at the kitchen table, his thin hair slicked back and his skin smelling of Lifebuoy.

Irma Klempner set a plate in front of him containing a baked potato and something black that might once have been a decent pork chop. She brought her own plate to the table and began to eat silently. He smiled at her, noticing that her old print dress was buttoned wrong and that her hair was badly in need of brushing. He hoped she didn't see him slip the charred chop under the table to Elmer.

"I'll give your hair a brushing tonight," he said. Irma didn't appear to have heard him, but she liked to have her hair brushed and later she would bring him the brush herself if he forgot. In this and other subtle ways they communicated, however obliquely.

They retired to the living room after dinner. Franz lit some kindling under a log in the fireplace and when the fire was roaring to his satisfaction, he took his seat under the reading lamp. Irma sat in her rocker and Franz read to her from John.

He read, "Jesus said to her, 'I am the resurrection and the life; he who believes in me, though he die, yet shall he live, and whoever lives and believes in me shall never die.'"

If he had been watching her, Franz would have noticed the sudden tightness around Irma's mouth. He would have seen her wrinkled lips pucker as she sucked at her cheeks, and he'd have seen her breath turn quick and shallow. But when reading the Bible, Franz sometimes felt himself transported. The room he was sitting in would vanish like an old dream, and Franz would be striding boldly among the Pharisees or giving sight to the blind or staggering down the streets of Jerusalem under the weight of his crucifixion cross, bound for Calvary. Tonight he was at Jesus' side for the resurrection of Lazarus.

"She said to him, 'Yes, Lord; I believe that you are the Christ, the Son of God, he who is coming into the world.'"

Irma gripped the arms of the rocker. Her fingers closed around the carved wood and squeezed it hard. The veins and tendons stood out under her thin, aging skin. She began to rock harder.

Franz continued reading. He read how Mary came to Jesus and fell at his feet, weeping in lamentation over her dead brother, Lazarus. He read how the Jews followed Jesus and Mary to the tomb of Lazarus and how Jesus commanded the stone over the tomb to be removed.

"Jesus said to her, 'Did I not tell you that if you would believe you would see the glory of God?' So they took away the stone."

Irma's old woman heart beat fast in her chest. Her body felt cold and frail. The dark unnamable thing rose from the horizon, blotting out all light, and towered over her. She saw it as clearly as Franz saw the words on the page before him, and when she closed her eyes she could feel it closing on her, engulfing her, swallowing her whole. . . .

"When he had said this, he cried with a loud voice, 'Lazarus, come out!'"

Irma felt the dark nothingness wrap around her and squeeze her in an icy fist. Her body was paralyzed, unable even to squirm in the grip of the thing. She felt herself being drawn away, down, down, down into the lair of the thing. In another instant she would disappear into the subterranean nether world beneath the feet of the living and dissolve into the suffocating being of the thing. She drew in her breath, filling her aging lungs until she felt they would burst.

Irma screamed with the terror that inhabited every nerve and vessel of her fragile body. She screamed from deep within her soul, screamed to shatter the grip of the black encompassing thing, screamed for her life.

Franz leaped from his chair and took his wife of forty-seven years in his arms. He held her close and whispered soothing words into her ear. He knew from experience that the words didn't matter. It was the sound of his voice that would draw her back from whatever oblivion she had witnessed. Just soothing words, nothing words, words spoken with love.

But tonight there was something sinister in the air. A sterile coolness. The dead smell of an ancient tomb. Something that whispered of death without redemption, of purgatory. Something that made Franz Klempner shudder and made Irma Louise Klempner scream and keep screaming until sheer physical exhaustion overcame her and she collapsed, spent, in her husband's arms.

Tom Culler took another swallow of beer and marveled at the profound effect digging a hole and filling it with water could have on a community of human beings.

That's all the Cooves County Reservoir was, really, just a hole with water in it. At some point in the history of Cooves County a bunch of enterprising men known as the Army Corps of Engineers diverted water from the river and regulated its flow into a big hole they'd dug in the countryside, and the reservoir was born. Trees were planted along the shore and a road was graded into being between the reservoir and the freeway, and the reservoir became a recreational lake. Bass were dumped into the water annually and pulled out again one by one by fishermen. Boats were launched, canoes paddled.

Area nudists had claimed one tiny cove as their own. They built a dock and were the scandal of the county for doing sober and in the daylight what decent folks did only after dark and half a bottle of Jack Daniels.

For many teenagers the reservoir was the make-out point of choice. These days, of course, a lot more went on than mere making out. Guilt—even Protestant guilt, which is a ninety-eight-pound weakling next to its musclebound cousins in the Jewish and Catholic faiths—was still a force to be reckoned with, and the natural setting lent a certain wholesomeness to all sexual proceedings, even the clumsy backseat fumbling of the young. Somehow slipping your hand under a girl's shirt didn't seem quite so sinful under a full moon beside a body of water under maples and oaks murmuring in the breeze.

No good free thing exists without opposition and the Cooves County Reservoir make-out point was no exception. Local authorities had tried to close the lake road after dark with a padlock and a chain strung between two poles set in concrete, but the effort was doomed from the outset. Horny teenagers quickly dug out the poles and left the whole works on the nudists' dock, hoping the nudists would get the blame. (They didn't.)

The authorities tried two more times to block the road and each time the roadblock found its way to the nudists. The third time it stayed on the dock until the nudists got tired of it and coiled it up on the shore. There it remained, finding function at last as a home to various beetles, snakes and pill bugs.

Tom turned these thoughts over in his mind until they seemed profound. They might have formed the spine of a "My Town" column if he was still writing it, if Brant Kettering didn't value subscription revenue over Truth. Tom should've known that Brant was a man of tin. Who else would end up in Anderson, the middle-aged owner/editor of a no-account weekly? That Tom had been taken in by such an obvious fraud made him feel even more like a small-town hick.

Then there was the whole Cindy affair.

Cindy Robertson was the other waitress doing time at Ma's Diner. She was a pretty redhead with a sweet body that tended to plumpness, which was fine with Tom who never cared for those boyish, thin-as-a-rail women in women's magazines anyway. Cindy had a quick mind and she made Tom laugh and she was the best kisser Tom had discovered in Cooves County. He'd been on the verge of discovering what other powers she possessed when he'd backed away instinctively.

Cindy was not going to be a casual thing, he could see that. He felt her pulling at him quietly, with a kind of gravity or magnetism or something, not with anything she said or did but simply with who she was. And unfortunately, who she was, was an Andersonite. She'd grown up in Anderson, was being schooled in Anderson, worked in Anderson, and worst of all seemed perfectly content in Anderson. Tom knew that Cindy would not be one of that majority of young people who moved away at the first opportunity. Even if she went to college, and she was certainly smart enough for that, she'd be back. Some miswired circuit in her brain actually liked small town life. She'd found her little plot of earth, it nurtured her, and she would gladly live there for the rest of her life, which struck Tom as a fate worse than death.

So he'd broken it off with her on the basis of a gut level feeling and left it until later to figure out why, when it was too late to explain. She'd run for her house trailing tears, with no notion of what she'd done wrong and no explanation from Tom to help her understand, and they'd barely spoken since.

After that, Tom had spent more time with the guys, all of whom shared his disdain for Anderson and his longing to be anywhere but.

"I've got to get out," he said aloud, to no one.

"I hear that," replied a voice behind him. Tom jumped. He'd known that Galen Ganger was there. They'd been passing a joint around only minutes earlier. But Tom's thoughts had led him to the edges of the Blacklands, a barren place inside his skull where he was the only occupant. Galen's sudden intrusion snapped him back to reality. "Anderson sucks." Galen punctuated his observation with a resonant belch fueled by a belly full of Coors.

The other boys muttered their agreement.

Darren, Buzzy and Kent sat on the hood of Darren's '66 Plymouth Satellite swigging beer. Darren figured he had about three thousand bucks invested in the Satellite, starting with the thousand dollars he'd paid for the body sans motor and transmission, then adding another couple thousand in swap meet parts, a '68 Chrysler engine, and fifty bucks worth of paint that he sprayed himself. He liked his car but he wasn't fussy about it the way Galen was about his '68 Charger with the overbored 440.

Buzzy drove a '74 Vega with a 454 big-block Chevy engine that, when it wasn't sitting in pieces in his father's garage as it was now, would give Galen's Charger a run for its money. Kent's taste ran to his '72 Super Beetle in which he was installing Weber dual carbs. He'd gotten as far as removing the old carburetor and opening the package from Fast Freddy's, but he didn't have the 12mm socket he needed and he wasn't too sure about relocating the coil to clear the linkage, so the project languished and Kent had been, for the last three months, without wheels.

Tom Culler rode a motorcycle, a used Honda he'd bought to dispel his egghead image and to keep from having to share a ride with Galen, Darren or Buzzy. Motorcycles were dangerous, but riding with any of his friends was pure suicide.

Car talk dominated the boys' conversation. Sex came in a close second. Everything else squeaked in around the edges.

Sitting on the fender, Darren blew a fart that rattled the sheet metal and prompted a lot of arm waving. Kent commented that it was lucky they weren't still smoking or they'd all have gone up in flames.

"That really happens to some people," Buzzy said. "They just go on fire for no reason."

"Bullshit," Galen said.

"No, it's true. They call it something."

"Spontaneous human combustion," Tom said.

"Bullshit. People don't just explode."

"Tell him about it, Tom," Buzzy said. "You know this shit."

All eyes turned to Tom, the former honors student. He sighed. It seemed like he was always playing Mr. Wizard for his friends.

"The human body's a controlled chemical reaction. We burn calories for fuel. That's why we have a temperature . . . ninety-eight point six, more or less. Only some people's thermostat goes haywire and their temperature goes up and up and doesn't stop. Eventually they literally burst into flame."

Galen stared at Tom. He cast his gaze around the group of boys, fixing each one for a moment before returning to Tom. "You're shittin' me," he said.

Tom shook his head. "It's the truth."

Galen considered for a moment, then he raised his beer can high and grinned. "To spontaneous human fucking combustion!" he yelled. The boys clinked their cans together and drank.

Galen sidled up next to Tom, wiping his mouth with the back of his hand. "Just one thing," he said.

Galen's arm whipped out and locked around Tom's neck. He bent Tom double and squeezed hard enough to show he wasn't kidding around. The other boys stiffened, but they didn't intervene. They'd learned better.

"If I find out you were shittin' me," Galen hissed through clenched teeth, "I'll break your fucking neck, you get me?" He squeezed harder, and Tom protested.

"I wasn't shitting you!"

Galen let Tom go. Tom backed away, saying, "Jesus, Galen!"

Galen took several animal steps around the small group, glaring a warning to each of them in turn, breathing hard through his nose. "And that goes for the rest of you, too," he said. The boys studied the ground intently.

The night grew quiet. You never knew what would set Galen off. These rages would just come over him and there was nothing to do but ride it out. Galen drained his Coors and threw the can in the water.

"Let's wake some people up," he said.

Darren and Buzzy got into Darren's Satellite, Galen and Kent rode in Galen's Charger. The engines roared to life and the cars peeled out, spraying dirt.

Tom, still smarting from his humiliation, kick-started the Honda and followed, wondering what in the hell he was doing but, at this moment in time, not really giving a good goddamn.

Annie Culler, five years old, lay in the hospital bed. Her eyes were closed as if she were asleep. They had been closed for eight months. Her face had become gaunt, her eye sockets sunken and gray.

The exuberant, teasing, giggling, willful little girl she had been was gone, and only the shell that had contained her spirit remained. But still the body lived. Doc Milford called it a "persistent vegetative state," but even that term couldn't capture the languor of her being. A vegetable was aware of the sun and the earth and the water and air. A plant could turn its face to the sunlight, could reach out limbs to gather the bounty of life, could seek and aspire and attain.

Annie did none of these things. She had not done them for eight months and was not likely to ever do them again.

The nurse's aide wadded Annie's old, soiled linen into a ball. She muttered to the orderly she glimpsed standing in the doorway.

"Hopeless," she said. "Waste of hospital resources. Ought to just pull the plug and be done with it."

"Not everyone considers her case hopeless," came the reply.

The nurse's aide looked up, startled. The uniformed figure in the doorway was not the orderly but was Peg Culler, still dressed in her waitressing outfit and destroying her with a look of perfect detestation.

"If you think you're wasting your time here," Peg continued, "maybe you should be the waitress and I should be the nurse."

Reddening, the nurse's aide hurried from the room clinging to the dirty bedclothes as if to a life preserver. She felt Peg's eyes on her neck as she stuffed the sheets into the basket and wheeled it away.

Peg's face softened as she looked on her daughter, her baby. Her precious. She walked over and brushed the hair off Annie's forehead.

"Hi, sweetie," she said.

Annie gave no sign that she heard the words or felt the warm kiss on her cool skin or sensed in any way her mother's presence. But still Peg pulled the plastic chair up close to the bed and withdrew the book from her purse, and, in her clearest voice, began to read.

Madge Duffy had turned herself in around two o'-clock, announcing to Sheriff Clark that she'd murdered her husband.

She'd actually done the deed an hour before. But whereas it had taken her only a moment to decide to open his neck with the filet knife, it took longer to figure out what to do next.

Madge did not want to be one of those people who blamed everything on the Negroes. She didn't want to concoct a black-skinned killer who fought with her husband and fled, though that was her first instinct. If they found her out later to be a murderess, she didn't want them heaping the name "racist" on her, too.

She worked on the problem as she picked things up and did a little dusting. The air seemed musty, so she opened a window. She knew that you weren't supposed to touch anything after a murder but she didn't want the place to be a total mess when strangers started tramping through gathering evidence and drawing outlines around things in chalk.

The sofa where John had fallen asleep, dead drunk, and the carpet in front of it were total losses because of all the blood so she didn't even bother with those.

She finished the dishes and left them in the drainer. By then she'd pretty well decided to make a clean breast of everything and just take her punishment. It was her first offense so maybe they'd go easy on her. She was barely forty, so even if she got fifteen years and served, say, eight of them, she could return to society (if not to Anderson) and live out her remaining twenty or thirty years knowing she'd paid her debt.

What were eight years, anyway? She'd been married to John for twenty, and they'd just flown. It didn't seem so at the time but looking back, the years whizzed by in a gray blur with very few high points to mark their passing.

Surely women's prison wouldn't be any worse than being married to a man who argued with her over every little thing and took his fists to her when he was drunk. She imagined prison as a kind of church social where she'd meet women of a like mind. They'd sit at folding tables and talk about their lives. The only difference would be that they'd wear uniforms, and she imagined that most women in prison smoked. She might even take it up herself, just to fit in.

She put on a fresh dress, worked on her hair a little, and then phoned Sheriff Clark.

"I've murdered John," she said. "I expect you'll want me to come in."

The Sheriff had told her to just stay put and he'd come to her. He showed up a few minutes later. She met him at the door and escorted him to the scene of the crime.

The Sheriff's mood had been black that day, he didn't know why. Staring at John Duffy's body swarming now with flies, he felt strangely unmoved. He knew that Duffy beat his wife and that she never had and never would press charges for fear of reprisals. The law couldn't have held onto Duffy for long, and a restraining order wouldn't mean squat to him once he got some booze in his belly. If she'd run off, he'd have gone after her and that would've been unpleasant, too. It could easily have been Madge Duffy lying somewhere dead instead of John.

He also knew that Madge's mother had committed suicide when Madge was a teenager in order to escape an abusive domestic situation. Apparently Madge had decided not to follow her mother's example. Madge was a decent if limited woman who'd married wrong, and she'd dealt with the problem the only way she knew how. Too bad she had to pay such a stiff penalty for it.

"Are you sure you did this?" the Sheriff asked. "Are you sure it wasn't a prowler, maybe? Somebody John caught in the act of burglary?"

Madge shook her head "no."

"I did it. There's the knife. I expect my prints are all over it."

Well, what could you do with somebody like that? Sheriff Clark handcuffed her according to the rules and took her to the jail. From there he called Doc Milford and Jedediah Grimm.

Now the dark had settled in. Madge Duffy lay asleep in the cell. She'd been understanding when the Sheriff told her no, she couldn't have her knitting supplies. He'd loaned her a book but the type was small and the light in the cell was no good and so she'd gone to bed early. He'd made a special trip back to the house for an extra blanket and her special pillow, the one she slept on for her neck, and she seemed comfortable enough. She didn't cry, which struck Sheriff Clark as odd.

Odd, too, was the feeling in the air. The Sheriff couldn't give it a name but it gave him the shivers. Something was going to happen tonight, he was sure of it. He'd even sent his deputy out to patrol the streets despite his protests that it was a waste of manpower.

Which it probably was. Probably, nothing would happen. Even if something did happen, Deputy Haws probably couldn't cope with it. The deputy wasn't good for much, but the job paid poorly and the Sheriff hadn't been flooded with applicants. Haws was a uniform on the street, at least.

Sheriff Clark was pouring water into the coffee pot when he heard the siren in the distance. It was drawing closer. He went to the door and stepped out in time to see the Ganger boy's souped-up old Charger tear down the street, followed by Darren Coombs' Satellite, both cars honking and the boys yelling out the windows. Tom Culler came next, quiet but riding hard, practically laying the Honda down as he rounded the corner.

Deputy Haws was in hot pursuit, the lights flashing and siren blaring.

Sheriff Clark considered joining the chase but remembered Madge Duffy in the cell. Besides, he could see Clyde Dunwiddey staggering drunkenly toward the office. He went back inside to put sheets on the cot in the second cell and the old soup pot beside the bed in case Clyde had to vomit in the middle of the night.

As he made up the cot, he prayed fervently that Deputy Haws didn't do anything stupid.

THREE

Deputy Harold Haws sat in the consarned patrol vehicle for no good reason he could determine.

Yes, it was Friday night, but so what? Friday nights in Anderson were not that much different from Tuesday nights or Wednesday nights or any night but Sunday which was so quiet you could hear a sparrow cough.

The Rialto was open on Friday and Saturday nights but that didn't mean much. Merle Tippert, the owner and operator, refused to show anything more rambunctious than PG so that limited his audience to a pretty docile bunch. The lights on the marquee were off already and the crowd— if fourteen people could be considered a "crowd"—was halfway home by now. They never stayed out late, the last show being at nine o'clock since Tippert liked to be home in time to complain at the eleven o'clock news.

Haws couldn't get his mind around what Sheriff Clark had said earlier in the evening, when he sent Haws out on patrol. Clark was a good lawman but his talk about a "bad feeling" and a "tightening in his scrotum" didn't cut much mustard with the deputy. Maybe Clark did have some kind of intuition slipping him warning signs, but it could just as easy have been that John Duffy's murder had left him with a case of the heebie-jeebies.

Now here was Haws, trying to fill his growling belly with the burrito he'd packed earlier in the day and not even able to heat it up because the consarned microwave was back at the consarned office. The steering wheel got in his way as he was raising the burrito to his mouth and he bumped his elbow and that caused him to squeeze the thing a little too hard and salsa squooshed out the bottom and dribbled on his shirt. When he tried to wipe it off with a paper napkin it only spread and made it look like he'd been stomach shot.

And now here came Clyde Dunwiddey, drunk as a skunk as usual. Clyde stumbled up to the police car and leaned on it like an old friend.

"H'lo, Deputy," Clyde said. His breath was flammable.

Deputy Haws made a face and waved a portly hand in the air. "Hoo, Clyde—you on your way to the station?"

"Yep. Headed for the hoosegow. How about a lift?"

"This ain't no taxi service, Clyde. Even drunk as you are, I figure your legs know the way by habit."

That's when the young hellions roared past in their muscle cars, whooping and hollering, stereos blasting rock music loud enough to deafen everybody in town, their tail pipes popping as if not one of them had the word "muffler" in his dictionary.

Haws shoved his half-eaten burrito at Clyde, who went another shade greener at the sight.

"Out of the way, Clyde. I've got work to do."

Clyde took a step back and inertia carried him a couple more. Deputy Haws hit the flashers and siren and gave chase.

Haws didn't like these boys. The Ganger kid in particular was a bad egg, and even the best of them, Tom Culler, was a wiseass. They reminded Haws of the bullies who used to torment him in high school because he carried a few extra pounds and because his slightly upturned nose called attention to his nostrils. The kids had called him "Hawg" of course, and that's why, once he graduated, he took the job as deputy. The uniform and badge gave him status. Now, at least, they had to call him "Hawg" behind his back instead of to his face.

That face was tight with determination as he chased the boys through the middle of town. Galen and Kent led, followed by Darren and Buzzy. Tom pulled up the rear with Haws hot on his tail.

Galen saw the flashing lights in his rearview mirror and mashed the pedal to the floor. Kent dug between the cushions for the seat belt that wasn't there. Galen called him a pussy and screeched around the corner that put them on the road to the highway.

Tom cut that same corner and jumped his Honda over a drainage ditch and onto the access road. He swerved into the far lane and nearly lost it on the turn, but the bike didn't fall and there was no opposing traffic so he twisted the throttle and kicked the gear shift and slid in ahead of Darren and Buzzy.

Tom had no specific plan but he knew he had to close the distance between himself and Galen. He wanted to somehow defuse the volatile situation that was brewing. Galen and Haws were like matter and antimatter. If they collided, there'd be hell to pay.

Now Darren had Deputy Haws on his ass and he didn't like it one bit. Surely Haws recognized his car even if he didn't get a good look at the driver, and surely Haws knew it was Galen leading the chase. Darren's mind could work fast when it had to and he made a decision. He whipped the wheel over to the right and hit the brakes, nearly catapulting Buzzy through the windshield as the Satellite screeched to a halt.

"What're you doin', man?" Buzzy yelled, bracing himself against the dash.

"Hawg doesn't want us. He wants to nail Galen."

Sure enough, the police car screamed past them and kept going. Haws had bigger fish to fry.

Darren wanted to turn around right then and go home but that would be chickenshit. Instead he waited until the flashing lights had vanished over the hill and then he crept forward. He'd watch the action from a distance, parking in the windbreak if he had to, so he could be there if anything happened. It was possible that Galen would reach the county line and escape the deputy's jurisdiction, but it was also possible that Haws would stop him first.

"Let's get the hell out of here," Buzzy suggested, but Darren shook his head and kept creeping.

Tom shot a fast look over his shoulder and saw the police car bearing down on him. It was faster than the Honda on the straightaway and its progress was relentless. By the time Tom decided to pull over the police car was so far up his tail pipe that Tom was afraid to slow down. Haws was stupid to be tailgating him so close but it was Tom who'd fly through the air and bury his head into a phone pole if they collided. That, or smear his face all over the highway.

Then suddenly the police car squealed as Haws jerked the wheel to the left and floored the accelerator. Tom instinctively steered to the right and the bike wobbled and Tom's heart went up into his throat, but Haws pulled around him with inches to spare. Tom eased back on the throttle and let the Honda slow itself down. When he was down to the legal limit he twisted the grip again and followed. Whatever Haws did to Galen, it should be witnessed. Maybe Tom's presence would avert disaster.

Kent was sweating hard as he saw the deputy closing on them. Normally the Charger would've shut the pigmobile out but Galen had been complaining about the timing and Kent could tell from the sound of it that the engine wasn't running up to snuff. He turned around and watched the steady progression of the flashing lights as they closed the distance between them.

"He's got us," Kent said.

"It ain't over 'til it's over," Galen said. He had the hard, immovable look in his eyes that told Kent they were edge-bound.

Haws pulled alongside and tipped a finger at Galen, telling him to pull over. Galen flipped Haws the bird. Then maybe because he had to take one hand off the wheel and there was a little dip in the road right then, or maybe because he did it on purpose, Galen nudged the wheel to the left and the Charger's front fender tapped the police car's hard enough to leave a dent.

Haws cursed and the police car fell back half a length. Tom saw the incident and winced mentally. "Pull over, Galen," he said, but it was more of a prayer. Galen couldn't hear him and wouldn't have pulled over anyway. Galen was in a Blacklands of his own, a world as narrow in options as the road he raced along. Galen barreled on toward his fate, mindless of consequence, deaf to logic and blind to peril.

Deputy Haws was no less determined than Galen to see this skirmish through to the end. A smarter man, a cooler man, a man with a larger view might have given up the chase and dealt with Galen Ganger in the morning. But Deputy Haws was not smart, his temper was up, and his mind was focused like a lens. He was going to pull that sonofabitch over if he had to chase him to Timbuktu.

Haws reached down and unsnapped the leather strap over his revolver. He pulled out the gun and floored the accelerator.

Kent saw the gun raised in Deputy Hawg's oversized fist and he freaked. He ducked, covering his head, and Galen looked over and registered the revolver pointed at his face. He knew Haws was dumb enough to pull the trigger.

Galen pounded the brake pedal and the Charger's tires
bit into asphalt. The car skidded and started to spin but
Galen pumped the brakes and brought it to a halt nose
down in the ditch by the side of the road. The engine was
dead and even as Galen cranked the starter, he saw Haws
up ahead, slowing, turning around, coming back at him.
The overheated engine didn't want to start and by the
time it did it was too late. Haws' police car was blocking the road and Haws was lumbering in Galen's direction,
gun drawn, screaming at him to get out of the fucking
car.

Tom decided to approach slowly. He didn't want Galen
to get shot but he didn't want to stop the bullet with his own
body, either. He had to arrive as a witness, not as another
target.

Deputy Haws pulled Galen's door open and yanked
him out of the car. He spun him around and threw him
to the blacktop, tripping him so he fell on the road face
first. Haws whipped around to aim the gun at Kent who
cowered against the passenger door, arms raised to the
roof.

"You set still!" Haws commanded, and Kent stammered
out a "Yes, sir."

Haws strode over to Galen and ordered him to his feet.
Galen's palms were scraped and stinging from the fall. He
raised himself slowly to one knee, his eyes locked on the
revolver that had begun to shake in the deputy's hand.
Galen stood and glared at Haws.

Haws yelled at him, his voice cracking. "You must be
wantin' to do time, boy!" he said.

"We were just lettin' off some steam," Galen replied.

"You want to let off steam?" Haws asked, and he planted
his fist deep into Galen's stomach, doubling him up. "I'll
show you steam," he grunted.

Tom pulled up and fixed the deputy in the glare of his

headlight. "Cut it out, Haws!" he yelled. The pistol swung in Tom's direction as Haws shielded his eyes from the light.

"Butt out, Culler. This ain't none of your business. And get that goddamn light out of my eyes before I shoot it out!"

Galen took advantage of Haws' momentary blindness to rush him, head down like a bull. He butted the deputy hard in the abdomen and knocked him backwards. Haws impacted against the Charger's door, slamming it shut, the door handle digging hard into his kidney. Haws cried out in pain.

Galen pummeled the deputy with his fists. He laid blow after blow on his body, his face, not planning where to hit, letting his fists find their own targets. Haws raised his arms to ward off the blows but it did no good. Galen was a flesh-pounding machine. He didn't think about the gun in the deputy's hand. He didn't think about anything. He hit and kept on hitting as Haws' knees buckled and he fell to the ground.

Galen kicked the deputy in the belly and Haws curled up into a tight ball, the revolver cupped to his stomach. Galen kicked again and there was a muffled bang that still was loud enough to sound like thunder to Tom, who went instantly white. Even Galen was shocked back to reality. He stepped away from the deputy as Haws slumped and his head fell to the ground.

"Galen, shit," Tom said. Inside the car, Kent fumbled for and found the door handle and gave it a yank, then tumbled into the ditch when the door fell open. He stumbled around to the front of the car and stared in disbelief at the body of Deputy Haws lying by the road like something out of a movie.

"Is he dead?" he asked.

Galen nudged Haws with his foot. "Fuck, yes," he said, and then he kicked the deputy again, meaning it.

Darren and Buzzy arrived, driving slowly like gawkers at a roadside accident. They got out of the car and all five boys gathered around the corpse, jaws slack, their minds trying desperately to interpret events in some way that didn't add up to deep, deep shit.

FOUR

Kent squatted with his head over the ditch. His body shook and pretty soon all the fear rose up inside him and expressed itself as an eloquent torrent of vomit.

Buzzy paced and flopped his arms as he looked up and down the highway. He kept glancing along the highway and muttering, "Somebody's gonna see us! Can't we just go?"

But Buzzy's ride, Darren, was hypnotized by the sight of Deputy Hawg lying in a pool of blood, dead as road kill. "Jesus," he kept saying, then as if he'd just noticed the body for the first time, he'd say again, "Jesus!"

"Don't tell me we have to tell the Sheriff." Galen's remark was directed straight at Tom.

"I didn't say we did," Tom snapped back. But it was true, his mind had been wondering what they'd tell Sheriff Clark. Would Clark believe that it was an accident? Would he believe that Deputy Hawg blew his cool and actually drew on Galen, and that Galen was afraid for his life, and that they'd tangled and the gun had gone off by accident?

Even if the Sheriff did believe it, could he admit that his deputy was more at fault than Galen, or at least as much so? There weren't twelve people in Anderson who didn't know Galen's reputation. It wouldn't matter what Tom and his friends testified to. Galen would probably go ballistic in court and start screaming at the jury and they'd find him guilty as sin.

Somebody had to have seen them racing through town with Haws on their butts. They'd get tied in with the body somehow. Tom and Kent were definite accessories to the crime. Darren and Buzzy might get off, seeing as how they weren't actually there when the gun went off. If the jury believed them.

Who would the jury believe? Haws had a reputation of his own. There was room for doubt.

They had to make a clean breast of things to have any credibility in the courtroom. Anything they did to cover it up would work against them. They just needed one juror on their side, just one. The worst thing they could do would be to try to hide the body.

"We have to hide the body," Galen said. Kent looked over his shoulder, sickness dribbling down his chin. Buzzy paced back and forth, his eyes on Tom. Darren's eyes tore themselves from the corpse. Tom stared at Haws's body and didn't say a word. He didn't have to see them to know they were looking at him. Him, the good kid. The smart one.

He'd known earlier that things were spinning out of control. This was just more of the same. He was in it now up to his eyeballs. It was no time to get into a pissing contest with Galen.

Galen went on. "We'll take it somewhere and bury it. Come on. Help me pick it up."

"Why don't we just get the hell out of here?" Buzzy said, his voice cracking.

"Because we need time, asshole! A couple of days. Time for it to rot so they can't pin down the time of death." Galen gestured, taking in the scene. "This here's like writing our fucking names in blood on the highway."

So Galen's mind was working, too. It worked differently than Tom's. It took paths that were more devious and treacherous. And yet, who's to say Galen wasn't right? The more confusion about what happened, the better. If the law couldn't absolutely pin them down, there'd be no case. Hell, if O.J. could walk . . .

"I ain't puttin' him in my car," Darren proclaimed.

But of course they did. Galen said it was because the Plymouth's trunk was bigger but that was bull hockey. He just didn't want any blood messing up his Charger, whether because of the evidence trail or out of plain fussiness, Darren didn't know and didn't dare ask. When Galen got like he was now, you just did what he said.

Haws's spine had stopped the bullet so by keeping him on his back they were able to keep the bleeding down, what with his heart no longer pumping. Darren was still lugging around a bunch of camping gear he'd never put back in the garage, including a sleeping bag that they spread out. They thought they were doing a pretty good job of keeping Darren's trunk clean. They'd think that way until the next morning when Darren could look it over in the daylight. Then it'd look like someone had butchered a hog back there, but right now they were proud of themselves.

They drove six miles down the road and then onto a pasture road and stopped when they crossed a creek. They hauled the body down the bank, each boy except Galen hanging onto one corner of the sleeping bag. They carried it along the creek a few hundred yards and then up to the bank again.

Darren had to go back for the camping shovel he'd left in the car. Kent passed the time by dry heaving at the creek. Buzzy gave up and just sat down on the ground and bawled his eyes out.

Galen paced angrily, nervously sweeping the hair from his eyes every few seconds. He kept up a steady stream of invective directed at Deputy Hawg whose fault this whole fucking unbelievable mess was. Now and again he'd kick something, often as not the deputy.

Tom retreated into the Blacklands where nothing

mattered, not even shooting a cop. The world around him vanished as if swallowed by fog. He watched from a hundred miles away as his hands dug a hole by the embankment. After awhile someone else took his place and he sat down and didn't see anything, nothing at all but shades of blackness swirling and roiling before his eyes in all directions.

He was caught up in events larger than himself by far. It was useless to fight them, useless to try to plan a course of action, useless to think, useless to do anything at all but to float on the wind like an expended husk.

After the deputy was planted and Galen had elicited the necessary oaths of silence, the boys headed home. Tom steered the Honda over roads so familiar he could have navigated them in his sleep.

He left his muddy shoes on the back porch, stripped off his clothes and climbed under the covers. As he closed his eyes it occurred to him that he had no recollection of the trip at all. He didn't remember entering the town limits or pulling up at his own house. He didn't remember anything after leaving the creek.

Except. . . .

One thing. Something he hadn't even noticed at the time.

When he'd passed the church, someone was ringing the bell. Funny. Who would ring a church bell at that hour? It must have been midnight, at least.

Franz Klempner woke in a sweat. He didn't think he'd been having a nightmare but the sheets were damp and twisted as if he had. He heard Elmer downstairs, barking his fool head off.

By habit, not quite awake, Franz reached over to touch Irma and discovered only the empty bed.

"Irma!" he called out, and by now the fog in his brain

had lifted and he began to connect his wife's absence with the frantic barking of the dog downstairs.

He rushed out of the bedroom and down the stairs, calling out her name. For some reason he paused at the foot of the stairs. Elmer the dog was in the kitchen and Franz could see that Irma wasn't in the living room. That's where he'd find her, for certain, in the kitchen. Then what impulse told him to take it slow? It just felt wrong, he couldn't say why.

Then the bell started ringing. The church bell, ringing in the middle of the night, calling to the faithful.

"Irma!" he called again. Elmer's insistent barking was ominous, intense. It wasn't like when he treed a possum or found a raccoon digging through the trash. There was a hint of fear in it.

"Irma!"

Franz padded on bare feet through the living room and toward the kitchen. The glowing hands of the mantel clock told him it was just after twelve.

He thought about turning on the light but the lamp was clear across the room. He wished he'd brought the shotgun but it was upstairs in the bedroom closet. He'd like to have felt something heavy in his hand . . . his flashlight would be good, but it was in the kitchen drawer. Why was everything always in the wrong place?

He reached the kitchen door. Elmer was going crazy inside. Franz reached his hand around the corner and felt for the light switch. Slowly his fingers inched along the wall until they found what they were looking for. He flipped the switch and the light came on just as the butcher knife stabbed the wall between his fingers. His middle and index fingers split open and trailed blood through the air as Franz instinctively jerked back his hand, screaming.

Franz looked up in horror at the terrified face of his wife. Her eyes were wide as she wrenched the knife from the wall and came at him again. The knife struck at Franz and his arm flew up in self defense and the blade sliced through his sleeve and bit into his wrist.

"Irma!" he yelled as she pulled the knife back to her ear and struck at him yet again. He grabbed her wrist and twisted. The knife fell and embedded its point in the linoleum.

Irma squirmed free and ran to the back door. She whined in panic as she fumbled with the lock. In moments Franz was behind her and had hold of her shoulders.

"Irma, it's me, Franz!" he said, "It's only me! There's nothing to be afraid of!" He managed to turn her around and commanded her to look at him. "Look," he said, "it's only me!"

She glanced at him. "Look," he said again. She found the courage to meet his gaze. He smiled at her. "It's just Franz. I won't hurt you. You know I won't hurt you."

She stared at him for several long seconds, and he kept smiling at her and telling her that everything was all right. Elmer's barking deteriorated to a sullen afterthought and then died out altogether. Silence embraced the room, then was broken by the reassuring lap of Elmer at his water dish.

Tears welled in Irma's eyes. She threw herself into Franz' chest and wrapped her arms around him and clung there for dear life.

Meanwhile, not many miles away in the morgue of the Cooves County Hospital, John Duffy, whose jugular had been severed by his wife less than twelve hours before, bolted upright on the autopsy table and wondered what in the devil was going on.

DAY TWO, SATURDAY

FIVE

Curtis Waxler was not warm to the idea of mopping out the morgue at midnight.

It seemed to him to be tempting fate, like walking through the cemetery on Halloween night or driving a car in Transylvania when the forecast called for rain. It was the sort of thing the obvious victims, the people Curtis and his friends referred to as "dead meat," do in monster movies.

But Doc Milford, who was also Chief Administrator of the Cooves County Hospital, was expecting the coroner to show up early for the autopsy on John Duffy and he wanted his facility to make a good impression.

They didn't perform many autopsies at Cooves County Hospital. It was usually pretty obvious what killed people when they got caught in the hay baler or had the tops of their cars peeled back like sardine cans and their heads sliced off by slow-moving combines driving the highway during summer harvest. It seemed obvious to Curtis, when he lifted the sheet over John Duffy's face and peered at the parted flesh and the exposed veins in the neck, what had killed the man. You didn't have to be a forensic scientist to figure it out. But the law required an autopsy and the coroner had been called and he would be there by eight a.m.

So here was Curtis and his bucket and his mop at the witching hour, down in the hospital basement with the corpse, doing as fine an impression of "dead meat" as any frustrated actor in Hollyweird ever dreamed when John Duffy's voice boomed out, "What in the hell . . . ?" and the corpse sat up, flailing its arms under the sheet and banging its head on the light over the examining table and groaning and cursing a blue streak.

The effect on Curtis was profound.

He emptied his bladder to shed the excess weight and ran so hard for the half open door that he reached it before he was ready and banged smack into it, slamming it shut. He grabbed the door handle with sweaty hands and wrenched it open but he couldn't help but glance back over his shoulder to see if something was gaining on him. He saw John Duffy writhing on the table, still kicking at the sheet over his legs and looking as perturbed as a badger in a gunny sack. Duffy and Curtis locked eyes.

"You there!" Duffy bellowed, and Curtis whined as he dashed through the morgue door. His shoes squeaked on the linoleum as he made a ninety-degree turn in the hallway and ran like Jim Thorpe had run in Stockholm in 1912 but with less grace and a lot more volume.

Curtis punched the elevator button frantically and gave the doors one half-second to open. When they didn't he headed for the stairs with the slap of Duffy's bare feet resounding down the hallway and Duffy's voice calling after him, "You! Hey you!"

To the night nurse on the first floor, Curtis was only a flash in the corner of her eye as he streaked past her station.

"Get out!" Curtis yelled, and then he was gone, leaving behind bewilderment and the faint odor of fresh urine.

Duffy appeared moments later. He'd wrapped the sheet around his waist and tossed the rest of the material toga-like over his shoulder, which may be why Claudia White, the night nurse, stammered out "Great Caesar's ghost!" rather than any of a hundred other possible exclamations. Later she would think it was funny, but it didn't strike her that way now. What did strike her was the corner of the counter as she fainted dead away.

"Sheriff?" Doc Milford said into the phone. "I think you'd better get out here to the hospital right away.

"No, if I told you what it was, you'd think I was drunk.

"No, I am not, thank you very much.

"I don't know if it's an emergency. I don't think so.

"Just come, Gene, please. I want somebody to tell me I'm not going crazy."

They had found Duffy's underwear by the time Sheriff Clark arrived. The rest of his clothes were bloodstained and were being held as evidence by the Sheriff's Department.

Duffy sat in Doc Milford's office in his boxers and a blood pressure cuff. He looked up when the Sheriff entered.

"Am I under arrest?" he asked.

It took Sheriff Clark a full fifteen seconds to summon up the word "no." Then he sat down to have a serious chat with the deceased.

They determined the facts of the case pretty quickly, as completely as they could without the input of Curtis Waxler, who had vanished like a vapor into the night. Duffy was informed that his wife had murdered him in his sleep and that he had been officially pronounced dead by Doc Milford. Then Duffy had been taken to the morgue awaiting an autopsy where he appeared to have returned to life.

"Thank Christ you didn't cut me open!" Duffy exclaimed.

"John," said Doc, "believe me—it wouldn't have made any difference. You were as dead a man as I've ever seen. Livor mortis had set in. Primary flaccidity of the muscles. You weren't in a coma, you weren't catatonic, you were dead."

Sheriff Clark flashed suddenly on an image of John Cleese pounding a dead parrot on the counter of Michael Palin's pet shop.

"I don't know about any of that," Duffy snarled.

Doc produced Polaroids documenting his diagnosis.

"Here. Look. This is how you were brought in twelve hours ago. Your throat was slit practically ear to ear."

Duffy glanced at the photos and then tossed them back at Doc. Sheriff Clark noticed the tightness in Duffy's jaw and the dark look in his eyes and was glad that Duffy wasn't drunk. With liquor in him, Duffy argued with his fists.

"I don't know what you're trying to pull," Duffy said, "but if you think I'm paying you dime one for this horseshit, you're wrong. My throat's fine. I've never felt better in my life."

"Sometime around midnight, you apparently returned to life," Doc said. "Your wound was completely healed."

Duffy snorted. He looked up at Sheriff Clark.

"You say Madge did that to me?" he said, gesturing toward the Polaroids.

"I have her taped confession at the station. She says you got drunk, beat her up and passed out on the sofa. While you were asleep, she cut your throat."

Duffy shook his head.

"I don't remember any of that."

A few moments passed in silence, during which Doc and Sheriff Clark exchanged looks and shrugs. Doc fought down an overwhelming urge to apologize, but what did he have to apologize for? For declaring a dead man dead?

"Where's she now?" Duffy asked.

"She's in a cell."

"But you got nothing on me?"

"We don't file charges against the victim, John, or against corpses. If Madge wants to file a domestic abuse complaint—"

"I don't remember any beating. I want to see her."

"I don't think that would be a good idea."

Duffy's mouth curled into a smirk. "Sheriff," he said, "you're gonna have a hell of a time convincing a jury that Madge killed me with me sitting there on the bench saying it ain't so. So you just let her out of that jail of yours and take her home and tell her I'll be there waiting for her."

Doc said, "I think you should stay here, John, at least until we can run some more tests. There will be no charge. But something awful damned strange is going on and we need to get to the bottom of it."

Duffy shook his head. He rose slowly and drew himself up to his full five feet and nine inches of height. He stood there in his boxer shorts and looked down his nose at Doc Milford.

"No, you might just decide I was dead again and I'd wake up in a pine box. You've wasted enough of my time. Now who's giving me a ride? I'd catch my death walking home like this."

Madge was awake when the Sheriff returned. She hadn't slept clear through a night for some years and sleeping on a cot in a jail cell didn't make it any easier. She wondered if she wasn't dreaming, though, when Sheriff Clark opened the cell door and invited her out to the office for a cup of coffee. That was nothing compared to what she thought when he told her that her husband didn't seem to be dead after all.

"Not dead?" she said, unable to keep the disappointment from her voice. "What did I do wrong?"

"Technically speaking, nothing. You severed a carotid artery which should have led to an immediate stroke. And even if he didn't die of stroke, the cut in his jugular was deep and ragged and he should have at least bled to death."

Madge prided herself on being meticulous, so it stung a

little to hear that her cut was considered "ragged" by professional standards. It was just like her, though, to bungle a simple job like killing her sleeping husband. Even more upsetting was the thought of what John would do to her when he got out of the hospital.

"How long will he be . . . confined?" she asked.

Sheriff Clark sighed, a habit he seemed to have acquired since getting the call from Doc Milford. "He isn't," he said. "Doc Milford drove him home a short while ago. He's waiting for you there."

Sheriff Clark saw the blood drain from Madge's face.

"Oh, my," she said.

"Is there someone you can stay with? A relative?"

No, there was no one.

"I just don't understand it," she said. "I know he was dead, Sheriff. A wife can tell these things. And Doc Milford—"

"Madge," the Sheriff interrupted, "I don't have an answer for you. We're all completely baffled. John should be . . . John was dead. There's no mistaking that. But he's very much alive again. There isn't so much as a scratch to indicate . . . what happened. I can't keep you here. You're a free person."

"No. I'm not," Madge replied, and Sheriff Clark knew what she meant.

They sat in silence for several minutes. Now and again the hairs on the back of the Sheriff's neck stood up for no apparent reason, and just as often Madge would shudder as if from a chill and take another sip of wretched, greasy coffee.

Madge looked over at Clyde Dunwiddey in his cell, snoring in drunken repose, and envied him. No spouse to answer to. No one to judge his every move and find it wanting. She had almost attained that freedom for herself, but somehow she'd mucked it all up the way she mucked up everything she tried. John hadn't come back from the dead, he couldn't.

Madge believed in miracles but they were for saints and such, and John was no saint, to put it mildly.

It was all a mistake. She'd done everything wrong. John was right about her. She was a waste, a sheer waste.

She said at last, "I'd better be getting home, then," but she sat in the hard wooden chair for another ten minutes picking at the Styrofoam cup of dregs until the lip was as ragged as an amateur wound in a husband's throat.

"I'll drive you," Sheriff Clark said. "Maybe I'll have a few words with John when I drop you off."

"Thank you," Madge replied. "I'll just get my pillow and we can go."

It was all clear to him now.

John Duffy had never been able to figure out the ways of the world before. It seemed so complex, like chess, where you could learn the basic moves in a few minutes but the strategy of the thing took some kind of genius to master.

School had been a nightmare, every day bringing a new humiliation. He hated the blackboard and every miserable math problem he couldn't solve and every lousy sentence he couldn't diagram. He hated spelling bees and oral reports and the way the teacher called on him whenever he didn't know the answer and never called on him when he waved his hand desperately in the air. He tried waving his hand when he didn't know the answer once and of course that was the time she did call on him and then he really felt like shit when he had to admit, his face turning radiant, that he didn't know it after all. How the kids had laughed at him that time.

No wonder he dropped out.

Working at the garage was no better. He was a good mechanic, he knew that, but the owner was always looking over his shoulder and second-guessing him, telling him that whatever he was doing was wrong. He couldn't please the guy no matter what he did.

No wonder he had quit.

Just as he had to quit every job he'd held since then. What cosmic law was it that made every garage owner either an idiot or an asshole and most likely both? If he could find one place that wasn't like working in an insane asylum, that treated him with the respect he deserved, that didn't play favorites, where you didn't have to be a goddamn computer expert just to change a set of spark plugs . . . that's all he wanted.

But he couldn't figure it. He couldn't figure how kids just out of school got the raises that eluded him. Or why supervisors who couldn't find their ass with both hands and a road map were determined to keep him down. Or how owners who were too dumb to cross the street without a dozen Boy Scouts made enough money to buy six-bathroom houses and fancy cars.

Meanwhile, here was John Duffy with not much of a formal education but more common sense than any dozen bosses he'd worked for, still bouncing from job to job, town to town, working his ass off for stinking wages that never even paid the bills.

It didn't make any sense.

Madge thought she knew it all, of course. Madge, with the I.Q. of a guppy, who'd never held a job in her life, thought she knew better than he did what went on at work.

"Maybe if you tried harder to get along," she'd say. Or, "Well, I can see his point." After he'd slapped her around a few times she'd learned to keep her mouth shut, but he could still see the disapproval in her eyes, the accusation that somehow all their troubles were his fault. Everything was always his fault. He couldn't bear it sometimes and he'd have to hammer something with his fists, just pound the living shit out of something, and Madge was always there, always there.

But it was clear now. He'd had time to think and to remember. He was confused at first, but it was all coming back to him now and the puzzle pieces were falling into place. All those thousands and thousands of pieces were forming a picture that he could see in its entirety. He had made the passage and it had opened his eyes.

The answer to life was simple after all, as he'd always suspected it was.

The answer was Seth.

SIX

The woods were lovely, dark and deep.

Not that Deputy Haws, trapped under eighteen inches of earth, was in any position to appreciate that loveliness.

His first impulse upon rising from the dead was to open his eyes. They filled instantly with dirt that lodged under his eyelids and scratched like sandpaper. Muddy tears flowed over his pounding temples.

He opened his mouth to cry out and dirt flowed between his lips. It mixed with spit to form a bitter black paste that clung to his tongue and the roof of his mouth. He sucked dirt into his nostrils. The dust tickled his nose but his lungs held no air with which to cough. His empty chest cramped painfully. Rivulets of muddy saliva worked their way to the back of his mouth and trickled down his throat. He felt his gorge rising.

His arms were pinned by the press of earth. His legs, immobile. He fought his lungs' demand to take in air, for there was none, only the engulfing residue of death and decay.

Haws lay in total darkness, unable to move an inch, the planet pressing him on all sides, earth insinuating itself into every wrinkle and crevice, no sliver of light, no air, no space. He couldn't pound on the constricting walls, couldn't scream. He was an object buried by children, sacrificed to the slow invasion of roots and water and the appetites of burrowing creatures.

His mind crackled with terminal efficiency. He had died and come back, and now he was about to die again, smothered in a blanket of crust, invaded through every orifice by the dust that was the beginning and end of life.

He remembered the hot sear of the bullet entering his belly and the taste of blood and bile from his shredded stomach that bubbled up through his throat. He remembered how time seemed to stand still, how the boys who'd killed him froze like slack-jawed statues. Galen Ganger was the first to realize what had happened, and Haws remembered the glint in his eyes, the flush of delight on his face, the sneering smile creeping over his lips just as everything misted over and then turned black and then white, white, white.

These memories flashed through Haws's mind in an instant, and in the next instant Haws vowed to get even with the Ganger kid and all the others, with everyone who'd ever tormented him or called him Deputy Hawg or laughed at him behind his back. Such was the promise he made to himself, sealed in the body of the smothering earth, suffocating, entombed. Buried alive.

He would get revenge. Seth would guide him, as Seth would help him now.

Fighting the panic Haws twisted his right hand palm up and worked the fingers like worms. He clawed at the dirt and his hand began to bore like a separate, digging creature for the surface.

He turned his left hand and it, too, clawed at the encompassing ground. How deep was his grave? Maybe inches, maybe feet.

He saw himself in his mind's eye as if in an ant farm, buried deep beneath grass and roots and rocks and bones, under the rabbit warrens and insect trails, his hands clawing pitifully at the earth, working their way in vain toward an airiness as out of reach as the moon.

Haws shook from the suppressed urge to fill his lungs. He clenched his teeth until his jaw ached. He felt the scritching of tiny legs in his left ear as a beetle, swollen with eggs, tunneled in. Something moist and silent slithered across his lips.

His hands continued their slow-creeping crawl. He found that he could raise his arms a little and then a little more. The earth was crumbling beneath his fingers. He swiveled his shoulders and turned his head from side to side, his nose digging at the dirt. But these were feeble victories, the last spastic twitchings of the fly caught in amber. His chest ached. He felt as if his entire insides were turning to stone.

He could hold it no longer. His lungs demanded air with which to scream. He would open his jaws and fill his lungs with dirt and let it gorge his windpipe and starve his brain. Anything was better than this dark torture!

And then his hands broke through to the cool night air.

They must have made some sight, his dirt encrusted fingers worming through the thin cover of leaves and then clawing frantically at the earth over his chest and face. Then his mud-streaked face heaved into view, gasping and coughing dirt, eyes bloodshot from abrasion and terror. He dug the dirt from his eyes and vomited it from his stomach and dug the kicking beetle out of his ear. He clawed the dirt off his legs and rose, choking and heaving, to his feet.

Ants, outraged over the night's excavations, swarmed over the deputy's feet and climbed his ankles. He stomped to the shallow river bed and let the current whisk them away. He scooped up water to splash his dirty face and washed the dried blood from his mouth and chin. A brown stain, blackened with powder, marked his shirt. Haws inserted a finger through the hole and prodded his belly. Then he opened his shirt and stared at the perfect, unbroken skin. Not even a scar or a scab commemorated his murder.

All around him was coolness and night. A breeze stirred

the branches, rustling leaves. Bats fluttered. Rodents scurried for cover under the rush of owls' wings. Crickets
chirped. Water bubbled and babbled and flowed ice cold
over the rocks of the riverbed.

Haws peered into the darkness with new eyes. His past life
seemed a million years gone. He saw everything with a new
clarity of mind and mission. He thought of the boys who'd
killed and buried him, and he remembered the vow he'd
made as he lay underground with the other subterranean
things.

The woods were lovely, dark and deep.

But Deputy Haws had promises to keep.

Madge politely declined the Sheriff's offer to come in
and speak with John. If anything, it would only enrage him
more. If it was remotely possible that John wasn't already
spitting nails over his murder, the interference of the law
would catapult him beyond the edge.

John had as little use for the police as did a serial killer.
How many times had the law brought him to the front
door, drunk, with blood caked under his nose and his jaw
bruised from a fight in some bar? Each time, she knew she
would bear the brunt of his fury.

Come to think of it, Madge didn't expect much from the
police herself. They couldn't protect her. They only brought
him home, time and again, to hit her with his fists or something harder. They took note of her complaints and filed
their reports, even hauled John off to jail a time or two. But
they always let him go. And he always came home madder
than when he left, and Madge always paid the price.

What would he do to her now that she'd tried to kill him?
And why, if he was going to be there waiting for her, was the
living room so dark?

She called his name. There was no answer. She turned

to lock the door and then thought better of it. The danger was not outside, but in. She had let the stranger in twenty years ago when she opened her heart to John. She left the door unlocked in case she had to run. Maybe, with luck, he would be too drunk to follow her and she could escape into the darkness.

She stood at the door and thought about running now. Why wait for the hand to grab her arm and twist it until she fell to her knees? Why wait for fists to knock her to the floor and hard-toed work shoes to bury themselves in her ribs? Why wait until she lay on the floor crying and begging his forgiveness and trying painfully to drag herself out of range of his anger? Maybe he'd break her leg again and she wouldn't be able to run at all. Why wait? Why not go right now? Why not run?

Because there was nowhere to run. Hadn't her sister warned her, after the last time, that she was tired of seeing Madge all bruised and broken, and that if she didn't leave John after this she could just run to someone else?

Leave. They made it sound so easy. As if a forty-year-old woman with no skills could just rent an apartment with no money, no security deposit, no first and last month's rent. As if John wouldn't find her and kick the door down and drag her back home wherever she ran.

She peered into the darkness. She turned on the switch but the light was off at the lamp. She called his name again and there was still no answer.

For a moment she dared to hope that he'd left her. Just packed his things and left. How could you live with a woman who had split your neck while you slept?

"John?" she called.

"Upstairs," he replied, and Madge's hopes died.

Well, what did she expect? She was a murderess, after all. If John did beat her, even if he killed her, it was no less than she deserved.

She flicked the switch that would illuminate the stairs. The stairway remained dark. Had he removed the bulb, or did he break it in a fit of anger?

She set her foot onto the first step and began to climb. She didn't have to see the wallpaper along the stairs to know it was faded or see the carpeting beneath her feet to know it was worn thin. The details of the house were as familiar to her as the lines in her own face. The shabbiness of it depressed her. This was her house, this was her self, shabby and worn to bare threads. If John did kill her, maybe he would have the courtesy to put a match to it all, destroying the evidence of his crime and sending her ashes into the sky, soaring at last.

Her mother must have felt this despair all those years ago, when she took her life to escape Madge's father. Madge had grown up with the fights and the beatings. Her sister had run away when she was fourteen, but Madge stayed behind. Someone had to stay with their mother. If now and again she could divert her father's anger away from her mother and onto herself, maybe her mother would find the strength to put an end to the abuse. Maybe she'd see Madge being beaten and something inside her would rise up and break the spell of fear her father had woven over them all. Maybe she'd grab something . . . a poker or a chair or anything . . . and bring it down hard over his head. . . .

Instead, her mother had swallowed poison and died a horrible death that left her husband's rage focused with unrelenting precision on Madge. When John Duffy started "sniffing around" (as Madge's father called it), he brought hope for Madge's own escape. He was strong and forceful. He would protect her from her father. And so they were married when Madge was nineteen and she passed from one hell to another.

She endured John's abuses but made one promise to herself. She would not die for him. She would not kill herself over a man the way her mother had done. She would find any other escape if it became too much to bear. Murder, if need be.

She continued her march. The railing wobbled under her hand, the stairs creaked in all the familiar spots.

As she neared the top of the stairs she could hear him up there, pacing. She looked up. The bulb in the overhead socket was gone, but there was a flickering light from down the hall. Not an electric light but something warmer and less steady, like a candle, but too bright for a candle. She reached the landing and saw that the light came from the bedroom.

"John?" she said.

"In the bedroom."

His voice was pinched, expectant. He was waiting for her, lying in wait like some great, hairy beast crouched in the corner of its cave, eyes afire, waiting for its prey to come stumbling in. Waiting to pounce.

She stepped hesitantly toward the open bedroom door. She could smell the burning wax. So it was a candle, or rather, many candles. Why did he remove the bulb? What was he planning that required candles? Some churches used candles. Some rituals. . . .

A sacrifice.

Her heart pounded in her chest. Her throat constricted so she could barely speak. Her voice, when again she spoke his name, was thin and wavering.

"John?"

"In the bedroom," he repeated. "I'm waiting for you."

She wanted to turn and run, to lose herself in senseless flight. But what was the point? She couldn't run forever. If it was going to end, let it be now. Let it be here. Let him beat her to death if that's what he wanted, but let it be over once and for all. She deserved it. She was a murderess in her heart. She didn't deserve to live.

Her only prayer was that he do it quickly. Maybe he would be so angry that couldn't hold himself back. He would hit her once and knock her out and she wouldn't even feel the killing blow.

She walked across the landing to a yellow trapezoid of light on the floorboards that issued from the open door. It beckoned her with its warmth. She reached the very edge of the light and paused. This was her last chance to run. If she entered the light, if she so much as let it touch the tips of her shoes, the decision would be made.

She took one more step and turned her head to peer into the bedroom.

He must have dug out every candle in the house, she thought.

The room was ablaze with candlelight. John stood in the middle of it. His hair was washed and neatly combed, slicked back the way he used to wear it, and smelled of Wildroot. He wore his only suit. The vest was tight across his middle and a button was missing from the jacket. His shoes were brightly buffed and shining in the candlelight. The pants, judging from the way the zipper opened ever so slightly in a V, must have been fastened with a safety pin around the waist. He hadn't worn the suit in years. Ages.

"Do you remember?" he asked. He stepped forward. "Our first night in our first house, the power wasn't on yet but you insisted that we spend the night there."

My God, she thought, that was a hundred years ago.

"I . . . bought candles," she said. And John had griped about what a waste of money it was.

"It was the beginning of a new life." He walked toward her slowly, as if afraid of frightening her off. "Tonight was another beginning. I was born again, Madge. I'm a new man. Maybe I almost deserved what you did to me, I don't know. But I don't hold anything against you. We're starting over again. Starting fresh."

He was close enough to touch her now. She tensed as he lifted his arms, afraid of what he would do, but he only rested his hands on her shoulders.

"We have work to do," he said. "We'll do it together, you and me. I can't explain it yet, but you'll understand soon enough. You'll see. Everything's going to be different."

Madge couldn't believe her ears. Was he reborn, really? His eyes were so bright, like they were twenty years ago before they'd grown cold and mean. In any event, what could she do about it? She was trapped there the same as ever. If things were better or worse, it didn't matter. There was nothing she could do about it.

His hands on her shoulders began to weigh her down.

"It's been a rough trip," John said. "It was quite a shock, waking up in the morgue. Then Doc told me I'd died, and the Sheriff came around and told me how. They showed me pictures, Madge. They weren't pretty. I'm not blaming you and I'm not mad. But I'm tensed up. Very tensed up."

The hands were pushing her down. She knew now what he wanted. It was one thing she'd never given him, not so much because she was against it, but because it seemed to be what he wanted almost more than anything else. It was the one thing he'd never been able to force her to do, despite the threats and the beatings.

She lowered herself to her knees. As she lowered his zipper, she told herself that she was not giving in. Maybe it was a new beginning. He wasn't threatening her. He'd forgiven her for a thing she'd done to him that was much worse than what he wanted now. It wasn't giving up to do this. It was an act of good faith. It showed she was willing to do her part.

The pressure on her shoulders remained as she drew him out of his pants, all hard and expectant. She looked up to see him standing like a saint in all that candlelight, the glow flickering over his face and glistening on his

Wildroot-slickened hair, his mouth set tight but curling slightly at the corners, and she wondered if she knew what she was letting herself in for. She decided that she did not.

Oh, well, she told herself, you never did.

SEVEN

Deputy Haws stood in the dark back yard of the Culler house and looked up at the bedroom window. Tom's Honda was parked beside the house, his muddy shoes were on the back porch. So the boy was home.

Haws forced open the back door with the strength of the undead and shuffled his way inside. One foot had stopped working somewhere between the grave and the house. His good foot, thick with mud, sucked at the vinyl flooring of the kitchen. The other, dragging behind, left a brown smear. Bits of decaying flesh dropped from his body, landing ker-splop ker-splop in his wake.

Somehow, without passing through the living room, Haws was on the stairs that led to Tom's bedroom. His dead foot knocked against each step as he painfully heaved himself up the long flight of stairs. He gripped the banister with a deteriorating, lichen-covered hand.

Haws gazed up with his one good eye. It was glazed over and yellow with pus. The other eye had fallen out in the woods. Earthworms oozed from the socket like meat through a grinder. Haws's teeth were decayed, some were missing, and his rancid breath issued through torn lips in a visible yellow-green vapor.

His head twitched. It seemed too heavy for him to lift. Sometimes it sagged until his chin collided with his chest, and then he'd raise it again, looking up, his Cyclops eye fastened on Tom's bedroom door.

Then suddenly he was standing over the bed where Tom slept fitfully, embroiled in a bad dream. Tom tossed his head from side to side muttering, "No, don't, Haws, don't, stay away, you're dead, dead, Haws, don't. . . ."

The room was starkly lit by the full moon shining in the window. Haws leaned his slack-jawed head over the sleeping boy. Drool hung from Haws's mouth and dangled over Tom's face. Longer and longer grew the thread until it broke free and deposited itself on Tom's lips.

Tom opened his eyes. He beheld the grinning face of Deputy Haws hovering over him, staring at him with one yellowed orb, haloed by the full moon in the bedroom window, breath hissing from his throat like gas through a cracked pipe, maggots overflowing his mouth and the stench of death exuding from his putrescent flesh.

Tom screamed.

He sat bolt upright to find himself in a bedroom bright with morning sun. A mockingbird outside the window chirped another bird's song. Tom shook his head to clear the cobwebs.

"Shit," was all he could think to say.

His mother called to him from downstairs.

"Coming!" he said.

He hauled himself out of bed and stumbled toward the bathroom. His foot slipped on something wet and gooey and he fell to the floor.

"What the hell . . . ?" he said, and then he saw the muddy footprints leading from the hallway to the bathroom. They weren't his. They couldn't be his. He'd left his shoes outside on the porch.

The bathroom door was closed. Carefully he climbed to his feet and followed the muddy prints to the bathroom. He threw open the door.

And stared into the grinning face of Deputy Haws peering at him with one yellowed eye, maggots overflowing his mouth and the stench of death issuing. . . .

Tom cried out as his eyes popped open and he found himself flat on his back in bed in a bedroom bright with morning sun and a mockingbird outside the window chirping another bird's song and his mother calling to him from downstairs.

"Jesus," he muttered, awake or dreaming, not certain which, "how long is this going to go on?"

Tom stared at the sunny side up eggs on his plate and wondered if he had ever seen anything more repulsive in his life. The bad dreams had left him with a queasy stomach that had been sour enough when he went to bed.

The events of the previous night were beginning to feel like a nightmare. He'd have given everything to make it a bad dream or make it right or just make it all go away. It was so weird to think of Deputy Haws lying out there in the woods, under the ground, and that it was Tom and his friends who'd put him there.

It was all Galen's doing, of course, but the law wasn't as lenient on accessories to crime as it used to be. Just being there when somebody shot somebody else was enough to get you a mandatory sentence if the circumstances were right. Didn't you have to be committing a crime or something for that law to apply? But shooting a cop . . . man, that was serious shit no matter what. And he knew that covering it up was a mistake that would come back to haunt them.

Was that what his dreams were about?

The swinging door to the kitchen banged open and Tom jumped a mile, expecting to see Deputy Haws's rotting face and moldy-green body come shambling through. He was only slightly relieved to see his mother, especially since Peg wore the tight-lipped, scowly look that said she was about to jump on his case about something.

"You look like crap," she said.

"Thanks."

"Late night."

"That's what Fridays are for," he said.

"Fridays are for going on dates with girls, going to football games, going out for dinner and a movie. For renting a tape and making out on the sofa after your mother goes to bed. Whatever happened between you and Cindy, anyway?"

Tom shrugged.

"Didn't work out," he said. He glared at her through his eyebrows to show her that any good humor she tried to spend on him would go unappreciated. He'd rather she just ragged him out. She got the message.

"I don't want you going out with that gang tonight," she said.

"It's not a gang."

"Then what is it, Tom? Please, characterize it for me. Is it a charitable organization . . . you're out doing good deeds for the underprivileged?"

He glared at her in silence.

Peg propped her arms on the table and leaned toward him.

"Look," she said. "You're old enough to be out after midnight. I don't care about any sort of curfew. You could stay out until six in the morning and I wouldn't care, not if I knew you were all right and weren't getting into trouble. But I don't like the boys you're hanging out with, and I especially don't like that Ganger boy."

"Why is he always 'that Ganger boy' to everybody? Why doesn't anybody just call him 'Galen?' "

"Because that's what he's made himself. And I don't want

people calling my son 'that Culler boy.' You used to be a good student, once upon a time. Until you started hanging out with those . . . with Galen and Kent and the others."

"They have nothing to do with it."

"They have everything to do with it. They're ignorant. They don't value education. They don't value anything but those souped up cars of theirs and getting drunk and—"

"You don't know that! You don't anything about them!"

"I know enough." She was thinking that they were just like Tom's father, but a comment to that effect would spin them off to a place she didn't want to go.

Peg sat there looking at Tom stonily. Tom stared at his eggs and they stared back. Big yellow eyes. The yolks looked like pus.

"Your eggs are getting cold."

"I'm not hungry."

Peg sighed. "They're a bad influence on you."

"Who? The eggs?"

"Don't be a wiseass. You know who I mean. They won't be happy until they drag you down to their level. You were a good student before. Now I never see you crack a book."

"You'd have to be home for that, wouldn't you?"

Peg's jaw set and Tom could tell from the way she started breathing heavily through her nose that he'd hit a nerve.

"What do you think waitressing pays in this town?" she asked after an ominous pause. "You think I'm rolling in twenty dollar tips out here? You think I want to work double shifts? I do what I have to to put food on the table . . . food you don't even care enough eat!"

The guilt was starting to roll in like a fog that settled over Tom's mind, obscuring everything. Where did it come from, this fog? He didn't have anything to feel guilty about . . . well, except the dead cop he'd helped bury in the woods. But what he was feeling now was old guilt. Old, familiar guilt.

He knew how hard his mom worked. He knew how hard it'd been on her since the divorce, and since she and Tom's dad weren't married when he died, there wasn't even any insurance money. He should've been working, but at what? Busboy in Ma's Diner? God, but Anderson sucked.

"I'll eat the eggs," he said.

Peg pounded the table. The dishes jumped and so did Tom.

"I don't care about the goddamn eggs!" she screamed. "I just want you to straighten the hell up! Quit hanging out with losers! Take school seriously! For Chris'sakes, Tom, I just want you to use your head!"

The implication that he was stupid cut Tom to the quick.

"Well maybe you've got two brain-dead kids in the family!" he snapped, with instant regret. That was low, bringing Annie into it. He wished he could call the words back and stuff them back down his throat where they belonged.

Peg's hand, moving with the speed of reflex, whipped out and slapped him hard across the face.

Tom sat back, stunned. He shoved his chair away from the table. It made a groaning noise and toppled onto its back, and he left it that way as he strode out of the room.

"Be here when I get home!" Peg yelled after him. She heard him tromp upstairs, heard his bedroom door slam shut.

Tom flopped down on his bed and somehow the motion made him think about Deputy Haws's body flopping into the hole they'd dug. He wished he could trade places with the dead deputy right now. He wished he was dead and buried and didn't have to hassle with all this bullshit.

"Shit," he said as the tears welled in his eyes.

In the kitchen, Peg considered allowing herself a good, hard cry. But she was already late and Ma was waiting for her at the diner, so she put it off, as she always seemed to do.

* * *

Doc Milford plopped the Polaroids one after the other in front of Brant, a stomach wrenching sequence detailing Madge Duffy's carving skills.

Brant merely glanced at the photos. He had no reason to doubt their authenticity or Doc's analysis of John Duffy's condition. Still, it seemed important to Doc to lay out all the evidence in favor of considering Duffy dead on Friday night. Maybe he was thinking of a malpractice suit. Or maybe he was doubting his sanity.

"The coroner showed up this morning and verified my diagnosis," Doc said. "He could tell from looking that these were pictures of a dead man, and he's seen his share. When I told him that this very same man had walked out of the hospital under his own power not eight hours later, he wouldn't believe me. And I don't blame him. It's the fruitiest goddamn story I've ever heard in my life. But it happened, I saw it, and all I have to prove it are these pictures."

"You aren't suggesting that I run these photos in the *Times*!"

"No, no, nothing like that. But you see why I had to show them to you. This wasn't some borderline case. Duffy showed all the normal symptoms of death—lack of respiration, no pulse—but for gosh sakes, look at the man!

"Normally I'd feel for a carotid pulse. In Duffy's case, with his neck laid open like that, I could see the carotid—plainly severed! The blood is not circulating in his body. Look how it's settled in the lower body area—they call it "postmortem stain." Livor mortis.

"And . . . there were the flies."

"Flies?" Brant asked.

"They smell death. Long before you or I would notice the smell of a dead body, the insects pick it up. We still don't know what produces the odor, but flies can smell a fresh corpse from a mile away. Madge Duffy left a window open. When the Sheriff got there, he said the body was swarming with flies."

Brant was silent. He didn't want to seem skeptical, but he hadn't seen the body himself. Could this all be a prank? Big city cynicism dies hard.

Doc Milford began to pace. He had a bad hip that wanted surgery but he kept putting it off, his own worst patient.

"I could've run an EEG," he said, "looked for brain death, but really, who would've thought it necessary?

"And even if I was wrong about the death . . . even if Duffy was just seriously wounded, where's the wound now? Where's the scar? It'd take hours of surgery to reattach those veins and arteries, and the stitches . . . he'd look like a damned Frankenstein."

His limping stride took him over to the goldfish bowl he kept in his office for its tranquilizing effect. He tapped some food into the bowl and the lone fish gobbled it up eagerly.

"People talk," Doc said as he fed the fish. "The news of the murder was all over town like a plague wind. Duffy's rise is already making the rounds. And you can bet that most people are saying what an incompetent old coot Doc Milford is and how he should have retired years ago before the liquor robbed him of his senses. Well I don't want to retire, especially not over something like this."

Brant's sympathy went out to the man. Doc Milford had devoted most of his adult life to the births and traumas of his small community and now he stood a good chance of being hooted out in disgrace. They wouldn't run him out of town, of course, but one great wave of gossip would wash out his sterling past and reduce him to another town character, like Clyde Dunwiddey the drunk. It was a fate worse than death for a proud man like Doc.

"I'll do what I can, Doc," Brant offered. "I'll point out

that the coroner agreed with you, based on the photos. If Sheriff Clark and Jed Grimm will back you up. . . ."

"You see," Doc interrupted. "If. You don't believe me. You think I'm off my rocker."

"I didn't say. . . ."

"Oh, I don't blame you. Yes, please, talk to the Sheriff. Talk to Jed Grimm. The night nurse, Claudia White, saw the body. Talk to her, too. But wait 'til she's off the sedatives. She got quite a shock last night."

"I imagine so."

Both men were silent for a time. Brant glanced at the photos on Doc's desk. John Duffy sure looked dead to him. He'd be interested to hear what the Duffys had to say about all this.

As much as he wanted to believe Doc and to believe that something incredible had occurred in this tiny town in the middle of nowhere, as much as he wanted to think that he'd somehow, magically been at exactly the right place at the right time to stumble onto the story of the decade, Brant knew better than to get his hopes up. There was probably a simple explanation. It was a hoax or a misunderstanding of some sort. He couldn't figure it out now but it would come to him or the right piece of the puzzle would fall into place and solve everything in a mundane, logical and very ho-hum manner.

If nothing happened to explain it, it would remain an anomaly. A tabloid item, MURDERED MAN RETURNS TO LIFE, photos on page twelve. Something to read in line at the supermarket, being sure to snort derisively in case anyone was watching, commenting as you put the newspaper back in the rack, "Can you believe the trash they print? Does anybody really believe this stuff?"

"Mind if I take these?" Brant asked. "I'll scan them into the computer, get them back to you."

"Fine, fine," Doc replied.

"I'll do what I can," Brant said again.

"I know you will," said Doc, but he wondered to himself if anybody could do anything at this point, or if events weren't already spinning wildly out of control.

Deputy Haws had been pissed as a bluejay that night to find himself more than six miles from his consarned vehicle. He'd walked along the highway without encountering a single car. These days anybody who was anxious to get anywhere took the interstate, leaving the old county highway to service the dying little towns that had sprung up along its path so many years ago. It saw some traffic in the morning and evening as the hardhats building the nuke plant drove to work or home, and you'd see combines working its length at harvest time, the migrant harvesters following the season from south to north. But much of the time, especially late at night, the road was just a black snake of asphalt running between Not Much and Used To Be.

Being dead didn't appear to have impaired Haws in any way. The bullet wound had healed completely, though he did wonder what became of the slug inside his gut. Had it been spit out like a cherry pit, or was it still rattling around his innards somewhere? Either way, it wasn't bothering him now.

He seemed to have more energy, which he appreciated as he hoofed it along the highway. He still carried about a hundred extra pounds of bulk, but that old feeling of weariness at the slightest exertion was absent. He breathed easier and had more get up and go. Maybe there'd been something wrong with his lungs or his arteries had been getting clogged or something, and now he was experiencing that unfamiliar phenomenon called "health."

He did cough up some dirt now and again and his mouth tasted like he'd been sucking on a toad turd, but that and a sort of roughness in his eyes, like the dirt had scratched his corneas, maybe, were about it for physical side effects.

His mind, however, had changed profoundly.

He preferred to view the world as black or white. Good was good and bad was bad and that was that. He liked it when a new subject of thought bounced down through his brain like a ball bearing in a pachinko machine until it settled into one slot or the other. Then he didn't have to think about it anymore.

But people liked to confuse him with subtleties, and that made him mad. Why, when a person had everything figured out, did they have to pull the rug out from under him? Just because they couldn't make up their own minds about a thing, that didn't give them the right to confuse everybody else.

Certain people always seemed to be laughing at him, like they knew something he didn't. And occasionally, that got to him. Late at night, lying in bed, trying to make shapes out of the shadows of the leaves crawling on the wall, sometimes he'd get to wondering if the world wasn't such a big, complicated work that it was foolish for an average sort of guy like himself to think he could make sense of it.

Maybe he was blind to something that only smart people could see, the way they say dogs can't see color. How could you explain color to a dog? Maybe he was just too thick-headed to understand what smarter people tried to tell him.

Well, if that was the case then there was nothing he could do about it, so it was stupid to even think about it. He got along okay, better than some of the so-called geniuses he'd known who ended up working in bookstores, selling books to other smart people for minimum wage. Or killing themselves because the world didn't fit their idea of how the world ought to be. They'd doubted themselves to death, some of those smart people had.

Deputy Haws wasn't going to lose any sleep thinking about how maybe everything he knew was wrong.

But still. . . .

Still. . . .

The uncertainty was always there, lurking in his nerves like a cold sore, ready to pop out under stress. It made him lash out over ridiculous things and get into fights when the conversation drifted to particular topics, like whether somebody who repeated third grade should be allowed to carry a handgun.

That night, though, trudging along the blacktop, he had no more doubts. Everything was crystal clear. Everything. And he was absolutely dead sure certain about it all. No crack weakened the armor of his certitude.

Seth had made everything clear.

Seth had spoken to him while he was dead. Seth had peered into Haws's brain on those lie-awake nights when the shadows crept along the wall, and Seth had examined the questions that haunted Haws's dreams, and Seth had provided the answer that Haws sought.

Seth was the answer.

No matter the question. All questions were one, really. All answers, one.

Seth.

All Haws had to do was believe in Seth and everything would be all right. All would be right. All . . . right.

There was an example right there of Haws' new clarity of thought.

It was Haws' mission to bring this enlightenment to the rest of the world, starting with those who needed Seth's wisdom the most.

Starting with Galen Ganger.

Haws retrieved his vehicle and drove home well before dawn. He laundered his clothes and sewed a patch over the bullet hole, doing both jobs much better than anyone in town would've expected him to.

He'd treated the bloodstains with pre-wash and liquid detergent and let them soak and then ran everything through the washer three times. Then he'd cut a circle of material from his shirt tail where it wouldn't be missed and used it to patch the bullet hole.

In truth, Haws was not half bad with a needle and thread. He'd all but raised his little sister, Lucille, his alcoholic mother not being of much use in that regard and his father being a "guest of the federal government" in Leavenworth, Kansas. With no money to waste on luxuries, Haws had grown up learning how to make do.

He hadn't anticipated needing more than one official police shirt and one pair of official police pants, so tonight he had to salvage his sole uniform so he could be seen around town later that morning. He wanted to mess with the heads of the punk kids who surely figured him for dead. Nothing heavy. He wouldn't run them in. He just wanted to be seen and let their own guilty consciences and fear of payback do the rest. For now.

Haws still lived with Lucy, who cleaned houses to bring in her share of the rent. Like her mother, she was a heavy sleeper, but for a different reason. Lucy slept because she was depressed. She was not an attractive woman by most standards and had given up on herself early in life. She rose from the bed only long enough to make her meager living, to watch a little TV, or to open a can and heat contents to boiling. Unlike her brother, Lucy was cadaverously thin. Her depression had been with her so long that she couldn't imagine life without it. She was not like other people, certainly not like the happy, buoyant souls she saw on the television screen, and she did not expect anything to change. She tried not to inconvenience her brother, whom she loved and relied upon, and that meant staying out of the way, in her bedroom, in her bed, the covers pulled up tight over her bony shoulders. It was as good a place as any to be, for her, and if that's how she wanted to live, it was okay by her brother.

Haws finished his washing and mending and pressing and draped his uniform on a wire hanger that he hung in a doorway. No point putting it in the closet when he was just going to put it back on in a few hours anyway.

He showered and put on clean underwear and went to bed, not really tired but figuring that he should try to get some rest. He fell asleep in moments and slept like a baby until late Saturday morning. He woke feeling like a million bucks. With a bit of luck, this could turn out to be the best day of his life.

EIGHT

Ma's Diner was already in pandemonium when Deputy Haws walked in.

Claudia White, the night nurse at Cooves County Hospital, was in a screaming match with the Ganger boy who gripped a teaspoon in his hand as if it was a switchblade and looked ready to spoon her to death. Jedediah Grimm, the undertaker, had hold of Ganger by both arms but that didn't stop Ganger's elbow from shooting back where it caught Peg Culler and made her drop two armloads of breakfast specials. Nurse White's mother seemed on the verge of a heart attack and Reverend Small was urging everybody to calm down and Merle Tippert, owner of the Rialto Theatre, pounded the table and screamed for boysenberry syrup. Ma screamed at Tippert from the service window but Haws had no idea what he was saying because he'd lapsed into Mandarin or something . . . it might have been Tongues for all Haws knew. Tom Culler sat at the counter looking sick and Brant Kettering sat next to him scribbling furiously in his notebook. Everybody else either observed nervously or wolfed their food like they planned to sneak out on their check during the hullabaloo.

Haws's arrival calmed the place down, but it wasn't because of the sudden appearance of the law. It was because, when he saw him, Galen Ganger's jaw dropped to the floor and he forgot all about Nurse White and the room spun and he fainted dead away. As a bonus, Tom Culler turned as green as a cartoon character and heaved his breakfast onto the countertop. It was everything Haws could have wished for, and more.

Brant knew that the article ran long and was too raw for publication, but he wanted to write it out like it happened first and save it for his book. He could water it down and objectify it later for the *Cooves County Times*. He wrote:

> John Duffy's alleged rise from the dead would be old news by the time the story made it to the *Times*. What I couldn't provide in terms of timeliness I determined to make up for with depth, or, failing that, width. I wanted to see what the town was thinking, and for that there was no better observation post on a Saturday morning than Ma's Diner.
>
> For many of the citizens of Anderson, Saturday morning breakfast at Ma's was the social event of the week. Ma's had its regulars, like Merle Tippert who lived alone and ate most of his meals out and who reserved Saturday morning for his weekly treat of waffles and boysenberry syrup, the hell with what Doc Milford said about his cholesterol. But anyone was likely to show up, if not for breakfast then for a donut and a cup of coffee, just to hear the current buzz. Any news worth telling would have made the rounds by telephone, but for a quick overview of public opinion about the co-op manager's new hairpiece or Carl Tompkins' decision to carry a line of Japanese power tools down at the hardware store, Ma's was the place to be.
>
> So I hied myself thither to get the lowdown on Duffy.

An angel got its wings as I entered. I presume an angel got its wings because a bell tinkled overhead.

I've often wondered exactly how that works—not the bell because I know how a bell works, but the angel business. How does it all stay in balance? What happens if there are more bells ringing than angels needing wings—do all the bells on Earth fall silent until the wingless angel population recovers? Or do the bells keep ringing and a lot of undeserving angels suddenly sprout wings and quickly and guiltily flutter off for a round of golf on the nearest par-seventy cloud bank? Did Frank Capra know what he was talking about or is it possible that he just made the whole thing up?

I was clearly in the proper frame of mind to debate life after death as I took my favorite stool at the counter, the one near the cash register where I'd receive maximum exposure to *la femme* Culler. I don't know why I can't get this woman out of my mind. For some reason I find her delectable. The fact that she's encased in her own world of troubles as rigidly as if sealed in lucite and is therefore unattainable only makes the attraction stronger.

Anyhow, I sat down and it was several minutes before Peg was able to take my order. The joint was jumpin', and the topic on everybody's lips was John Duffy. I tried to tune my hearing to a single conversation at a time, aurally table-hopping the way I do with the television and the remote control. Eventually, though, the debate took on a more diner-wide scope with people shouting from one table to the next as the issue got deeper and murkier and closer to deeply held, heartfelt beliefs.

The brouhaha seemed to start with Claudia White. Claudia is the night nurse at the hospital and was on duty that night when Duffy appeared from the stairwell in pursuit of Curtis Waxler, the janitor. Doc Milford had prescribed sedatives for the shock Claudia had received to her psyche and ibuprofen for the pain from the bump on her head she took when she fainted at the sight of a man she knew for a fact to be dead throwing open the stairwell door and calling out, "You there!" Maybe she'd stopped taking the sedatives or never took them or they weren't strong enough or she was one of those people on whom drugs have the opposite effect, but for whatever reason Claudia was clearly not sedate. Her voice was up an octave and her hands were waving in the air as she told the story to her mother, sitting across the table from her ignoring a bowl of oatmeal.

"He weren't dead," opined Merle Tippert sitting at the next table by himself. "And this here syrup's maple, not boysenberry. Peg!"

Peg looked his direction even though she was busy filling a coffee cup. He held up the syrup dispenser and hollered out, "Maple!" as if he were saying "Hemlock!" or "Radioactive toxic waste!"

"Sorry, Merle, I'll be right there," Peg answered.

"He was so dead!" Claudia called over to Tippert. "You think I don't know a dead man when I see one? I've been a nurse for fourteen years and I think I know a little more about death than you do who wasn't even there!"

"He weren't dead," Tippert maintained. "Doctors!" He practically spat the word. Merle Tippert practically spat most of his words, which is probably why business was down at the video rental store he ran right next to his movie house. "Videos!" he'd spit at customers. "Television!" He didn't like to rent out movies on videotape. If twenty people would just decide to watch *His Girl Friday* on the same night he'd show the darned thing at the Rialto and they'd see it the way it was meant to be seen, on a big screen with an audience. But society was splitting off into one's and two's who sat in their separate houses and watched movies on little screens all by themselves because they had to watch what they wanted to watch when they wanted to watch it and just stop it right in the middle if they felt like taking a bath or something, which you might as well do since nothing made after 1945 was worth seeing anyway. And don't even mention that direct-to-cable crap.

"Doctors!" Tippert spat. "Don't know nothing! And Doc Milford hasn't had a sober day in twenty years!"

"Don't you go bad-mouthing Doctor Milford!" Claudia warned. If Doc Milford had been running for Pope he would not find a more ardent supporter than Nurse Claudia White. She overlooked his occasional afternoon nip from the flask in his bottom left hand desk drawer because she knew that he'd devoted his life to their little town and she, for one, was grateful for it. Maybe the rest of the people in Anderson didn't appreciate how rare a dedicated physician was these days or how many towns bigger than theirs went begging for a good doctor, but Claudia knew. She knew. And she wasn't going to let a comment like Tippert's go by without calling him on it. "He's given a lot more to this town than that ratty little movie house of yours ever did," she said.

"Yes, and he's done it half-drunk most of the time, too," Tippert countered.

"He was stone cold sober when they brought John Duffy in," said Claudia, "and Duffy was dead as a door nail."

Claudia turned to Jed Grimm, the local undertaker, for confirmation. "You saw him, Mr. Grimm. Of everybody in town, I expect you've seen more dead people than anybody. Was Duffy dead or wasn't he?"

Jed Grimm was working on a short stack with fried eggs and a side of bacon but he didn't waste a second before announcing loudly, aware that eager ears were waiting for his verdict, "That he was, my dear. He was as dead as they come."

Claudia shot a there-you-see look at Tippert who just humphed and called out again for his boysenberry syrup, his waffles were getting cold.

"Then you would agree that Duffy came back from the dead?" I asked of the mortician.

"Now that's another question," Grimm replied. "I haven't seen him since that afternoon, so I don't know that he's alive again. Besides," he chuckled, "resurrection's not really my area of expertise, is it? Perhaps the Reverend Small . . . ?"

And he gestured toward the newest member of the Anderson community, the newly-arrived Reverend Small who was even now mentally preparing the next day's sermon while picking at Ma's version of a fruit plate—a sliced banana and a few wedges of apple topped with fruit cocktail from a can. He did not seem comfortable with the topic. Or with the fruit plate, either, for that matter.

"Well," he said as all eyes swiveled in his direction, "there are precedents, of course, for this kind of thing."

"Louder!" called a voice from the far side of the room. It was Carl Tompkins, still smarting from the past two weeks' grilling over his Makita decision and eager to see someone else on the hot plate for a change.

Reverend Small adjusted his volume upwards and continued.

"There are precedents," he said. "Lazarus. And the Savior himself, of course."

"Are you saying it's a miracle?" Peg asked, adding, "More coffee?"

"No, thank you," Small replied.

"No, which?" Claudia White asked. "No coffee or no miracle?"

"No coffee. As to the miracle, well, who can say?"

"If you can't say, Reverend, who could?" some smart aleck asked. I think it was me.

"Well, of course, I didn't see the deceased. I'm sure Mr. Grimm's credentials are impeccable, but—"

"Louder!"

"I'm sure Mr. Grimm knows what he's talking about!" Small repeated. "Still, such a bold display of God's work as resurrection—well, the Church doesn't sanctify such things without considerable evidence. Now, near-death experiences, thanks to modern medicine, have become almost commonplace, but Duffy—"

"Never happened!" Mr. Tippert snorted. "Like my boysenberry syrup!"

Peg turned red, said "Sorry!" and scurried back behind the counter. Ma stuck his head out of the service window.

"I have cat once that come back," he said. "Back in China. Cat have kittens and no one to take care of. My father, who was very kind man, have unpleasant task of drowning kittens."

I noticed a cloud pass over the face of Carl Tompkins' wife, Bernice.

"He wrap up in sack all kittens and he take sack to river to drown, only when he open sack to place in stone to make heavy, he see all little kittens and they so cute he can't stand thought of trapped in sack and drowning. So he take stone and he hit kittens bang, in head, so death come quick, and then he put stone in sack and kittens and throw in river.

"Next day, one kitten come back. Blood on head, very sad, and my father see kitten and can not bring self to kill kitten again, so I get to keep. Only, stranger thing.

"Kitten never grow up. Kitten stay kitten, many years. Live to be old kitten, but never cat. Very strange."

Ma was shaking his head as he drew it back into the kitchen leaving a stunned silence in its wake, as if everyone had been hit in the head with a stone. Bernice Tompkins nudged her husband Carl and they gulped their coffees and Carl put a half-eaten donut in his jacket pocket and a five dollar bill beside his plate and they hurried out, Bernice leading the way. Bernice was known to have a soft spot for felines, owned twelve at present, and so I guess Ma's story hadn't set well with her.

Then the door opened and Tom Culler walked in with the Ganger boy.

Peg looked up with a smile ready, but it turned into a scowl for some reason (sharing her opinion of Galen Ganger, I can guess what it was) and the two boys took the Tompkins's former seats at the counter. Peg quickly scooped up the five-dollar bill as she shot a hostile look at the Ganger kid, as if she expected him to steal it. The boys ordered Cokes and the conversation returned to John Duffy, Merle Tippert providing the transition.

"The cat weren't dead," Tippert said. "Neither was Duffy. People don't come back from the dead."

"So you're not buying into the miracle theory, Mr. Tippert?" I asked.

He snorted. "Dead's dead."

"Well I know what I saw and I saw John Duffy dead and I saw him a few hours later walking down the hallway toward me healthy as a horse." Claudia White was not giving an inch.

"Perhaps it is the Second Coming," her mother suggested.

"From what I hear of Duffy, he's a pretty unlikely candidate for Savior," I said.

"What're they talking about?" Tom asked his mother as she brought them their Cokes.

"John Duffy," she said. "His wife murdered him yesterday afternoon and now apparently he's come back from the dead."

Tom and the Ganger boy exchanged incredulous looks. They both seemed to turn a shade paler.

"You're kidding," Tom said. Peg gestured toward the assembly.

"Ask them," she said.

A chorus of voices validated her story, all except Merle Tippert who snorted derisively.

"I don't believe it," Tom said.

"At least somebody in this town's got some sense," Tippert said.

"It's the Second Coming," said Mrs. White, expounding her theory. It seemed to have gained solidity in her mind from having sat there for a minute, kind of like what Ma's pancakes do in your stomach. "Jesus has come to Anderson and he's working miracles," she announced with conviction.

"Bullshit!" the Ganger boy said.

A hush fell over the diner. No voice spoke, no fork rang against plate, no ice jiggled, no coffee slurped. The people of Anderson were accustomed to profanity, but they kept it in their fields and houses and workplaces where it belonged. It arrived at Ma's Diner in the middle of a discussion about life everlasting and the Holy Christ like a bandito at a bar mitzvah.

The Ganger boy continued: "Like Jesus would have anything to do with this shithole!"

"I happen to love this town," Claudia White said, "and I do not appreciate your calling it . . . what you did. And I don't think anyone else did, either." She looked around for approval and received enough nods and murmurs of agreement to spur her on. "I'd like to know just what you find so offensive about this town," she added snippishly, which with Galen Ganger was a lot like asking a Libertarian what was so wrong with the federal government.

Ganger swiveled off his stool and headed for Nurse White's table. Tom put out his arm to stop him, saying, "Galen . . . don't." Ganger shoved the arm aside and sauntered toward the nurse with fire burning in his eyes.

"Let's see," Ganger said, "how about the fact that it's in the middle of no-fucking-where, halfway up the ass of the universe? How about the fact that there isn't dick to do except fuck sheep or watch shit movies in some piss-smelling movie house."

Merle Tippert bristled visibly.

The Ganger boy was closing on Nurse White and I saw something glisten in his hand and for a moment I thought he'd pulled a switchblade, but then I saw it was only a teaspoon that he was twiddling between his fingers.

"I don't like your tone . . . or your language," Claudia White said.

"And I don't like your fucking face, so that makes us even," Galen replied, and he kept walking.

Reverend Small looked like he was going to crawl under his table as the Ganger boy passed, but then he sat up straight and ventured to say, "Young man. . . ." Ganger whirled around and pounded the Reverend's table with the flat of his hand and yelled "Shut up!"

and made everybody jump. That put an end to the Reverend's interest in discourse.

Jed Grimm was watching the scene unfold as if expecting he might get some business out of it. He started slowly inching out of his booth as the Ganger boy walked by. I couldn't tell if he was going to make a run for it or what.

"But what I hate most about this stupid, fucking, ugly little town," Ganger said, "is the people. The boring, stupid people." He leaned in at Claudia White, and though she backed away from him, she held his gaze. She looked right at him, right into his eyes, and she never blinked. Her jaw was clenched tight and her own eyes were invisible behind narrow slits, but she never looked away.

"Boring. Stupid. Ugly people," Ganger said, "like you, Nurse White. People who believe every stupid fucking story they hear."

I don't know what devil possessed Nurse Claudia White to spit in Galen Ganger's face, but I'll bet he earned his pitchfork for it. She could hardly miss at that range. It took Ganger by surprise, that was for sure, and he jerked back reflexively. The next instant he was cocking back his arm, his hand balled into a fist, and he'd have planted it on the woman, I'm certain, but for Jed Grimm.

Grimm is a big man, big like a football player, and normally the most easygoing guy you'd ever hope to meet. But for a big, easygoing guy he moved damned fast and he was behind the Ganger kid before anybody knew it, his arms wrapped around the boy's chest, pinning his arms to his side.

Claudia White, who moments earlier had been chastising Ganger for his language, begin to spew out such a barrage of obscenities at such volume that

I half expected her head to spin around in a circle vomiting pea soup.

Ganger yelled back using words that made his earlier profanities seem like sweet nothings by comparison. He squirmed free of the undertaker's grip but Grimm was on him again instantly and grabbed his arms as he pulled him back. The kid's elbow shot out, trying to catch Grimm in the jaw but instead hitting Peg Culler who'd been watching the whole incident, dumbfounded, with plates of eggs and pancakes and sausage balanced all up the length of both arms. The plates went flying and crashed on the floor and Ma stuck his head out of the service window and started yelling something in his native tongue.

Merle Tippert yelled at Ma demanding boysenberry syrup and Ma yelled back in Chinese and the Ganger kid shook his spoon menacingly at Nurse White. They kept up their exchange of threats and vilification as Grimm dragged Ganger toward the door and nearly backed into Deputy Haws who stood there with one hand on the door and the other on his weapon.

The Ganger boy took one look at the deputy and must have thought he was about to get shot because every last drop of color drained from his face in about one-hundredth of a second and his eyes rolled back into his head and he fainted dead away. I turned around to locate the source of the wet, retching sound behind me and saw Tom Culler emptying his stomach all over the counter.

Deputy Haws said he'd take it from there and dragged the Ganger boy off and Jed Grimm helped load the body into Haws' police car. Then Haws drove off for the Sheriff's office, grinning like the cat who swallowed the canary.

All in all I'm not sure what I learned about Anderson's collective attitude toward John Duffy's return from the nether world, but I did have a hell of an exciting Saturday morning.

Merle Tippert never got his syrup.

Brant read through the words on the computer screen and was generally pleased. He had to find a more original metaphor than "the cat that swallowed the canary" but other than that, it was a pretty fair first draft.

He was ready, now, to go have a few words with John Duffy.

Madge was certain that something awful was about to happen to her.

She couldn't put her finger on why, but the premonition was there, like when she felt . . . just felt before anyone in town had the slightest reason to suspect it . . . that the Mathewson girl was going to run off with Bobby Speers.

"I just had a feeling," Madge would say when others asked her how she'd known that Elaine Mathewson would throw over her steady boyfriend, Herman Johnson, and ride off with Bobby in his red Mustang convertible to Las Vegas. "I guess you could call it a 'premonition' if you wanted to."

Madge had another premonition now.

John had been sober and industrious since his rise, but it made Madge uneasy, like when Jimmy Swaggert cried on television. It wasn't natural. Not that she wanted the old John back, not by a long shot, but deep down she wasn't so sure he was gone. People don't change like that overnight.

He'd said that they had work to do, but he didn't say what it was. He'd busied himself around the house, fixing dripping faucets and the like, but surely that wasn't what he meant. The way he'd said it made it sound more like some kind of mission, but John hadn't breathed a word about anything like that. She wondered what he was waiting for.

It was the waiting and the not knowing that made her nervous. That, and the voice in the back of her head that kept whispering its warning in her ear. She was feeling the premonition as a coldness in her veins when Brant Kettering drove up and tooted his horn.

The toot was a kind of courtesy in Anderson, extended by visitors who hadn't phoned before dropping in. It gave you time to button your pants or get your hands out of the dish water before you had to respond to the knock on the door, and if you didn't want to be home to visitors, it let you quiet down and make yourself invisible until they left.

Madge had often had reason to take advantage of the toot. When she had a bruise she didn't want anyone to see or her eyes were swollen from crying, she'd hear the toot and move quickly to switch off the radio she was listening to and hide in the pantry. They couldn't see her, then, even if they peeked in the windows, but she couldn't see out either and had to stand very quietly so she could hear when the car drove away. One day she'd seen Bernice Tompkins walking her way with a basket of kittens and Madge had a black eye and hid in the pantry and she'd stayed there for forty-five minutes, imagining Bernice circling the house and peering like a spy through every window.

Hiding was Madge's impulse now, but she couldn't say why.

John was working on the back porch banister that'd been wiggly as long as Madge could remember. She could see him through the back door and saw him look up and scowl when the horn sounded, as if he didn't want to be dragged away from his work. That wasn't like John, either, who was usually happy to put off any chore, especially if it meant a sociable drink or two.

She went to the door and was there when Brant knocked. His appearance was no surprise to her. He'd approached her before, when she was a murderess, but she'd refused to say anything for fear that the first word would be like the first tiny rock in the dam to give way, and that after that would come the torrent of abuses and complaints bottled up over twenty years of marriage. She didn't want to complain then, and she sure as heck wasn't going to get into it now.

Brant studied the Duffy place as he walked from the car to the front porch. It was shabby, not quite ramshackle but needing a lot of tender loving care. He knew from the gossip that tender loving care was a rare commodity in the Duffy household.

Madge answered his knock. Brant had no idea how he was going to get this ball rolling considering her sphinx-like silence when he'd tried to interview her in her cell, but he hoped that talking to her in her own home would be more productive.

He couldn't imagine how Duffy would respond, but Brant was prepared to duck.

"Hello, Madge," Brant said warmly.

Madge returned his "hello" but didn't invite him in.

"I guess you know why I'm here," Brant said.

"I expect it's about John," Madge replied.

"It's a big story. I thought he might want to tell it from his point of view. I'd like to talk to you, too, of course."

"There's nothing to tell." It was John Duffy's voice, and it had an edge to it. He'd appeared from the kitchen. The grim look on his face made the hammer in his hand seem more like a weapon than a tool.

"Must have been quite an experience," Brant said, trying to sound conversational. When Duffy didn't take the bait, Brant dropped another worm into the water. "Waking up in the morgue like that, must have been a shock."

"It's over and done with," Duffy said, advancing. He put his hand on the door as if to slam it shut.

"Maybe for you," Brant said, "but all of Ma's Diner was debating the principles of the thing this morning. Darn near started a riot. Any light you could shed—"

"It just happened, that's all."

Brant sighed and scratched his head. "Well, if that's the quote you want me to run. . . ."

Sometimes the best way to get a subject to talk is to just shut up and let the silence become a void that they feel compelled to fill with words. As the seconds ticked by, Brant got the impression that he could stand on that porch for seven days and seven nights without John Duffy ever uttering another syllable. Madge, though, was another matter.

"He's changed," Madge said, almost without moving her lips.

Duffy whipped his head around and glared at her like a rattlesnake suddenly aware of a descending boot. Madge knew that glare even without actually seeing it, but the test of John's redemption had to come sooner or later and so maybe this was it. "I don't know what he saw on the other side," she said, "but it changed him."

"In what way?"

Madge chose her words with great care. Practically everybody in town knew her and John's history, but there was no need to splash it all over the front page for those who didn't. On the other hand, she wanted people to know that he was reformed, and having it reported in the *Times* made it somehow truer.

"For the better," she said at last, and then added, "and that's my last word on the subject."

Brant opened his mouth to speak but the door swung suddenly toward him and shut with a finality that told him the interview was over. He turned away from the Duffy place and got back in his car and drove off, not knowing that behind those walls John Duffy had just knocked his wife to the floor.

NINE

"You're shitting us," Darren said. He looked from Galen to Tom, desperate for a sign that this was all some kind of sick joke. A smirk, a snicker, a twitch of the lip. Anything. Finding nothing.

"It's true," Tom said. "Haws is alive."

"Again," Galen added.

Darren regarded Kent and Buzzy. Kent sat on the fender of Darren's Satellite looking so sunken and morose he barely seemed to be breathing. Buzzy sat beside him, his leg twitching nervously, his mind working a mile a minute.

"I don't believe it," Darren said.

"You heard about Duffy," said Tom.

"Yeah, I heard. And I don't believe that crock of shit either."

Galen paced like a caged hyena, his teeth clenched, his breath huffing through flared nostrils. He turned on Darren and punched a palm hard into his chest.

"Fucking believe it!" he said.

"Hey!" Darren protested.

Galen was in his face.

"I saw the asshole! I woke up in the back of his fucking car! The fucker is alive!"

Galen had indeed come to in the back seat of Haws's patrol vehicle and stared up at Haws's red neck, and then Haws had turned around and grinned at him and Galen had figured he'd died and gone to Hell. "Feeling better?" Haws had asked, and all Galen could do was lie there on the stinking seat while his brain performed its impression of the *Lost In Space* robot blowing a fucking fuse. Haws had reached over and jacked open the door behind Galen's head and said, "Be home tonight," and then told him to get the hell out of his patrol vehicle. Galen had scrambled out of the car without even sitting up, just scooted out like a lizard and flopped onto the pavement and Haws slammed the door shut and drove off, his back tires spinning and spraying Galen with road debris. When he'd stopped shaking, Galen had called the guys and told them to get their asses out to the reservoir pronto, some serious shit was going down.

"You'd better believe it," Galen said, resuming his pacing. Then he yelled out "Shit!" and kicked the fender of Darren's Satellite hard enough to leave a dent.

Darren leaped at Galen and gave him a shove before his good sense had time to stop him.

"Asshole!" Darren yelled and Galen whirled on him and grabbed the front of his shirt and muscled him over against the car and backed him against the window.

"Who are you calling asshole, asshole?" Galen demanded.

"You dented my fucking car!" Darren yelled back.

Galen and Darren faced off for a few seconds and then Galen glanced over at the fender. He looked at the dent as if seeing it for the first time.

"Shit!" he said, giving Darren a shove as he turned loose of his shirt. "Shit shit shit shit!" It looked as if he was going to kick the car again but some force restrained him.

"If Galen says he saw him, he saw him," Buzzy said.

"I saw him, too," said Tom. "He's alive."

"So Galen didn't kill him."

"No, but we sure as hell buried the fucker," Kent said.

"So why didn't he arrest us when he had the chance?" Tom asked. "He saw me there. He didn't even arrest Galen. He just loaded him in his car and let him go."

"He told me to be home tonight," Galen said.

"But he didn't arrest you. He didn't do shit to me. He didn't go after Darren or Buzzy or Kent. Why? What's he waiting for? Maybe you didn't kill him but you put a bullet in his stomach! You think he's just going to forget that?"

"Shut up!" Galen yelled. "How can I think? Shit!" He kicked at some dirt and everybody gave him some time to wind down.

"We're fucked," Buzzy intoned.

"This isn't real," Darren insisted. "This is fucking *Twilight Zone* shit."

"It's real," Tom said, "and we have to figure out how to deal with it. And we can't do that until Haws makes his move."

Tom felt abnormally calm. After the nightmares and the shock of seeing Deputy Haws alive at the diner, a strange resignation had settled over him. If Haws was alive, they hadn't killed him. So no matter what revenge Haws tried to take, it wouldn't put them in jail for life with no chance of parole. They faced the unknown, but it couldn't be worse than what they'd faced before. It just couldn't.

"I hate this shit!" Galen said.

Galen paced and Tom thought, This is it, Galen, the moment you've been hurtling toward for the past eighteen years. The moment of truth.

He'd often wondered what force of nature kept somebody like Galen Ganger in Anderson. He'd thought that Galen's rage would have taken him somewhere else long before this. Ironically, he realized, Anderson's provinciality, against which Galen struggled and cursed and railed, was the glue that held him fast. The town was like the forced perspective room in a funhouse that makes giants of midgets. Viewed against any larger backdrop, Galen Ganger would diminish. He might even disappear.

And now, something enormous had come to Anderson, and Galen had set himself against it. It dwarfed him utterly.

It was roaring over him like an avalanche. To defy it was useless.

"You going to be home tonight like Haws wants?" Tom asked.

"I don't know!" Galen snapped.

"I think you have to."

Galen stopped abruptly at the words, his back to the other boys, his eyes on the water. The air was heavy and still. Tom felt his palms moisten—Galen did not like being told what to do. He looked at the others and noticed how carefully they avoided his gaze.

After several moments of leaden silence, Galen looked over his shoulder at Tom.

"Fuck," he said flatly. He looked at Buzzy and Kent, both studying the ground, and at Darren who glared at him, still mad about the dented fender, then fixed his eyes on Tom.

"When you're right, you're right, Einstein," Galen said. "It's me and him. That's what it comes down to. Me and him."

Tom nodded.

"Yeah," he said, "pretty much."

It wasn't just Galen and Deputy Haws, of course. It was all of them, and it was something much bigger than the bunch of them put together. He didn't see any use in pointing that out, though, not yet.

They'd find out soon enough.

Brant wondered if he should contact the Associated Press.

He'd never had a story go out over the AP wire, and the way news traveled over the grapevine somebody in the outside world would hear of Duffy's rise soon enough and he'd be scooped in his own backyard. On the other hand, he didn't want to be branded a kook and the facts in the case were as wonky as a shopping cart. Doc Milford could be counted on for a solid "no comment" and the Duffys certainly weren't talking.

No, if there was a story here, it'd take more digging to unearth it. At least, those were his thoughts as he drove by Carl Tompkins's house and saw him crawl out from under the foundation in coveralls and a filter mask and dragging a five-gallon stainless steel sprayer.

Brant pulled onto the wrong side of the street and rolled down his window and hollered at Carl.

"It's the damned cockroaches," Carl explained. "I've done everything, but with all the cats . . . I don't want to complain, but you know how it is. Cat food left out all the time, and they eat like pigs. Bernice tries to keep the place clean but . . . twelve cats. Jeez!"

Brant asked Carl if he'd thought about tenting the house.

"No, that's for termites," Carl informed him. He hoisted the sprayer into view. "I've sprayed with everything in the store, even stuff I'm not supposed to sell without a permit. I thought I had them licked there for awhile, but. . . ." He shook his head. "I could swear I heard them in the night, in the walls, under the floor, made a helluva racket. Regular cockroach jamboree down there. Joists were thick with them when I looked this morning. Damn brazen, too. I shined the light on them and they just stood right there looking back at me like to say, 'What the devil do you want down here?' They're dead now, though. Bernice threw a fit about the poison. Say, you wouldn't want to keep a cat or two for a couple of days?"

Brant said "No, thanks," and wished Carl luck and drove on to the hospital.

He had to wait to see Doc Milford. Annie Culler was having trouble breathing and Doc suspected fluid in her lungs. They'd taken her in for x-rays and Doc had a few minutes while waiting for the results. Brant told him about his interview with John and Madge Duffy.

"It sounds to me like they just want to put the whole thing behind them," he said.

"I wish it was that easy for me," Doc replied. "Did you get a look at him?"

"Just as you said, not a mark on him."

"You're not a religious man, are you, Brant?"

Brant acknowledged that he wasn't.

"Neither am I," Doc said, "not in the strictest sense. Still, there isn't a doctor living who hasn't had a miracle case or two in his career. Someone who shouldn't make it, does. Someone who shouldn't wake up, wakes. The little Culler girl, for instance. I'd bet a dollar to a donut that she never regains consciousness. If she were my own daughter, I'd have pulled her off life support months ago. But Peg has faith, so who am I to say that Annie won't be that one in a million who pulls through against all odds? She could go on to be a normal little girl and a sullen teenager and the mother of three and the first lady President of the United States for all I know.

"But John Duffy, he's something else. Duffy's right up there with multiplying loaves and Sunday strolls on top of Lake Erie. It couldn't happen, but it did."

Doc Milford chuckled.

"I even tracked down his birth record," he said, "to see if he might have been twins. You know, somebody pulling a switch on me. No such luck. Not even a brother or a sister. So, there is no rational explanation for John Duffy whatsoever. Unless you believe in miracles."

Brant shifted uncomfortably in his chair. If Doc was talking miracles, there might be something to it, and that meant the inevitable interview with the local guru. "I guess I'd better see Reverend Small this afternoon," he said. "Come with me."

"Why? Do you need help finding the church?"

"No, but I'd like a doctor there in case I break out in boils. Got a free hour?"

"I'll make one."

Brant did not break out in boils or burst into flame when he set foot inside the First Methodist Church, but his stomach did flip-flop and he felt his forehead bead up with sweat. He wondered, because of his obvious aversion to all things religious, if he weren't suppressing memories of being molested by a church leader as a child, but since he hadn't been raised Catholic he didn't think that was likely.

Reverend Small was setting out hymnals for the next day's services when Brant and Doc walked in. The sanctuary smelled, well, like a sanctuary, and the scent was probably what triggered Brant's gastronomic response. It was the unforgettable mixture of wood and Pledge and holiness that defines middle American churches from east coast to west, from North Dakota down to Galveston Bay.

They exchanged greetings and quickly got down to business.

"You have a very spirited community here," Small offered, and Brant smiled.

"You mean that little fracas at Ma's this morning? That was nothing. Wait'll an election year and you'll see some real fireworks."

"What do you make of the Duffy situation, Reverend?" Doc asked. "Are we talking 'miracle' here?"

"Well—and no offense intended, Doctor—but it's either that or gross medical incompetence. Not having been at the hospital. . . ."

Doc whipped the Polaroids out of his inside jacket pocket with a speed that would have dazzled a gunfighter. To his credit, Reverend Small was noticeably unsqueamish as Doc led him through the photos one by one, describing

Duffy's state in medical terms that led inevitably to the same conclusion: Duffy was as dead as a holiday ham when they wheeled him down to the morgue. If his death was a hoax, it had taken the participation of John Duffy, his wife, the Sheriff, Doc Milford, Nurse White, and Curtis Waxler the janitor (who had eventually turned up at the grade school playground on top of the jungle gym with no recollection of how he got there) to pull it off. Not to mention the able assistance of a top special effects makeup team.

And for what? If John Duffy were a glory hound of some sort, it might make sense. But why stage such an elaborate hoax just to retreat and clam up like an indicted Senator?

"For one," Reverend Small said, "I'm perfectly willing to accept the notion that the Good Lord, in His generosity, chose to smile upon the Duffy family, if not for John Duffy's sake, then for his wife's. Miracles happen. After viewing your photos, Doctor, I'd say I'm convinced. Thank you."

"For . . . ?"

"For giving focus to tomorrow's sermon. Congregations don't respond well to ambiguity. They worship conviction. A minister who isn't sure about things soon finds himself without a flock."

"Like a shepherd with no sense of direction," Brant suggested.

"That's a good analogy. May I use it?"

Brant nodded his assent. "Myself, I've always been skeptical of people who had all the answers," he said. "Take the good doctor, here. I'm sure he'd freely admit to certain gaps in his knowledge of medicine."

"Medicine often seems to be more gaps than knowledge," said Doc. "Everything we learn somehow raises more questions."

"So it stands to reason that when it comes to comprehending the basic forces of the universe—God, in other words—we pitiful little human beings would be as much at a loss as, say, a housefly to understand Wall Street, molecular physics, or the federal income tax. Yet we're surrounded by people—the holy men of every denomination—who claim to have the inside scoop." Brant shrugged. "I'm skeptical."

"As well you should be," Reverend Small replied. "Nonetheless, your fellow houseflies demand such answers, and we clergy do the best we can to provide them."

"Even when you have to make something up."

"Unlike reporters, you mean." The preacher smiled.

Doc Milford had been regarding the exchange with amusement. "What strikes me," Doc said, "is how this 'miracle' occurred fewer than two weeks after your arrival. I guess if a preacher wanted to impress his new town, a resurrection's one way to do it."

"Well," Small replied, "with Anderson, I wanted to hit the ground running."

"Maybe I wasn't kidding," replied Doc.

"Maybe I wasn't, either."

The sanctuary fell deathly quiet for some moments. Then Brant's bowels gurgled and he suggested that they'd taken enough of the Reverend's time.

It was as if someone had left the window to Peg's brain open and flies had gotten in, but it was only her own thoughts that were swarming. She was worried about Tom's growing bond with the Ganger boy, she kept flashing on the morning's altercation at the diner, she didn't know what to make of John Duffy's miraculous rise from the dead, and there was the persistent and familiar question that cropped up at every occurrence of stress: What does this mean for Annie?

If people could come back from the dead, couldn't they just as easily ... even more easily ... come out of comas?

Why was John Duffy, a known wife-abuser, chosen for this miracle over her own sweet, innocent baby?

Did anything at all make sense? Or was the whole world some sort of monstrous practical joke on humankind?

Against the buzz of thoughts like these, who ordered dressing on their salad and who wanted it on the side could not compete. On top of that the diner was uncommonly busy, and John Duffy was the hot topic at every table. Peg found herself at times wishing the man had stayed dead.

People tend to gather together in a crisis and the fact that they were gathering now made Duffy's rise that much more ominous. Peg had to make more apologies to customers that afternoon than she'd made all year to date, which Ma was quick to point out to her. She looked so miserable, though, that he offered to call in Cindy Robertson and let Peg off early. She took Ma up on his offer and left as soon as Cindy arrived. She drove straight to the hospital to check on Annie.

She noticed Brant's car in the lot and learned that he was in Doc's office. The admissions nurse told her that Brant and Doc had just returned from a confab with Reverend Small and Peg could guess the subject of the conversation. She knew Brant well enough to take his visit to a church as another bad omen.

Her outlook, then, was bleak when she stepped into Annie's room and saw the stranger bending low over the bed, obviously not a nurse or even an orderly. She couldn't see his face or what he was doing, but he was dressed in worn-out blue jeans and a shirt that badly needed laundering and Peg's protective instincts kicked into overload. She yelled out, "Hey!" and marched in ready to leap on his back.

The stranger whipped around like a mongoose at the hiss of a cobra. "Mom!" Tom said, "Jesus, you scared the shit out of me!"

Peg was suddenly lightheaded. I didn't even recognize my own son, she thought. There had been a time when she could have picked him out on a playground among thirty other kids at five hundred feet. She'd have known the way he ran, the way he stood and fidgeted with his fingers, his laugh even when mingled with a dozen others. She'd known his every pair of pants and every shirt and how long he'd worn them without changing. She could have picked out his silhouette at twilight, running toward her along the sidewalk or dangling from a tree limb or just sitting on the riverbank lost in his own thoughts. That was years ago, and every year since had seen that intimacy erode, had brought her closer to this single, pulse-fluttering, upside-down moment when she looked upon her son and beheld a stranger.

My God, she thought, I've lost him.

"She isn't breathing right," Tom said. "Listen."

Peg put her ear to Annie's chest and listened to the rasp of her breath. "Get Doc," Peg said, and Tom dashed out of the room. He returned with the doctor and Peg spied Brant hovering around the doorway, watching.

Doc put a stethoscope to Annie's chest and gave a listen. "We detected this earlier," he said. "I think it's just a little water that's collected in the lungs. We x-rayed her to check for pneumonia, but the x-rays were clear. We're giving her a diuretic now. If the drug doesn't take care of the problem, we'll go in with a tube, but I'd like to avoid that if possible."

After a few more reassurances Doc left and Brant entered.

"I don't want to intrude," he said. Peg told him not to be silly and to pull up a chair.

"I understand you've become a church-goer," she said.

Brant laughed and told her about his visit to the Duffys and his and Doc's conversation with Reverend Small, and Peg filled Brant in on the general buzz at the diner. Tom listened with what Peg took as polite interest. She expected him to excuse himself at any moment, but maybe the gathering instinct was working on him, too. Something had brought him to the hospital, and something held him here now. For some reason the image of crows grouping on a wire before a storm came into Peg's mind.

"The big question in town," Peg said, "seems to be, 'Why Duffy?' What makes him so special?"

"It certainly wasn't his karma," Brant agreed.

Tom studied the pattern of the tiles on the floor. As usual, the populace of Anderson was off on a tangent. Duffy wasn't the only one chosen, but how was anyone except Tom and the other boys to know that? Not that Deputy Hawg was any more deserving of divine intervention than John Duffy was, but if anybody was likely to figure this thing out, it might be Brant, and he was as far off base as everyone else.

Tom felt himself stuck between a rock and a hard place. Brant needed facts that only Tom was able to provide . . . well, that only Tom was likely to provide. He might do it, too, if Peg weren't there. She'd run to the Sheriff for sure, Galen being involved and all. For that matter, so might Brant. Then again, Brant would grasp the concept of confidential sources, or should, anyway. There was a time when Tom would've taken Brant into his confidence immediately, but that was before the "My Town" business. Brant might not have the guts to do what was needed now, but who knew what was needed? Damn, this shit was confusing. Tom felt himself sliding into the Blacklands, but he fought it. This wasn't the time or place. . . .

"Tom?"

Tom started. He hadn't noticed that Brant was speaking to him.

"Sorry," Tom said.

"Lost in thought?" Peg asked. "I know how it is. I was the same way all day."

"I was just going to get us some coffee," Brant said. "Want a cup? It's even worse than Ma's."

"I'll go with you," Tom said. He got out of his chair and then for some reason he bent down and kissed Peg on the forehead. It took her by surprise. He hadn't done that since . . . ever. "Back in a minute," he said.

"I'll be here," Peg said.

Brant and Tom left and Peg was grateful for a few minutes alone. For one thing, she felt like she was going to cry, and she wanted to give in to it this time, and she wanted to have it over with before they got back.

"What's on your mind?" Brant asked.

He and Tom stood in front of the coffee machine in the waiting room. Brant held one cup of foul black liquid in his hand and another was filling as they watched. Clearly there was something Tom wanted to tell him that he couldn't bring up in front of his mother. While eager to rebuild the bridge between himself and Tom, Brant still hoped that Tom's next sentence wouldn't contain the phrases "a few bucks," "there's this girl," or "a single homosexual experience." What Tom did say was not much of a relief, though.

"Can you keep a secret?" Tom asked.

"Helluva thing to ask a reporter," Brant said. "But if it's something personal. . . ." He pried the second cup of coffee out of the machine.

"It's about Duffy. I mean, sort of. I think it's about Duffy." Tom was well aware that he sounded like a typical tongue-tied teenager and he struggled to transcend the stereotype. "It's serious," he continued, "and I need advice, and it might help you . . . figure things out. But I need your word."

"To keep it to myself?"

"Right."

"I don't know, Tom. I want to help, and if you know anything that'd make sense of this Duffy business. . . ."

Tom told himself that he was an idiot. Brant was no different from any other adult in Anderson. "Forget it," he snapped. He spun on his heels and was headed for the door when Brant called after him.

"Wait!"

Tom turned and glared at Brant as the reporter hurried to catch up with him, scalding hot coffee spilling across the backs of his fingers.

"This secret," Brant said, "were any laws broken?"

"Yes."

"Was anybody hurt?"

That was a tough one. "Not permanently," Tom said.

Brant thought it over for a second. "Okay," he said, and then he told Tom to meet him in front of his office in an hour. Tom nodded his agreement and headed into the deepening twilight.

So he had an hour to think about what he was going to say, if he decided to show up at all.

Peg was reading to Annie when Brant got back to the room. He entered quietly, set the coffees on the bedside table, and peered over Peg's shoulder.

" 'So Booboo Bunny,' " Peg read, " 'although she was very afraid, poked her tiny pink nose out of her den and said, "What do you want, Mr. Bear?" Mr. Bear smiled his best smile and said to Booboo Bunny—' "

Brant put his hand on Peg's shoulder and read, in a voice that he hoped was suitably bear-like, " 'Come out, come out, Booboo Bunny! I want to see your long, beautiful ears!' "

Peg smiled up at him. He gave her a look of mock reproach and she quickly jumped into the role of Booboo Bunny.

"'Do you really think I have beautiful ears?' asked Booboo Bunny. And she poked her head out of her den just far enough to show Mr. Bear her tall, fluffy ears."

"'Oh, you have very soft, fine ears!' said Mr. Bear, 'but I'm sure the fur on your lovely neck is even softer and prettier!'"

Peg felt the hair on her neck stand at attention as a chill ran up her spine. "'Really?' said Booboo Bunny. She took the little-bittiest bunny hop and eased her neck out of her safe, warm den. . . ."

Madge Duffy nursed her bruised jaw with the ice pack. John sat across the kitchen table from her, looking sorrowful.

"I said I was sorry. I just lost control for a minute, that's all," he said.

So this was the way it was going to be. Abuse and control, the same as always, followed by remorse that appeared genuine yet failed to move Madge emotionally—except to instill in her a profound sorrow for her never-changing state.

She wondered: What kind of half-baked miracle was it that taught a man remorse but left the evil within him intact?

She didn't know if she could endure more years of this life. Was this living, to be reduced to a machine that followed orders like a robot, to be a punching bag for a sick man's anger? Was this the Madge she wanted to be, would consent to be, would settle for being for the rest of her days?

She glanced over at her husband, whose head was bowed in shame. He'd apologized for hitting her and she hadn't said a word. She'd just calmly walked into the kitchen and taken the familiar ice pack out of the drawer and filled it with cubes from the freezer and sat down to think things over. He'd come in and sat across from her and for half an hour neither had uttered a syllable.

Odd state of affairs, sitting at the table with a man who, about this time the day before, she'd killed with a kitchen knife. Yes, killed. Who would have thought she'd be capable of such an act? Yet she had done it, and she would do it again, do it in a New York minute, if she thought there was any point. But who's to say he wouldn't come back as often as she could murder him? He was like a stain that wouldn't come out, or that crack over the mantel that, no sooner would she get a coat of spackle and paint over it than the house would settle another sixteenth of an inch and there it would be again.

It was just hopeless, her situation. Hopeless. She thought about the pistol that John kept in the drawer in the night table beside the bed.

She wondered if this was how her mother had felt. Had she sat in her own kitchen with an ice pack on her jaw while the poison under the sink whispered to her?

"I'm going to go lie down for awhile," she said flatly.

John watched her leave. Moments later he heard the bedroom door shut.

This was the part Seth loved most—early on, when there was time to play.

Soon enough events would whirl and spin under their own momentum. Soon enough they would tear through the middle of town, crashing and roaring and ripping up lives by the roots, tossing them this way and that, exuberant and destructive as a storm. Death would crackle like lightning, victims would howl like the wind. It would be a fine spectacle and he anticipated it eagerly.

But now, he played a gentleman's game of carefully

maneuvered pawns and cunning traps. Now was the time to manipulate, to roll the first pebbles gently down the hill and delight in the mathematical beauty of their inevitable collisions.

John Duffy was such a stone. No doubt, a miserable stone at this point, stupefyingly predictable and dull. But Madge was a delight. A good woman by any measure, she'd surprised him with the delicious murder of her husband. And now . . . well, that remained to be seen.

Then there was the Ganger boy. If any soul in Anderson was ripe for seduction, it was the Ganger boy.

Twilight, and the air was getting chilly. Seth started a fire in the fireplace and poured himself a glass of a surprisingly piquant pinot noir from California.

And Peg Culler, he thought.

Yes. That would be the test, wouldn't it?

TEN

Brant sat at his desk in the *Times* office and tried to pretend that he wasn't paying any attention to the teenager huddled in the shadows, knees drawn up to his chest, whose low voice quietly and matter-of-factly detailed one of the most deliciously lurid stories Brant had ever been privileged to hear. Brant's fingers flew over the Mac's keyboard, trying to get it all down and get it right. It seemed typical of Brant's career—and of the whimsical humor of the journalism gods—that Brant was able to obtain this story only by swearing on his dear mother's grave not to publish it.

Tom had objected at first to Brant's note-taking, but he accepted it when Brant pointed out that any other activity would arouse suspicion on the part of passersby. Besides, if Brant was supposed to help Tom puzzle something out, having a few written notes would save Tom a lot of repetition.

It was Tom's idea to leave the overhead lights turned off and to locate himself where he was invisible from the street. Deputy Haws drove down Main Street several times every night and Tom insisted that it would do no good for them to be seen talking together. Tom had gone so far as to park his Honda in front of the Rialto a couple of storefronts away, buy a ticket to see *A Little Princess*, and then sneak out the exit and over to Brant's office, wondering as he did so if he was the first person to ever sneak *out* of a movie theater.

They both realized later that they could have met at Brant's home, but there were risks associated with that, too—where to hide the Honda, for instance—and decided to stay put after they got the basic seating arrangement worked out.

Tom started slowly, but once he'd decided to tell all and let the chips fall where they may, he seemed unable to hold the words in. When he reached the part about Galen kicking Deputy Haws and the gun going off and the deputy falling dead onto the pavement, Brant called a time out. Since Brant had seen Haws himself earlier that day, alive and apparently healthy, he could divine where Tom's story was headed. So many questions rushed into his head, pushing and crowding like lemmings rushing to the sea, that Brant decided to hear the whole story first and try to fill in the whys and wherefores later.

Tom told about burying Haws's body in the woods and then about his and Galen's shock at Haws's sudden appearance at Ma's. Galen's fainting spell made a lot more sense to Brant now, as did Tom's regurgitation. Tom went on to describe later events as related to him by Galen.

"So now it's wait and see, is that it?" Brant asked.

"Yeah."

"Haws didn't say when he'd be stopping by Galen's?"

"Just that he should stay home tonight."

"And Haws never said what he wanted?"

"I don't think it's to give him a merit badge for grave digging."

They sat in the quiet office for some time without speaking, Brant in an island of light from his desk lamp and the glow of the computer screen, Tom hunkered in the shadows.

Brant did not question Tom's story for a minute. Incredible as the story was, he took it completely at face value. Duffy's rise had become real enough, and what can happen once can happen twice, but mainly it was Tom's demeanor that convinced him that the boy was telling the truth. Sure, the boys might have been mistaken about Haws being dead. They weren't doctors or coroners or undertakers, after all. But the coincidence was too strong—two people apparently rising from the dead on the same night . . . it could be some kind of contagious hysteria, he supposed. But that wasn't what his gut was telling him.

As for Tom, he found comfort in the shadows. His heart was lighter now, and Brant wasn't calling him a fool or accusing him of being on drugs or belittling him in any of the myriad ways adults have of reducing a young person's self-esteem to zero. He was glad he'd told Brant about the incident. It was too large a burden to carry by himself, and lord knows Kent and Buzzy and Darren were more problem than solution. And Galen, of course, was the embodiment of the term "loose cannon." As he sat there in the dark, Tom felt that perhaps the worst was over. He'd found a kind of peace.

Then Haws's police car slid in front of the office silent as a shark and coasted to a halt, and Tom thought that he was about to replay his diner performance all over Brant's floor.

Tom hissed to Brant and pointed to the window and Brant saw Haws and jumped in his seat the way the movie audience did in *The Tingler* in 1959 because the producer had wired shockers into the theater seats. The car door opened and Haws stepped out, and Brant hurried to get his notes off the computer screen while Tom scurried for cover. He punched "command-w" to close the file but the notes stayed right there while the helpful Mac reminded him that he hadn't saved his document. Haws was lumbering toward the office door as Brant punched the "return" key to save the file, but the stubborn notes refused to budge until Brant gave the file a name. The door opened and Haws said, "Evening, Mr. Kettering," and Brant's mind seized up like an overheated engine. Brant always thought that he worked well under pressure but suddenly he was as incapable of thinking up a coherent file name as his Uncle Irvin who'd been dead for twelve years would've been—in fact, the way things had been going lately, Uncle Irvin might've stood a better chance.

"Working late," Haws observed, heading his way, his footsteps crackling on the ancient linoleum. Brant said "Yep" while he trilled his fingers along the keys, named the file ";lkj" and punched "return" and the notes disappeared just as Haws leaned over his shoulder to peer at the now-blank screen. "Just finished up," Brant said.

Haws grunted and stood back. He cast a look around the darkened office.

"Dark in here," he said.

Brant stared at Haws' stomach. There was a hole in Haws' shirt, neatly patched, like a little porthole over his navel.

"What?" said Brant.

"I said it's dark in here. Saving on the juice?"

"Yeah. Saving juice." Brant had never been a good liar. He felt like he was diving off the high board and making a belly-flop landing in a dry pool.

"Um-hmm," Haws said skeptically. He took a few steps toward the dark corner where Tom had insinuated himself and now stood, his back pressed against the wall, holding his breath and hoping he wasn't sweating too loudly.

"I don't mean to be rude, Deputy," Brant said, "but I have work to do. If there was something you wanted. . . ."

"I thought you said you were finished."

"I was. With that. Now I have to do . . . something else."

"What?"

"What?" Brant echoed.

"What do you have to do?"

Brant feigned a laugh. "Maybe I should have my attorney present," he said. "This is beginning to sound like an interrogation."

Deputy Haws showed his teeth. An anthropologist from Mars might have called it a smile. "Just making conversation," he said. "It's the uniform. It makes people nervous."

"That it does," Brant said, thinking of the hole in Haws's shirt.

Haws took another couple of steps toward Tom's corner, squinting into the darkness.

"Lose something?" Brant asked.

"The Culler boy," Haws said. "He couldn't've snuck in here, could he, while you were working?"

"No. Why? Is he missing?"

"Tippert remembers him buying a ticket, but he didn't see him leave after the show. All this computer gear of yours makes a pretty tempting target."

"He might've left early."

"Motorcycle's still parked out front."

"Maybe he's hiding in the theater," Brant suggested. "Maybe he was going to vandalize the place after Tippert locked up for the night."

Haws halted in his tracks and whirled to look at Brant. He aimed a meaty finger at him.

"You could be right about that," Haws said.

"Yeah," Brant drawled, "if I were you, I'd check that theater from stem to stern. You know, I think I might remember seeing him at the hardware store earlier. Buying spray paint."

Haws's brow furrowed. He shot Brant a quick "thanks" and strode out of the office. He got back in his patrol vehicle and drove the hundred feet to the Rialto. Brant watched him from the front window as he tried the theater doors, found them locked, then returned to his car and drove off to bother Merle Tippert for the key.

"Coast is clear," Brant said.

"I've gotta go," Tom said, emerging from the shadows.

"Listen . . . what about tonight . . . you know, about Haws and Galen?"

Brant pressed his lips together, thinking. "I don't think there's anything to worry about," he said after a few moments. "Haws seems as thickheaded as ever. He was probably just trying to throw a scare into the Ganger kid."

The Ganger kid, Tom thought. *Et tu*, Brant?

Tom was surprised when Brant held out his hand. "Thanks for telling me about Haws. I saw the bullet hole, by the way."

Tom shook Brant's hand.

"So what do we do?" Tom asked.

"Let me think on it. Peg asked me over for Sunday dinner. I thought I'd take her up on it. We can talk then, okay?"

"Yeah. We'll talk then."

Tom sneaked out of the *Times* office and dashed over to his Honda. He drove off, his thoughts bubbling like a stew. His mom and Brant Kettering. When they'd had one date and then never a second one, he'd figured they hadn't hit it off. Now she was inviting him over for Sunday dinner, the most serious dinner of the week. Had something been going on that he'd missed?

Man, life was getting more complicated by the minute.

Madge had never shot a pistol before but there didn't seem to be any trick to it. She could see that it had bullets in it, and she'd seen the men on television pull the thumb-thing back until it clicked. She did that and the thumb-thing stopped and she noticed that the trigger had moved back quite a bit.

"Ready to rock and roll," she said.

She'd never liked rock and roll, of course. She always used to say, "Give me Patsy Cline over the whole lot of those skinny boys and their noisy guitars. Why, they don't even sound like guitars, they sound like something's wrong with the speakers. I don't see how people can stand to listen to that stuff." She imagined it was rock and roll that Bobby Speers played over the radio in his red Mustang convertible that had seduced Elaine Mathewson. Las Vegas was probably full of people in red convertibles playing rock and roll.

But here she sat on the edge of her bed with a loaded pistol, ready to rock and roll for the first and last time in her life.

She pointed the pistol at her temple and held it there for maybe half a minute. Then she remembered reading about how sometimes people did that but the bullet just bounced off their skull and they woke up in the hospital still alive and embarrassed that they'd caused everybody so much trouble. Madge didn't like the idea of bothering all those people for no reason, so she lowered the gun and tried to remember the other way people shot themselves, the better way. After some consideration she remembered that they put the gun in their mouths.

Madge got up and opened the bedroom door a crack, just enough to see if John was out there. She didn't see him and so she tiptoed to the bathroom. Maybe he'd fallen asleep on the sofa.

She reached the bathroom and closed the door behind her before turning on the light. It was a habit she'd gotten into because John said that the light from the bathroom in the middle of the night was like a searchlight in his face.

She set the pistol on top of the toilet tank and ran water in the sink until it was warm. She dampened a wash rag and soaped it up, then washed the outside of the gun barrel thoroughly. There was no way she was putting that filthy thing in her mouth without scrubbing it first.

When the gun barrel was washed and dried she tiptoed back to the bedroom and fluffed some pillows up against the headboard and sat back with the pistol in her lap. She looked at the glowing numbers on the alarm clock and saw that it was after eleven o'clock. She hoped the sound of the gun didn't wake the neighbors.

She laid the barrel of the gun on her tongue, closed her eyes, and squeezed the trigger. Before she thought it would happen the thumb-thing snapped forward and that was that.

It was late and Doc Milford was drunk and he knew it and he didn't care.

The fireplace in his study roared, warming Doc's feet through his socks. He swallowed the last of his Glenlivet and set the glass on the end table beside the mammoth, probably hideous, old overstuffed chair that had been his for thirty-some years.

It had been a rough day.

Merle Tippert had come in that afternoon complaining of chest pains. It turned out to be heartburn—he'd had sausage with his waffles this morning, Doc guessed—but Tippert had to get in his dig.

"You going to declare me dead?" he asked. "I'd sure like to know when I walk out of here whether I'm dead or not."

Doc had smiled.

Vance Stephens had been rushed in with the end of his finger half off from cutting a bagel. He said he was glad Doc could see him right away because he always fell asleep in the waiting room and he was afraid he'd wake up in a pine box.

Doc had smiled.

Even little Josh Lunger who'd sprained his wrist when he fell off the garage roof had told him about all the comic book characters who'd died but come back in the next issue.

And Doc had smiled.

So it had gone all day long. Everybody had a quip and Doc had a smile for every one of them. He got through the day by telling himself that this, too, would pass, but he wondered if he was lying. Small towns had long memories.

This was no way to end a long and, by local standards, distinguished career.

Doc became aware of a draft in the room and assumed that one of the French doors had blown open again. He heaved himself out of his chair and stood for a moment to let his head stop spinning, then walked carefully over to the French doors that his late wife had insisted on installing against Doc's better judgment. He thought they were too easy to get into from outside, a security risk, but she liked the way they opened onto the garden. He thought of her whenever he looked through those doors. Some of the hardier perennials still came up, but most of the flower beds had been taken over by some kind of little white-bloomed weed that she used to complain about. Arturo, who he hired to mow the lawn and trim the bushes, kept the jungle at bay, but he lacked the artistic touch. The garden was neat but uninspired now and it made Doc miss his wife very much.

The doors were latched but unlocked, so he locked them and moved himself toward the bedroom. He noticed as he glanced up that one of the dueling swords that he kept on the wall, crossed of course, had fallen down. Strangely, he didn't see it on the floor. Well, he was drunk and it was late and dark, and swords don't walk off by themselves. Not like corpses, he thought ruefully. The sword would show up.

As Doc made his way down the hall he became aware of a presence waiting for him at its end. He would have been more alarmed if he weren't in the habit of seeing his wife's ghost at times like this, when he'd been hitting the scotch.

"Hello, Ellen," he said warmly, and he was about to apologize again for neglecting the roses when the figure stepped from the shadows and Doc started.

"Reverend!" he exclaimed.

Reverend Small said "hello" and drew closer. When Small was less than a stride away he produced the missing sword and ran it smoothly through Doc's abdomen and then jerked it up hard until it came to a halt at his sternum.

Doc's jaw dropped open in bewilderment, then he fell to the floor. Reverend Small withdrew the sword as Doc fell, watching Doc's demise with something close to distraction. He knelt beside the body and lay the sword across Doc's bloody chest.

He checked his watch. Eleven-thirty.

Haws should be picking up the Ganger boy about now.

Galen Ganger took another deep drag on the joint.

His mother had gone to bed two hours before. She liked to be well rested for church. It wouldn't do for her friends to see her with bags under her eyes. She lay upstairs wearing the gel-filled mask that she cooled in the refrigerator during the day, under the spell of the sleeping pills she bought over the counter, the sound of an artificial sea broadcast to her ears from the plastic synthesizer box beside the bed. Her bathroom was an arsenal of creams and lotions and pastes and jellies designed to keep time at bay.

Time was the ravager that Galen's birth had loosed upon his mother's body, to hear her tell it. His fault were her splayed hips, the stretch marks on her tits, the cellulite in her butt, the bulge of her abdomen. She had been young when he was conceived and would have remained young eternally if not for his departed ("not dead, just departed," she liked to say) father's vicious seed that battled its way through a defective diaphragm and up her uterus to fertilize the innocent egg that waited there, creating the metabolism-shifting, flesh-rending, fat-producing creature that was himself.

She didn't know that her son was waiting for a dead man to knock at the door. She and Galen had little to say to one another. She'd snip at him about drinking the last of the milk and he'd snarl back something obscene, and every now and again they'd rage at one another like mad dogs, and that was the mother-son relationship as practiced in the Ganger household. She predicted that Galen would meet an evil end. It was the only thing they agreed on.

The means to that evil end was even now pulling up in front of the house. Deputy Haws had wrangled a key to the Rialto out of Merle Tippert, interrupting the evening news to do so, and returned to find the Culler boy's motorcycle gone. Haws played his flashlight around the outside of the theater but found no graffiti, and he checked the inside and everything seemed to be in order. He didn't waste any more time on Tom Culler. He had bigger fish to fry.

Galen heard the car door slam. He snuffed out the joint and tossed it and the ashtray in the Tupperware container he used for a stash box and slid the container under the sofa. He wiped his sweaty palms on his jeans and waited for the inevitable knock. It came.

Galen opened the door and Haws said, "Let's go," and that's what they did. As he walked down the sidewalk to the street, Galen felt as if he were a condemned man marching to the gas chamber. The solemn way in which Haws held open the door to his patrol car reinforced that feeling. Inside, the car smelled like fast food and old farts, which shattered the gas chamber illusion without improving on it.

Haws drove slowly down the dark streets of Anderson. They were deserted, naturally. Cars were safely parked in driveways or garages. Lights glowed from a few houses but most were dark. Main Street and the town square looked like a miniature set waiting for a giant hand to reach in and reposition a tree or move the Optimists' cannon to the other side of the park. The Rialto's marquee was dark. The sole lighted storefront was Captain Humphrey's Tavern, Anderson's only bar.

The Captain, as he liked to be called though he'd never sailed any ship larger than a bass boat, had grown adept at turning Clyde Dunwiddey out before he reached the vomitous stage. Clyde was staggering down the street in a style he'd learned from Hal Smith, better known as "Otis" on the old *Andy Griffith Show*, when Haws caught up with him. Haws turned on the flashing lights to catch Clyde's attention and pulled up on the wrong side of the street. Clyde angled their direction.

Clyde collided with the driver's side of the car and leaned in to exhale fumes at the deputy. Galen could smell Clyde's breath even in the back seat. It did not smell like roses.

"Where to, Clyde?" Haws asked.

"Headed for the hoosegow," Clyde's tongue replied by habit.

"I'll take you," said Haws. He unlocked the back door with the power switch and Clyde yanked it open and fell in. Galen gave him as much room as possible, wondering if this was part of whatever torture Haws had in store for him, making him ride with a stinking drunk who'd likely urp in his lap.

Haws drove around the town square and headed along Main Street. He passed the Sheriff's Office without stopping. Galen noticed immediately but fuck if he was going to say anything about it. Haws was calling the shots and Galen knew it. The deception didn't sit well with him, though. Clyde didn't know the difference but at that point in the evening Clyde probably didn't know his own name.

Haws took the access road to the highway and Galen guessed that he was returning him to the scene of the crime. Instead, Haws drove a few miles and then cut the wheel hard and turned onto a dirt road that ran along a windbreak of trees between a pair of fields. He drove another half mile or so and put on the brakes.

Galen saw that Clyde had fallen asleep. He lay with his head on the rear window shelf, mouth open, snoring. Haws turned around and smiled at Galen and asked how he was doing and Galen said he was fine.

"Good," Haws said, and then he produced his police revolver and aimed it at Galen's face. Galen's heart stopped in his chest.

"You wouldn't shoot me," Galen said, not believing a single word.

"Wouldn't I?" Haws asked. "You did a pretty lousy thing to me, kid." Haws rearranged himself on the front seat, rested his gun hand casually on his forearm as he spoke his piece to Galen.

"I never meant to kill you," Galen began, but Haws cut him off with a curt "Shut up."

Haws continued.

"Let's get one thing straight," he said. "You're dog shit. I'd scrape you off my shoe right now if it was up to me. This would be a pretty fair little town without the likes of you and your gangster buddies. I'd pull this trigger right now. Don't move."

Galen was dizzy with fear as Haws stepped out of the car and pulled open the back door next to the drunken Clyde. He held the gun on Galen as he grabbed Clyde's arm and dragged him out of the car. Clyde fell on the ground and woke up and muttered some jumbled syllables of protest. Haws put his foot on Clyde's chest and held him down. It didn't take much effort.

"Get out," Haws said to Galen. Galen climbed over Clyde and Haws backed off a few feet. There was no way Galen could get the jump on him, not with the pistol pointed straight at his chest.

"Can you imagine what it's like waking up in a grave?"

Haws asked. "Can you imagine laying there, covered with dirt? Can't move. Can't see. Can't breathe. There's no way for you to know what that's like, no way at all, unless you was to experience it for yourself."

He's going to make me dig my own grave, and then he's going to bury me alive, Galen thought. Well, fuck him! I'd rather be shot!

Haws checked his watch.

"It's time," he said, and he angled the barrel of the gun down to point at Clyde Dunwiddey's head. He pulled the trigger. The gun barked and Galen cried out and bits of skull and hair and flesh flew as a hot slug of lead drilled its way straight through Clyde's besotted brain and planted itself in the ground. Clyde's body jerked once and his jaw went slack and air hissed out as his lungs collapsed, and then he lay still.

Galen backed away as Haws raised the pistol. He lifted his hands. "Don't," he pleaded, and again Haws told him to shut up.

"Is he dead?" Haws asked.

"Fuck yes he's dead!" Galen replied, his voice creeping up an octave.

"Like I was," said Haws. He checked his watch again and Galen thought for a moment about running, but he knew that Haws would just shoot him in the back. For some reason Haws was keeping him alive and it'd be stupid to try anything now. He noticed that Haws was unbuttoning his shirt and Galen thought, Oh, Jesus, he's going to fuck me!

"Look at that," Haws said, exposing his belly. "Not a scratch. Can you believe it?"

From town, the bell of the First Methodist Church began to toll. "Midnight," Haws announced, and he pointed to Clyde with the pistol. "Watch," he said.

Galen looked down at the body at his feet. It twitched a

time or two and then started convulsing like an epileptic in the throes of a grand mal seizure. Galen leaped back and yelled out "Holy shit!" as Clyde's corpse flopped around spastically before him.

Then Clyde's body stopped its dance and something even more astounding made Galen's sphincter tighten. The bullet hole in Clyde's shattered skull was closing. Even as Galen watched, shattered bones knit themselves together and flesh grew over the mended skull and hair pushed itself up through the new skin and in a matter of moments—before the church bell had finished tolling—Clyde Dunwiddey was a whole man once more.

Clyde opened his eyes and looked around, stared up at the trees and the sky, turned his head to look out over the dark expanse of field. He felt the cold ground under his palms and registered the grinning deputy and the scared-shitless teenager gawking down at him.

"What's going on here?" he said, befuddled but with no hint of drunkenness in his voice.

"Welcome back, Clyde," Haws said. He clapped Galen on the back. "Let's have a talk," he said, and all Galen could do was nod his head dumbly and walk with Haws back to the patrol car, Clyde Dunwiddey following like some dumb animal.

DAY THREE, SUNDAY

ELEVEN

"Do you know Seth?" Deputy Haws asked Clyde Dunwiddey.

Clyde's mind was muddled. Not from alcohol, for once, but from having made the journey through death. Waking up in the field with no recollection of getting there had been a shock. He was used to waking in a jail cell without remembering the trek from Captain Humphrey's Tavern to the Sheriff's Office, but the field was something new.

He was becoming aware of memories that he didn't know he had. Sorting through them was like looking at photos of a family vacation you took when you were a child. That's you feeding the okapi at the zoo or holding up one end of the balancing rock or sitting on top of the stuffed bronco, but you don't really remember doing any of those things.

Clyde didn't remember dying and he didn't have any specific memories of what it was like on the other side. But he did remember meeting Seth and he remembered an impression of transcendent wisdom, of life's truths revealed, of his own inadequacies laid out before him like a Sunday brunch. He remembered an offer of redemption and guidance. Of course he had accepted. Anyone would've.

"Yes," he said with an uncharacteristic clarity that Galen found disturbing, "I do. I do know Seth."

Haws nodded his approval.

"Who's Seth?" Galen asked.

"Seth is the answer," Haws replied.

"The answer to what?"

"The answer, that's all. You'll see, once you've met Seth."

Galen looked at Haws and at Clyde, two men he'd seen die and rise from the dead. He studied the floor of the patrol car.

"I suppose that means I have to die," Galen said.

Both men answered simultaneously. "Yes," they said.

They looked at each other and smiled. Galen recalled something Haws had said earlier, about being buried alive. He'd said that Galen would never understand the horror of it unless he experienced it himself. He'd feared, as Haws marched him out behind the windbreak, that he was going to be forced to dig his own grave. He wasn't free of that dread even now.

"How?" Galen asked.

Haws answered, "Seth hasn't said. Maybe he hasn't decided."

Galen mentally breathed a sigh of relief but kept his eyes glued to the floor. He was afraid, yes, but he was ex-hilarated as well. Something big had come to Anderson, and he was in the middle of it, and there was a chance that it was not intent on destroying him.

"You should feel privileged," Haws said. "Seth has re-vealed his work to you. I could've just shot you like I did Clyde, but it wasn't Seth's will. I don't know why, but Seth's chosen you."

"For what?"

Haws shrugged.

"You'll find out," he said, "when it's time."

* * *

   Madge Duffy did not expect to have to clean up after her
own suicide. If she had, she'd have done it in the bathroom,
in the tub, where she'd just have to wipe down the tile
walls with a wet sponge and some Fantastik. She might
even have chosen a different method. She might have cut
her wrists or stuck her head inside a dry cleaning bag.
Now that she thought of it, just about anything would've
been better than blowing her brains out all over her expensive pillow—the one with the well in the middle so she
didn't get a stiff neck—and her mother's handmade quilt
and the sheets and that's not to mention the bedroom wallpaper (though she'd wanted to replace that ugly stuff ever
since they'd moved in). She'd chosen the gun because she
expected it to be sudden and painless, and it was, and it
gratified her that she'd been right about something she'd
never done before.
   The cleaning up gave her something to do while she
sorted through the whole life-after-death experience.
John had offered to help but she'd said, "No, it's my mess.
I guess you'll have to sleep on the sofa tonight." He'd
bid her good-night and left her alone with her thoughts,
confident that everything would sift out to his benefit.
   And it was doing exactly that. Now that she knew Seth
she realized how unguided and random her first life had
been. She'd just reacted to one thing and another, like one
of those toys that turns around every time it bangs into
somebody's foot and eventually ends up in some corner
banging banging banging and going nowhere. Knowing
Seth meant that she'd found direction. Seth would guide
her. All she had to do was let Seth take her by the hand and
lead her around life's numberless obstacles, and she'd be
fine.
   It was very strange, picking up bits of bone and flesh
and hair and, she supposed, brain, and knowing they were
hers. She didn't seem to miss them. Her skull had repaired

itself and her body worked—not like old Mrs. Crenshak whose brain stroke had left her partially paralyzed—and she couldn't even tell, looking in the mirror, where the old skin met the new. She'd seen pictures of the boy who'd shot off his face with a shotgun and even after plastic surgery he looked, well, kind of like Popeye, his features all sunken in. She'd have expected the back of her head to look like that, but it was as round and full as ever. This was truly a miracle.

She'd thought that John had bled a lot when she slit his throat, but his mess was nothing compared to hers. His blood had flowed down onto the sofa and soaked the carpet, but hers had blown all over the place. The bedroom looked like an explosion in an Italian kitchen. Her mother's quilt was ruined and probably the blanket and sheets and everything, clear down to the mattress. It would all have to be replaced, and considering the cost of a new mattress and the sentimental value of the quilt, that was a darned shame. Maybe the quilt could be saved, but she didn't know if the hand stitching would stand up to a vigorous cleaning. Maybe Seth knew a good way to remove bloodstains, since he seemed to know everything else.

It did not bother her anymore that she was trapped in her life with John. Getting beaten up now and again didn't hold as much terror for her as it used to, though she didn't quite understand why. She guessed that dying and coming back had broadened her perspective, letting her see that Madge Duffy was just a tiny cog in a vast machine that existed to serve Seth's will. If she broke, Seth would make her whole. And John was not the powerful machine that she'd always imagined him to be, but another cog like herself. They would work together from now on to do Seth's bidding.

She understood John's personal struggle better, too. Like her, John was okay as long as things went smoothly, but as soon as life took one of its inevitable turns for the worse, he lacked the internal compass that would guide him back to the good times. He would get angry and lash out and look for someone to blame. Madge, on the other hand, would curl up like an armadillo and trust trouble to wear itself out beating against her shell. You could say that she and John were made for each other. He was the some-kind-of force and she was the something-or-other object.

But now they had Seth as their compass. Whatever trouble they faced in the future, Madge knew they could turn to Seth and he'd lead them out of it. She didn't know why she felt that way but she did. She supposed it was a matter of faith.

Well, she and John would work it out. She smiled as she wrung out the bloody sponge into a pail of water. After all these years, she and her husband finally had something to talk about over breakfast.

Doc Milford knew intellectually that it could have been the surge of chemicals into his brain that caused him to see a brilliant white light and to feel as if he were flying at immeasurable speed over a vast distance toward an inevitable destiny. He'd felt very much this way at the dentist, once, when the nitrous oxide was turned up too high. But this time it was much more.

He felt at peace, pervaded by a sense of well-being that was unprecedented in his experience, as if he'd finally shaken off some kind of flu that had poisoned his cells for sixty-odd years. He had no body, but he had no need of one. He felt like a child again, like a small boy hurtling downhill on roller skates and then glancing down to see that his skates had vanished and he was flying over the sidewalk on a cushion of air.

He heard his deceased wife Ellen calling his name and

he sensed her presence. She was beckoning to him, welcoming him and telling him not to worry, as if worry were even a remote possibility in this swooping, gliding, transcendental moment. Time had no meaning here so he couldn't say how long his journey took him or where, but suddenly he was there and Ellen was with him and his joy was literally boundless. He felt them moving together toward an even greater fulfillment, nothing he would personify as God, but an energy of such overwhelming rightness that it held no terror for him. Once more he had to reach to his childhood to remember any moment one-millionth as lovely . . . images of a birthday cake and singing and presents and a loving family and the feeling that he was the center of the most benign universe imaginable. All of that he was feeling now, and so much more.

Then it all went horribly wrong.

The headlong rush ended as if he'd crashed into a wall. Ellen flew away from his being, her soul ripped from his, and spiraled into infinity wailing in desolation at his loss. The glorious light flashed and winked out and he was no longer flying but plummeting, falling helplessly through a dark well whose sides he could not see, but he could feel them closing on him, threatening to crush him like palms around an insect. He heard the moans of the lost and the shrieks of the tortured. But worst of all, he could feel himself forgetting. . . .

Forgetting the light. . . .

Forgetting the joy. . . .

Forgetting it all as if it had never existed.

And when it was forgotten and he stopped falling and he stood forsaken and bewildered in the dark void of nothingness, wondering if this truly was death and this truly was his fate for all eternity, to wander blind over a dark, featureless plain with the cries of the damned in his ears, he became aware of Seth.

Seth would lead him out of the void. Seth would be his guide. All he had to do was follow Seth and everything would be all right. . . .

Doc scrubbed at the blood on the hardwood floor. His blood. He should have felt weak and dizzy from losing so much blood, but he didn't. In fact, he didn't remember ever feeling better in his life.

He didn't remember.

Without knowing Seth, they obeyed him.

It was an instinct they had, like the instinct to mate or to seek food and water or to flee the light or to run along the floor with the press of the wall on their backs, the instinct to seek the crevices and secret places of the earth, to nest in the houses of the sloppy giants who fed and sheltered and reviled them.

They wanted to roam now, but Seth told them to remain still. They wanted to explore, but Seth told them to hide. They wanted to swarm, but Seth told them to conceal their number. Seth spoke with a voice louder than their own inner voices. He spoke to calm them and make them wait. Their hour would come, he promised, but it was not yet.

Until then, the resurrected roaches beneath Carl Tompkins's floors would cling to the joists and water pipes and electrical wires. They would huddle in masses in the dirt of the crawl space. They would wait in the walls, silent as the darkness. They would wait, unthinking and uncaring and voracious, for Seth to tell them it was time.

Clyde Dunwiddey, Town Drunk.

He'd lived with the title for so long, he'd thought about having business cards printed that way. Then he figured out that the cards would cost as much as an evening at

Captain Humphrey's and common sense won out over whimsy.

When Clyde was sober, which was from about ten in the morning to four in the afternoon, the time when he was on what he called a "maintenance dose" of spirits, people sometimes asked him why he drank. He supposed they were looking for some tragedy in his life, and Clyde wished he had one to offer. But he didn't, unless it was a tragedy to be born with a gift that set you apart from others when all you ever wanted was to be one of the gang.

Clyde was cursed with intelligence and a prodigious skill at mathematics. Neither of these attributes earned him any friends in Anderson. The young people in town were more impressed by the size of a person's baseball card collection than the size of his intellect, and Clyde was smart enough to realize this fact early.

In school, his grades, except in math, were never more than adequate because he studiously avoiding studying. His parents accused him of goldbricking and his teachers accused him of under-achieving. In truth, Clyde was achieving his own goals quite nicely. He turned his intelligence to memorizing and making up jokes, a skill that diverted more beatings and won him many more friends than knowing how to diagram a sentence. When it comes to surviving any place as hostile as a school ground, shortish, fattish, too-smart boys like Clyde Dunwiddey would do well to follow his example.

When he was a few years shy of doing it legally, he started drinking. Alcohol was the great equalizer, making idiots of smart and dumb alike. He occasionally made use of his mathematical prowess to win free drinks by adding long columns of numbers in his head, but he was careful to dismiss the ability as a bar trick.

Clyde felt good when he drank and not so good when he didn't. He enjoyed the camaraderie of drunkenness. He fed on it as a plant feeds on sunshine. The dark basements where young men gathered to drink were like wide, grassy meadows bathed in sunlight to Clyde. They were his element. As the years wore on and Clyde watched his high school chums get married and settle down with a passel of kids and a ton of responsibilities, he often found himself drinking in the company of strangers. Alcohol had been the mortar that bound him with others, and Clyde learned in his twenties what every schoolchild knows, that alcohol evaporates.

As he entered his thirties, Clyde thought it might be nice to be married, but he knew that no woman he'd settle for would put up with a drunk. He might've been able to join a program and stop drinking, but when he thought about it a little longer he always came to the conclusion that drinking was nearly the only pleasure he got out of life—there surely wasn't anything he enjoyed more—and why sacrifice his greatest joy for the uncertain and very mixed pleasures of marriage?

Clyde lived with his mother until he was old enough to start thinking about it the other way around, that she lived with him. She tolerated his drinking. She'd tolerated her husband's drinking, too, until the night he'd wandered over the center line and into the path of an Exxon tanker truck.

His father's incendiary death and that of an innocent truck driver shook Clyde to the bone. He never drove after that, not even when he was relatively sober, not trusting himself to make the judgment call. He'd tried walking home after Captain Humphrey kicked him out of the Tavern each night, but navigating the dark residential streets of Anderson was more of a challenge than he liked to face in that condition. Once or twice he'd made himself unpopular by pounding loudly on the wrong door, baffled why his mother wouldn't let him in.

When Sheriff Clark offered him nightly lodging in cell B, Clyde took him up on it. The Sheriff even drew a line from the Tavern to the jail to make it easier for Clyde to find his way. He got Stig Evans, the local handyman, to rub a length of mason's string with blue chalk and snap it on the concrete so the line would be nice and straight, then he darkened the line by hand. By the time the chalk line wore away, Clyde's clever brain had memorized the route and could call it up under any level of inebriation that didn't knock him clean off his feet.

Clyde made his drinking money as a freelance mathematician. Most of the work arrived in the mail. Sometimes it was delivered personally by men in dark suits and dark sedans. Exactly what the work might be was a topic of speculation in Anderson, but most of it came from the National Aeronautics and Space Administration so that seemed all right. Still, people could not imagine what sort of problems Clyde Dunwiddey was able to solve that NASA with all its computers couldn't, and Clyde refused to give them a clue even when thoroughly drunk. Even the government agents who periodically infiltrated Captain Humphrey's Tavern to evaluate Clyde's security clearance couldn't finagle so much as a stray algorithm out of him. Clyde maintained a clear separation between his thinking life and his drinking life, toeing that line as carefully as he'd once towed the chalk mark between tavern and jail.

Now Clyde was in his forties, approaching his fifties. The alcohol had made a road map of his nose and his color was that of a man dying of slow poison. Doc Milford said his liver must look like a lace doily, that most likely Clyde's mother would see Clyde buried. Deputy Haws's bullet had cut Clyde's life short, but it hadn't cut it by much.

This morning, looking at his face in the mirror after a night of sober repose, Clyde asked himself, Who is that young man? The face that stared back at him sported a healthy, rosy complexion that he hadn't seen in ages. His eyes were clear, his nose seemed actually to have shrunk.

The veins that had wormed their way to the surface had submerged. He felt vibrant and strong.

Clyde was healthy again.

He had been granted a chance to start over. He could begin anew with a robust liver and a fresh outlook and all past physiological sins wiped out. Some beneficent, Clyde-loving force had graced him with nothing less than a miracle and Clyde appreciated that fact and vowed that it would not go unrecognized.

This called for a bender.

But first it was his duty to acknowledge the miracle, as Seth instructed. Seth had given and Seth could taketh away. It would not do to seem ungrateful to his benefactor.

So Clyde admired his face in the mirror as he shaved, as he combed his hair, as he fumbled with the necktie he'd dug out of the bottom of his bottom drawer. He splashed on a sprinkle of Old Spice, buffed his shoes with an old rag, and headed off to church.

A hole must have opened into another universe while Peg slept. She'd rolled over and fallen through it in her sleep, and that's why she was now living in an alternate reality. There was no other explanation for the words that had just spilled out of Tom's mouth.

"What?" she said, dumbfounded.

"I want to go with you to church this morning," he repeated. Tom looked uncomfortable in the suit they'd bought him for his father's funeral, a tie fixed with a crooked knot, his leather shoes, and he'd shaved the patchy stubble that passed as his beard. He added, "And please don't give me any shit about it, okay?"

"Okay," Peg replied, and while she wondered if John Lennon was still alive, if pudgy women were now considered sexier than skinny ones, if there was still such a thing as rap music and if Ma was serving haute cuisine down at the diner, she helped her son adjust his tie.

Franz Klempner brushed his crazy wife Irma's hair.

It had been another bad night. He'd heard the midnight bell again, and again Irma had rushed from the room in a terrified frenzy. She'd made it as far as the living room before Franz caught up with her and held her and reassured her as he had done so many times before. Eventually she'd let him lead her back to bed where she fell into a deep, sheltering sleep.

Franz debated taking her to church today. These spells were nothing new but they'd become too frequent and too severe. He didn't want her making a scene before half the town, not because he would be personally embarrassed but because he'd be embarrassed for her. He thought about not telling her it was Sunday, but she had set out her church dress first thing upon rising that morning so she knew what day of the week it was.

Resigned, Franz ironed the dress and brushed Irma's hair and they seated themselves in Franz' Chevy station wagon and made the drive into town. Rumor had it that the new preacher was going to address this fool notion that John Duffy had come back from the dead.

The bell of the First Methodist Church was ringing in the faithful as Brant Kettering pulled into the parking lot. He worried that regular members of the congregation might have their own parking spots, unmarked but honored by everyone else as a matter of courtesy. If he took the wrong space, it might force someone else to take someone else's spot, setting off a domino effect that would resonate through Anderson's entire church-going community. To play it safe he took the furthest spot from the church that he could find, one in the corner where the asphalt was buckling and cracking, and then worried as he made the long trek churchward that he was, perhaps, being too ostentatiously humble.

He noticed raised eyebrows and heads tilting together as he walked along, as if he'd forgotten to put on pants. His worries about being chucked out on his rear dissipated as he was descended upon like the prodigal son by enthusiastic well-wishers. He exchanged greetings and accepted welcomes, promised one or two wags that his appearance wasn't just to drum up subscribers for the *Times*, and then escaped thanks to the miraculous appearance of Clyde Dunwiddey, a son even more prodigal than himself.

Brant slid as quietly as possible into a pew in the back of the sanctuary.

He saw Tom Culler walk in with Peg and knew that Tom was there for the same reason as everyone else, to hear Reverend Small's analysis of Duffy's trip to the Other Side. Brant caught a glimpse of Small and could tell from his beaming face that this was a capacity crowd, surely the biggest since Small had taken over from Reverend Paulsen three weeks ago.

Tom and Brant had another agenda, though. Only they, among all those gathered, knew that Duffy wasn't the only "Risen" person in town. They wondered if Small's comments would reveal any knowledge on his part about Deputy Haws.

Brant scanned the crowd for familiar faces. There was Haws, in uniform but for his hat, sitting on the outside aisle. Brant didn't know if Haws was a church regular or not. While he was thinking about it, a hand clamped onto his shoulder and Brant jumped six inches.

"Got you, too, I see," said Doc Milford.

Brant put his hand to his chest and said, "Christ, Doc, you nearly gave me a heart attack. I thought I was busted."

"Some crowd," Doc said, "bigger than Easter. That's usually when all the borderline cases turn out. I suppose you're here for the same reason I am, to hear the Reverend's official stance on the Duffy business."

"You've got it. Look—there's the town deputy. He's never struck me as the religious sort."

"You can't always tell. Maybe I'll go have a few words with him. Enjoy the sermon."

"I'm sure I will."

Doc walked over to Deputy Haws and they put their heads together for a minute or so, then Doc took a seat elsewhere. Brant continued scanning the crowd. While he was picking out familiar faces a silence fell over the room, washing over the congregation like a wave. Row by row the heads turned to see who had just now walked in the door.

It was John and Madge Duffy.

John wore the suit he'd pulled out of the mothballs the day before. Madge had mended the jacket with a button off the vest that she assured him he didn't need to wear, and she'd let out the pants a little. John was ill at ease, uncomfortable as the center of attention, but Madge marched with her head high as if she owned the mortgage on the church and everything in it. She didn't care what people thought. She walked with Seth's spirit, as everyone in this room would do, one day soon.

They took seats in the middle of the sanctuary. For all the buzzing that had been going on about John, no one seemed particularly eager to talk to him. Cindy Robertson was there with her mother and sister, and she ended up sitting next to John. He caught her staring at him and nodded a polite greeting, and she smiled back at him nervously and said, "How are you?" "Tolerable," he said, then he sat down and stared straight ahead and so did Cindy.

Ruth Smart took her seat at the organ and played "Lead, Kindly Light" and "Come, Thou Almighty King" and

"The Way of the Cross Leads Home," and then Reverend Small made his appearance and led the congregation in the opening prayer. Choir master Jimmy Troost stepped up and directed the choir in "Are You Washed in the Blood," and after that everyone rose and gave voice to "Abide With Me" and "O God, Our Help In Ages Past." A kid Brant recognized from the grade school, Josh Lunger, gave a prayer. Then Jimmy Troost took center stage again to lead the choir in "The Blood Will Never Lose Its Power." Either Jimmy had a thing about blood or he was working a theme, Brant decided. Finally it looked to Brant as if they were closing in on the sermon.

To Brant's relief, Reverend Small was not one of those pulpit-pounding orators who mouthed every word as if God had His hand up the preacher's backside like some kind of cosmic ventriloquist act. Small spoke warmly but intimately, as if in consideration for those who might be sleeping in the pews. He welcomed the crowd and made a couple of announcements concerning the Youth Group. Then he got down to business.

"There lives among us—and I'm delighted to see him in our congregation this morning—one who has made the ultimate journey. No trip to Yellowstone Park or Greece or even to the moon can compare with the incredible odyssey of John Duffy. For he has been to infinity. To death. And he has come back again.

"What are we to make of this journey, this miracle? Some have suggested that it's the work of a new preacher trying to impress his congregation."

There was some scattered laughter.

"Well," he continued, "as much as it would please me to take credit for John Duffy's resurrection, I can not. Such powers are not granted to ordinary men like myself. And besides, I wouldn't want Jed Grimm accusing me of stealing his business!"

Jed Grimm called out, "Just don't make a habit of it, Reverend!" and the congregation laughed again.

Brant hadn't noticed Grimm in the crowd before. It made sense that he'd be a church-goer, though. The work of a preacher and that of a mortician are intimately bound.

"We think of miracles as something that happened long ago and far away," Small said. "We don't really believe that they happen anymore, and that's sad. For the work of the Lord is all around us. We witness the miracle of each new spring, of each baby born, the miracle of the breeze in our hair and the sunshine on our backs. We take these miracles for granted.

"But when it comes to miracles of a less-common variety—the multiplying of the loaves or resurrection of the dead—we assume that those miracles belong to the distant past. If they were to happen today, they wouldn't happen here, they wouldn't happen to us.

"Now why would we think such things? Do we truly believe that the Good Lord watches over us and protects us and keeps us in His Love, or do we not? Is it pessimism that makes us think such thoughts? Or is it fear? Fear that maybe God is dead after all, and we are on our own.

"I still believe in the Lord, and I still believe in miracles. And to any of you who don't, I say, Look over there. Look at John Duffy. Living, breathing, hale and hearty after a fine doctor and every scientific principle in the world had declared him dead. Look at him. Look at him and tell me that miracles don't happen anymore, that they don't happen here, that the Good Lord isn't watching over every one of us.

"Look at John Duffy and tell me that God is dead. If you can do that, then I'll say to you that none are so blind as those who will not see. Because miracles are there for the seeing, if we but open our eyes."

Brant had to admit that Small was getting to him. Even

as a boy, Brant had wondered why all the magic happened two thousand years ago. Why, if there was a Lord and He gave a fig about mankind, did He appear for one brief show, like a Las Vegas act, then hustle everyone off to the casino leaving later generations nothing but a tattered program to describe the wonders their ancestors had beheld? Shouldn't He be making occasional reappearances to keep the material fresh in people's minds?

Maybe Duffy was the modern miracle that Brant had needed for so long, if he'd just choose to believe it.

He might have had something like a revelation if Irma Klempner hadn't suddenly leaped out of her seat and aimed a craggy finger at Reverend Small as if to smite him with a thunderbolt and yelled out, "Devil! Satan!" The congregation gasped. Heads turned and bodies swiveled to get a good look.

Franz tugged at Irma's dress and hissed, "Irma! Sit down!" but he might as well have been a mouse pulling at the tail of a tiger. Irma was incensed, every synapse in her poor, mad brain firing at once.

"You think nobody remembers, but I do!" she screamed. Her body shook with emotion, the finger waved. "I remember Eloise! You think everybody's forgot, but I remember! I remember!"

Franz was on his feet now and trying to escort Irma out. His look of chagrin was apology enough to the Reverend, he didn't try to say a word. Irma was doing plenty of talking for the both of them.

"Devil!" Irma shouted as her husband ushered her to the back of the sanctuary, down the aisle under the stares of two hundred pair of eyes. "Satan!" she cried. "I remember! Eloise! Eloise!"

All eyes were on Irma Klempner as Franz took her by the shoulders and, shushing soothingly in her ear, walked her out of the church. All eyes but two.

Brant scanned the murmuring crowd with the scrutinizing gaze of a reporter. He saw the hateful stare creep unbidden onto Small's face and then vanish, subdued by a master actor, suppressed for the sake of appearances.

"If God can resurrect, then God can surely heal," Small said. "Let us pray for those who need His healing touch." As two hundred heads bowed in prayer, Brant saw Deputy Haws steal toward the exit. After a few moments, Brant followed.

He stood on the steps of the church and looked around. Haws seemed to have melted into the earth.

Brant went around to the parking lot and watched the Klempners make the contentious journey to their car. Irma was quiet now, but sullen. She'd take a few steps and then stop and glare balefully at Franz. He'd pretend to ignore her, then he'd walk back and grab her hand and pull her along for a few steps. She'd shake her hand loose and seem to follow and then stand stock still again and wait for him to come back for her. If he hadn't, she'd have stood there for days, it seemed to Brant.

It took them several minutes to reach the car, long enough for the congregation to sing two mournful choruses of "The Little Brown Church in the Vale." Franz opened the door for Irma and she slid in and sat there staring straight ahead. The frost from her icy demeanor threatened to crack the windshield. Franz walked around to the driver's side and got in, and then he leaned over and fiddled with something on Irma's side of the car. She slapped his hands away. He seemed to argue with her for a bit and then gave up. Brant guessed that he was trying to buckle her seat belt but that Irma was having none of it out of pure cussedness.

Franz backed out of the parking space and drove through the lot and into the street. The right rear tire of the Chevy bounced over the curb as Franz cut the corner a little tight. Brant watched until the Klempners' car was out of sight.

"Shouldn't let the old fool on the road," Deputy Haws said a few inches behind Brant's ear. Brant jumped. Haws noticed.

"Didn't mean to scare you," Haws said, hauling his bulk alongside Brant.

"You took me by surprise," Brant said. "I thought you'd left."

"Had to make a phone call. You probably walked right by me." Haws nodded in the direction Franz Klempner had taken. "Ought to yank his license, I suppose, but everybody around here knows to give Franz a wide berth."

"There's always room in law enforcement for compassion," Brant said.

"You got to know when to be tough, too," Haws replied as Galen Ganger's Charger pulled into view and parked across the street. "That boy knows better than to park in front of a hydrant."

Apparently the Ganger boy didn't know he was parked illegally because he sat right there as Haws sauntered up. Maybe Ganger was picking his mother up from church—Brant had caught her heavily painted face when she'd turned to watch Irma Klempner's exit—but if that was the case, why didn't he pull into the lot? Maybe because Brant was there, but what difference could that make?

It occurred to Brant that Haws may have phoned Ganger from the church and commanded his immediate appearance. The Gangers didn't live far away—nowhere in Anderson was far from anywhere else in Anderson—but even so Ganger must've hauled some hasty butt to get there so soon. Was Haws blackmailing him? That seemed logical, given the circumstances. But what could the Ganger boy have that Haws wanted?

Theirs was a short conversation. Without writing a ticket, Haws stepped away from the Charger as Galen Ganger started the engine. He made a fast three-point turn and tore off in the wake of Franz Klempner.

TWELVE

Galen floored the accelerator and heard his Charger roar and felt the satisfying press of his body against the seat. He felt like an astronaut lifting into the cosmos. Indeed, this was the beginning of his own journey into the Great Unknown.

It was a kick, roaring through town on an otherwise sleepy Sunday morning without worrying about Deputy Hawg lurking behind every bush. But even more, Galen felt like a revolutionary.

His rebellion up to now had been random and unfocused, a stubborn digging in of his heels and thumbing of his nose at a bunch of narrow-minded old farts who'd gotten stale and set in their ways long before their time. Even the so-called young people in Anderson were old, old because they were afraid to be young. They were afraid to step outside the limits and do their own thing, to run right up to the edge and leap off, screaming and kicking, into the abyss.

Not Galen. He embraced the unknown, and he rebelled against everything comfortable and safe.

Today he rebelled for a larger cause. The exact nature of that cause and the motives of its mysterious leader, Seth, weren't clear to him, but Galen could feel the force of it, like a thunderstorm gathering on the horizon, and he wanted to be part of it, wanted it to be part of him.

He sure as hell didn't want the revolution to happen without him.

He hit the access road to the highway and squealed around the corner, running the stop sign. He knew the direction the Klempners would be taking and followed in their path. Soon he caught up with the old man, a positive hazard on the two-lane blacktop as he poked along at forty miles an hour, barely staying within his own lane as he wove back and forth between the lines, his bald head visible over the headrest.

Galen kept up his speed as he closed on the station wagon. He flashed his lights and honked his horn as the distance between the cars narrowed. It was almost as if the wagon was sitting still as Galen's Charger closed the gap. He jerked the wheel at the last minute, just seconds before the Charger climbed up the wagon's rear bumper, and pulled into the on-coming lane. He honked the horn and gave Franz the finger as he roared past. The old man just stared straight ahead, colorless lips pressed together tight, cloudy eyes glued to the road. Galen wondered if the old coot had noticed anything, if he ever looked in the rear view mirror to see the Charger bearing down from behind, if he could hear the horn honking or see the flashing lights, if he even knew that Galen's upraised middle finger meant "stick it up your ass!"

Galen yanked the wheel hard as he cut in front of the Klempners' wagon and then roared off ahead of them. In case the old man hadn't seen it before, Galen stuck his hand with the upraised digit out the window and pumped it up and down.

The Charger left the Chevy wagon in the dust. In just a couple of minutes, the Klempners had disappeared from Galen's rear view mirror, as if they'd never existed.

* * *

Franz Klempner was old but he'd had stature in his time—he'd never be one of those shriveled husks who had to peer through the steering wheel to see the road. His vision was clouded a little by cataracts and the Chevy station wagon's steering hadn't gotten any tighter over time, but Franz felt that he was a good enough driver, even if his reflexes weren't as sharp as they used to be, if he just kept his speed down. He had common sense and wasn't out to prove anything with his driving, didn't have all that macho bullcrap stewing in his head like the teenage boys who were the real menaces on the road.

He looked over at Irma sitting there like a statue.

"You only hurt yourself with that crazy talk, you know," he said. His voice had an edge to it, but darn it, he had a right to be mad. He'd dressed her and prettied her up and driven her all the way to town to go to church, and then she'd made a damned fool of herself in front of the whole congregation.

"How can I take you to church if you're going to make a spectacle?" he asked.

Irma was deathly silent. She sat there cocooned in her own dark thoughts.

"Who the hell is Eloise, anyway?" Franz said. "You don't know any Eloise."

Irma turned her head to look at him and Franz glanced over at her, reluctant to take his eyes off the road, things changed so fast. But he stole a glance at her and what he saw in her eyes made the blood rush to his head. What he saw in those eyes was fear. No . . . more than that. It was terror, nothing less.

His eyes burned, seeing the awful fright that resided in his wife's soul. It made him want to cry. He made sure the road ahead was straight and then he took one hand off the steering wheel, something he never did, and reached over and patted her arm.

"We'll be home soon," he said. "Everything will be all right then."

Something attracted his attention in the rear view mirror. It was a car flashing its lights.

Franz was used to cars flashing their lights at him, unable to pass on the two-lane road, in a hurry to get somewhere and wanting him to pull over and let them by. He did it, too, most of the time.

But this driver had plenty of room and there wasn't any traffic at all. Why was he flashing his lights that way? And honking, too, like a dang fool. Was something wrong? Was he trying to point out a loose wheel or something Franz couldn't see? Maybe he should pull over after all.

Then he saw the Ganger boy's face behind the wheel, lips curled in a snarl the way they always were. He saw the contemptuous grin and he could guess at the black thoughts circling in the boy's brain. He knew what kids like that thought of old people, as if brute strength and vigor were the measures of a man, as if they themselves would never be old. He thought of that moronic phrase they bandied about these days, the one about dying young and leaving a good-looking corpse, as if getting old was a fate worse than death, as if life had no value if you weren't a young buck raging with hormones.

Franz noticed and thought all these things in an instant. His eyes didn't see sharp but they saw deep, and there was nothing wrong with his mind. He knew where he stood with kids like the Ganger boy. The best thing to do was to ignore them, just pretend that you didn't see, didn't hear, didn't know.

He locked his eyes on the road ahead. Ganger's car roared to within a few feet of the station wagon and then pulled suddenly away and in an instant Franz and the Ganger boy were driving side by side. Ganger made an obscene gesture but Franz kept staring straight ahead, eyes fastened on the blacktop. Irma seemed genuinely oblivious to the drama unfolding just over the white line.

The Ganger boy pulled ahead of Franz and swerved his car in front of the station wagon and zoomed off down the road. Ganger stuck his hand out the window and repeated the pitiful gesture that passed, on the road, for eloquence. Soon the boy's car was well ahead of him, and in another couple of minutes it had disappeared from sight completely. It was over.

Franz looked over at Irma. Her expression hadn't changed for better or worse. Soon they'd be home and Elmer would bark his greetings to them and Franz would make them some tea and she'd calm down. Maybe they'd go for a walk through the field, it was such a warm, pleasant day, almost hot which was strange for this time of year. Yes, that was what Irma needed. Some tea, and then a nice little stroll in the warm sunshine.

Franz squinted and peered into the distance. A car was approaching. It was that boy's car again, and the damn fool was driving on the wrong side of the road.

When he was sure he was out of the geezer's sight Galen hit the brake and spun the wheel and the Charger's tires squealed as it skidded in a sharp turn that left it pointed in the opposite direction. Galen slammed it into gear and laid rubber as he headed back toward Franz Klempner and his bugfuck wife.

Some tiny voice in the back of his mind told him this was crazy. It was a voice that rarely spoke to him anymore. After years of being ignored it had at last gone mute, but what he was doing now would surely and truly and irrevocably put an end to the being that was Galen Ganger. He wasn't just flirting with death this time but embracing it, plunging into it like a circus performer into a barrel of

flaming water. Blood rushed from Galen's pounding heart
and pulsed in his ears and made him deaf to the voice of
reason. This was literally the thrill to end all thrills.

Until Seth brought him back.

Galen thought about Clyde Dunwiddey. He saw his
skull explode from the bullet hit and his body slump in
death, and he saw the wound heal and Clyde rise at the
stroke of midnight. Galen had seen the power of Seth. He'd
seen it in Deputy Hawg and again in Clyde, and it had
made him a believer.

He glimpsed the Klempners' Chevy in the distance as
he topped a small rise. His mouth spread into a grin. He
floored the accelerator and watched the needle climb past
the eighty mark and ease toward the ninety. The Charger
vibrated from the effort and Galen knew that, in its un-
tuned state, it would never hit its top speed, but this was
good enough. Plenty good enough.

It occurred to him then that he was making the supreme
sacrifice. Not his life, which he would get back, but his
car. Unless Seth had the power to bring back totaled cars,
this was the last ride Galen would ever take in his beloved
Charger. The grin fell from his face. So the ultimate thrill
had its price.

He nodded. Very well, then, he thought, if that's the
price of the ticket, that's what I pay. He reached down and
patted the seat beside him. You were a good old girl, he
thought, and this is an honorable end.

The Charger and the station wagon approached each
other on a nearly level stretch of blacktop. The old man
could surely see him now, and even an old buzzard like
that would realize soon enough that they were headed
for a crack-up. For good measure, Galen flashed his
lights a couple of times and then left them on, brights
included.

He took a fraction of a second to check the gas gauge.

More than half full. Good. Though he wouldn't see it himself, he hoped for a nice fiery finish.

Why wasn't the geezer honking? Galen had played chicken with unsuspecting travelers before and they always laid on the horn. Nobody was going to back off because he got honked at, but it was part of the ritual. Maybe Klempner was blinder than Galen thought. Maybe taking the old man out was the biggest favor Galen could do for Anderson.

The boy is crazy, Franz thought as the Charger roared toward him.

He'd had young Turks play this game with him before. They'd flash their lights and honk and threaten to run him off the road, but they didn't know Franz. They didn't think about what it must have been like growing up in the mid-40s when all the world was at war with Germany, growing up in the United States with the first name "Franz." He'd gotten into plenty of scraps, you'd better believe it, and he'd learned quick not to ever back down or they'd beat you that much more. He'd learned to ball his hands into fists or grab a stick or a length of pipe and lay into them, however many they were, with everything he had, not to think he was getting out of it but to concentrate on getting through it. The bullies learned something, too. They learned not to pick on Franz unless they were ready to go home with a bloody nose or worse.

But this Ganger boy, he didn't see the bantam rooster that still lived inside Franz Klempner. He saw an easy target, somebody to push around. Well by God, he was going to learn different.

Franz didn't honk, he didn't flash his lights, he didn't accelerate. But he kept going. He squinted his eyes and looked straight into the on-coming headlights and he gripped the steering wheel tight and he just kept going, knowing that the boy would turn away at the last second. The boy wanted to live, and once he saw that Franz wasn't budging, he'd yank the steering wheel and his car would leap into the other lane and the contest would be over. Franz just had to get through it, that was all.

So he kept going and the Charger kept charging and soon there was no more than a hundred feet between them. The boy had to turn away soon or it would be too late. He was cutting it too close. Too close!

Crazy! Franz thought as the Ganger boy's grinning face raced at him, and he knew in that split second that this was not a game, that it had never been the boy's intention to turn away. This was suicide, and the boy would take Franz and Irma with him.

Franz mashed the brake pedal hard and the Chevy's tires cried out as they slid on the blacktop. He cranked the steering wheel and the wagon spun but the Charger was on top of it in a heartbeat. Franz heard the tortured metal scream as the cars hit, their massive, steel frames crunching. The steering wheel collapsed under Franz' momentum and his rib cage cracked and out the corner of one eye he saw Irma's body fly forward and hit the glass and he heard the glass shatter.

When he opened his eyes he saw that his car and the boy's had become one twisted mass of metal. Only a miracle had left him more or less intact. Irma's body lay across the hood on a bed of broken glass. Flames licked out from the burning engines of both cars. Blood was everywhere, everywhere. He couldn't see straight, couldn't focus his eyes, and maybe that was a blessing. Blindly he fumbled for the seat belt and freed himself.

The door was jammed shut but the window glass was gone. Franz crawled out of the wreckage, knowing that his chest hurt and unable to feel anything at all in his legs. He hauled himself out and tumbled through the window and onto the asphalt. He tried to stand but his legs went out from under him and he fell to the ground. He must have passed out because, when next he opened his eyes, he was lying on the highway and the car was burning and somebody was yelling, "Get him away from the car! Get him out of there!" He felt hands grab him under the arms and pain shot through his body like fire. Then he heard a loud ka-whumpf! and the wreckage that had been the cars and his wife and the Ganger boy became a flaming torch.

Bright light, white hot, washed over him and a jumble of voices filled his ears. Then everything turned into a loud, chaotic roar and he let go, he didn't care, he just let go and the black wave washed over him and, for a moment, nothing hurt at all.

This was the way life was supposed to be.

The sun shining and water gently lapping at the dock and a warm breeze sighing over your naked body. It didn't seem to Merle that it was so much to ask, just to be left alone when you needed it, to get rid of the press of the city and strip bare and bask in the sun for a few hours like a lizard or a butterfly or a lazy old dog. Harming no one, not meaning to offend.

So why were Merle and his fellow nudists so persecuted?

They'd been granted the dock, but it was a fragile treaty, written on the wind. Every time some Mrs. Grundy filed a complaint with the county they had to go through the same song and dance to keep their hundred square feet of space, even though it was set back in the farthest cove where only the most diligent seekers could find them. As if it was going to kill anybody to glimpse a bit of bare skin now and again, anyway.

It was one more sign that civilization was going to hell in a hand basket, according to Merle.

Merle Tippert, the town grouch, wasn't what most people thought of when they thought of nudists.

They might think of well-proportioned young women playing volleyball or riding horseback or sunning themselves in the company of other well-proportioned young women. Certainly that was the image promoted by the "social documentarians" who published nudist magazines in the 1950s, before Hugh Hefner demonstrated that you didn't need an anthropological reason to print pictures of naked young ladies.

They might think, right or wrong, of bare bodies engaged in fruity New Age rituals involving body paint, Gaia the Earth Mother, and flutes.

But they certainly did not think of an ancient grouser sitting naked on a dock at the Cooves County Reservoir. Merle with his family-rated movie house would seem like a particularly unlikely candidate for parading around "nekkid," as uncomfortable as he was with sexual matters. But as any true nudist (or "naturist" as the group preferred to be called) could tell you, the surest way to short-circuit sexual impulses was to eliminate the tease factor, for what is sex without mystery?

That most people could not think of nudity without connecting it to sex was more evidence to Merle that most people had shit for brains.

Merle was not alone on the dock this Sunday afternoon. Also enjoying the unseasonably warm weather were Jack and Dolores Frelich—he was an engineer on the nuke plant construction project, she was a bookkeeper there—and Hiram Weems, an insurance agent for the tri-county area who made a point of stopping by when he was in the vicinity, weather permitting.

Merle sat on the edge of the dock on a ragged towel he kept for this purpose and dangled his feet in the water. Sometimes fish would nibble at his toes, but he didn't mind. He wished that he and his Indian maiden, Princess Tall Pine, had had a lake such as this to swim in back in 1932. Back then, when there was still a decent patch of country between towns, this land had belonged to farmers like his father and mother, and kids like Merle grew up half wild. Trees grew along the river and he and Princess Tall Pine spent many hours among them, running from the cavalry and building lean-to houses and cooking meals stolen from their families' kitchens. They ran around naked much of the time, sometimes fashioning loin cloths out of rags, but there was nothing dirty about it. They never even played at any of the sex games kids play. Theirs was a pure love, innocent and timeless. Naked was the way to be when you were seven years old and lived in the woods and you were Indians and it was 1932.

Princess Tall Pine's Christian name was Ellie Driscoll and she was one of seven Driscoll kids whose parents farmed a poor piece of dirt not far from the Tipperts' place. Her hair was dishwater blonde but Merle always thought of it as jet black as befitted an Indian princess. Merle's Indian name changed from day to day. Often he was the powerful Great Bear, sometimes he was Sees Like A Hawk, sometimes Chief Many Scalps. Ellie was always Princess Tall Pine.

One day Ellie's younger brother got tonsillitis and the doctor came to the Driscoll house to snip out the boy's tonsils. They had him breathe chloroform until he was woozy and laid him on the kitchen table and the doctor performed the surgery. Even though Ellie wasn't sick, she was the only other Driscoll kid who hadn't had her tonsils out and so the doctor snipped her, too, while he was there.

Ellie's brother recovered but Ellie caught some kind of infection and they took her to the hospital to die. They didn't let Merle see her but they said he could go to the funeral. He saw the doctor there and glared at him all through the service. Outside the cemetery, as they were leaving, Merle chucked rocks at the doctor's car until his father boxed him on the ears, saying, "What's the matter with you?" and commanded him to show some respect for the dead.

Merle, now in his early seventies and never married, muttered the word "doctors" and leaned over and spat into the reservoir. His old tanned hide was loose and baggy and folded many times over his pot belly and a lot of folks would have found it a disgusting sight, but Merle thought, So what? He came into the world naked and, God willing, he'd go out the same way. Who cared what anybody thought in this ass-end-up world anyway? In his mind he was still young and he still sported with Princess Tall Pine in a world that existed only in the memories and dreams of old coots like himself.

He jumped at the explosion behind him.

"What in the hell—?" he said and he turned around to see Deputy Haws standing over the body of Hiram Weems, the traveling salesman, holding a smoking pistol. Jack and Dolores Frelich stared at the deputy in stunned disbelief. Haws moved his gun over to point at Jack and shot him through the forehead. Dolores screamed and tried to get up and run but she was too slow. Haws fired again, shot her right through the chest, and she fell to the dock with a dead thud.

Merle took all this in and couldn't believe it. He couldn't get his mind around it somehow, it made no sense. He didn't have time to summon up remorse at the loss of three lives or even to be properly frightened for himself. Then the gun barrel was pointed in his direction and Haws was looking at him coldly and there was another explosion.

Merle knew he was dying as the impact caught him in the sternum and blew him off the dock. He fell into the cold water and blood streamed from his chest. He surfaced, gasping for air, and Deputy Haws stepped over and got down on his hands and knees and reached down, laid a heavy hand on the top of Merle's head, and pushed him back under. Merle struggled but couldn't break the deputy's grip. After a few moments he gave up. He floated there under the surface, his chest on fire, and watched his blood gush into the water and swirl before his eyes. He watched it and he felt the coldness creep into his limbs and he thought, Here I come, my princess, here I come. . . .

In the office of the *Cooves County Times* where Brant had gone to write up his impressions of the morning's service while they were still fresh in his mind, the phone was ringing. Brant didn't answer. He'd already heard about the accident that claimed the lives of Irma Klempner and the Ganger boy and put Franz Klempner in the hospital, and he was busy in the bathroom with his bowels doing a damn fine impression of Mt. Vesuvius. They always turned volcanic when events weren't adding up the way Brant wanted.

He sat on the toilet and thought about all the things that were vexing him:

—That people were coming back from the dead.

—That Deputy Haws could be murdered and risen and not tell anybody about it, not even his boss and supervisor, Sheriff Clark.

—That Haws had met with his alleged murderer, the Ganger boy, outside the church just a few minutes before Ganger's so-called "accident."

—That Irma Klempner perished in a car crash before Brant or anyone else could ask her about the enigmatic "Eloise."

—That Haws knew that Brant had seen him with the Ganger boy and might do something about it.

It was all very strange and unsettling and terrifying. No

wonder Brant's guts were in an uproar. They didn't want to believe what seemed to be going on any more than his brain did.

Brant sat with his spinning head in his hands, his pants wrapped around his ankles and a telephone ringing off the hook on the other side of the wall and his bowels threatening to blast him halfway to Timbuktu. He rubbed the palms of his hands together. They were sweaty and cold.

He felt like a condemned man. He sensed unknown forces descending on him as Galen Ganger must have descended on the Klempners, swooping in like a hawk on a field mouse.

He had to do something, and soon. But what, damn it? What?

THIRTEEN

Peg thought that Brant was pale as he walked into Ma's Diner and ordered a cup of coffee. She smiled at him and he sort of smiled back but his heart wasn't in it. She prepared herself for a let-down.

All afternoon, all she could think about was tonight's dinner with Brant. She still didn't know what to make of John Duffy's resurrection but her brain had quit thinking about it, bombarding her instead with questions like, Should I mash some potatoes? and What if he hates creamed corn? She was a fluttery school girl again. Brant had brought back to life a part of her that had been dead. Chalk up another miracle resurrection in Anderson.

Now here Brant came dragging himself in like a whipped dog. He looked shifty. His eyes darted this way and that and he was jumpy. If he'd been a stranger Peg would've figured him for an escaped convict. He even asked if Deputy Haws had been in lately. Since he wasn't on the lam, he must have been planning to break their date and he was just waiting for the right moment to tell her. He kept ordering coffee and watching the people in the diner come and go.

She decided she had to talk to him.

"Cindy's filling in for me this evening," she said. He jumped at the sound of her voice, as if he hadn't seen her coming. In fact, he'd been staring into his coffee cup like a gypsy reading tea leaves for the past five minutes. "So I can get off early and fix us a nice dinner," she added.

He replied, "Oh. Good."

"It'll be a treat for Tom, too. He hasn't had a home-cooked meal in I-don't-know-how-long."

"Um," Brant said. He stirred his coffee, though Peg hadn't seen him put anything in it.

She felt like she'd just walked up to a boy at a high school cotillion and flirted with him and now she was standing there waiting for him to ask her to dance and instead he just looked at the floor and looked at the ceiling and made some comment about how hot it was. Obviously she had to take the bull by the horns.

"I figure about seven," she said.

"Seven what?"

"Dinner at seven. You're coming, right? You're coming to dinner?"

"Sure," Brant said flatly, "I'm looking forward to it."

"Well okay then," Peg said a bit snappishly.

"Okay," he replied.

"Okay."

She spun on her heels and marched away and became very busy with some little boxes of breakfast cereal. He would call her, she knew, about ten minutes 'til seven, after she'd bought groceries and cooked dinner and fretted and stewed and cleaned and made sure everything was just so, and tell her he couldn't come, that something had come up. She started preparing what she was going to say to him then to cut him down to size.

Brant hadn't completely forgotten about dinner with Peg but it wasn't uppermost on his mind anymore, either. The longer he thought about the day's events the more sinister they became. He remembered how, on Saturday morning, Jed Grimm and Deputy Haws had loaded the Ganger boy in Haws' police car. Was Grimm in on it, too? Had he had a stroke or something in the night and risen and nobody knew it?

Hell, people could be dying and coming back all over town and who'd know? How could he tell who he could trust and who he couldn't?

Paranoia is a terrible thing, especially when people are out to get you. If he wasn't careful, Brant could cut himself off from friends and foes alike.

Okay, Deputy Haws and John Duffy were definitely Risen. What about Reverend Small? No hard evidence of it yet, but he was a maybe. Then again, everybody in town was a maybe. Jed Grimm was doing what anybody would have done in his place, he didn't necessarily know that he was putting the Ganger boy in the hands of the man he'd murdered. Tom Culler wouldn't have confided all his fears about Haws if he was one of the Risen, so he was safe . . . unless he'd died after leaving Brant's office on Saturday night and come back.

Wasn't there some test Brant could perform to find out? In the movies, when people were under the control of aliens there was a parasite or little metal doohickey in the back of their necks. Or that other one, the terrifying one . . . *Invasion of the Body Snatchers*. The pod people didn't have emotions. But according to Madge Duffy, John had come back better than he was before.

What was he doing, basing life and death decisions on B-pictures? It was a sure sign that he'd lost the ability to distinguish between fact and fiction!

Time to return to Planet Earth. Drink his coffee. Have a nice dinner tonight with Peg.

He watched Peg busying herself behind the counter. She looked at him only once, and then he thought he could see Bowie knives hurtling at him from her eyes. He realized that she'd been flirting with him a few minutes ago and he'd been too busy piling stones over his own grave to notice.

With typical male single-mindedness he had let a bunch of nonsensical and probably groundless fears sidetrack him from attending to the real business of life.

He imagined himself explaining it all to her. Even in his head it sounded absurd. Peg's affections were a locked room which she had opened the barest crack. If he came across sounding like a madman, it would slam shut in a heartbeat.

No, there would be no explaining. Apologizing. Groveling if needed. But no explaining. He'd confide in someone else, but not Peg, not yet.

He waited for her to glare balefully at him again. When she did, he smiled and gave her a wink. She glanced away before he could read the expression on her face.

He drained his coffee and walked over to the register. She was already ringing him up before he got there, as if she was anxious to see him go.

"I'm looking forward to tonight," he said.

"Oh?" she said. "That'll be a dollar."

He had a dollar bill but he dug for a five. If she had to make change, he'd have about ten more seconds to redeem himself. He leaned in and spoke with a voice he hoped was rich with sincerity.

"Listen, I was distracted there, a few minutes ago. Things on my mind. I'm sorry. I get too wrapped up in my own thoughts sometimes. If it happens again, it'd help if you'd call it to my attention. Any subtle hint—pour coffee in my lap, slap me with a waffle. . . ."

"I'll remember that," she said, handing him his change. Her gaze was encouragingly knifeless.

"I thought I'd stop by the hospital and have a chat with Doc," he said. "I'll look in on Annie and explain that you're at home whipping up a gourmet dinner, okay?"

"Okay," she replied. Warmly, this time.

He peeled a dollar bill out of the four she'd handed him

and left it on the counter. "For the waitress," he explained. "You wouldn't know if she's seeing anyone . . . ?"

"I think she is," Peg said. The way her lips curled into almost-a-smile gave him the shivers.

Brant was on his way out when he turned with an afterthought.

"Say . . . do you know where Tom would be about now?"

"Oh, are you two partners again?"

"In a way. Does he hang out anyplace particular on the weekends?"

"You might try the reservoir. Other than that. . . ." Peg shrugged.

Brant thought for a moment, tapped his finger on the cash register, smiled. "Well, if I don't run into him before, I guess I'll see him tonight," he said, and Peg nodded.

Brant turned and nearly bumped into Madge Duffy. They exchanged greetings and Madge made a beeline for Peg.

Brant started across the street. He stopped in the middle and pretended to pick up a lucky penny, but actually he was sneaking a peek back at the diner. Madge still hadn't taken a seat. She and Peg were chatting about something, and the look on Peg's face told him it was serious. Peg nodded to Madge and then both women unexpectedly looked at Brant. He hurriedly pocketed the nonexistent penny and walked off with what he hoped was a jaunty air.

"He's damned lucky to be alive," Doc said, referring to Franz Klempner. "He's got some cuts and bruises and a few cracked ribs, probably some whiplash, but a wreck like that? I'd have expected worse. Much worse. He's got a guardian angel, that's for sure."

Brant nodded. "You never know. When I was. . . ." He caught himself. He'd almost said, "When I was a reporter."

"I've seen people walk away from wrecks that should

have killed them, and I've seen the opposite. Maybe the Reverend pulled some more strings."

Doc chuckled. "At this point I'm ready to believe anything. You saw Duffy at church, didn't you? The man hasn't looked that healthy in ten years."

Brant weighed his options carefully. Should he tell Doc about Deputy Haws or not? His paranoia urged him to proceed with caution.

"Maybe Duffy isn't the only one," he said. "Maybe there are others who've risen."

Doc seemed taken aback.

"Why would you think that?" he asked.

"Just thinking out loud. There doesn't seem to be any reason for Duffy to be picked for resurrection. Maybe the phenomenon is more widespread than that. Maybe Death's on a holiday or something."

"That would be my cue to retire," Doc offered. "But surely if there were others, we'd know, wouldn't we? If you came back from the dead, wouldn't you tell somebody about it?"

"I would, if I didn't mind sounding like a nut. Duffy's death was well documented. He couldn't come back quietly and go on about his business. But if I died, say, in my sleep one night, say I had a stroke, and I came back the next day, I might not even know it myself. Except for any changes, of course. And I wouldn't go buttonholing people and saying, 'Look at me! I died and came back!' They'd measure me for a strait jacket."

"I see your point. I think."

"I'm just saying . . . what if Madge Duffy hadn't phoned the police after killing her husband? What if she'd killed him and buried him under the petunias? Then he'd come back, claw his way out of the flower bed, and how would we have known? Madge wouldn't have broadcast the information, and even now, Duffy isn't saying a word."

"But she did call the police. We know he died."

"We know that about Duffy, but what about everybody else in town?"

"Such as . . . ?"

"Such as everybody! You, me . . . everybody!"

"You think the entire population of Anderson's come back from the dead?"

"No! I'm just saying that they could! Christ, when I say it out loud, it sounds crazy."

Doc raised one eyebrow. "You said it, Brant, not me."

Brant leaned forward, propped his arms on Doc's desk. "What if I could cite a specific case, a person who died and came back, but for some reason kept the information to himself?"

"Who?"

"I'm speaking hypothetically. If I did find someone like that, what would it mean?"

"It would mean he didn't want his name in your newspaper."

"But it could mean a lot more, couldn't it? Like, a conspiracy."

Doc's patience seemed to reach its end. "Brant, for godsakes, listen to yourself! I'm tempted to sign your commitment papers myself, right now!"

Brant sighed. "Yeah, I know," he said. "But something in this town has changed. It's the air or the negative ions or something. Don't you feel it? The town just feels different."

"Maybe it's you who's changed," Doc said. "Maybe you need a rest. Take a week off and quit stewing about things you can't do anything about. If the Grim Reaper's taken Anderson off his rounds, we'll know soon enough, won't we? Here. I have some medicine for you."

"I don't want any medi—" Brant began, then he saw that Doc was reaching into his bottom desk drawer and pulling out a bottle of Maker's Mark and a couple of shot glasses.

"I keep this handy to steady my hands before surgery,"

Doc said. When he saw the look on Brant's face, he added, "I'm kidding."

"Don't kid like that around Merle Tippert," Brant advised. "He already thinks you're a drunk."

"Don't I know it," Doc said. He filled the glasses and handed one to Brant. "Cheers."

"Cheers."

Brant drained his glass and set it on the edge of the desk. He waved off Doc's offer of a refill.

"I promised Peg I'd look in on Annie, and I think I'd like a word with Franz Klempner. Can I talk to him?"

"Out of my jurisdiction," Doc said. "He isn't with us any longer."

"Died?! But you said—"

"He went home. Oh, I tried to keep him here, but the stubborn old goat wouldn't hear of it. He asked if he was going to die and I said 'Not today' and he said, 'Then I'm going home.' Against my better judgment, but. . . ." Doc shrugged.

"Doc, you don't suppose . . . ?"

"Suppose what?"

"That Klempner didn't make it out of that wreck alive. That he died and came back."

Doc Milford reached across his desk for Brant's shot glass. "I'm cutting you off," he said, "You've bagged your limit. I'll walk with you to Annie's room."

During the walk along the corridor, Brant acknowledged that Doc was probably right about Klempner. "If Franz had come back, why didn't Irma and the Ganger boy? Say . . . the leg must be doing better."

Doc's limp had disappeared.

"What? Oh, you mean my hip. Never underestimate the power of a good whiskey," Doc said with a wink.

* * *

Brant explained to Annie that Peg wouldn't be in to see her because she was cooking a special meal for a special night. He told her he was sorry to take her mother away even for one evening but he hoped that she wouldn't hold it against him. He spoke to her just as if she could hear and understand, and he stroked her forehead and confided to her that he thought he was in love with Peg and he was going to try hard to be worthy of her. He said he had a lot to learn about love and faith and determination, and he figured that Peg was as good a teacher as he'd find anywhere.

For some reason none of this seemed foolish to him. Maybe he was buying into the myth that Annie was more than a human vegetable, and maybe she had come to symbolize something to him about his own life and the part of it that needed fixing. If he needed to find a miracle to believe in, the miracle of this little girl's recovery would suit him better than a hundred John Duffys and Deputy Hawses.

As he walked to the parking lot he was unaware of Doc Milford standing at his office window watching him go. Doc's goldfish lay on the doctor's desk, asphyxiated. Doc had pulled it from its tank and plopped it on his desk blotter and watched it flip-flop around for the time it took it to die. He'd never sat back and watched something die before, not when there was something he could do to forestall that death. Life had always seemed so precious.

Now Doc was wondering what the fuss was all about. The fish swam around in its bowl, around and around, with no meaningful direction to its life. What did it matter if this one fish stopped swimming? He watched it die and felt no remorse. Did Seth watch over the little fishes in the sea as he did over humankind? Doc felt that he must. Would the fish know the blessing of Seth's love as Doc did? He felt it would.

He picked the fish up by the tail and dropped it back in its bowl where it floated on its side.

Doc picked up the telephone and dialed the Sheriff's Office. As he'd hoped, Deputy Haws answered.

"Harold?" Doc said, "it's me. Brant Kettering just stopped by. I think we have a situation." He recounted the conversation with Brant, particularly Brant's theory that the town could be secretly infested with Risen citizens.

"I'll deal with it," Haws said.

Brant found Tom at the reservoir, all right, talking with the rest of the gang—Kent Fredericks, Buzzy Hayes, and Darren Coombs. They all seem subdued and for once it wasn't attributable to the joint that Kent tried to hide inside his cupped palm when Brant drove up.

"Hi, troops," Brant said. They mumbled their greetings back. "I guess you heard about the . . . about Galen Ganger."

"We heard," Tom said.

"I'm sorry."

"I know how sorry you are," Darren said. Apparently he was taking over Galen's angry-young-man duties.

Brant blew out his cheeks and stared at the water.

"Well," he said, "Galen wouldn't win any popularity contests with most of the town, but it's hard when you lose a friend. So, Kent. . . ."

Kent looked up as if he'd been called on in class.

"You going to Bogart that joint or pass it around?" Brant asked.

"Huh?"

"Sixties talk," Tom translated. "It means he wants a hit."

Kent was baffled for a few moments, then he held the joint out to Brant. "It's out," he said.

"Got a light?"

Buzzy gave Brant the loan of his Bic and Brant lit up. He hadn't smoked marijuana for fifteen years and he'd heard that today's weed was a lot stronger than the homegrown he'd smoked in college, but he had to knock a hole in the wall between himself and these kids. Somehow he had to tap into their thoughts on the Deputy Haws matter without revealing what he knew about the murder. If the other boys learned that Tom had confided in him, they were likely to kick Tom out of the group and Brant would lose his "mole."

The stories about modern weed were correct. It was all Brant could do not to collapse into a coughing heap on the ground. He fought the constriction in his throat and held the smoke in his lungs as long as possible, then let it out slowly. He did what the boys did, just stared quietly at nothing for the time it took to smoke the joint down to a nub. Buzzy had a roach clip on his key chain that looked like a house key, Brant noticed.

Brant's head was spinning pretty good when Darren asked him, point blank, "Why'd you come out here?"

Brant studied the ground for an honest-enough answer.

"Something's bothered me about the accident," he said. "It struck me as odd."

"How so?" Tom asked. He knew why Brant had come to the reservoir—he'd come to see Tom. Brant had to appear more ignorant than he was in order to protect his source, and Tom could help by asking leading questions.

"Well, it's just that I always figured that Galen and Deputy Haws weren't exactly buddy-buddy," Brant said. "In fact, I pretty much figured they hated each other's guts."

Dark, worried looks circulated among the boys.

"So?" Kent asked.

"It just struck me funny," Brant said, "to see them together outside the church this morning." He told them about Galen's surprise appearance and his quick huddle with the deputy. "I guess Deputy Haws and myself were the last people to see Galen alive, except for the Klempners, of course. I wondered why Haws and Galen would be talking, is all."

"You said he was parked in front of a hydrant," Buzzy offered.

"That was another funny thing. Haws never wrote him a ticket. Didn't even pull out his book. The whole hydrant business sounded like, I don't know. . . ."

"Like an excuse," Tom said. "Like he needed some reason to talk to him."

"Yeah," Brant said, as if the idea hadn't dawned on him before. "That's exactly what it was like. Then the . . . then Galen peeled out like, I don't know, like he'd just been given orders or something. Not that Haws told him to smash head-on into the Klempners and kill himself and them both. That'd be crazy. But it was like that. That's the kind of feel the whole thing had. Pretty strange, huh?"

"Pretty strange," Tom agreed. Looks shot around among the boys so fast it was like watching a juggling act.

The seed had been planted. Tom would do Brant's talking from this point on and report back to him at dinner. Brant, who'd been leaning against Darren's Satellite, stood up straight and stretched.

"So Haws knew you were watching?" Tom asked quickly. Brant noticed an urgency in his voice. Tom had something to tell him, but it was going to be awkward.

"Yeah. He saw."

The boys were all looking at Tom. What he wanted to say was, "Then you could be next," but he couldn't be so blunt.

"So?" Brant prodded.

"Nothing," Tom said. He looked around as if taking in the reservoir for the first time. "Warm today. Nice day to take a drive in the country or something. Spend the whole day away from the hassles of home."

"Yeah, I was thinking the same," Brant said, picking up on the veiled suggestion to make himself scarce. "Get out of the house. Stay as far away from the office as I can." He slapped Tom on the arm, said, "Hey, I may even check out the nudists' dock!"

He and Tom forced laughs and the other boys smiled. But nobody was laughing as Brant got back in his car and drove off. In the rear view mirror, he saw the boys talking and Buzzy pacing and Darren yelling about something to Tom. Kent just looked sick.

"Why would he do it? It doesn't make sense!"

That was Buzzy, talking and throwing his hands around as he paced back and forth in front of his Vega. He'd spent the morning getting it running again and was timing the engine when his dad came out to the garage and told him about Galen. A chill had gone up his spine then, and another one had appeared when Brant told them about Galen's meeting with Deputy Haws. The boys accepted as fact all that Brant had said and implied.

"Haws threatened him. Haws said he'd kill him if he didn't do it," Darren said.

"So he killed himself instead of getting killed? That's stupid," said Kent. "Either way he's dead."

"It makes sense," Tom said. He was teetering on the edge of the Blacklands, but he wasn't going to go over no matter how tempting it was. He wasn't going to space out.

"How?" Kent asked, almost pleaded.

"Because he plans to come back."

"Shit!" Buzzy said.

"Just because Haws came back doesn't mean Galen will," Darren stated.

"John Duffy came back, too."

"So what are you saying," Kent demanded, "that everybody that dies from now on is going to come back?"

"I don't know," Tom said. "But Galen wouldn't have killed himself if he didn't think so. Even if Haws threatened him with something. If he was that scared of Haws, he'd have just kept going. He'd have driven off and we'd never see him again."

"Maybe it was an accident," Buzzy suggested. "Maybe he didn't mean to kill himself at all. Maybe he was just fucking around with the old man and something happened."

"If you believe that, you wouldn't be peeing your pants right now."

"I'm not peeing my pants."

"Anyway, I guess we'll know soon enough."

"What do you mean?" Kent had gone a couple of shades whiter since Brant left. He looked like a little boy who'd been bedridden for a month and this was his first day in the sunshine.

"I mean we'll know soon enough if Galen's coming back. I figure it'll happen tonight or not at all."

The boys gathered around as Tom laid it out for them.

"From what I've heard about John Duffy's rise, he came back around midnight. It was before midnight when we buried Haws. We don't know when he came back but if it was the same time as Duffy. . . . "

"This kind of shit always happens at midnight," Buzzy said. "I mean, when it does happen, it's at midnight."

"What do you know about it?" Darren asked sarcastically.

"As much as you."

"You know what this means, don't you?" asked Tom.

"No, please tell us, O Wise One." Darren's attitude was grating on Tom's nerves. Tom made a point of looking at Darren when he told them.

"It means we have to be at the mortuary tonight at midnight to see for ourselves."

"Shit! If he comes back, I do not want to be there!"

"You'd rather sit around all day waiting for the phone to ring?" Buzzy asked. " 'Hello, this is Galen, I'm back from the fucking dead, man!' "

"First, I want to see the corpse," Tom explained. "I want to see it now so I know he's really dead."

"The corpse is a fucking charcoal briquette."

"So they say. I want to see it for myself. And if it comes back, I want to see that, too. I've got to know, all right?"

"Then you're going alone, man," Darren declared, "because I am not getting anywhere near a mortuary at fucking midnight."

"I don't blame you," Tom said, "for being afraid. If you want to stay home in bed. . . ."

Darren was up like a shot with a fist headed for Tom's chin. Tom was expecting it and sidestepped, holding his foot out so that Darren took a header as he went by. Darren got back on his feet and charged Tom again, head down, and Tom got him in a headlock and swung him around and into the side of Buzzy's Vega. He still had a hold on Darren's head when he swung him the other way and let go and Darren stumbled a few steps but didn't fall. He had his fists balled and charged again but this time Buzzy stepped between them and pretty soon Kent and Buzzy both had hold of Darren and were holding him back.

Darren let forth with a stream of obscenities and struggled against Kent and Buzzy for about a minute before running out of steam and dirty words. They were surprised when he fell limp and they almost dropped him to the ground. His head was down so they didn't notice right away that tears were running down his cheeks.

Darren fell to his knees. He wasn't able to hold it in any longer. He started sobbing. Tom felt sorry for him, not because he was crying but because he needed Galen more desperately than anyone, including Darren, would have guessed.

Come midnight, Tom knew, Darren would be there at the mortuary with him. And if Darren came, then Kent and Buzzy would, too.

* * *

Brant could almost believe, standing there on the dock in the sunlight with the occasional fish jumping in the water and the breeze caressing his face, that there was nothing at all wrong anywhere in the world, particularly in Anderson. It was so quiet, so peaceful.

Kind of amazing that he had the dock to himself. He'd expected to find a few naked bodies there, anyway, on a day that came like a present the way this one had. There were cars parked nearby, but they could belong to hikers or boaters. He recognized Merle Tippert's Studebaker. Merle wouldn't have been at the dock, though, not an old prude like Merle. Would he?

If Brant had seen anyone there he wouldn't have intruded. He didn't want to gawk. But the dock was empty and he had a day to kill. He wanted to clean up before dinner at Peg's, but Tom's thinly disguised warning had hit home. He'd had those same thoughts himself. Better to avoid the usual places. It seemed unlikely now, standing in the sun on the most perfect of autumn days, that Haws was stalking him, but you never know. You just never know.

The longer he stood on the dock the more secure he felt. He told himself that his imagination was working overtime. Maybe he just wanted so badly for something worth reporting on to happen that he'd built the whole thing up in his head. There was a rational explanation for everything that had happened. He just didn't know what it was. He was chasing ghosts. If he stayed on the dock long enough he'd talk himself out of everything.

He felt so comfortable that he considered getting naked after all. There was no one around to see, and if someone showed up, they were probably a nudist. What would it hurt? No, he couldn't do it. But he could take his shoes off. He could at least take his shoes and socks off.

He leaned down to unlace his shoes and that's when he noticed the stains under his feet. He'd visited enough crime scenes to recognize them. They were blood, and they were fresh.

Brant cast a quick look around and then strode back to his car. He drove off with his heart pumping a mile a minute, never discovering the four bodies Deputy Haws had pulled into the brush and covered with branches and leaves, waiting for midnight to work its magic.

Haws cruised the town several times looking for Brant's Toyota, but he didn't see it anywhere. Brant could usually be found at home or at the diner or at his office and he was at none of these places today. Haws figured that he might have gone to Junction City, the nearest town with a five-digit population, to pick up some things he couldn't find in Anderson.

He was tempted to drive back out to the reservoir and check on the bodies he'd left there. He'd been careful to cover them up but, since he didn't want any of them going through the ordeal he'd suffered upon his rise, he didn't dig any earth or do any burying. He dragged them off to the side and covered them with debris and figured that was good enough to last until midnight. He wasn't too worried about anyone stumbling across them—it was getting cooler as the sun headed for the horizon so the dock would see no more business today—they just crossed his mind off-and-on the way things were prone to do.

He wondered about Seth's command to kill the nudists, but he didn't consider not doing it. Everyone would come to Seth sooner or later. He didn't see why they received such a high priority, that's all. Maybe it was a matter of opportunity, them being out there by themselves, easy targets, or maybe their nakedness was an offense to Seth in some way, a blasphemous celebration of the earthly flesh or life itself.

He didn't think of it as killing. He thought of it as introducing them to Seth, and dying was part of that process. When he'd drawn his gun and shot them one by one, he'd been puzzled by the terrified looks on their faces. But of course they didn't know that he was just sending them on a journey, that Haws was more of a conductor than an executioner. They thought they were really dying. Haws tried to see it from their perspective, but even with his newfound mental robustness he couldn't make that leap for more than a few moments at a time. There was only one way to see things, ultimately, and that was Seth's way.

Brant Kettering had gone to the head of the list of people who needed to meet Seth. The conversion process was at a critical point. As far as most of the people in town knew, John Duffy was the only person to come back. A few more knew about Deputy Haws, but the main troublemaker, Galen Ganger, would meet Seth tonight. He'd take care of the others.

Brant was a bit of a puzzle, though. Did he know about Haws or didn't he? Even Doc Milford wasn't sure and he was the one who'd talked to him. But it didn't really matter. Haws would introduce Brant to Seth and then everything would be all right.

All. Right.

Haws decided to park his car outside Brant's house. If he'd gone to Junction City, he'd be back shortly, and Haws could take care of him then.

It was warm inside the patrol vehicle so Haws rolled down the windows and let a breeze wander through. He scooted the seat back for more leg room and leaned his porky neck against the head rest. He decided to rest his eyes and listen for Brant's car to drive up. Five minutes later he was fast asleep.

He didn't see Brant ease his car through the intersection at the far end of the street, but Brant saw Haws and kept going. Maybe he'd just chosen Brant's street for an afternoon siesta, but Brant was taking no chances, not until he knew more. He was still operating on hearsay and conjecture and with an acute shortage of hard facts. Not a comfortable spot to be in. Part of him wanted to leave town and never look back, but another part reminded him of the words of Edmund Burke, a sentence he'd once, in his younger, fiery days, typed out and pinned to his bulletin board: The only thing necessary for the triumph of evil is for good men to do nothing.

He couldn't go to the authorities—he didn't trust Sheriff Clark, and anyone else would instantly write him off as a loony—and he couldn't go home. So he hit the highway and drove out to the Klempners' farm, thinking of Eloise. By all standards of decency (except those of television reporters, who had none) it was too soon to interview the grieving widower, but another day could be too late. If he had to err. . . .

He knocked softly, figuring that Franz Klempner was probably in bed asleep. A dog barked inside, a fairly large one by the sound of him. Soon the old man appeared at the door. The dog scooted in between Brant and Franz and barked fiercely while his tail whipped the air, slapping against the old man's shins. Franz looked like he'd been beaten up but was remarkably hale for someone who'd been through such a serious accident. He should have been in a hospital bed, swathed in bandages, with tubes in his arms and a beeping monitor at his bedside.

"I'm Brant Kettering," Brant said. "I run the *Cooves County Times*. I was hoping—"

"I don't want to talk to the papers," Franz said, and he started to shut the door. It might have closed in Brant's face but for the dog who was in the way, trapped between the big door and the screen.

Brant quickly added, "I'm not here on business. In fact, I'd rather talk to you 'out of school,' as it were."

"Come back later," Franz said, shoving at the dog with his foot.

"It was no accident that killed your wife."

The words popped out of his mouth before Brant had time to think about them. It was a cruel and careless thing to say, but it worked. Franz held the door open and peered out at him, sizing him up.

"Something very strange is going on in town," Brant said. "Your wife may be the only person who knew exactly what it was."

The old man stood in the doorway for several long seconds. Finally he unlatched the screen door and turned his back on Brant saying, "You'd best come in. The dog won't bite."

Franz hobbled into the living room, obviously in considerable pain. He walked hunched over and picked his way slowly. When he lowered himself into an overstuffed chair that should have been sitting outside waiting for the trash truck, he moaned and freefell the last few inches. He fingered his side, where Brant could see through a gap in Franz' shirt that Doc had wrapped the cracked ribs.

Elmer the dog gave Brant the once over and received a scratch behind the ears, then he curled up at Franz' feet, lay his head on his paws and proceeded to ignore the ensuing conversation.

Brant sat in the rocking chair, the only other chair in the room. He expressed his condolences and Franz waved them away and steered him back to the main topic. Now that Brant had the audience he'd wanted, he wasn't sure where to begin.

"You heard about John Duffy," Brant said, and Franz acknowledged that he had. "Do you believe it?"

"I don't know," Franz answered. "If I'd seen it with my own eyes, maybe I would."

Brant angled his chair to point more squarely toward Franz and leaned forward. "It's true. And what's more, John Duffy isn't the only one. There are others. I don't know how many, but there's at least one more. There was no way to keep Duffy's rise a secret, but others could be dying and coming back and not telling anyone about it."

"Why would they do that?"

"That's the worrisome thing. One of them . . . well, it's Deputy Haws."

"I know him."

"He was shot the night John Duffy came back. He was shot and killed. The next day he was back, good as new, with a bullet hole in his shirt. He never said a word to anybody, not even to Sheriff Clark. Mr. Klempner, the boy who shot him was Galen Ganger."

Franz stiffened in his chair.

"I saw Haws talking to the Ganger boy shortly before your accident. I don't know for sure, but he may have ordered him to . . . do what he did. It may have had something to do with what Irma said at the church."

Brant became highly aware of the antique clock ticking loudly on the mantel. Either Franz or Irma had probably bought it new. The clocked ticked off a good three minutes before Franz said anything.

"I thought it was me," Franz said. "Because I drive slow, the boys have their fun with me."

"Mr. Klempner, who is Eloise?"

Franz shook his head. "I don't know anyone by that name."

"Did Irma know anyone named Eloise?"

"Not that I recall."

"Maybe someone from long ago."

"No, no. I don't remember anyone by that name. I'm

sorry. My wife, she wasn't right, you know, in the belfry. But she was a good woman."

Brant nodded with a sympathy that he discovered, to his surprise, was genuine. Maybe two years in Anderson had softened him more than he knew.

They sat in silence for some time, Franz in his big stuffed chair, rigid as a statue, the dog at his feet. Brant noticed the Bible on the lamp table next to him, well worn.

"She had nightmares," Franz said. "Always had them, but they were worse as of late. It was the bell that set her off, though. Scared her half to death."

"The bell?"

"The church bell. Some fool's taken to ringing it late at night. Midnight. It's that new preacher, I'd guess. It just set her off something awful."

Brant sat back and subconsciously began to rock. "Hm," he said, and he rocked slowly, back and forth, forward and back, while the mantel clock ticked and Elmer the dog chased a rabbit in his sleep, and Franz Klempner sat like a stone in his ratty old overstuffed chair, occasional tears running unashamedly down his cheeks.

As dusk fell in Anderson, Deputy Haws jerked in his sleep and his elbow honked the horn of his patrol vehicle and he woke with a start.

Tom Culler arrived home and helped his mother by peeling some potatoes.

Doc Milford called it a day.

And the roaches under Carl Tompkins's floor picked clean the skeleton of a cat who'd crawled under the house a few hours before, seeking someplace cool.

FOURTEEN

Tom felt like a time traveler in the Grand Ballroom of the Titanic watching the doomed dancers in their finery twirl and laugh, watching star-crossed lovers nuzzle each other under the chandeliers, knowing that soon the alarm would sound and there would be panic and the mad scrabble for the lifeboats would begin as the unthinkable happened, as the unsinkable ship sunk to an icy grave.

The unthinkable was happening here, now, to Tom and everyone else in Anderson. Like the dancers on the Titanic, most of the town was unaware of the impending horror. His mother flitted about the kitchen, tearing lettuce and slicing carrots and celery and mushrooms for the salad, checking the roast in the oven, buffing the silverware with a kitchen towel, putting out dishes and finding chips on all the plates and digging through the shelves to find three perfect ones. She didn't know what was going on, and Tom didn't want her to know, not yet.

Obviously she was in love.

It made him feel good to see her excited about something again, but he felt shame, too, that he wasn't the one who'd snapped her out of her grim obsession with Annie. Brant had better not let her down as he'd let Tom down. If he thought for a minute that Brant was just using his mother for sex, he'd kill him. Not that that would do much good, apparently. Not in this town.

Tom peeled the potatoes and whacked them into fourths and put them on the stove in a pan of water. He marveled at the way life went on in its usual patterns while momentous events seethed beneath the surface. Everyone knew that a man had risen from the dead and they realized what an outstanding and uncommon thing that was. The news rattled through the community and set tongues wagging and raised some hackles. But after the gossip and the arguments and speculations, they went back to their houses and their families and their ironing and mending and sports on television, and come Monday morning they'd wake up and go to work or to school just the same as always.

What would it take to break the grip of the mundane? What would it take to shake people up enough to say to hell with school and the workplace and all the stupid minutiae of life, and compel them to dive deeply into unknown waters? A disaster, maybe. A flood, an earthquake, a war.

Miracles were happening in Anderson. Were they good miracles or bad miracles?

Are you a good witch or a bad witch?

Tom told himself that he had to start writing again and get some of this crap out of his head or he'd go crazy, if it wasn't already too late.

He heard a knock at the door and Peg dashed into the bathroom for some last minute adjustments, wondering why Brant didn't give her a warning toot. Tom let Brant in and they had a few hurried words in private while they could. Tom had noticed that Brant's car wasn't out front.

"I parked in the alley," Brant said. "Haws had my house staked out earlier. I spent most of the day with Franz Klempner. He doesn't know anything about Eloise, but Irma had been having nightmares. It had something to do with the Reverend ringing the church bell in the middle of the night."

Tom said, "I heard it! It was ringing the night we buried

Haws." He told Brant about his "midnight" theory and Brant said that it fit the facts, what few of them he had.

"Maybe it's some kind of signal or catalyst or something," Tom suggested.

"Irma Klempner might've been able to provide the link, but. . . ."

"Hi, Brant," Peg said brightly as she waltzed into the room. She was so pretty and chipper that Brant's gloom was brushed into the corners of his mind. He smiled at her and offered up a compliment and the three of them shared an awkward moment before Peg rushed out to check on the dinner. She told Brant to have a seat and instructed Tom to find him something to drink. Brant asked for a glass of water. Tom returned with the water and the news that dinner would be another few minutes. They huddled in the living room and tried to keep their voices down.

"Peg doesn't know about any of this, does she?" Brant said.

Tom shook his head. "I keep wanting to tell her. I keep thinking that she ought to know what's going on. But damn it . . . you should have seen her this evening. You've made her happy somehow. I want it to last as long as it can. Until we know what's really going on. . . ."

"I know what you mean." So, he made her happy, did he? "Still, she's in a position to hear things."

Tom shook his head. "I know her better than you do. It's too soon."

Brant acquiesced. He could hear the resentment in Tom's voice. Brant had given Peg something Tom couldn't. Tom probably knew what a shit he'd been lately and confessing his role in a murder, however accidental, would leave him open to all manner of accusations and I-told-you-so's. Brant had screwed up with Tom once and didn't want to do so again, especially not with things on the mend.

And Tom was right in that he had a clearer picture of

Peg's mental state than Brant did. Brant had never believed, as some people did, that God didn't give you more
than you could handle. If that were the case, where did all
the nervous breakdowns and suicides come from? Between the divorce and the accident, Peg was already
walking the edge. He'd let Tom call this shot, for now.

"What did the boys say after I left?" Brant asked.

"They're freaked out. If it wasn't an accident, Galen
must've been expecting to come back like Haws did. It's
a freaky thought but, shit . . . anyway, we're going to check
it out tonight."

"Oh?"

"We're meeting at the mortuary at a quarter to twelve."

"That'll test the 'midnight' theory, too. How do you plan
to get in?"

"Kent. He got fascinated with Houdini in junior high,
wanted to be an escape artist. He can open about anything."

Brant shivered. "If what I saw of Galen can come back,
then anybody can."

He filled Tom in on his other thought, that there could
be more Risen than John Duffy and Deputy Haws.

"I've thought of that," Tom said. "For every one we
know about, there could a dozen others. People could be
dying right and left and coming back before anybody
knows about it."

"Or getting murdered. I saw blood stains on the dock
this afternoon."

Tom's eyes went wide. "We heard shots across the
water. A long ways off. We didn't think much of it. Jesus!
Did you look around for bodies?"

"No, I got the hell out of there."

"You should've looked. We'd know who they were if they
came back. I'll check it out tonight, before the mortuary."

"Be careful, Tom. If half of what I think is going on is

really going on, we should just pack our bags and get out of town while we still can. Right now. Right this minute."

"Mom wouldn't go, not with Annie in the hospital. We'd have to get her released, get her transferred. That'd be a risk. Mom wouldn't do it, not based on what we have now."

That point struck Brant as one more reason to tell her what they knew. He started to say something when Peg appeared in the doorway.

"My, don't you two look serious," she said. "What's the topic of conversation?"

"Politics," said Tom before Brant could answer.

"We're against them," Brant added.

"I don't allow any political talk at my dinner table. It's bad for digestion. Come take a seat. Dinner's ready."

Peg decided early that the meal was a disaster. The roast was dry and the potatoes competed with the gravy in the category of Most Lumps. She noticed that Brant ate around the mushrooms in the salad and neither he nor Tom asked for seconds of anything.

Conversation lagged. Brant seemed interested in the town's reaction to the Duffy business, but every time he brought the subject up, Tom sidetracked it by complimenting the food he'd barely touched. Peg couldn't seem to start a sentence that didn't begin with "Annie . . ." and that made her realize how insanely narrow her life had become in the past eight months. She dredged her memory for an amusing anecdote from the diner but couldn't come up with anything that didn't involve Cindy Robertson, another touchy subject with Tom. She tried to tell a joke that she'd overheard Carl Tompkins telling Stig Evans but she only remembered after it was all told that the three guys in the rowboat were Lutheran ministers, which was the point of the whole thing.

She couldn't fathom the reason for Tom's sullenness. She'd have assumed that he was jealous of Brant, but they'd seemed to be getting along so well in the living room. Maybe it was the you-can't-replace-my-father thing. He kept shooting hateful glances at Brant as if mentally kicking him under the table.

She saw echoes of the haunted, escaped convict in Brant's face. He'd said at the diner that he had things on his mind. Apparently a plate full of dry roast and lumpy potatoes wasn't enough to make him forget his troubles, whatever they were. He'd catch himself now and again and make the effort to smile, but clearly something was on his mind.

Something was on her mind, too. As an act of desperation during one of the long, tense silences that had become the hallmark of the evening, she said, "Madge Duffy has some strange ideas."

"Oh?" Brant said.

Tom's jaw tightened the way his father's used to do before he flew into a rage, but Peg couldn't take the strained silence any longer. She had to get this notion out into the open or she'd burst.

"She says that John's changed since he came back. He used to have bursitis in one arm. Did you know that?"

Brant said that he didn't.

"Neither did I, but I guess Madge would know. Anyway, it's gone. Just completely gone. Other things, too, little physical ailments that aren't there anymore. She said. . . ."

Peg toyed with the green beans on her plate.

"She has this idea about Annie. She thinks maybe if it had been Annie instead of John . . . if Annie had come back . . . maybe she'd be better. Maybe. . . ."

"Fuck Madge Duffy!" Tom's angry exclamation was like a firecracker exploding under the table.

Peg looked at Tom and saw her ex-husband staring back at her. He wore the same beastly look that she'd seen on

Rod a hundred times, usually when he'd been drinking, or when he was laid off, or when fate had dealt him any unjust blow. The look spoke of a savage anger with its roots thousands of years in the past, when the line between human and animal was thin as dust and the difference between survival and extinction depended on sheer ferocity.

"Madge Duffy is an idiot!" Tom continued.

"She was only saying that—"

"She was talking bullshit!"

"What did she say exactly?" Brant asked.

"It doesn't matter!" Tom shouted.

He set his hands on the table and leaned toward Peg as if getting ready to pounce. "Annie's gone! You have to face facts, Mom! She isn't going to get better and if you kill her—which is what Madge Duffy was suggesting, right?—she isn't coming back from the dead!"

"You can't know that," Peg replied coldly, returning his stare with one of her own. "John Duffy came back."

"So what? That doesn't make it right! Jesus! Can't you see that? Can't you see how fucked up that is?"

"Tom, maybe we should—" Brant began, but Tom cut him off, stabbing a finger at him.

"Brant, shut up," Tom commanded. "I know what you're thinking and you're wrong, so just shut the fuck up!"

"Tom!" Peg admonished.

"It's okay," Brant said.

"No, it isn't okay!" Peg said. "We have rules in this house, and I'm pretty damned sick of being the only one who follows them!"

"I don't need this," Tom said, and he shoved his chair away from the table. It fell over with a bang and he kicked it aside as he marched out of the room. Peg heard the kitchen door slam shut, then the engine of Tom's Honda coughed and roared and finally faded into the distance.

Brant saw that Peg was trembling. She wadded up her napkin and threw it to the table.

"Shit!" she said.

Brant went over and put his hand on her shoulder.

"I am so sick of his shit!" Peg's voice shook with fury.

"Don't be too hard on him," Brant said.

Peg brushed off Brant's hand and turned to look at him incredulously.

"Me, hard on him?" she said. "Weren't you here? Didn't you see that? What did I say that deserved that?"

"I'm sorry. I didn't mean to imply that it was your fault. It wasn't. But it wasn't his, either."

"Then whose? Madge Duffy's? Yours?"

Peg got up and started clearing the table, forcing Brant to answer over the clatter of dishes as she angrily stacked plates one on top of another.

"There's something going on in this town," he said. "It's thrown everybody out of whack. You saw the fight at the diner. Everybody's on edge. Would you mind not doing that right now?"

Peg slammed the plates to the table and whirled to look at him, arms folded over her chest.

"Okay, tell me how to raise my kid," she said.

"I'm not telling you how to raise Tom."

"Then what, Brant? What are you saying?"

"I'm just saying that . . . kids like to think the world is a stable, secure place that makes sense. When they hit Tom's age they start finding out that it isn't so, that it never was that way and never will be. Then there's the Duffy business and the Ganger boy's accident . . . Tom doesn't know how to deal with it all, but he's grown up enough to think he should. That's all I'm saying."

Peg closed her eyes and sighed. Some dinner. Any normal man would've made his excuses and fled. What planet did Brant come from where people were so patient and kind?

"Oh, Brant," she said. She felt suddenly very tired. "I'm such a mess."

She opened her eyes to see him looking at her and smiling for no damn reason, and when he opened his arms to her she didn't know what to do. He stepped up and embraced her and without thinking about it she threw her arms around him and held him tight. She didn't realize until she did it that this was what she'd been needing for way too long. She wondered if Brant noticed that she'd started crying and decided that he'd figure it out when the tears soaked through his shirt.

Brant couldn't think of anything to say, so he just said "It's all right" about a hundred times or so. Finally Peg pulled away and looked up at him, swiping a palm across her red, wet eyes, and sniffled.

"Dessert?" she said, and Brant said that dessert sounded good.

Peg and Brant sat on the front porch in a swing that groaned under their weight. It had been there for twenty years, long before Peg and Rod moved in, and had seen its share of lovers' autumn moons. It was an old-fashioned thing to do, and Brant was thinking that it was one of the finest pleasures life has to offer.

"It was a stupid thought," Peg said after a long period of neither of them saying anything. "About Annie. I don't blame Tom for getting upset."

"It's not all that farfetched," Brant said. "If John Duffy can get his throat cut and come back from the dead, you'd have to think that anything was possible."

"Are you saying you believe in miracles?"

"I believe things happen that I don't understand. What I can't figure is why Duffy would be the one it happened to."

"I don't think it was meant for John's benefit. He was brought back for Madge. Otherwise she could've spent the rest of her life in prison. I think it's her miracle."

"She deserved it more than John did," Brant said. "But still, why Madge? What makes her so special?"

"She's a good person."

"So are a lot of people. You're a good person."

"I try," Peg said. "Maybe if I keep trying, I'll get a miracle of my own."

Brant was finding it hard to keep biting his tongue. He had to beat down the urge to tell her about Haws and the Ganger boy and about all his fears and suspicions. On the other hand, he didn't want to be the one to rat on Tom—he wanted and needed the boy's trust—and didn't want to sound like a paranoid idiot. As if those reasons weren't enough, he wasn't sure Peg could take any more pressure. Her daughter was in a coma, her son could be the poster boy for teenaged angst. She didn't need something else to worry about, especially something as unsubstantiated as his anxiety over the Risen.

What had they done, actually, for a fact? Nothing.

"Don't wish too hard for a miracle," he said. "It might not look so good to you, once it came."

"But I do want it, Brant," Peg said. "I want it more than you can imagine. Like you probably wanted a BB-gun and tickets to the Beatles and your first woman, all rolled into one and multiplied by a hundred. I think about the way she used to be, how curious she was about absolutely everything. I can still see her when I peek into her bedroom at night. She's all I think about. I'd do anything to get her back. I want it so bad. . . ."

She felt herself choking up again. Brant must have noticed because he folded his hand over hers and smiled at her. She smiled back and he put his arm around her. She scooted over closer to him and before she was sure it was going to happen, they were kissing.

Down the street, sitting in his patrol vehicle with the lights out, Deputy Haws watched. He'd stopped by to check on the Culler kid and he'd spotted Brant's car in the alley. Funny place to park, as if Brant was hiding or something. He must know that Haws was looking for him, but he must also know that he couldn't hide forever, not in a town the size of Anderson.

Haws fingered his police special. He could do both of them right now. But Seth had warned him against converting Peg. Seth was saving her for some reason, and Haws did not question Seth. It would be so easy, though, to sneak up behind them and put a bullet in each head. If they were kissing he might get both with one shot. He'd have to line it up just right, but it could be done.

No doubt about it, it could be done.

Frank Gunnarsen hadn't wanted to stop by the Duffys' house for coffee after dinner, but his wife Doris insisted. It wasn't every day that they were invited. In fact, Frank and Doris hadn't exchanged more than six words a month with the Duffys in all the years they'd lived next door.

Doris didn't like John Duffy. She'd heard the gossip and knew it was true by the look in his eyes the day she showed up at their door with a fresh peach cobbler. Bernice Tompkins had told her about bumping into Madge Duffy in town and that she had a black eye she tried to hide with makeup but you could still see it as plain as day. The Duffys had lived in Anderson for a few months, at that time, and Doris had heard John's yelling from time to time, but this was the first concrete evidence anyone had of physical abuse. It had to be verified before Doris could pass it on, naturally, so she had rushed home and whipped up the cobbler and taken it over to Madge with her story all ready.

"You know how it is with peach trees," she planned to say, "it's feast or famine. We're practically swimming in the darned things now so I just thought . . . well, here. I love to bake but Frank's already eating peaches for breakfast, lunch and dinner."

All the time, of course, she'd be checking out Madge's eye for herself and when she got home she could start making her calls.

It hadn't worked out that way because it was John who answered the door. The way his eyes seemed to burn right through her, she knew he was a wife-beater and he knew that she knew and that frightened her. Besides, she could smell the bourbon on his breath and that made him even more unpredictable. Instead of her elegant story about the peaches she mumbled something that probably didn't make any sense and shoved the cobbler at him and practically ran back to her house.

Later she caught sight of him scooping her beautiful peach cobbler, one of the nicest she'd baked, into the trash, though Madge returned her baking dish a week later ("after the swelling had gone down and the bruise had healed, no doubt," Doris had told Bernice) and lied about how delicious it was.

Doris kept her distance after that, and Frank was never one to socialize, preferring to come home from work and put his feet up and watch television over going out and seeing anybody. To him, visiting with people was a chore. "It's all that talk," he complained, and Doris never understood what was so hard about talking, it came so naturally to her.

When Doris learned that Madge had cut John's throat, she breathed a sigh of relief. It was like living next door to a time bomb, being neighbors with the Duffys. She felt sorry for Madge, figuring that she'd go to prison, but they'd never gotten close and maybe somebody less troubled would move into the house now, somebody Doris could talk to over the fence and sit beside with a glass of lemonade on a hot summer's afternoon and have over for coffee on Saturday mornings to catch up on the week's happenings.

Then when it turned out that John wasn't dead after all and Madge was being released from jail, she felt let down. It had annoyed her that Madge couldn't tear herself away from her no-good husband, and now Doris was even more annoyed. Couldn't the woman do anything right? As the facts poured in over the telephone line, however, it seemed that Madge had done a pretty thorough job of killing John after all and that, through no fault of her own, the man had somehow cheated Death.

In short order Doris and Frank found themselves living next door to celebrities of sorts. People slowed their cars as they drove by, and the telephone hardly stopped ringing as everybody called to find out the latest. Doris would tell them, "I haven't heard anything, not a peep," or "He's outside, working on the porch railing. Yes, right this very minute, he's hammering away loud enough to . . . oh! I almost said 'wake the dead!'"

Doris was spending so much time on the phone that her ear started to hurt. She told Frank that she was thinking of buying one of those headphone-things so she could do her cooking while she talked and not get a crick in her neck, or at least one of those stick-on shoulder pads. He'd just harumphed and clicked the channel changer, looking for a game.

So when Madge called her and invited her and Frank over for coffee after dinner, she'd accepted at once. Imagine! A chance to hear the whole story directly from the horse's mouth! She'd been watching from the window when the Duffys gave Brant Kettering the cold shoulder, and now she was being handed the inside scoop on a silver platter. Maybe she could sell Brant the story. "Personal Interview with Madge and John Duffy" read the headline in her mind, "by Doris Banks Gunnarsen." Or maybe she'd leave off the "Gunnarsen" and write under her maiden name as other independently minded women did. Wouldn't that be a kick in Frank's pants!

Frank had told her, of course, "You go if you want," but Doris said, "What, me go all alone into that house? Do you think I'm out of my mind?" Frank moaned and grumbled but he put his shoes on after dinner and Doris handed him a clean shirt and they were off to the Duffys'.

There was something different about them, no doubt about it. Madge had lost that hunted look she'd always worn, the worried brow and a slightly hunched-over way of carrying herself, as if something was going to leap out and get her. She was relaxed and exuded a charm that quickly put Doris at ease. As for John, he looked like an ordinary human being, which for him was a step up. If Madge had looked like something's prey, John had always looked like the predator. But this evening he seemed more like one of those full-bellied lions on the nature shows that scratches its back in the grass and lets the little cubs tumble all over it without a snap or a snarl.

They talked about almost everything there was to talk about in Anderson except the main topic of conversation, which was John's rise. Doris had enough good gossip at her disposal to keep the ball rolling and the Duffys had all the right reactions to the various tidbits of news: it was shocking, the Maeders girl getting pregnant out of wedlock and the abortion on top of that; it was a disgrace that Carl Tompkins didn't give his number-one man at the hardware store, Jimmy Troost, more of a raise after all his work getting the place in shape—everybody knew who really ran that store; the new reverend seemed like a good egg, if a little young, but then the whole world seemed to be getting younger these days—they couldn't be getting older, could they? And so forth.

Sitting there in the living room, sipping coffee with the Duffys, Doris felt that a corner had been turned. Madge might be the neighbor she'd always wanted after all, and if John and Frank could find common ground, they might all become fast friends.

After a time the women retired to the kitchen, ostensibly to make a fresh pot of coffee but really to get away from the men. Once the women were out of the room John offered Frank a taste of the good stuff and Frank gratefully accepted, and they headed for the basement. John hollered in to the kitchen that he was going to show Frank the workshop and to give them a yell when the coffee was ready.

John's workshop consisted of a handmade table with a vise screwed into the top that had been there when they moved in and an assortment of familiar tools hung in no particular order on a pegboard. A gray wooden cabinet, another legacy from the previous occupant, held a bottle of Jim Beam. John rustled up a couple of glasses and handed one to Frank, advising him that he might want to wipe it out a bit. Frank gave the glass a perfunctory swipe with the tail of his shirt and said that it didn't matter, the whiskey would kill the germs anyway.

After a couple of shots, Frank ventured to ask John how he was feeling.

"Never better," John said. "You can call me crazy, but the whole business was the best thing that ever happened to me. It opened my eyes. There's a whole world out there we don't even know about. Another?" He hefted the bottle of Beam.

"Don't mind," Frank said, holding out his glass.

John poured it a little higher this time.

"Now I hope you don't take this the wrong way," John said, "but when Madge said she was inviting you over, I kind of didn't think much of the idea. We've been neighbors for some time and I'd gotten the feeling that you were a little stand-offish."

"Well, you know how it is," Frank said. He started to talk about working all day and coming home and just wanting to put your feet up and watch a little television, but he remembered that John had been out of work a good many of the months they'd lived next door, so he let his comment hang and hoped that John would put his own spin on it.

"Don't I though," John said. "I said that you'd never invited us over to your place, but Madge said, 'The phone works both ways, you know,' and I had to admit she was right. Once I figured out what she meant, anyway."

The men had a good laugh.

Frank said, "Doris did bring over a pie or something once."

"Did she?" John said, cocking an eyebrow. "She did, didn't she? I think I remember that now. Yes sir, you're right! I'd completely forgotten about that pie."

They drank a toast to the pie and John poured another splash of whiskey into their glasses.

It seemed like he and John Duffy were getting along pretty good so Frank decided to go for the gusto and asked him what it was like being dead.

John's face took on a thoughtful look. "I don't remember much about it," he said. "I remember darkness, and a kind of sense of things I couldn't see moving around. There were sounds but I couldn't make out any of them. I hadn't heard sounds like these before. It wasn't good, I can tell you that.

"When I woke up . . . that's what coming back was like, it was like waking up . . . I didn't know what had happened at first. You know how it is when you wake up in a strange place and you're kind of fuzzy for a bit. It was like that. I'd gone to sleep on the sofa and I woke up in the morgue. What came between I didn't remember right off the bat. It came back to me in bits and pieces."

Frank shook his head. "I don't know," he said, "but that I'd be pretty disturbed."

"I would've been, but for Seth," John said.

"Seth? I don't believe I know any. . . ."

"No, you wouldn't. Seth was my guide through the afterlife. It was Seth who brought me back. Seth showed me the error of my past life and the path to follow in my new one. He brought me and Madge back together again."

John stood up and offered Frank another whiskey. Frank's brain was afloat by now, but not unpleasantly, so he accepted just a drop more. John poured it and put the lid back on the bottle and set it back in the gray cabinet. He picked up a claw hammer that was lying on the shelf.

"We'd drifted pretty far apart," John said, turning to face Frank. "It was my fault, I suppose. You have to make the effort to stay connected, it doesn't just happen by itself. You have to work at a marriage. I guess I'd let things slide. But we're working it out. Things have been better since I came back."

Frank was listening to John but he was concentrating more on not falling off the metal stool he sat on. He used to have a good head for liquor but Doris didn't like the smell of the hard stuff so Frank had gotten into the beer habit. The Jim Beam was hitting him harder than he'd expected.

He was staring down at the floor through most of John's talk about marriage. He raised his eyes to an unbelievable sight. John Duffy had a hammer in his fist and was raising it up and bringing it down like he was going to hit Frank in the head with it.

"Hey," Frank said, and then the hammer crashed against his skull and there was a crunch and Frank was falling off the stool and onto the concrete floor. Lights danced before

his eyes and there was a roaring in his ears and a godawful pain in his head. He was aware of a blur of motion, the
hammer rising and falling. His face mashed itself against
the cold floor and a liquid, warm and sticky, flowed over it
and into his mouth. When he tasted it he knew it was
blood. Then everything went completely black.

Madge called from upstairs that the coffee was ready
and John said, "Be right up." His hand was dripping with
blood and bits of Frank Gunnarsen's brain. He rinsed it and
the hammer in the Fiberglas sink. Frank could clean up the
rest of the mess when he came back. Madge would take
care of his bloodstained clothes.

John trudged up the stairs clinging to the handrail. He
felt buzzy and agreeably woozy, either from the whiskey
or the exercise, he didn't know or care which. He walked
into the kitchen where Doris Gunnarsen sat at the table,
her head flopped back with a telephone cord wrapped
tightly around her throat, tongue protruding from her
gaping mouth. John nodded toward the cord.

"Better get that loose before she comes back or it'll
strangle her again," he said.

Madge filled their cups. "Plenty of time for that after
coffee," she said, smiling, then she added, "It was a nice
evening, wasn't it?"

Lucy Haws was used to being cared for by her brother
Harold. He'd done it as long as she could remember. He
sheltered her from their mother's alcoholic rages. He
went with her to pick out her school clothes and he kept
them clean and neat. He tried to help with her school-
work but he was such a poor student himself that, even
with a two-year lead (which would've been three if he
hadn't repeated), the experience was too painful for both
of them. He ended up telling her just to do her best and

not to worry about it. He'd be the one signing her report card, anyway.

It was evident early on that Lucy wouldn't find a man. She wasn't pretty but she wasn't horrid, and she wasn't smart but she wasn't stupid, so there was certainly someone out there for her if she troubled herself to look and didn't set her standards unreasonably high.

No, Lucy's problem was of the emotional sort. Put simply, she didn't have many, or maybe she did but they were of such a low intensity that most people failed to notice them at all, like earthquakes at the bottom end of the Richter scale. She didn't attract men naturally and didn't feel compelled to attract them through cosmetics or sex. Men didn't seem worth the energy it would take to snare one and then put up with his demands and messes and idiosyncrasies. A lot of things were that way, like pets and cars and motorboats and fancy clothes and nearly everything, come to think of it.

Lucy settled easily for not much. She had to eat, she had to work, and she had to pass the rest of her time tolerably. But she didn't expect romance or success or children or status in her community or wealth or anything, really, except for what she had: a roof over her head and a television set that worked. When Harold bought cable for her, she felt like someone had gifted her with the Hope diamond, it was so far above her expectations.

She was proud of her big brother. People had expected him to wind up on the wrong side of the law but instead he'd embraced it, and now people had to do what Harold . . . what Deputy Haws . . . told them to do. He'd become a big shot, but you'd never know it from the way he treated Lucy. He still looked after her. He was still probably the only person in town who cared if she lived or died.

She heard him come home around eleven o'clock. He'd

usually busy himself downstairs for awhile before coming up to bed, but he'd always take a moment to look in on her. If she was still up they'd have a few words and then he'd say goodnight. He wouldn't kiss her, he never had and never would and she never needed it to know that he loved her.

Harold came straight upstairs tonight. She thought, as she followed his heavy footsteps on the stairs, that it must have been a busy evening for him to want to go straight to bed. She hoped those boys hadn't been giving him trouble again.

The floor boards squeaked in the hallway and pretty soon he was standing there at the open door. He didn't look tired at all. In fact he was smiling.

"Hi," she said.

He walked in and sat on the edge of the bed. He had a different look on his face, like the way he'd looked when he told her they were coming out to install the cable TV.

"You have a surprise for me," Lucy said. "I can tell by the look on your face."

"I could never hide anything from you," Harold said. "Close your eyes."

She did. "Should I hold out my hand?" she asked.

"No," he said. "Lean up."

She leaned forward and he took the extra pillow from behind her head, the one she used when she watched television.

"Lie down," he said, and she thought that was strange but she did as he told her.

"Are you going to smother me with that pillow?" she joked.

She felt the pillow come down over her face.

"Yes," he said, and he leaned on it with all his weight so she couldn't draw a breath, and no matter how hard she kicked and pummeled and tried to yell out that this wasn't funny, he wouldn't let up.

* * *

Clyde Dunwiddey stood at the front door of his house and stared through the screen at the quiet town beyond. It looked to him as if time were standing still. No cars plying the streets, no boys skateboarding along the sidewalks. Cicadas buzzed and crickets chirped to tell him that life did proceed, if invisibly. A bat flashed from a tree and was gone again by the time Clyde swiveled his eyes to look at it.

This was a time of hidden songs and furtive flights, of mice dashing along baseboards and cats skulking through quiet yards. It was a time for the night predators to emerge from their dens to prey on the sleeping, a time for the dark-adapted seers to roam, seeking out the blind.

The air was cool, bracing. "Nice night," he said. His mother, sitting in her rocking chair with her knitting in her lap, didn't answer. "Odd to see it so clearly, instead of through an alcoholic haze."

Not that he was completely sober, but neither was he drunk as a skunk as he usually was by this hour. He felt that something within him had changed. He still enjoyed the taste of liquor and the burn as it slid down his throat, but the compulsion for more and more and more had slipped out of his being the way a bad dream fades under the morning sun. He gave credit for this cleansing to Seth.

Seth had healed that part of Clyde that was, by nature, defective. Many inducements to alcohol remained, but the addiction was gone. Captain Humphrey would see much less of Clyde Dunwiddey in the months and years to come, that was for sure.

"You're usually in bed by this time," Clyde told his mother. "I guess I haven't given you much to stay up for. Things are going to be different from now on, though. No more binges. No more staggering home after the Captain kicks me out. We'll have more money, too, without me

spending it all on booze. I'll put it into fixing this place up.
I didn't realize how I'd let it run down. The first thing I'll
do is give it a coat of paint. It's an embarrassment, all the
other houses on the block look so nice and ours. . . ."

His voice trailed off. The house seemed like a metaphor
for Clyde himself. He'd spent decades nurturing his addiction and letting the rest of himself decay. That was over
with. He had his priorities straight now.

He looked over at his mother, still in the chair where
she'd been sitting when he strangled her. He'd slipped up
behind her as she worked on her knitting and wrapped his
necktie around her baggy-skinned throat and pulled it
tight. She was frail and didn't put up much of a fight.
When it was over Clyde had put the necktie in his pocket
and opened the front door and gazed out at the night. It
was so peaceful, so eerie.

He pulled the necktie out of his pocket and ran it between his fingers to smooth out the wrinkles. He looked at
himself in the hallway mirror as he tied the tie, then loos-
ened it a bit. He pulled his shirt tail out part way and
mussed his hair. He always looked disheveled when he left
the Tavern late so he should look disheveled now.

He had to pay a call on the Sheriff, and then he could go
to bed.

It was around ten o'clock and Sheriff Clark was turning
out the lights and calling it a night when seven-year-old
Josh Lunger, dressed in cartoon character pajamas, hit the
door running and rushed in as if the Devil was on his tail.
Clark tried to calm him down and get a few coherent
words out of him but it was plain that the boy was scared
to death. The Lungers lived out on the edge of town so
Josh had made quite a run. The cuffs of his pajamas were
wet with dew.

"It's all right," Clark said, "you're safe here. Nobody can hurt you here. Calm down. Take a deep breath and tell me what happened."

The boy swallowed hard and wiped the tears off his face with the back of his hand. It took him a few minutes to get his wind back. Clark sat the boy in a chair and draped a blanket over his shoulders and told him to take his time and tell him what happened. Josh was almost settled down when Clark made the mistake of asking him where his mother was.

Instantly the boy was out of the chair, his eyes wide with panic, and yelling, "She's the one! She tried to kill me! She choked me! I was just laying there asleep and I couldn't breathe and I woke up and she was choking me! You gotta help me, Sheriff! She's trying to kill me, I swear it, she's trying to kill me!"

"Are you sure it wasn't a bad dream, Josh?" Clark asked. The Lungers were a good family with no history of abuse, rock solid, no drinking or criminal offenses.

"No! It happened! My mom, she tried to choke me, I swear I'm not making it up!"

Sheriff Clark put his finger under Josh's chin and lifted it. There were red marks on his throat and the beginnings of a couple of thumb-sized bruises. He looked at the side of Josh's neck and found more marks, marks that could've been fingers squeezing tight. He decided he'd better call Doc Milford.

"Hold on a minute, Josh," he said, and he went to the telephone and dialed Doc's number. He described the situation and Doc said he'd be right down to take a look. Before Clark could hang up the phone, Josh screamed.

His mother's car had just pulled up to the curb.

Josh ran to the Sheriff and wrapped his arms around Clark's legs, begging him not to let his mother get him.

"I won't let her get you," Clark promised, but he knew

that unless Doc could tell him something about the marks on Josh's neck, something that pointed clearly to child abuse, chances were excellent that Josh would be back in the custody of his parents within the hour.

The telephone rang. The Sheriff thought it might be Mark Lunger, Josh's father. If Josh had suddenly gone missing, Mark might stay at home working the phone while Carol, Josh's mother, drove around looking for him. Clark answered "Sheriff's Office" but even as he was speaking the caller hung up. He clicked the button a couple of times but there was no response. Funny. That was the second such call he'd received that night. Probably the same person, dialing a wrong number, but it set off a warning buzzer inside Clark's head. He made a mental note to remember these calls, and he checked the clock to see when this one came in. Ten after ten.

"So there you are," Carol Lunger said, and she strode into the Sheriff's Office toward Josh. Josh cried out and hid behind Clark's legs, pleading with Clark to keep her away.

"I think you'd better keep your distance, Carol," Clark said, "until we find out what's going on here."

"He had a bad dream, Sheriff, that's all," Carol replied calmly, but with a thin edge of annoyance creeping into her voice. "He woke up screaming and I rushed into his room. He was in bed, and his pajama top was all twisted around his throat. . . ."

"No!" Josh screamed. "That isn't what happened! She's lying!"

"He was choking, having a nightmare."

"No! She's lying! It was her! She was choking me! It was her!"

"Josh, stop this nonsense immediately!" Carol commanded. She took a step forward and reached for the boy but Sheriff Clark interposed himself between them.

"I can't let you have him," he said, "not just yet."

"I demand that you release my son!" Carol said, drawing herself up tall.

"We'll see," Clark said. "Doc Milford's on his way over. He'll tell us if the marks on Josh's throat could've been made by pajamas."

"Are you accusing me of child abuse?"

"I'm not accusing you of anything. When Doc gets here—"

"This is ridiculous!" Carol snorted. "He had a bad dream! That's all there is to it!" She looked at Josh. "Tell them, Josh! It was just a bad dream!"

The boy wasn't about to say anything of the sort, Clark could tell. He was genuinely afraid for his life. And the marks on his neck and throat didn't look a damn thing like a pajama top.

Doc was taking his own sweet time getting there so Clark sat Carol Lunger down at Haws's desk to wait. Carol asked if she could call her husband and Clark said she could. This was developing into a fine mess. Stir in one irate father and things were sure to get fiery. He wished Doc would hurry it up and verify his suspicions. The red marks looked like finger bruises to him and it was certain that young Josh didn't try to strangle himself.

As he looked at Carol Lunger he noticed that the makeup over part of her face was extra heavy. She might be covering up a mark of her own, where Josh had struck her, for instance, trying to get free. He'd ask Josh about that later.

Sheriff Clark didn't like what was happening in his town, and he didn't even know what it was. Madge Duffy's murder of her husband was unusual enough. Having the deceased seem to rise from the dead was damned disturbing. The business with the Ganger boy and Franz and Irma Klempner smelled fishy as all get-out, and now this, a boy from a perfectly healthy family claiming that his mother tried to strangle him to death, and with the physical evidence to substantiate it.

Something was going on. Something dark and evil. And all Sheriff Clark had to go on in figuring it out were a bunch of bizarre but unrelated incidents and about a hundred tiny hairs rising on the back of his neck.

Mark Lunger showed up and demanded to know what the hell was going on. If he felt any relief at the sight of his missing boy, he didn't show it. He threatened Sheriff Clark with a lawsuit that would make his head spin and Clark replied that that was his right, but until Doc Milford arrived he wasn't releasing Josh to anybody.

The boy was terrified. With every passing minute Clark grew more certain that handing him back to his parents would be the worst thing he could do. Maybe there was a relative who'd put the boy up for the night.

What was keeping Doc Milford, anyway? It was after eleven o'clock.

The sight of Clyde Dunwiddey staggering down the sidewalk toward the jail was reassuringly familiar. Some of the old patterns still held, anyway. Clark checked that cell B was ready and unlocked so he didn't have to spend any more time with Clyde than necessary.

Clyde stumbled in and Sheriff Clark said, "Evening, Clyde," and Clyde gave him a drunken wave as he "headed for the hoosegow."

Mark Lunger chose that moment to get belligerent again.

"Look here, Sheriff, this is no place for a young boy!" he yelled. "There's school tomorrow and he needs his sleep! He shouldn't be hanging around jails with derelicts!"

Carol Lunger joined in and soon they were both yelling at Sheriff Clark while Josh cowered behind Clark's legs. Clark decided to fight volume with volume and yelled back and didn't notice Clyde Dunwiddey lifting the shotgun out of the rack on the wall until he pumped a shell into the chamber and aimed it at him.

Sheriff Clark drew his police special and got off a round as Clyde pulled the trigger and sent a flurry of pellets into Clark's gut. The Sheriff's shot hit Clyde in the leg and Clyde cried out and nearly crumbled, but he caught himself with one hand on Clark's desk. Bracing himself against the desk, Clyde pumped the shotgun again and fired, this time hitting Josh Lunger in the throat and throwing his blood all over the office walls.

Clark's head was spinning and he was kneeling on the floor, but he and Clyde traded shots again. Both shots connected and the two men collapsed as one, stone dead.

Carol and Mark Lunger surveyed the damage. The walls dripped blood. Their son Josh lay on the floor, his head nearly severed from his body. This wasn't the way they'd wanted it to be, but come twelve o'clock they knew that everything would be set right. Seth had promised.

Doc Milford drove up at last. He walked through the front door, looked around, and whistled. He saw the Lungers standing in the corner, holding hands.

"Do you know Seth?" he asked, and the Lungers allowed that they did.

"It wasn't supposed to be like this," Carol said.

"It'll be fine," Doc said, "come midnight."

He adjusted Josh Lunger's head squarely onto his shoulders, and then he turned out the lights so no one driving by would notice anything amiss. In case someone did poke his nose in the door, Doc picked up the shotgun and pumped a fresh shell into the chamber. He and the Lungers took seats in the dark office and waited.

* * *

Bernice Tompkins couldn't sleep.

"I can't find him anywhere," she said. "I haven't seen him since noon." She was looking for Groucho, a black-and-white cat with a dark patch over his mouth that had earned him his name. He'd shown up last summer and, recognizing a good thing when he saw it, had made the Tompkins house his own. He had gotten heavy over the last year, and it wasn't like him to roam. Bernice could always count on spotting Groucho lounging in the shade in the summer or hogging a sunbeam in the winter. He was less like a pet and more like something someone forgot to put away.

"He'll turn up," Carl said, turning over and adjusting his pillow. It's what Carl always said and he was always right.

"But it isn't like him to stay out late," Bernice insisted. "Something's wrong." Then she added almost under her breath, "Something's wrong with the whole town."

"There's nothing wrong. Go to sleep."

"There is. I can't put my finger on it, but it's there. Something in the air, like a storm ready to break. And that business with John Duffy. It isn't natural. The cats feel it. They've been nervous the last three days. You've seen how they pick at their food."

"Uh-huh," Carl said, though he had noticed no such thing. They were still eating him out of house and home, as far as he could tell.

"Now this. I'm worried about him, Carl."

"Bernie, I'm not getting up and looking for a cat in the middle of the—"

"I'm not asking you to. I'm just saying that something's wrong, is all. I don't know how you can sleep, anyway, with Groucho missing."

Bernice threw back the covers and got out of bed, displacing Sputnik and Heather and Zoe who liked to sleep on and around her legs, and annoying Pumpkin who was curled up in the crook behind Carl's knees.

"For gosh sakes, Bernie, what are you doing?"

"I'm going to look under the house. Remember the time he got trapped there? You were looking for that leak and when you left you put the screen back on and Groucho was trapped inside. I still think you did it on purpose."

Carl sat up, which caused Pumpkin to stand and glare at him impatiently.

"I did no such thing," Carl said. "And you're not going to go crawling around under the house at this hour! It's insane!"

"I'm not going to crawl around. I'm just going to peek in. Where's the flashlight?"

"Use the rechargeable. It's plugged into the socket by the back door."

"You're really going to let me do this myself, aren't you?" Bernice said. "Any decent husband—"

"All right, all right!" Carl complained, throwing back the covers and swinging out his legs. He found his house slippers and pulled on a robe. "I knew I'd get sucked into this one way or another."

He yanked the flashlight out of the socket and walked out the back door with cats milling around his feet. Bernice followed him calling for Groucho.

Carl went around to the back of the house where the access door to the crawl space was. He'd been under the house the day before, spraying for cockroaches, and he hadn't done a perfect job of putting the door back. The door was a window screen, actually, and it had plenty of "give" in it. A space on one side could have admitted a cat. It was only a couple or three inches but he'd seen the cats squeeze through smaller spaces, and if Groucho could've gotten in, he could've gotten out again. But Carl was there now and he might as well look around for Bernice's sake. He pulled the door off and set it in the wet grass and crouched down to peer inside.

"Groucho?" he called, shining the flashlight around.

Bernice peered over his shoulder, saying, "Here, kitty, kitty, kitty!" The light bounced off concrete blocks and pipes and wires and joists, all dripping with spider webs, but there was no sign of Groucho. Carl couldn't see into the farthest corners, of course, and he wasn't about to get down on his belly in his pajamas and crawl inside, but if Groucho was in there and wanted out, he'd have seen the light and heard Carl and Bernice calling to him and he'd have shown himself.

"He isn't under here."

"Are you sure? How can you see from way out here?"

"Bernice, I am not crawling under the house in my bathrobe. It's filthy under there." He gave the crawl space another sweep with the flashlight and this time the light came to rest on a skeleton lying in one corner. "Well, I'll be damned," Carl said.

"What is it? Is it him?" Bernice asked anxiously.

"I don't know what it is." The skeleton was almost out of the flashlight's range and Carl couldn't get a good look at it from where he sat. He duck-walked another step closer and bent his head down, poking it just inside the access hole. He smelled the lingering perfume of poison mixed with the dusty, musty odor of the crawl space. "It's some kind of skeleton," he said.

Bernice drew in a breath of horror. "Oh, Carl! You don't suppose. . . ."

"No, no, it couldn't be him. It's picked clean, like something in a museum. It's been here awhile. Could be a squirrel. Or a skunk. Possum, maybe."

"Can you reach it?"

"Not from here."

"You have to get it out! I don't see how I can sleep tonight knowing that thing's under there!"

"It's been under here for weeks, maybe months. Funny I didn't notice it. . . ." His voice trailed off. He didn't want

Bernice to know that he'd just been under the house spraying poison around.

Then he got to thinking: Where are the dead roaches? He shined the flashlight around the sewer pipe where he'd seen so many of them. He'd hit them with the spray, he'd watched them die and drop off into the dirt. There should be hundreds of roach corpses under there. Where had they all gone? There wasn't a one that he could see.

Bernice could tell that he was puzzling over something. "What is it?" she said.

"Nothing. Just looking," Carl replied. "I thought he might be hiding behind a pipe or something."

He backed out of the access hole and stood up, his legs and back aching. He stretched, swiveled his shoulders.

"He isn't under there," Carl said. He bent down and replaced the access panel.

"You're sure? Absolutely sure?" Bernice asked.

"I'm sure."

Carl's house slippers were soaked with dew and he was anxious to get them off and to warm his feet up under the covers. He was wide awake now, of course, and worried about the roaches. He didn't understand where they could have gone. He'd seen the cats eat bugs before. Could Groucho have gotten under the house somehow and gorged himself on dead roaches? Was he lying under a bush, dead from ingesting bug poison? But Groucho couldn't have eaten every single one.

It couldn't possibly be Groucho's skeleton under there. It couldn't.

"I won't be able to sleep a wink," Bernice said, "knowing poor Groucho's out there suffering."

"Groucho's probably out there getting laid," Carl muttered under his breath. He left his wet slippers by the back door and tiptoed across the cold hardwood floor of the hallway to the carpet of the bedroom. He dived beneath the covers and kicked his feet to warm the sheets that had cooled in his absence. He heard Bernice opening cabinet doors and running water in the kitchen. She was probably taking a pill.

"I took a pill," Bernice said as she crawled into bed. "Otherwise I'd toss and turn and worry about Groucho all night."

Bernice found a reason almost every night to take a pill.

"He's fine," Carl said. "You'll see. He'll be here for breakfast in the morning."

Carl leaned over and gave his wife a kiss and said "Goodnight." He turned his back to her and pressed his butt against hers and lay that way for a few seconds. Then the arm he was lying on started to hurt and he turned onto his back. He didn't like sleeping that way but he had a pinched nerve or something in his left arm that bothered him when he slept on it. He'd been meaning to talk to Doc Milford about it but he knew that Doc would just tell him it was old age creeping up, and Carl didn't want to pay good money to hear that.

It took Carl about four minutes to go to sleep. Bernice was asleep sooner than that, not because of the pill that hadn't even entered her system yet, but because she knew she'd taken the pill and therefore had an excuse for not lying awake worrying about Groucho any longer. Heather and Zoe and Pumpkin returned and took up their places on the bed covers. By eleven o'clock, the Tompkins household was sleeping soundly.

None of them noticed the first cockroach slip under the carpet by the wall and into the bedroom, its antennae feeling the air for signs of life.

Following the first cockroach there came another, and then a steady stream of roaches flowed into the bedroom with a mathematical precision that would have impressed Clyde Dunwiddey. Their numbers seemed to explode exponentially as they poured from the walls, skittering through every crevice. They moved like liquid, oozing up through the cracks and over the carpet toward the bed where Carl and Bernice slept, deep in their dreams.

The cats woke and meowed in alarm. They padded around on top of the bed, meowing, but Carl was a heavy sleeper accustomed to ignoring cats, and Bernice would not be roused from her drug-induced slumber. Heather leaped from the bed into the sea of roaches and bounded out of the room. Zoe and Pumpkin followed her.

The roaches engulfed the bed posts. They clambered over one another as they climbed, their sharp insect legs scritching against the wood and scratching for purchase on the slippery shells of their brethren. Roaches swarmed over the bed from all four corners and engulfed the sleepers. They crawled into ears and nose and mouth, slid under the sheets and inside Carl's pajamas and under Bernice's night dress. Their mandibles tore at soft flesh.

Carl was suddenly aware that he couldn't breathe. He woke with a mouth and nose stuffed with wriggling roaches. He tried to cough but he couldn't dislodge the roaches from his throat. Vomit rushed up his esophagus and into his mouth and slipped down his trachea into his lungs. He crunched roaches between his teeth as he heaved and more roaches descended over his face, pouring in from everywhere. He dug at them with his hands as he tumbled out of bed and onto a floor undulating with roaches.

He groped for the light switch and flipped it on, hoping the light would scare them off. He saw that his bed had become a sea of roaches. He saw Bernice's body as an unmoving lump beneath the mass of insects, already dead. The sleeping pill had spared her this horror.

The roaches bit at his eyes and Carl squeezed them shut. He couldn't get a breath, couldn't expel the roaches from his airways. He brushed frantically at them as they swarmed over his body. He staggered over the carpet of roaches that crunched and spat gore with every step. His chest was on fire. His stomach heaved. He doubled over, gagging. His foot slipped, and he felt himself falling, falling. He landed on his back in the middle of the writhing mass.

They swallowed him whole. They covered his eyes and face and crawled deeper into his ears. He heard their clicking mandibles through a hurricane roar as they dug in. He was dizzy from lack of oxygen, his head swam. He knew he was dying, knew that Bernice was already dead, knew what had stripped the flesh from the skeleton in the crawl space, knew that the same fate lay in store for him, for Bernice. He knew that nothing in death could match the horror of these, his last living moments.

Oblivion came as a blessing.

FIFTEEN

Brant sat next to Peg on her bed and carefully unbuttoned her blouse. They'd made out for awhile on the porch swing and when she'd pulled away from him, Brant had expected her to tell him it was time to go. Instead she'd said, "Let's go inside," and she'd led him up to her bedroom.

Brant opened her blouse down to her waist, where it was tucked inside her skirt. She sat up straight so he could pull it loose and finish his unbuttoning. He took his time, and Peg found the sexual tension exhilarating. Brant was stretching out the moment, obviously savoring the thrill. This was a good portent of things to come, and Peg let herself imagine that an orgasm lay in her not-too-distant future.

God knows they'd been few and far between with Rod.

She sloughed off her shirt and reached around to unfasten her bra but Brant stopped her, wanting to do it himself.

"Removing a bra was the only useful skill I learned in high school," he said, "besides typing."

The bra came loose and Peg's breasts fell free. There had been a time when they would have stood out firm and pert. She wished Brant could have seen them then, men have such an obsession with tits. She hoped they didn't look too motherly to be erotic. She tugged at his shirt and he took the hint and pulled it off. She put her hands behind his neck and pulled him close, kissed him deeply on the mouth. He leaned into the kiss and their bodies met. Soon they were fumbling with snaps and zippers, then his fingers were exploring between her legs and she was holding him in her hand.

He seemed determined to kiss every inch of her body before entering her, even rolling her over onto her stomach and kissing the back of her neck, down her spine, kissing her bottom, her hips, the inside of her thighs. It felt like forever before he was inside her and they were rolling together in passion.

She climaxed first. Then almost immediately, as the hot waves crashed through her, she felt him come. For Brant, the long denial paid off with rush after rush, every second drawn out in time until it seemed that he'd never stop. When he did finally roll over in exhaustion, Peg rolled on top of him and planted a long kiss on his mouth.

They lay together in post-coital reverie, Peg nestled into Brant's shoulder, and let the breeze from the window cool their bodies. Brant glanced at the alarm clock on Peg's night stand. Its glowing face told him it was nearing midnight.

For awhile he had completely forgotten about Duffy and Haws and whatever other Risen were lurking outside. Tom would have met his friends at the mortuary by now, and in another few minutes they might be witnesses to a miracle.

Brant looked at Peg and observed that he had a miracle of his own right here. It took the form of a woman he cared about and who cared about him and who was pretty and unmarried and good in the sack. It seemed to Brant as if every event of his life had existed for the sole purpose of propelling him toward this moment.

It surprised him to realize that somehow, amid a lot of extremely strange and menacing goings-on, life had become quite good.

* * *

The dock looked the same as ever to Tom. The cheap flashlight he'd snatched from the refrigerator when he stormed through the kitchen kept going out. When he was able to pound it into working, the glow it gave off was feeble and yellow. The waning moon wasn't much help, either.

Apparently blood stains weren't as dramatic in real life as they were in the movies. If someone had been killed here, it would've been easy for the killer to douse the dock with a bucket of water and rinse it clean. The stains might be obvious to a reporter like Brant, in broad daylight, but to Tom and his dime store flashlight with the dying batteries, they remained invisible. He'd seen the cars, though, parked at the edge of the woods, and people didn't leave their cars at the reservoir overnight unless they were camping out. He didn't see or smell any campfires.

It was a beautiful night. The air was cool, the sky clear and starry. Tom slapped at a mosquito that came to dine on his cheek. He picked the dead insect off his face and held it between his fingers. He remembered reading that all blood-sucking mosquitoes were female. This one must've had a hardy meal before zeroing in on Tom for dessert because her smashed body was bloody and red. Would she, too, come back at midnight? Tom wished he'd brought a jar to keep her in and find out, but since he hadn't, he kneeled down and washed her off his finger in the water of the reservoir.

Tom shined the light at the surrounding trees. Somewhere out there was a body, probably more than one. He thought about himself and his friends on the other side of the lake getting high and talking about Deputy Haws and Galen, hearing gunshots and thinking nothing of it, while across the water the nudists were being slaughtered. They must've made easy targets, lying there lolled by the sun, rather obviously defenseless. What kind of person could walk up and blow people away in cold blood?

A religious fanatic, it had to be. Who else would care? Normal people who didn't want to see naked bodies just stayed away. Only someone who thought he had God on his side would feel compelled to . . . what was the word they always used? Smite. Only religious fanatics went around smiting people. What the hell was "smiting" anyway?

You're losing it, he told himself.

Whoever did it, he could be watching Tom this very minute. Maybe he was lurking in the trees, waiting for his victims to come back to life. That could be the thrill, the rising, not the killing.

He could be out there right now with his gun trained on Tom's back. Tom scanned the trees again with the flashlight. An ice worm crawled up his spine and made him shiver. This is how Brant must have felt this afternoon, how the nudists must have felt, naked and helpless. It would have been worse in the daylight.

He shined the light on his watch. Almost eleven. He was meeting Darren, Buzzy and Kent down the street from the mortuary, and they'd sneak around to the back where the bodies were kept, where Galen would be now. Kent was supposed to bring the lock picks he'd bought in junior high from the mail order place.

Jed Grimm lived in the house next door to the mortuary. There was an apartment above the mortuary itself but the previous owner had bought the adjacent property when it came on the market a few years ago. This was good for the boys. Breaking in with Grimm sleeping upstairs would've been quite a risk.

Tom heard frogs croaking as he walked away from the dock. Whatever monkey wrench had been thrown into the cosmic works, certain wheels kept turning, and the lure of a mate was one of them. Life expressed itself everywhere, in all parts of the world, under the Arctic ice, beneath the sea where no light penetrated and the pressure would crush a man's bones, in the microscopic ecology of an eyelash. There was no more potent force on Earth than the replication and spread of life.

But life changed form, identity was lost and reshaped in the eternal process of birth and death and decay and rebirth in the cells of new organisms. Life was eternal but identity was not.

Until now. Something new had come into being, a kind of super-life that thumbed its nose at death, that refused to give up the who and what of its being.

It might be a miracle to some, but to Tom it had the stench of abomination.

He kick-started the Honda and steered it toward the mortuary. Darren and Buzzy and Kent . . . and Galen . . . would be waiting for him there. He smiled wryly as he realized that he had, quite literally, a rendezvous with death.

On one side of the mortuary was the house that Jed Grimm lived in. On the other side was a park. It was a small park, just a few picnic tables, a barbecue pit made out of cinder blocks, and some trash cans.

Darren, Buzzy and Kent sat on a picnic table, getting high.

"He won't show," Darren predicted.

"He'll show," Buzzy said.

The boys looked toward the mortuary as they heard a car engine crank and start. The car, a recent model Dodge, was parked in front of Grimm's house. It made a U-turn and headed their way. When it passed, the driver shot them a look.

"Who was that?" Darren asked.

"The new preacher," said Kent. "Do you think he saw us?"

"He looked right at us!" said Darren.

"Maybe we should call it off."

"No way. We've come this far. What time is it?"

Kent looked at his watch. "Quarter 'til."

"He won't show."

"I hear his bike."

They saw the single headlight of the Honda moving toward them and thirty seconds later Tom pulled into the tiny parking lot at the park's edge. As he walked up to the boys, Darren said, "You're late."

"Sorry. Kent, can you still get us in before midnight?"

Kent nodded.

"Then let's go."

They climbed the six-foot chain link fence that separated the park from the mortuary grounds and dropped to earth on the other side.

"Grimm's light is on at the house," Tom said.

Buzzy informed him, "He had company. The preacher just left."

"I passed him on the road. Did he see you?"

"Hell, yes." Darren spat onto the dewy ground. He was still in a pissy mood. The more he thought about Galen purposely killing himself and leaving the rest of them alone, the madder he got. Tom's stepping in and acting like he was everybody's boss pissed him off even more.

This was not how it was supposed to be, and it didn't have to be like this. Galen's suicide had screwed everything up. If he'd really died in an accident it'd be different, but the longer Darren thought about it the surer he was that Galen had taken himself out on purpose, because of the Haws thing, because of Duffy, because he had it in his stupid head that he'd come back. Now they were going to find out if he was right or not, and either way, Darren didn't like it. He wished Galen hadn't died, but the thought of him coming back from the dead creeped him out. He didn't know what he was hoping for, and that pissed him off, too.

Tom kept an eye on Grimm's house, as much as he could before the mortuary building blocked his view. Why would Reverend Small be visiting the town mortician in the middle of the night? Tom had seen two lights on, one in the living room and one upstairs in what must be a bedroom. The upstairs light was faint, it could be a reading light. If Grimm was upstairs when the doorbell rang, but not yet asleep, he might have left that light on when he answered the door. Why didn't he turn out the downstairs light after Small left? At this hour, he'd probably be headed upstairs before Small's car pulled away from the curb.

All sorts of possibilities presented themselves to him. Maybe Grimm was watching television downstairs or reading a book or the latest issue of *Modern Embalming*. Maybe Grimm naturally kept late hours or had insomnia. Maybe he was a drunk and had passed out on the sofa while Small was there.

It was only a couple of lights in the windows. It didn't have to mean anything sinister.

But it was odd at a time when oddity walked hand in hand with death, and death itself—good old dependable, enduring death—came packaged with a surprise.

The steel door at the back of the mortuary had a good lock on it, and it'd been a long time since Kent had used his lock picks. Kent supposed that there were all kinds of pervs and weirdoes who'd like to get into a mortuary at night. Necrophiliacs, for example. The very thought made him shudder.

"Hurry up, man!" Buzzy urged.

Kent tried to ignore him. This was delicate work and it took all of Kent's concentration. Buzzy was always in a hurry and he couldn't stand still when he was agitated. He paced nervously behind Kent, his hands twitching.

"Ten minutes," Tom said.

"I'm working on it," Kent snapped.

"This sucks," Darren announced. "Let's just kick it down."

"It's a steel door. You could pound on it all night and all you'd do is wake everybody up." Tom tried to keep his voice steady while his heart beat like he was running a hundred-yard dash. They had to get inside before midnight or it would all be for nothing. He had to see the body and see for himself that it was dead, feel the cold flesh and even stick it with something sharp if necessary. Then he'd see if it came back. He had to wash the uncertainty out of his mind. Two days ago he'd been sure enough that Deputy Haws was dead to help put him in a hole, but two days was time enough for his mind to manufacture doubts. Galen would be the crucial test.

"Fuck it," Darren said, and he turned to walk away when there was a pronounced click from the door and Kent pulled it open.

"We're in."

Kent played doorman as the boys entered. Tom led the way using the flashlight Buzzy had taken from his dad's camping gear, an expensive aluminum number that produced an achingly white light. Tom shined it into the middle of the room and immediately discovered the bodies.

One of them lay on a steel table, the other on a gurney. Sheets covered both.

The air in the room was sharp and unpleasant, reeking of germicide, like a hospital, but overlaid with the chemical smells of a janitor's closet and a biting stench that had to come from the bodies themselves. The air was cold. An air conditioner hummed, keeping the temperature in the low sixties.

Tom played the light around the room, illuminating steel shelves holding chemicals and containers and latex gloves

and needles and tubing and wax and cosmetics and surgi-
cal instruments and mysterious, knobbed rubber items
Tom could not readily classify.

"What time is it?" Darren asked.

Tom held the light on his watch. "Eight minutes to go,"
he said.

"Look at this," Kent said, picking up a sharpened metal
tube with a handle on one end. He made fencing motions
at Darren with the tube but Darren was in no mood to
horse around.

"Quit fucking around," Darren said.

Kent looked at the object in his hands.

"What do you suppose it is?" he said.

"It's a trocar," Buzzy said. "They use it to drain gas and
liquid out of corpses." All eyes turned to Buzzy as if he'd
suddenly started speaking Italian. He looked back at them
nonchalantly. "What?" he said.

"How do you know that?"

"I don't know. I read it somewhere."

"What's this for?" Kent asked, kicking at a machine on
the floor attached to various tubes.

"That pumps preservative into the body when they
embalm it."

"What're these?" Tom asked, picking up a couple of the
knobby rubber appliances he'd noticed on the shelf.

"Mouth formers. They put one under the skin before
they sew the mouth shut, to make the mouth look right.
Those round ones are eyecaps. They keep the eyelids
closed, but sometimes morticians use Superglue."

Kent was feeling nauseous.

"How do you know all this shit?" he asked.

Buzzy shrugged. In fact, he was fascinated with the
mortician's art and had read more about it than most people wanted to know. He'd only been to one funeral, that of
an uncle who'd fallen off his tractor and run himself over.

Buzzy had been impressed with how good his uncle looked as he lay in the coffin. His nails were trimmed and clean, his hair styled more neatly than Buzzy had ever seen it before, his skin was rosy, and his face wore a look of contentment that had eluded this particular uncle while he lived. It had seemed like a miracle to young Buzzy, the transformation of a coarse and quarrelsome uncle into a man of refinement and peace. It set Buzzy on a path of private study, one he knew that other people wouldn't understand.

He picked up all the technical details of body preservation that he could discover. His proudest volume was a textbook on embalming printed in the 1930s. At first Buzzy had been appalled, though no less intrigued, by the crude methods old fashioned undertakers used to keep corpses from rotting and to make them presentable for viewing by the grieving family. Things like using barbed wire to hold the mouth shut seemed unbelievably gross, and he felt sure that some better way had been invented in the sixty years since the book was written. Later he learned that barbed wire still was used, or the lips might be sewn shut, and that overall the process hadn't changed in any fundamental way since the Civil War. The last big thrill had been in 1867 when they discovered formaldehyde.

Buzzy even considered undertaking as a career. He hadn't said anything to his parents. He'd mentioned it in passing when the guys talked about what they were going to do after high school, but they always treated it like a joke. He knew it was weird but he couldn't help himself. This shit fascinated him.

Darren walked over to the corpse on the embalming table. The boys had avoided the bodies, cruising the perimeters of the room instead, zeroing in on the true target of their curiosity.

He raised the sheet over the body and peered in. The

blackened thing that greeted his eyes could have been
Galen or Irma Klempner or Freddy Krueger. It was still
recognizably human, but the flesh had burned into a black
parchment over the bones and the bones, too, were burned
black. Looking closer he saw that the body parts weren't
even attached properly. Pieces rested loosely on the table,
connecting tissue burned away. He couldn't stomach the
sight for more than a few seconds.

"Tom," he said, and Tom looked over at him. Darren nodded toward the corpse. "This thing is not coming back."

Kent angled around behind Darren and glanced at the
corpse and instantly turned away.

"How do you even know it's him?" Kent said.

"There should be a toe tag from the morgue," Buzzy
answered.

Tom lifted the sheet over the corpse's feet. There was no
tag.

"That's weird," Buzzy said. "How does he know which
one's which?"

"Maybe there's a tag on the other one."

They looked at the corpse on the gurney, head and toe,
but it too was unlabeled. Looking from one body to the
other, it seemed that the one on the table was larger. They
decided it was Galen.

"How do you embalm something like this?" Kent asked,
directing the question to Buzzy.

"You have to vat it. Soak it in chemicals. He might not
even do that if they're going to be cremated."

"They're already cremated," said Kent. "Why didn't he
just throw them in the oven instead of letting them sit here?"

"It's the law. You have to wait forty-eight hours."

"Man, it creeps me out that you know this shit. You
ought to leave a fucking job application on your way out."

"Stupid question," Tom said, "but is everybody satisfied
that he's really dead?"

"Hell, yes," said Darren, "and he's staying that way."

"It might not be Galen," Kent said.

"What if it doesn't come back at midnight?" Buzzy asked. "How long do we give it?"

"I don't know. Ten or fifteen minutes."

"This is fucked," Darren said, pacing. Tom looked at his watch. As he did so, the church bell began to toll.

The boys tensed. Simultaneously, the corpses started to jerk, one body slapping against the steel table, the other on the creaking gurney.

"Fuuuuck!" Darren said, backing toward the door.

"Wait!" Tom cried out.

Kent was the first to bolt. Tom heard him bang into something and he shined the light in the direction of the noise. Kent's face was drained white and his eyes were as big as an alien's. He was feeling his way along the wall, looking as if he might crawl right up one of the metal shelves and curl up on top of it in a fetal position. The light helped him find the door and he was out of the room like a shot.

Darren was trying to hold back. He watched the corpse on the table as scorched lungs healed and organs were born anew. Black parchment skin fell away as limbs swelled and veins filled with blood. Features appeared in the face, familiar contours. It was Galen on the table, and he was alive, dragged back painfully across the boundary that separated the living from the dead. In Galen's empty sockets, eyes were born, eyes that stared out blindly as his body continued to reflesh, jerking and writhing uncontrollably.

When he saw the eyes, Darren lost it. He turned and ran, following Kent's footsteps across the dewy grass between the mortuary and the park.

Buzzy stood transfixed. He saw blood rush through vessels and pink new skin grow across fresh muscle that flowed over Galen's body like a wave. Galen's chest heaved and his lungs drew in air through a ravaged throat. Muscles formed in his jaw and pink skin grew to cover it and Galen worked his mouth soundlessly. He drew a ragged breath and let out a tortured scream.

His shriek was joined by Irma Klempner's. Tom and Buzzy glanced over to see the old woman's body twisting in the pain of rebirth. She screamed as she had screamed from her nightmare fears.

Buzzy clapped his hands over his ears but he couldn't draw away. He couldn't take his eyes off the corpses. Hair pushed its way through new skin. The convulsions ceased, replaced by a tortured writhing as nerves knit into a network of electric pain.

Two new bodies lay among the ashes and the burnt, useless tissue of the old. Their shrieks died in their throats. They clenched and opened their fists as new blood flowed to their extremities. Buzzy turned to run, but Galen's hand whipped out and held him fast.

"Tom!" Buzzy yelled, and Tom shined the light on Buzzy and saw Galen's hand clutching a fistful of Buzzy's shirt. Galen turned his face to look at Buzzy. He moved his mouth, his lips forming words that his newborn throat struggled to voice.

Buzzy tugged at his shirt, trying to free it from Galen's grasp. Galen's mouth took on its signature sneer and his voice croaked, "Date . . . with an angel?"

"Go!" Tom yelled and Buzzy pulled away with Tom shoving him toward the door. Cloth ripped and Buzzy was free. The boys reached the doorway and Tom paused, shined the light back at Galen. Galen still clung to the scrap of shirt. He swung his legs off the embalming table, moving like a paraplegic, grinning. Nearby, Irma Klempner sat up on the gurney. Tom spun on his heels and ran.

Darren and Kent were already hightailing it in their cars when Tom and Buzzy reached the fence. They launched themselves at the chain link and climbed up as if rottweilers were snapping at their heels.

Buzzy dashed for his Vega and Tom hopped onto his Honda and put his weight into the starter. He heard Buzzy's Vega roar to life and Buzzy peeled out in a cloud of dirt that stung Tom's eyes and made them water as he followed closely behind.

Tom shot one quick glance back toward the mortuary. He could barely see, through the dust and tears, in the near darkness under the crescent moon, two figures standing near the mortuary door. Galen Ganger and Irma Klempner.

Running toward the mortuary from the house was Jed Grimm, the undertaker.

DAY FOUR, MONDAY

SIXTEEN

It was supposed to be the man who fell off to sleep and the woman who lay awake, her brain buzzing, but Peg and Brant had exchanged roles somewhere along the way. Peg slept with her head in her pillow, her butt snuggled against Brant's side, and he lay on his back, eyes wide open, worrying about Tom.

The further it got past midnight, the more Brant stewed. He should've made some excuse to Peg and pursued Tom to the dock to poke around for bodies. Instead, while Tom was confronting the forces of darkness, Brant was safely under Tom's roof boffing his mom.

He'd gone from anticipating Tom's report to dreading it to fearing that Tom wouldn't come back at all. Now his mind was exploring the possibility that Haws or someone else had found him snooping around the dock and shot him, and he'd come back, and he'd show up and tell Brant that everything was fine, and they'd been worried about nothing. How would Brant know if Tom was Risen? This idea scared him more than any others. He should have gone after him, damn it, and might've if he hadn't been thinking with the wrong head.

He looked over at Peg and knew that he was being too hard on himself. It wasn't just sex with Peg. This was the real thing, the love that had eluded him through his big city life and big city marriage and divorce. He hadn't come to

Anderson looking for it, he'd come to get away from everything he knew wasn't what he wanted, but here it was. It had been right here waiting for him to get his mind clear enough to recognize it.

Now that he had it, he was going to be damned sure it didn't slip away from him.

He checked the clock. Twelve-fifteen. He'd heard the church bell. He wondered if Franz Klempner had heard it, too, and what he thought of it. There were secrets locked in that silent farmer's head, secrets so deeply buried that Franz Klempner himself couldn't divine them. Somehow Brant had to dig them out. He had to find Eloise. Maybe there was a photo album stored in a trunk or letters that Irma kept hidden in a drawer that would provide a clue. He needed a last name. He could search public records for every "Eloise" in the county and hope that it wasn't a long-lost cousin in another state or an old school friend who'd gone away to college and never come back. Tom could help him.

Where was Tom anyway? What was he doing? What had he seen? What did he know?

The boys hadn't planned to rendezvous at the reservoir. They hadn't planned anything to do after the mortuary. Tom realized that, in his mind's eye, he'd seen them milling around at the mortuary until a few minutes after midnight, after nothing had happened, with Darren bitching about what a waste of time the whole thing had been and how stupid it was to think for one instant that Galen would come back from the dead, and then they'd all go their separate ways and that would be that. It would be over. It would turn out that Haws was never really dead and Doc Milford was drunk when he diagnosed John Duffy. Whatever happened between Haws and Galen, it was settled with Galen's death. It would all have been a bad dream, something Tom cooked up in his imagination, fueled by Brant Kettering's desperate need for a story.

But things hadn't gone that way at all. Tom had witnessed the miracle of rebirth, and it had been horrifying. Emotionally, it was like being in an earthquake. They'd had one once, a couple of years back. It hit from out of the blue, no warning, in an area not known for earthquakes or faults, and it had scared the hell out of everybody. The earth wasn't supposed to move. The roaring that came from nowhere and everywhere spoke to some ancient memory that resided deep inside Tom's soul. He'd wanted to run, but with the floor and the walls and the ceiling shaking, with objects hurling themselves off shelves, with the awful roaring in his ears, where could he run? Where a moment ago had been solidity and strength and order, was now chaos. Nothing made any sense. What could he do in a world that, in one fraction of a second, suddenly changed all the rules? The earthquake had lasted fifteen seconds, and those seconds changed Tom's outlook forever. You couldn't count on anything, not even the ground beneath your feet.

He felt that same disorientation now. The one great certainty of life was that it was temporary. Death waited at the end. Maybe the soul lived on. Maybe there was a world beyond. But bodies died, flesh died, cells died, and they didn't come back.

Until tonight. He'd seen it for himself. He'd actually seen it happen, and it sent his mind into the Blacklands. He sat at the edge of the water with the chill night air stirring the hairs on the back of his neck, on the edge of a black lake in a black, scorched world obscured by smoke. The cicada buzz filled his ears like a mantra, transporting him beyond the world of men and out to the barren plain of nothingness. Voices spoke around him but their words had no meaning, like the water lapping at the shore, like the ci-cada thrum, like the dark thoughts buzzing around inside his skull.

"Fuck you, man!" Darren screamed, but Tom sat with his back to the other boys and didn't flinch, as if he hadn't heard.

"He's out of it," Buzzy said, pacing, wiggling his fingers.

"Fuck you!" Darren yelled again, practically in Tom's ear.

"I've seen him like this before. He's spaced."

Kent was shivering.

"That wasn't natural," he said. "That was freakin' weird."

"You didn't see shit," Buzzy said. "You were out that door so fast!"

"I saw enough."

"This is so incredibly, incredibly fucked!"

"We should go back."

Darren and Kent looked at Buzzy like he was nuts.

"Galen's our friend," Buzzy said. "This isn't some hor-ror movie where zombies start eating people's brains. He came back and we ran. What're we gonna to do when he calls us? Hang up? Not answer the door when he comes around? We should be glad he's back. We should have a party or something."

Kent stared uncomprehendingly at Buzzy.

"You are so weird," he said.

"What do you think, Tom?" Darren asked loudly, speak-ing to Tom's back. "Should we throw a party for Galen? Put up a big banner . . . 'Welcome Home From Hell?' "

"Leave him alone, Darren."

Darren walked over to him and Buzzy was sorry he'd opened his mouth. He was sorry, but he was tired of Darren's shit.

"What're you gonna do about it?"

"Back off, Darren." Apparently Kent was tired of Darren's shit, too. "Leave him alone."

"I don't believe this," Darren said. "Look at you guys. Sitting around like bumps on a fucking log. Do something, for Chris'sakes!"

"Like what? What are we supposed to do?"

"Something! How the hell should I know what?"

"Galen would know what to do," Buzzy said.

"Galen!" Darren said. "It's Galen that's got us all fucked up!"

"He would know! If it was one of us instead of him that got killed and came back . . . he'd know what to do about it!"

"Well it wasn't! And Brain Boy over there's gone into the asshole zone, so that leaves you and me and Kent to figure things out!"

"The blind leading the blind leading the blind," Buzzy said.

"Just shut the fuck up."

"I'm going home," Kent announced. He picked himself off the ground, dusted his behind. "Tomorrow, whatever happens, happens." He headed for his car.

"That's it? 'Whatever happens, happens?' "

"That's it," replied Kent.

"Works for me," Buzzy said. He walked over to Tom, patted him on the shoulder. "Hey. We're going home. You coming?" He went around and waved a hand in front of Tom's face. "Hey!" he said.

Tom started, blinked. He saw Buzzy's face looking down at him, asking him if anybody was home.

"I spaced out," Tom said.

"No shit," said Darren.

"Listen," Buzzy said, "we're calling it a night. Can you get home okay?"

Tom nodded.

"Okay, then. We'll see you tomorrow. You going to school?"

"I don't know."

"Give me a call, okay?"

Tom said he would. He heard the cars start and drive off. He waited until he could no longer hear the engines, then he stood up, threw a rock into the water and watched the ripples spread.

He wondered what Anderson would make of Galen's rise, of Irma Klempner's. He and Buzzy and Kent and Darren had all seen them come back. Jed Grimm saw them, too, was probably one of them, another Risen. Would they try to keep it a secret and deal quietly with the boys the way Haws had dealt with Galen? Or would they figure that the cat was out of the bag?

It was late. Brant would be wondering what happened to him. He should go home and tell Brant what he'd seen, get some rational advice.

Unless someone had gotten to Brant in the meantime. Haws could've killed his mom and Brant both, before midnight. They could be Risen by now.

He shouldn't have left Brant behind. Now Tom didn't know who to trust again.

The ripples on the water were dying out. Tom thought: What if they didn't stop? What if, instead of getting weaker as they spread, some force made them stronger? What if they kept spreading and spreading, and nobody could do anything to stop them?

Tom felt a sudden longing to be somewhere familiar and safe. He wanted to be someplace where the basic rules of the universe hadn't been turned upside down and inside out, where corpses slept the big sleep and you knew who your friends were.

But he no longer knew where that place would be.

Brant was about to fall asleep despite himself when he heard Tom's Honda pull up. He slid out of bed and pulled on his pants and shirt. He'd decided to play it cagey with Tom. He'd ask him about how it went and appear to take him and everything he said at face value, but he'd watch for blood stains and suspicious holes in his clothing, anything suggesting that Tom might be Risen. If he decided that Tom could no longer be trusted, Brant would tell Peg that Doc had called and they should come to the hospital. That would get her in the car. Then he'd hit the highway and tell her everything he knew while she had no choice but to sit there and listen, and he'd hope for the best.

He heard Tom rustling around in the kitchen, fixing himself a snack. Tom dropped a knife when Brant entered, asking, "How'd it go?" The kid was jumpy. What did that mean?

Tom tried not to stare at Brant, but it was hard to act casual after all he'd been through.

"He came back," Tom said. He cut himself a slice of roast for a sandwich. "So did the Klempner woman."

"You saw it?"

"Yeah."

Brant walked up and pulled out one of the kitchen chairs, sat down. "Well, what was it like? Tell me!"

Tom concentrated on digging bread out of the plastic bag, cutting the meat to fit, spreading it with horseradish.

"It was awful. The bodies were so burned, you couldn't tell which one was which, not really. I mean we had an idea, but they were in bad shape. Skin all black or burned off. Hardly more than skeletons."

"Did it happen at midnight?"

"On the dot. The church bell rang. Then the corpses started jerking and flopping. Some of the guys ran right then."

"But you stayed."

"I had to know. Then after it started, I couldn't take my eyes off it. The old, dead, burned stuff just fell away. I saw muscles reforming, new skin growing over it. It was like some weird time-lapse movie or something."

Brant's heart was beating fast and he had to remind himself to breathe. Tom seemed to be taking it so calmly—was that a normal human reaction? He just stood there making a sandwich and talking about it as if giving a book report in school that day.

It was now one o'clock. Tom had had an hour to react. Maybe he'd been sick to his stomach at the time, maybe he screamed or cried and was hiding all that from Brant under a facade of teenage stoicism. Or maybe he was Risen and was trying to downplay the whole thing to catch Brant off guard.

"You're taking it well," Brant said. "I'd be reaching for a bottle right now."

"You want a beer?"

"At one in the morning? No thanks. Got any whiskey?"

Tom shook his head "no." He pulled out a chair and sat down facing Brant. He took a bite of his sandwich and chewed, not really hungry, playing for time while he studied Brant's face. So far his reactions had been what Tom had guessed they'd be if Brant was still Brant, but how would he know? He didn't even know what kind of sign he was looking for.

"So, they came back. Then what?" Brant asked.

"Then we ran. Galen grabbed Buzzy's shirt and he panicked. So did I. We were shook up pretty bad and we just got the hell out of there."

"You didn't talk to Galen?"

"We just ran."

"Did they come after you?"

"No. I . . . I saw Jed Grimm. He knows we were there."

Brant scowled. "I was hoping they hadn't gotten to Jed. He'd be a good man on our side. What do you think?"

"Reverend Small was there before us. I think . . . I don't

know. I can't prove anything. It's just a bunch of feelings and shit."

"Then tell me what you're feeling."

Tom was silent. He glared across the table at Brant.

"I don't know what I feel!" His voice was edgy, climbing in register. "I don't know what to make of anything, all right?"

"But Galen did come back, you're sure of that."

"I saw it! One minute he was this . . . this burnt out husk, not even a body but a . . . thing! Then he came back, and he was alive! And I don't . . . I don't know. . . ."

"What don't you know, Tom?"

"The only goddamned thing I need to know! Is it good or bad? I don't know!"

"But you ran."

"Yeah, I ran! I said that, okay? I got scared and I ran!"

"Your gut knew what to make of it. It told you to run."

"So?" Tom was mad at himself. He'd let too much slip. He was going to hold something back but he'd lost control. Brant was infuriatingly calm and insistent.

"Something I learned as a reporter," Brant said. "Trust your gut. It'll lead you straighter than your head will. What's your gut telling you, Tom?"

"To get the fuck out of this town!"

"Then that's what we'll do." It hadn't taken much to crack Tom's facade enough to see the terror lurking behind it. As soon as he discovered that fear, Brant knew that Tom was still himself. If he was Risen he'd have tried to sell Brant a miracle, but Tom had described something quite different. Miraculous, yes, but wonderful? Spiritual? Transcendent? No. What Tom had seen scared the bejeezus out of him.

As for Tom, he still wasn't sure about Brant, not one hundred per cent, but as long as things moved in the direction Tom wanted them to go—as long as they were getting out of Anderson Tom would give him the benefit of the doubt. He would also watch his back.

"We'll talk to Peg in the morning," Brant said, "and somehow convince her that we have to go away."

Peg's sleepy voice spoke to them from the doorway.

"Who's going away?" she asked.

Tom looked up abruptly. Brant twisted his head around to look over his shoulder and became painfully aware of how the tensions of the past couple of days had settled there. He scooted his chair around to regard Peg standing in the kitchen doorway in her house robe. He wondered if Tom could tell that she had nothing on underneath. He felt himself rising and thought about junior high school and how erections always came at the most inappropriate moments, like when the bell rang for class change. It had been a long, long time since that had happened. Peg had worked some kind of change on him, that was for sure.

"Join us," Brant said. He and Tom exchanged looks. The conversation they'd thought to put off until morning was already steamrolling along. They might as well get it over with.

Peg shuffled to the cupboard and got out a glass. She poured herself some water and carried it over to the table. She propped her chin in her palms and looked at Brant and then Tom.

"Well?" she said. "What has the two of you skulking around the kitchen in the middle of the night? Plotting to blow up City Hall?"

Neither of them spoke. Neither knew how to begin. Peg looked again from one to the other. "Hello?" she said.

"I don't know where to start," Tom said.

"I guess you have to start with Friday night," Brant said. "Yeah."

Tom looked at his mom and thought about exacting the promise that can never be kept, the promise not to get mad.

But that was useless and juvenile. He'd just lay it out for her and deal with whatever came.

"I was out with the guys, and there was an accident," he began.

God, this was going to be rough.

Peg sat in the kitchen alone. It was after three, she had sent the men to bed promising Brant she'd be along shortly. The way she felt right now, she might never go to sleep again.

Listening to Tom tell about Deputy Haws's shooting had tied her stomach into knots. It was terrible, awful, but exactly the sort of thing she'd feared would happen when he started running with the Ganger boy. As he'd told the story, her mind raced through the possibilities. Where was she going to get a lawyer? How would she pay for it? What in the world could she do to keep her son out of jail?

Then it had occurred to her that she'd seen Haws herself over the weekend, alive and well. Whatever else Tom told her, then, the story didn't end in murder. It was a mistake of some sort, Haws was only wounded. She was so wrapped up in listening to Tom that her mind wasn't piecing things together yet. It wasn't linking Haws and his murder with John Duffy, the man who came back from the dead.

Until Tom described burying the body.

Then something had clicked. The murder, the grave in the woods, memories of a drive-in movie she'd seen when she was no older than Tom, her talk with Madge Duffy . . . they all fell into place in a single, plummeting moment in which Peg felt the earth disappear beneath her. She fell like Alice down the rabbit hole, into a place where everything she knew was twisted into a bizarre caricature of itself.

When Tom had started to falter, Brant jumped in. He told about seeing the bullet hole in Haws's shirt and how

Haws had been nosing around on Saturday night, looking for Tom. He told about seeing Haws and the Ganger boy together on Sunday morning, about finding the blood stains on the nudists' dock, about coming home to find Deputy Haws staked out across the street from his house.

At that point, Peg had called a time out. She couldn't sit still any longer. She stood up and paced. She was angry and confused. She demanded to know why they'd kept all this from her. She heard terrible words pouring out of her mouth, bitter accusations directed at Tom that she regretted instantly, apologies and tears. Finally she'd broken down completely and sat at the table and sobbed while Tom and Brant hovered around her, uncomfortable and helpless.

When she had recovered, emotionally exhausted, confused, resentful, she looked at them both and could tell from their expressions that there was more. She guessed that the worst was yet to come.

"I went to the mortuary tonight," Tom had said, "to see Galen. To see if he came back. I saw it, Mom. I saw his burned-up corpse, and the old woman's, too, and I saw them come back. I can't describe it. It was like they were being built all over again. They were brought back as good as new. I guess it was a miracle, but it scared the shit out of me. The other guys—Darren and Buzzy and Kent were there, too—they ran, and so did I."

She'd said that she couldn't believe it, and Tom said he wouldn't have believed it either except he was there, he saw it with his own two eyes. The other guys could back him up. It happened all right.

"Peg," Brant had said, "the thing is, we think there could be more Risen. The people on the dock, for instance, if they were killed. They could've come back just the same as Irma Klempner and the Ganger boy. And there could be others. How many people might have died, maybe even been murdered, and we don't know about it because they came back and seemed as good as new?"

"Madge Duffy," Peg said to the empty kitchen. She spoke the name flatly, without inflection. She thought about their conversation and remembered how Madge had seemed different. Better somehow, stronger. Whenever she'd spoken to Madge before, she'd always had a defeated manner, like an animal resigned to its cage. She hadn't had that manner on Sunday afternoon. It was remotely possible that John had killed her on Saturday and she'd come back that midnight. But if so, she'd come back better than before.

Seeing his friend come back had terrified Tom. Then again, he was just a teenager, and what did teenagers know about life? Witnessing any birth would be frightening to someone who'd never seen it. Peg had given birth twice and she knew it was a painful, bloody process, the stuff of horror stories. But giving birth was such a common occurrence that people had to make it beautiful in their minds. Birth was the physical expression of the divine spark, after all. It was God's gift.

Maybe the Risen were a new gift. Just as off-putting, perhaps, to those who witnessed it unprepared, in the wrong setting—in the middle of a mortuary, for Chris'sakes, at midnight—but it was no less a gift to be granted a second chance than to be given the first one.

What had happened, after all? The Ganger boy had shot Deputy Haws, and Haws had risen. What was so horrible about that? Strange, yes, even bizarre. But the end result was that Haws wasn't dead, there was no murder . . . wasn't that better than the alternative? Brant had seen them talking after church. Reconciliation?

As for Haws staking out Brant's house, that could've been Brant's imagination. Everybody knew that Haws could often be found on a hot afternoon parked under a shade tree, head lolled back, snoring. It could've been pure coincidence that he took his nap in front of Brant's house yesterday, and Brant overreacted after seeing what he thought were blood stains on the dock, stains that Tom hadn't been able to find later that night.

Brant and Tom wanted to leave town. They wanted to run away from something they didn't understand. A child might be frightened, too, by a spectacle of clowns and elephants and wild animal tamers, but he'd learn eventually that a circus was indeed something uncommon and even grotesque, but it wasn't anything to be feared.

Why shouldn't miracles be frightening, too, to the uninitiated? A magician sawing a woman in half could be unsettling to someone who'd never seen the trick before. Why shouldn't real magic be even more disturbing? But that didn't mean it was bad. And if it meant that Annie could be returned to her. . . .

It was four o'clock. She'd sat in the quiet kitchen for an hour, turning these thoughts over and over in her head. Brant and Tom wanted to pack up first thing in the morning. They wanted Peg to arrange with the Cooves County Hospital to move Annie to a hospital in Junction City. She'd promised to look into it, and she would.

But she wasn't going anywhere, not yet.

She had to see what the day brought, and what it promised for herself and her girl.

Downtown, Doc Milford and the Lungers and their son Josh and Sheriff Clark and Clyde Dunwiddey had scrubbed down the Sheriff's Office and gone home.

Carl and Bernice Tompkins slept peacefully and the cats had settled down and the cockroaches had retreated to the nether regions under the house and inside the walls, some making the journey through the grass to the neighbors' houses on either side.

Frank and Doris Gunnarsen finally got their coffees and had a long chat with John and Madge Duffy. They left the Duffys' after two, promising to get together more frequently from now on.

Merle Tippert, Jack and Dolores Frelich, and Hiram Weems the traveling salesman had awakened shivering in the woods, found their clothes stacked and folded neatly nearby, and dressed quickly. They hurried to their cars, making a date to reconvene at Ma's for breakfast in the morning.

Jed Grimm had had a long talk with Galen Ganger and Irma Klempner, and they'd decided not to go home right away. The boys had seen them, so word would be spreading quickly. As far as the town knew, they were the first resurrections since John Duffy, so it was important to treat them with precisely the right "spin." Jed called Reverend Small over to help plan an event for Monday morning.

Seth tossed another log on the fire. He stood in front of it and warmed his hands, smiling.

Things would really start happening now.

SEVENTEEN

Despite their late night, everyone in the Culler household was up and around before eight o'clock the next morning. Brant was in the kitchen making coffee when Peg came in. They exchanged greetings and a quick kiss and a hug. They stood in one spot for more than a minute, holding onto one another as if it might be the last time. Peg sighed and Brant said it felt good to hold a woman who wasn't made of inflatable vinyl. Peg said that surely it hadn't been that long and Brant replied that it had and they kissed again, for real this time.

Tom was upstairs sitting on the edge of the bed, breathing hard. He'd had another zombie nightmare. This time it wasn't just Deputy Haws but Galen and Jed Grimm and Brant and it seemed like half the town who was after him, chasing him through the mortuary, through the park, and somehow he found himself at the reservoir, his back to the water while the zombies closed in. He ran into the water and started to swim, but then he couldn't move his legs and he felt himself spinning down into the black depths, and he couldn't breathe and he knew he was going to die, and he was going to come back, and when he did, he would be one of them.

He went to the bathroom and was going to splash some water on his face but decided, once he was there, on a nice, hot shower. When he came downstairs he could smell freshly brewed coffee and bacon frying on the stove. He walked into the kitchen where Peg sat at the table with Brant. They both looked grim. Tom checked on the bacon, which should have been turned over a minute ago.

"Should I flip this?" Tom asked, and Peg said she'd do it. She didn't get up immediately, though, but sat there looking sadly at Brant, so Tom got out the spatula and turned the bacon over before it burned.

Peg said, "I'm sorry" and put her hand over Brant's. He took her hand and squeezed it, said, "Me, too." Tom watched them over his shoulder.

"You guys have a fight?" he asked.

Brant let go of Peg's hand and picked up his coffee cup.

"Your mother says she's not ready to leave town," Brant said. "She thinks we're full of beans."

"I didn't say that," Peg protested. "I said I didn't want to risk moving Annie until we knew more."

"Mom, I saw it. I saw Galen come back."

"I know you did. I believe you."

"Then why won't you . . . ?" Tom's voice trailed off. He knew why. "You're thinking about what Madge Duffy said, aren't you?"

"If there's a chance, if there's any hope at all, no matter how slight—"

"You can't trust her! Don't you see that? She's one of them! You can't trust anybody in town! Anybody could be Risen! Anybody!"

"He's right," Brant said. "John could've killed Madge."

"I know that! I understand everything you've said . . . I'm not a child and I'm not stupid!"

"I didn't mean—"

"Look," Peg said. She was trying hard to keep the discussion from turning into an argument, but she wasn't going to give in to what the men wanted until she was convinced it was the right thing to do. She was beyond acquiescing automatically to the male of the species.

"You say people are coming back. You've seen them, and it's frightening. Of course it's frightening because it's the unknown. It's something we don't understand. But that doesn't make it bad. Maybe it's the best thing that ever happened to this town. Maybe we aren't even the only ones. Maybe leaving town wouldn't accomplish anything! Whatever's going on, I'm not going to risk moving Annie until I know . . . until I'm certain it's the right thing to do!"

There was a long moment of silence broken only by the sizzling of the bacon. Tom folded some paper towels and laid the bacon strips out to drain, and Brant sat back in his chair and sighed.

"Well," Brant said, "I guess we've got our work cut out for us, Tom. Obviously you aren't going to school today."

"I hadn't thought about it."

"And this is Peg's day off, right?"

Peg nodded.

"So let's do this: Peg, you check into Annie's transfer. Meanwhile, Tom and I will go to Junction City and look through the morgue."

Tom started to protest, but Brant cut him off.

"I mean the newspaper morgue. Back issues of the paper."

"Looking for what?"

"Somebody named Eloise, for one. Anything about people making miracle recoveries, being pronounced dead and coming back . . . you'll know it when you see it."

"What about Galen?"

"What about him?"

"He's back. Some kind of shit's going to go down."

"Then it's just as well you won't be here for it," Peg stated. Tom glared at her, but he knew she was right. Peg excused herself and went upstairs to shower.

Brant took over the cooking duties from Tom. He broke four eggs into the bacon grease.

Tom said, "I knew she wouldn't leave."

"She just needs more convincing," Brant replied. "I can't say I blame her. We laid an awful lot of stuff on her last night. We have to find out about Eloise."

"Irma Klempner's been out of her gourd as long as I can remember. Eloise could be the name of her sled for all we know."

"Yeah, but it's all we have to go on."

"Well, she's back. Maybe we should just ask her."

"If she's one of them, it's too late. No, the newspaper's our best bet."

"Okay. Big city, here we come."

"It's boring, godawful work, sifting through the morgue. You sure you're up for it?"

"Can't be any worse than school."

"Don't believe it. How do you want your eggs?"

Tom said "over easy" and they spent the next few minutes in silence, eating breakfast, mulling things over, pondering the imponderable. Peg came down dressed in jeans and a t-shirt and drying her hair with a towel, and Brant headed upstairs for his turn in the shower. Twenty minutes later he and Tom were in the car, headed for Junction City.

They'd no sooner pulled into the street when the telephone rang. Peg answered. It was Doris Gunnarsen, and she had remarkable news.

The excitement in Doris's voice was infectious. She began with "You remember John Duffy?" as if anyone in town could've forgotten, and slid right into, "Well, it's happened again!" without waiting for a response.

"It's Irma Klempner and the Ganger boy. They're back from the dead, I swear to God. I heard it myself straight from

Madge Duffy who got it straight from Reverend Small, and he got it straight from Jed Grimm who was right next door when it happened. Now, I didn't see the accident but you can imagine . . . I mean, those cars were burning like I-don't-know-what and the bodies . . . well, it doesn't take a rocket scientist to know what the bodies must have looked like. We're talking crispy critters, here, no disrespect intended.

"So Jed wakes up in the middle of the night and for some reason he's thinking about those bodies in the embalming room. Maybe he had a dream or something, I don't know, but whatever . . . he wakes up and those bodies are on his mind and he decides to go next door and take a look. And what does he see when he gets there but Irma Klempner and the Ganger boy, alive and whole and as pink as a baby's bottom, standing there outside the mortuary without a stitch. So he throws his robe around Irma and takes them both back to his place and calls Doc Milford.

"Can you imagine? A crazy woman and a teenaged hoodlum in your house, both of them fresh off the slab . . . you wouldn't find me in that house, let me tell you! But anyway, Doc shows up and runs a few tests and . . . well, the upshot is that they're both in perfect health. And Irma Klempner! From what I hear she's as clear-eyed and right in the head as Doc's seen her in forty years!

"Can you believe it? I don't know what's going on in this town but it's something else, that's for sure. The Reverend's having a special service this morning, ten o'clock, to announce the news and to, you know, help people sort it out in their heads. I hardly know what to make of it myself. People coming back from the dead . . . doesn't it give you the shivers?

"Listen, I'd love to chat but the Reverend's depending on me to get the word out. Be a dear and call the diner? See you at church! Bye, now!"

The phone clicked and, without saying a word since she

answered "Hello," Peg hung up the receiver. She phoned Ma and talked to Cindy who promised to spread the word to the breakfast crowd. She figured that Ma would be willing to close up for an hour or so since he wouldn't have any business anyway. Then Peg ran upstairs to do something simple and quick with her hair and to put on a nicer shirt.

At about a quarter to ten, the church bell started to toll.

Brant and Tom drove by the church on their way out of town. Brant slowed for a better look. He recognized Jed Grimm's car out front and the old Chevy pickup he'd seen at Franz Klempner's farm. Tom pointed out Janis Ganger's car.

There were other vehicles, too. Merle Tippert's Studebaker was unmistakable, which made them think that some of the other cars might have been the ones parked at the reservoir all day yesterday. One of them had out-of-county tags and a Hartford Insurance bumper sticker. They attributed it to Hiram Weems who sold insurance and did a little claims adjusting in the area. Brant recognized Carl Tompkins's truck, and Deputy Haws's squad car was there. Others, too.

"If we knew who all those cars belonged to," Brant said, "I'll bet we'd have the beginnings of a list of Risen. They're gathering."

"But for what?" Tom asked. For some reason he thought of the crows massing on the jungle gym in the Hitchcock movie.

"Maybe we should stay and find out."

Tom shook his head "no."

"Let's do this newspaper thing," he said. "It's all just guess and speculation until we get some facts. Find out who Eloise is, or was. See if there's any record of this kind of thing happening around here before. Anything we can use to convince Mom to move Annie."

Brant told Tom about his alternate plan, to lure Peg into the car under false pretenses and drive her out of town.

"Wouldn't work," Tom said. "Mom would jump out of a speeding car for Annie."

Brant noticed the bitterness underlying Tom's remark.

"She spends a lot of time with Annie, doesn't she?" Brant said. "Too much, maybe."

"It's her obsession. It's like, if she's awake and she isn't at work or with Annie, she thinks she's doing something wrong. As if it was her fault Annie's in a coma."

"Not that I'm any expert on the female psyche," Brant said, "but it seems like some of them have a special gland for producing guilt. Peg's probably played the 'if' game so much about the accident that she feels responsible. You know 'If I hadn't divorced Rod, this never would've happened.' 'If I'd gone to pick her up instead of letting Rod drive her. . . .'"

"Right, right. I keep telling her, 'Mom, it's not your fault.' But she won't listen."

"She's got the gland, for sure. It doesn't make her a bad person, though."

"I didn't say she was. It just gets frustrating, that's all."

"Tell me about it. I tried for months to get a free day out of her. In a way, you lost both parents in that wreck. She's as much a victim as your dad was, only she has to go on living and deal with the aftermath. It's tough as hell."

"I guess so. I never thought of it like that."

They didn't talk for the next few miles. When they hit the highway and passed the sign telling them Junction City, 62 miles, Tom picked up the conversation again.

"I love my little sister," he said. "I always did. But the way she is now, it's like she's dead but some part of her brain didn't get the message. Do you think she's got a chance?"

"There's always a chance. Very small, of course."

"You read about people coming out of comas after years."

"You read about them because they're news. They're the exceptions. You read about people who win the lottery but nothing about the thousands of losers. That's what the news is all about, life as it isn't. A reporter in the city spends all his time looking for the hook, the angle, the sensation. You can start to feel like a charlatan after awhile."

"Is that why you came out here and started the *Times*?"

Brant shrugged. "I probably romanticized it. I thought it'd be spiritual somehow, immersing myself in births and deaths and farm sales and hail damage and high school graduations. There's just one problem with reporting life as it really is."

"What's that?"

"It's real damn boring."

Tom let out a short laugh. "Yeah, that's Anderson."

"I have to admit, this 'Risen' thing had me fired up as a reporter. For a time."

"What about now?"

"Now?" Brant considered the question. "Now I just want to get out of it alive."

"I thought that was the problem."

Brant gave Tom a questioning look.

"An excess of life," Tom explained. "The wrong life. Like a cancer or a virus."

Brant glanced over at Tom. "Jesus," he said, "you put your finger on it. The Risen are like a virus, some kind of strange thing that isn't living or dead but capable of taking over living cells. You know, viruses can lie dormant for years. Then they find a suitable host, start reproducing, and all hell breaks loose."

"You think this is a virus?"

"Not in the strictest sense, no. But metaphysically, maybe. Maybe that's not a bad way of thinking about it. I mean, what do the Risen want, the ones we know about?"

"Nothing," Tom said, "except maybe. . . ."

"Except to make more Risen. Maybe that's all that matters to them."

"Shit," Tom said. He thought again of the ripples that didn't die out, that got stronger and spread wider and farther, never stopping. "Shit," he said again. "It'd be like a virus that nobody was immune to. It could mean the end of the world."

"Yes, it could," Brant said.

The church was packed. Even people who hadn't attended Sunday's service were gathering to hear about the latest miracles. The parking lot was full and people were parking along the street for several blocks in either direction. As Peg hurried toward the church she fell into step with Bernice Tompkins and her husband, Carl.

"Can you believe something like this is happening in Anderson?" Bernice asked. "I think everybody in town's here. I told Doris when she called that if I got Carl to come to church, it'd be another miracle. But here he is!"

"Biggest thing that's ever happened in this town," Carl said.

"You don't think it's a little creepy?" Peg asked.

"Creepy!" Bernice laughed. "I guess you could call it that, but I suppose the people who saw Lazarus rise from the tomb thought that was pretty creepy, too."

"Biggest thing to happen in the whole state," said Carl. "You watch. It won't be long before the TV networks pick this up. They'll all be here. NBC. CNN. You just watch."

"I imagine you're right," Peg said.

"ABC. Fox."

"The shows, too," Bernice agreed. "What's that one . . . *Hardline?*"

"They'll be here, soon as the word gets out."

"I just hope they don't make us all look foolish the way they do."

"There's nothing foolish about coming back from the dead. I expect they'll treat it like a joke at first, but once they see that it's on the level . . . you watch. It'll be big."

By the time Peg reached it, the sanctuary was standing room only. She looked around and spotted John and Madge Duffy in the pews. Madge sat with her back as straight as a wall, and Peg knew that she was beaming with pride. As a murderess, she had been shunned by polite society; John's rise had granted her a kind of "social pardon," but at the cost of identifying herself with an oddity, acknowledged by the mainstream, perhaps, but separate from it. Now she and her husband were at the forefront of an apparent movement, and their social coin had soared in value.

The Duffys sat next to Frank and Doris Gunnarsen. Frank Gunnarsen, John Duffy, Carl Tompkins . . . the room was filled with husbands who generally chose the sports section of the Sunday newspaper over the word of the Lord. As Peg scanned the crowd she located quite a number of newcomers. Merle Tippert, who never missed a chance to disparage organized religion, was there, as was Deputy Haws's reclusive sister, Lucy, and that salesman who breezed through town every so often. Others, too, who Peg knew by name or only by face, swelled the ranks.

Doc Milford worked the center aisle, smiling and shaking hands like a politician. This was his moment of vindication. Everyone who'd seen the bodies of Irma Klempner and the Ganger boy knew beyond a shadow of a doubt that these two people were as dead as a pair of roasted game hens. If they'd risen the way Doris Gunnarsen and the grapevine said, it couldn't be because an aging dipsomaniac who should have retired from medicine ten years ago had forgotten to feel for a pulse.

Sheriff Clark and Deputy Haws handled crowd control. The rules about maximum occupancy and fire aisles had flown out the window as more people crowded their way in. The sanctuary began to resemble an overloaded ferry boat headed for disaster, people were wedged in so tightly, until Clark and Haws moved some of them outside while Jimmy Troost hooked up a makeshift speaker system so the latecomers on the lawn could hear the Reverend's address.

The place roared with conversation. Gone was the reverential silence of the sanctuary, the hushed tones and breathy whispers, replaced by a clamor as pounding and energetic and incomprehensible as the din of an engine room. People wore jeans and t-shirts, baseball caps, boots and sneakers, khaki pants and slacks and house dresses and work uniforms. They jostled and angled for position. They joked and scoffed and fretted and proclaimed.

It seemed to Peg as if the entire town had been resurrected. A few days ago, Anderson had been a sleepy little town massaged by the humdrum into a state of relaxation so deep it could have been mistaken for a coma. Now it was alive and buzzing. Peg's heart was beating fast as Reverend Small led Franz Klempner and the Ganger boy's mother in from the sacristy.

Franz looked like hell. His eyes were dark and he moved slowly and stiffly, as if every joint and muscle in his body ached, which they probably did. He seemed to have no strength as Small helped him to sit down in the front pew where spaces had been reserved for the two of them. Franz, even in his so-called "declining" years, had shown the vigor of a much younger man, but this morning he looked his age and more. The shock of the accident on his body was taking its toll, as was the shock to his spirit upon learning of his wife's rise.

Janis Ganger appeared shaken. She wore the same dress

she'd worn to church the day before, and even from the back of the sanctuary Peg could tell that she was not quite there, as if she were watching herself from some hidden corner and operating her body by remote control. Awakened in the early morning hours to find that her son was back from the dead, then rushing to the funeral home to witness the miracle herself, then hours spent wide awake in her living room smoking cigarettes and nipping at a bottle of Gilbey's gin while Galen lay in bed asleep, all of it had left her feeling dissociated from the events playing out around her. It was all happening without her, had nothing to do with her except for the accident of birth that linked her and one of the morning's celebrities. So complete was her estrangement from her son that coping with his death had been easier than this, his unexpected and (yes, why not admit it?) unwelcome re-entry into her life. Yesterday had been a day of closure. Today was a day of riddles and uncertainties and doubts, and she had to fake her way through it in front of the whole town, nursing a hangover and draped in a day-old dress.

Reverend Small stepped to the pulpit and waited for the crowd to quiet down. He spoke a few words to test the sound system, made sure the people on the lawn could hear, and began his speech.

"Just over twenty-four hours ago," he began. "I stood at this pulpit and addressed a similar group—many of you were among them—concerning a miracle. It was the miracle of John Duffy's rise from the grave.

"Today, that miracle has been repeated twice over. Killed in a tragic automobile accident, their bodies burned beyond recognition, there could be no doubt but that the spirits of Irma Klempner and Galen Ganger departed their physical bodies to join the Holy Father in Heaven.

"For reasons unknown and perhaps unknowable to mortal man and woman, the Good Lord saw fit to return those spirits, those souls, to Earth. The bodies that had housed them were ravaged beyond the skill of any surgeon to repair. But God is no ordinary physician. He healed those bodies as you or I would rebuild a house or, more appropriately, a temple, for the body is the temple of the soul, and it is well within the power of the Lord to restore that temple to its former glory, whatever violence it has suffered.

"It is normal to fear that which is beyond our comprehension. From the time when our earliest ancestors huddled in caves, terrified of the thunder, fear has been the curse of humankind, for there are so many, many things even to this day that we do not understand. But the Lord gave us courage, also, and even more importantly, he gave us the faith to accept these things as part of His grand scheme for the universe, to accept them and their goodness as His work.

"I urge you, in God's name, to cast your fears aside and to welcome Irma Klempner and Galen Ganger into your hearts. Welcome them for what they are, the work of our heavenly Lord and Father from whom all good things must come. Welcome them as living testaments to the faith that you nurture in your breast. Welcome them as you would a newborn child, for they truly are reborn. Welcome them as Irma's husband, Franz, and Galen's mother, Janis, welcome them. Welcome them as the true miracles they are. Welcome them now."

Peg had not noticed Ruth Smart at the organ, but now the strains of "Holy, Holy, Holy" filled the sanctuary and Reverend Small turned toward the sacristy door. The door opened and Galen Ganger stepped through followed by Irma Klempner.

Galen's hair was trimmed, washed, and neatly arranged. Peg wondered what barber or stylist had been summoned in the middle of the night to tidy the boy up, and then she remembered that one of Jed Grimm's talents was preparing

corpses for public viewing. He was probably a pretty fair
hand with a pair of scissors. Galen wore a button-front shirt
instead of his usual ragged tee, and slacks that Peg could not
imagine were his own, probably borrowed for the occasion
from Reverend Small, who was about Galen's height.

But the true miracle was Irma Klempner. She wore a
plain house dress, her Sunday best having burned in the
crash, but she carried herself with the composure of a sea-
soned socialite. She graciously accepted Small's arm and
smiled at him, a genuine smile for the man who, a day earlier, she'd branded a "devil" and "Satan."

The crowd buzzed. Heads craned and someone lifted
himself out of his seat ever so slightly to get a better look,
and the person behind him stood up, and soon the entire
assembly was on its feet jockeying for a better view. Franz
rose slowly and painfully and stepped forward and took his
wife in his arms and they embraced. Galen held his arms
out to his mother. Janis Ganger must have been moved by
the sermon because she stood and, with tears streaming
down her painted cheeks, took his hands in hers. She drew
him close and held him as she had not done since he was
a little boy.

It was enough for Peg. As everyone else surged forward
and Reverend Small and Sheriff Clark tried to throw together a reception line of sorts, Peg slipped out of the
sanctuary and hurried along the sidewalk toward her car,
anxious to spend the rest of the morning with Annie.

EIGHTEEN

Franz Klempner lay in bed with the Bible in his lap, more exhausted than he had ever been in his life. Farmers are used to feeling physically spent at the end of a long day, but the past eight hours had been too much for Franz.

First he'd been roused in the middle of the night by Elmer's passionate barking and somebody's pounding on the front door. Franz thought his house was on fire. He'd clawed his way out of a deep sleep and heaved his aching body out of bed, his heart racing, and shuffled across the cold wooden floor while his muscles protested every step and his nose tested the air for smoke.

He'd flung open the door and there stood Reverend Small. The light was dim under the crescent moon and Franz had navigated his way to the door without turning on a light, so at first he didn't recognize the woman who stood just behind the preacher. When she stepped forward and said his name, he figured he was dreaming. Things like this don't happen.

"Irma," he said, and she'd smiled at him. The simple exchange of a word and a smile was a miracle to Franz. It was like turning the key on his pickup truck and having the engine grab and start in an instant. He was used to cranking it for awhile first and fiddling with the choke knob until he coaxed a few labored coughs out of the engine, and then having it die a time or two before it was finally running strong, and that's what it was like talking to Irma. Most times she didn't respond at all, and when she did, it could be with tears or a laugh or anything in between, there was no telling. To speak her name and receive a smile was a transaction of such clarity that it took him aback for a moment, adding to the dreamlike impression.

Elmer kept barking. Franz assumed he was barking at the Reverend, a stranger to Elmer, and told him to hush up but it did no good. When he looked down at the dog with the intention of thumping him on the head, he saw that it was not the preacher that had riled Elmer but Irma.

"Hush, Elmer! Hush!" Franz had scolded. The dog stopped barking but paced behind Franz, whining nervously.

"God has granted you a miracle, Franz," said Reverend Small.

Irma had moved closer and took one of Franz' hands in hers. Her touch was warm, her skin soft. She lifted his hand and brushed the back of his fingers against her cheek. She looked up at him with clear, blue eyes.

"It's the miracle you've prayed for," she'd said. "You've been asking the Lord to make me well for the past forty years, and now your prayers have been answered."

"This is a dream," Franz had replied. He took Irma's face in his hands and stroked it with his thumbs. She smiled at his touch, tears welling in her eyes, and rushed forward to bury her head in his chest. His hands fluttered for a moment before settling on her back.

"Then hold me till you wake," she'd said.

Franz had wrapped his arms tighter around Irma, as tightly as he'd held her during her night terrors. The press of her body against his was comfortable and familiar, but she clung to him now, not to allay her own fears but to put his at rest. They embraced in the doorway while Elmer circled and Reverend Small watched from the front porch, smiling.

That was at two o'clock in the morning. Finally Reverend

Small had said his good-bye. Irma thanked him for the dress he'd brought her from the church thrift and for bringing her home. He'd said it was his honor to play any small role in such a wondrous occasion, and he'd exacted Franz's and Irma's promise to come to church tomorrow for the special service.

"After all," he said, "you and the Ganger boy are the guests of honor."

It was the first Franz had heard that Galen Ganger had come back as well, and the news shocked him. Now, in the glare of the day, having endured the church service and the voices and handshakes and well-wishes of the community, now, sitting in his own bed in his own house, he wondered what kind of force it was that would return his wife and her killer both, that would regard and treat them as equals. Was it a spiritual power of such love that all sin was forgiven, even the sin of murder? Or was it simply a force of nature, like a tornado, that was oblivious to all moral distinctions?

His Bible lay open to Matthew. He read aloud: "He maketh his sun to rise on the evil and on the good, and sendeth rain on the just and on the unjust."

Elmer lay in the corner, chewing a place on his leg. Harsh words and a few thumps from Franz had taught him to treat his risen mistress with civility, but he was visibly anxious when Irma was in the room. He wouldn't lie still when she was there, but would stand and sometimes pace back and forth, whining softly. He'd reverted to certain puppy behavior, spotting the kitchen floor once and chewing obsessively, turning his teeth on himself and worrying angry red spots on his legs and tail.

Franz put great store in the behavior of simple creatures. He trusted the weather predictions of cows and woolly caterpillars over those of the U. S. Weather Service who, for all Franz knew, were looking at cows and caterpillars, too. Elmer's reluctance to accept Irma reinforced Franz's own doubts. It was Elmer who'd barked incessantly at the Scotsman they hired to build the fence, the one who'd done such a poor job that Franz had to go out and hammer nails in all the boards himself when the staples the Scotsman had used failed to hold. Ever since then, Franz had considered Elmer a shrewd judge of character.

Franz heard Irma approaching with his lunch. He'd smelled the stew she was cooking and it brought back memories. He thought about the first few years they were married. Irma had been a good cook and Franz had put on some extra pounds early on, before he'd learned to control himself around her desserts. The aroma of the stew took him back to those days. Was it really possible that his bride was back from whatever mental purgatory she'd inhabited for the past four decades?

He could hear her singing as she walked down the hall. It was a hymn, one of Franz's favorites.

"There's a church in the valley by the wildwood," she sang, "No lovelier place in the dale."

Franz mouthed the words, singing low, under his breath: "No spot is so dear to my childhood/As the little brown church in the vale."

The door opened and Irma walked in bearing the steaming hot bowl of stew on a bed tray. She beamed at Franz as she settled the tray over his legs. Franz had not seen a smile so lovely in forty years.

She caught him looking at her face and turned away.

"What's the matter?" he asked, and she replied, "I'm old."

"We've both seen a few years," Franz said.

"It isn't fair to you. You married a young woman and she left you. I left to go live someplace in my mind. You were young and handsome, a hard worker . . . you could have found a proper wife to take my place. No one would have blamed you."

"That was a long time ago."

"You'll never get those years back, Franz, the ones I took from you. You could have had a family. Children, grandchildren. Instead, you had a crazy woman living under your roof, one who burned the food and woke you with her nightmares. A burden. . . ."

"You were no burden."

"Don't be foolish. Of course I was. But you looked after me and cared for me, loved me, and what did I do in return? I got old. I got old and came back and here you were, as kind and loving. . . ." Franz saw the tears welling in her eyes. He took her hand.

"There, now," he said as he always did when he didn't know what to say. She tried to smile at him.

"You're a saint," she said.

"Bull," he answered.

"You are. You are the sweetest, sweetest man." She leaned down and kissed him.

"Careful," he said, "you'll spill my lunch. I've waited forty years for that stew."

Irma laughed. She wiped at her tears with the back of her hand.

"I'll leave you alone," she said. "Is there anything else you need?"

Franz said no, he was fine. As Irma headed for the door, he had a thought and called to her.

"Who's Eloise?" he asked.

Irma halted. When she turned around to face him, Franz saw that her smile had altered somehow. The smile was there, but so was a hardness around her eyes, a baleful look that the smile could not soften.

"I don't know any Eloise," she said.

"In the church, last Sunday. . . ."

The smiled faded. Plainly, this was not a subject she

wanted to explore. "I didn't know what I was saying. I was out of my head."

"You called the reverend a devil."

"It was nonsense. I wish you'd forget it. That's all behind us. We have to look to the future." She nodded toward the bowl of stew in his lap. "Don't let that get cold."

She left, shutting the door behind her.

Franz leaned over and let the aroma of the stew fill his head. He felt like he was visiting his own past. The sense of smell had that power, to take you back. On evenings when the barometer fell and the earth released its scents, Franz often felt transported to the days of his youth and the magic of twilight, those precious moments before his mother called from the kitchen door that it was time to come in. Irma's stew worked its magic now. He fell spinning into the good old days. He knew even then to appreciate that time, his strength, their love, the struggle itself, but he couldn't know how fleeting those years would be, and how few.

His darling bride was back, forty years older but with many good years yet ahead of them. And yet, like those picture puzzles in the Sunday funnies, there were things that weren't right. Elmer's behavior was the most worrisome, but there were other signs. Why didn't she remember Eloise? Though spoken in dementia, the name connected somehow to Irma's history. Her mind was sharp, she should have remembered what it was. Maybe she did remember and maybe it was the key to understanding all that was going on, like that reporter thought it was, but now she had to bury it somehow because the situation could not withstand such scrutiny.

The Bible had fallen to the floor. Franz wanted to retrieve it and leaf through its well-thumbed pages, searching for answers, but the tray on his lap prevented it. The Bible, the Farmer's Almanac, and Nature itself . . . these were the wellsprings of knowledge. What would they tell him, if he only knew where to look?

He glanced over at Elmer lying in the corner, head on his paws, looking to Franz for answers to his own questions even as Franz looked to Elmer.

Franz picked up his spoon and sampled the stew. It was delicious, as he knew it would be, but his body and mind were spent and he had no appetite. He let his mind wander on its own. Perhaps in its unguided ramblings it would stumble on the truth that Franz's logical processes had failed to discover. He let his eyes relax until the room was a soft blur, and when his eyelids got heavy he closed them, and when his chin headed down toward his chest, he let it. He fell asleep sitting up.

When he woke, he felt a weight on his legs. The scent of stew in his nose had been replaced by that of a farm dog. He opened his eyes and beheld Elmer lying on the bed, on Franz's legs, slurping up the last of Franz's lunch.

Franz shooed Elmer off the bed and called to Irma. She entered promptly and Franz said, "I hope there's more stew."

Irma smiled and said it was a good sign that Franz was getting his appetite back, and Franz was tempted not to tell her what had really happened. He did tell her, though, and she scowled at Franz and glared at Elmer with a ferocity that would have stopped the heart of a lesser beast. She took the tray and the empty bowl and marched out of the room.

Franz was scolding Elmer for getting him into trouble with his wife when he noticed the dog's rapid breathing. He was sitting in the corner, panting as if he'd run a mile.

Franz threw back the covers and walked over to Elmer, his muscles and joints protesting every step. He bent down and made Elmer lie down and Franz put his ear to the dog's chest. Elmer's heart was racing like a sparrow's.

Franz yelled for Irma to call the vet, that something was wrong with Elmer. Suddenly Elmer's body convulsed and he flipped across the wooden floor like a dervish. He thudded against the wall and jerked obscenely as Franz hurried over to him and tried to hold him still. This had happened once before, when Elmer got into the pesticide. . . .

Elmer whined and then his body went limp. He stared up at Franz with wide, unseeing eyes, and Franz's heart felt as if it had frozen solid in his chest. His mind searched furiously for any explanation other than the obvious. He did not want to believe that Elmer had been poisoned, or that the poison was in the stew, or that it had been meant for him.

He looked up as something rushed at him and he realized that it was Irma. A beam of sunlight glinted off the butcher knife in her hand.

Franz cried out and fell backward as the knife sliced the air and whistled past his ear. He hit the floor and Irma came at him again. She raised the knife and Franz tried to scramble to his feet, but Irma was too quick for him. He kicked at her and the knife came down and embedded itself in his calf. Irma jerked the knife free and Franz saw his blood arc in the air.

He backed into a wooden chair, twisted around and grabbed it in one hand. It took all his strength to hurl it at Irma. The chair caught her in the knees as she strode toward him. She cried out from the impact and cursed as the chair tangled her legs and she fell. She stabbed weakly with the knife as she fell toward Franz. The blade bounced off one of his cracked ribs and the hot rush of pain made him cry out. His head swam and the room became a red, pulsating blur and he felt Irma's body collapse on top of his.

He rolled over and lay on top of her while he searched through the veil of red mist for the knife. He saw it, still in Irma's hand. He shifted his weight to her forearm to pin it to the floor. They wrestled awkwardly until Franz's sight cleared and the dizziness left his head. He worked the knife out of her grip and threw it skidding under the bed.

He straddled Irma, pinned her wrists to the floor. "Why?" he asked, gasping for breath. His ribs ached and he felt warm, sticky blood oozing down his wounded leg.

"To bring you to Seth," she replied.

Franz stared at the face he loved so dearly. The madness was gone from her eyes, replaced by a cold sanity that he found even more terrifying. He didn't want to ask more questions. He didn't care about the answers. He thought about the Ganger boy and Deputy Haws, and the reporter's words echoed in his head. There are others. I don't know how many. All Franz wanted to do now was to get away.

"I'm leaving," he said, and Irma told him, "You can't."

Darren, Buzzy and Kent had fled to school that morning like refugees seeking sanctuary. They figured correctly that it was the last place Galen would look for them.

The rumor mill told them that Principal Smart had come that close to canceling classes so that everyone could attend the special church service for Galen Ganger and Irma Klempner. It was one more sign of how topsy-turvy everything had become that they were actually glad he'd decided against it on the principle of separation of church and state. It bothered them that Tom had not shown up. Had Galen gotten to him already?

They stood in the hallway beside Buzzy's locker and speculated.

"I think he hit the highway last night and just kept going," Buzzy said.

"Like we should have done," offered Kent.

"Maybe we should have gone to that church thing," said Darren. Some of the kids had gone, knowing that whatever punishment they'd face for gypping would be slight. Some had ditched classes and the church service both. They began to dribble back in during lunch, finding that the tedium of school was matched only by the tedium of being nowhere, doing nothing.

"What are we afraid of?" Darren asked. "I mean, it's Galen. He's our friend. What's there to be scared of?"

"Haws came back, and he hasn't hassled us," said Kent.

"Right! And hell, we killed that bastard!"

"We didn't. Galen did. And look what happened to Galen."

"So what? He came back! It's like that play we read, where Death gets stuck in the tree or something."

"Yeah! I remember that!"

"Great retention, Kent. It was last week."

Kent gave Buzzy a shove for being a smartass and Buzzy muttered a word that sounded to Kent like "dumbshit" and Darren stepped in to keep things from getting ugly.

"This is no time for bullshit," he said. "We have to stick together."

"Then where's Tom?" Kent asked sullenly.

"Who gives a fuck where Tom is? He's probably halfway to Canada by now. The question is, what are we going to do? We can't go on ducking Galen for the rest of our lives."

"I just have to duck him for six months and then I'm outta here." Buzzy looked up to see the other two boys staring at him.

"What does that mean?" Darren asked.

Buzzy began to feel sheepish. "I mean once I graduate, I'm leaving town. I'm going to stay with my uncle for the summer, then I start school in the fall. I'm going to State."

"Jesus!" Darren said. It was first any of the boys had heard of Buzzy's college plans. Darren paced, chewing the news like a tough piece of meat. "It's all falling apart," he said. "It's all turning to shit."

"Why didn't you tell us?" Kent said.

"I just did."

"You had to know for months!"

"We just made the plans last week. I didn't know for sure before then." Buzzy was starting to get pissed. What did they think, that high school was going to last forever? That they'd all spend the rest of their days hanging around the reservoir smoking dope and lying about the sex they got?

"We have to see Galen," Darren said. "We need him. Everything goes to shit without him." He turned to Buzzy. "Last night you wanted to throw him a party. Now today you're ready to run him out of town."

"I didn't say that. Jesus! Maybe we should throw him a party. Maybe that's what we should do. I mean, if he'd come back from some war or something that's what we'd do, right?"

"Right," Kent said.

"Then that's it," Darren said. "We throw him a fucking party. After school, at the reservoir. Who has money for beer?"

Kent made a face as he dug into his pocket and pulled out a wad of ones, slapped the wad into Darren's palm. Buzzy did the same.

"Don't get the tall cans," Buzzy said. "They get hot before you finish."

"That's because you drink like a wuss. But okay, whatever Campus Joe wants."

"What about Tom?" Kent asked. "I mean, if he shows up?"

"If he shows and wants to kick in for the beer, he can come. Otherwise, fuck him."

"Man, I need a joint," said Kent.

Darren slipped a hand into his pocket and pulled out a reefer that looked like it'd gone through the wash. "Ten minutes to the bell," he said.

"I'm in," said Kent. "Buzzy?"

Buzzy waved it away. "I've got a test next period. Pass."

Darren angled a thumb at Buzzy and shook his head in puzzlement. "You see?" he said. "You see what I mean? It's just turning to shit."

He threw an arm around Kent and they headed for the parking lot. Buzzy watched them go. "Fuck you," he said quietly to Darren's back, "I'm getting out."

When the other boys were out of sight, Buzzy opened his locker, dug out his chemistry book, plopped to the floor and started to cram.

Outside, Galen stood at the chain link fence and watched Darren and Kent get in Darren's car. Darren and Kent would be the easy ones. Buzzy would be harder.

He'd deal last with Tom.

After the events of the night, Carl Tompkins was not eager to crawl under the house to check out the skeleton.

Contrary to Carl's belief at the time, Bernice had not slept entirely through the ordeal. She had swum her way into semi-consciousness as the cockroaches filled her throat and was dimly aware of her stomach heaving and of gasping for air that would not, would not, would not come. She had passed out without fully comprehending her situation.

Waking up, though, had been a full-blown nightmare for both of them. Their throats were still stuffed with roaches when they returned to life, and those roaches, too, had returned. Those that Carl had bitten in two or crushed between his teeth came back and fled from his mouth, although some fled the wrong direction and headed down instead of out. Carl and Bernice both vomited live cockroaches and cockroach parts onto the bedroom floor. Bernice fell out of bed, gagging and spitting, and Carl stood on all fours in the middle of the room doing the same.

Eventually the last roach was expelled and ran skittering for the woodwork. The process left a taste in their mouths that no amount of toothpaste and mouthwash would expunge, and then there was the mess to clean up. As they scrubbed the floor with soap and water, Carl and Bernice assured one another that the worst was over and finally headed downstairs. Bernice put on a pot of coffee and Carl got out the bourbon. They sat in the kitchen and talked about the man they met on the other side, the one who called himself "Seth," until they found themselves yawning, grainy-eyed, and went back to bed to catch a few winks.

The phone woke them at eight-forty-five. It was Doris Gunnarsen.

It was only when they pulled into the driveway after the service that Carl remembered the skeleton in the crawl space. He walked around to the back of the house. Before he reached the access hole he heard Groucho's unmistakable cry. Groucho peered at Carl from the other side of the panel, meowing plaintively. Carl pried the panel loose on one corner and Groucho squeezed through the opening and proceeded to rub one side and then the other against Carl's leg, meowing in gratitude and hunger.

Bernice, of course, was delighted at Groucho's rise and fixed him a special bowl of food since he had missed yesterday's feeding. The whir of the can opener summoned the other cats but Bernice kept them at bay while Groucho filled his empty belly.

Carl got out the flashlight and returned to the crawl space. He removed the access panel and pointed the light at the corner where the skeleton had lain. It was gone, as Carl expected it would be.

He went back inside and explained things as best he could to Bernice. Seth, it appeared, was a lover of animals, and Groucho had received his blessing right along with Carl and Bernice. And the cockroaches.

"Well, then," Bernice said, "I guess we know what needs to be done, don't we?" Carl nodded.

Bernice went back upstairs and changed into her old clothes. Then she put on her gardening gloves and gathered the cats for strangulation.

NINETEEN

Tom watched another page of *The Junction City Beacon* blur past on the microfilm reader.

From the outset, he and Brant had decided to limit themselves to front pages and the obituaries. Each had assembled a short list of Eloises, mainly from the obits, but few of them died of unnatural causes and not one of them came back. One Eloise had been murdered. The killer had been her husband and he'd been swiftly brought to justice. Another had died in an auto accident, and the others—there weren't many—passed away from cancer, heart disease, and, as Tom delved deeper into the past, in childbirth. His back hurt, his neck was stiff, and his stomach gurgled from too many Snickers bars, cheese curls and cans of soda. It occurred to him that in one day of reporting he'd picked up the ailments it had taken Brant a lifetime to assemble.

He leaned back in his chair and swiveled his neck and glanced over at Brant who was doing the same. They saw each other and smiled.

Tom looked at his watch. It was nearly three o'clock, which meant they'd been poring through old newspapers for over four hours and neither of them had found anything of note.

"Ready for a break?" Brant asked.

"I'm almost at the end of this spool," Tom replied. He sat up and twirled the little handle and confronted another

Beacon front page. A small headline caught his eye: Police Close Book on Eloise.

"Holy shit," he said aloud as he began reading.

"What?"

"Come here."

In a moment Brant was leaning over his shoulder and reading the short article along with him.

"Holy shit is right," Brant echoed. "Go back. Find the first report."

"Must be on another spool. I've been through this one."

"Get the previous year."

Minutes later Tom and Brant were staring at the headline that set their abused stomachs churning big time. Tom felt something cold climb up his spine and wrap itself around his heart.

SLAUGHTER IN ELOISE, it proclaimed, and the article began:

"Police are baffled by the murder overnight of all but two residents of the small town of Eloise. Forty-eight bodies were counted by police sent to investigate. The bodies were discovered early Tuesday morning. . . ."

"God," Tom said as he continued reading.

The article described a "tableau of death unparalleled in a civilian population during peacetime." Corpses were found in bedrooms, kitchens, porches and outhouses; in front of houses and behind; in cars; everywhere. Some had been murdered where they lay. Others seemed to have been killed elsewhere and deposited in a favorite chair or behind the wheel of a wrecked automobile.

"There was no sense to it," according to one frustrated policeman. "No sense at all. It was as if the whole town went mad. But even then, there are things about it that . . . I can't explain it. It doesn't make any sense."

The only hope for an explanation lay with the two survivors. One was a child, Irma Louise Pritchett, age five.

"I'll bet a dollar that was Irma Klempner's maiden name," offered Brant. "It says she was sent to stay with relatives, her own mother and father having been murdered. Her mother's throat was slashed, but they don't say what killed the father."

" 'Unknown causes,'" Tom read. "Poison, maybe. There wouldn't have been time for an autopsy before the story was written."

"Good guess," Brant said.

Irma had been found in a kitchen cabinet, hiding under the sink behind a tiny curtain of fabric, terrified. Police had had to crawl in and drag her out.

The other survivor and the only suspect in the case was Irma's older brother, Donald Adam Pritchett. Donald was eighteen years old. It was Donald who telephoned the police on Tuesday morning.

"What made him a suspect?" Tom asked.

"It only says he was behaving erratically. Maybe we'll learn more in later editions."

They did learn more as they followed the story through the pages of the *Beacon*.

Eloise, Unincorporated, was tiny, barely more than a collection of houses along the road that would later become the highway. No post office, no governing body, no schools. There was a bar and a church, both constructed during more optimistic times, both badly in need of repair. Not too far away, off the main road, there was a cemetery named "Wildwood."

Calling Eloise a "town" at all was like calling a patch of wild daisies a "garden." The house and the people were just there, with road signs on either end to inform travelers that they were entering and leaving something. The people who made up the population of Eloise were bound only by coincidence. Looking for a place to live, they stopped in the same vicinity, like pennies rolled down a sidewalk that happened to lose momentum and fall over in more-or-less the same spot.

Much of the population was black, slaves and their descendants who'd fled north within living memory and now worked on neighboring farms. Most of the people living in Eloise would be considered poor, but too many people were poor at that time for the word to carry any weight of special tragedy. The Pritchetts did all right, thanks to an oil well on their property, a modest producer that didn't make them rich but which allowed the purchase of an automobile and a few other niceties. It was a common sight, that of a well-head bobbing in the middle of a field of wheat or milo, but yields were marginal and no fortunes were being made as they were in boom states like Oklahoma and Texas.

Nature's bounty lay closer to the surface around Eloise, in the rich topsoil that farmers were only now, in the barest beginnings of the dust bowl years, wishing they'd done more to protect.

Maybe it was the wind and the drought that set the people of Eloise on a murderous rampage, though the true hardship had barely begun. A psychiatric authority labeled it a "mass psychotic episode." Even if Donald Pritchett had tried, he couldn't have murdered them all. In fact, there was no evidence that he'd killed anyone beyond the man he'd buried in Wildwood Cemetery outside of town, the one he'd buried alive.

The man's clothes were ripped as though he'd been stabbed several times, but his body, when it was exhumed, was completely intact. There was dried blood on his collar, a lot of blood, but no corresponding neck wound to account for it. It was as if he'd put on the clothes of a man who'd been stabbed to death, but what, other than insanity, would possess a man to do such a thing?

The only evident trauma was in the man's fingers and legs, and those were explained by his premature burial.

The flesh of the fingertips was scraped away and the nails all but ripped from their roots by his frantic clawing at the pine box Donald Pritchett had buried him in. The coffin had been built for a much smaller man, and Donald had had to break the man's legs to fit him inside.

Tissue samples were taken to test for poison. (Weeks later, the tests would come back negative.) Donald Pritchett insisted that he'd stabbed the man repeatedly, killing him, and that he'd risen to life inside the coffin. His account of the mass homicide in Eloise was similarly fantastic.

Due to overcrowding at the morgue, the man had been interred again before nightfall, buried in the same undersized box utilized by Donald Pritchett, broken legs and all. No one knew his name and, in the months following the slaughter, no one had identified him from the autopsy photos.

Donald was incarcerated, tried, found insane, and committed to a state-run facility.

His little sister, Irma Louise, was sent to live with an aunt and uncle in the town of Isaac.

The other bodies were identified and buried at Wildwood Cemetery. The houses were abandoned and eventually torn down, the road signs removed when the road was paved and widened, and the town of Eloise passed into history the same way it had come into being, without fanfare or ceremony, never inspiring a mark on any map.

Tom read the articles in the *Beacon* and felt as if he were gazing into a crystal ball. Change "Eloise" to "Anderson," bump up the numbers, and he could've been reading the epitaph of his own town.

He continued searching back, forsaking the front pages in favor of human interest articles that might hint at persons who'd come back from the dead. There was one, a farmhand who'd been struck by lightning. With the storm raging, his body had been carried into the barn where he was left until the weather cleared and the corpse could be properly disposed. His appearance at a farmhouse window in the wee hours of the morning had caused a pregnant woman's water to break and a child to be born a week early. Several hours later, all three patients . . . farmhand, mother and child . . . were doing fine.

That was less than a week before the Eloise slaughter.

Ripples, Tom thought, and he showed the article to Brant.

"There's a fable," Brant said, "about a peasant who saved a king's life. The king offered him a reward, and the peasant said that all he wanted was a gold coin today, and for his reward to be doubled every day for a month. The King agreed. By the end of the month the king owed the peasant half a billion gold coins."

"So the peasant took over the kingdom."

"Well, he was probably dragged out behind the castle and killed for being a smartass. But the same math would apply to Risen."

"If each Risen created another one, how many would you have in a week?"

Brant and Tom did some quick multiplying and came up with the number sixty-four.

"Of course," Brant observed, "there's no reason to limit each Risen to a single murder per day. If each one killed two or three, you'd accelerate the curve dramatically."

"Then, what stopped them in Eloise?" Tom asked. "They died on Tuesday. Why didn't they all come back on Wednesday?"

Tom and Brant arrived at the answer simultaneously.

"Donald Pritchett," they said, practically in unison.

Galen's welcome home party consisted of Galen, Darren, Kent and Buzzy, a twelve-pack of Bud and the last of Darren's grass, which was mainly stems, seeds, and recycled roaches.

"Jesus," Galen said, wincing and stifling a cough after his first toke, "you trying to kill me again or what?"

"Hey, how's the weed in hell?" Kent asked.

"Like Darren's," Buzzy said. "All the good dope's in Heaven."

Galen snickered.

Darren was relieved to see Galen's mood lightening up. He'd seemed pissed off when he met them at the school, yelling at him and Kent as they headed back in after getting high over lunch break. He said he'd been hanging out, walking around town and letting people get a good look at him. Hardly anybody spoke to him, he said, they just gawked and kept their distance, like he was some kind of freak.

"Which I guess I am," he said.

The boys didn't know what to say to that since it hit so close to home. If they could've, they'd have avoided Galen themselves. So they muttered something about what assholes people in this town were and hung around until after Buzzy's test. They convinced Buzzy to blow off the rest of the afternoon, popped the Buds, rolled a joint out of Darren's trash and headed for the reservoir.

Buzzy was glad to be getting high and drunk. The test had gone poorly, to say the least. He'd been sliding this semester and he knew it, getting high too much, not studying. He'd gotten into State on the basis of his junior year grades and now he was wondering if they'd change their minds when they received his final transcript. Then again, it was only a state university and not M.I.T. They took anybody with tuition and a pulse, at least for the first year. There was still time to turn himself around. He'd start first thing tomorrow.

"So," he said, "what's it like being dead?"

"It sucks," Galen replied, turning somber.

He described the crushing void and the monstrous sounds, the terrible wails of lost souls. He told them about wandering, hands stretched before him, feeling his way step by step through the relentless dark. He told them about kneeling down to touch the earth beneath his feet, and how it was coarse and sharp and left splinters like glass in his fingertips. He told about stepping into nothingness and falling, about sliding and tumbling down the lacerating rock until it seemed no shred of skin remained, yet how the wounds refused to bleed. Somehow he knew they would just as stubbornly refuse to heal.

Galen's eyes went blank as if again confronting that limitless night, and he told about staggering along after his fall, his exposed flesh screaming from a thousand cuts, pain shooting through a battered ankle. Tears burned their way down his ravaged cheeks and his cries joined those of the invisible damned he could sense but never find, hear but never touch.

He told of the stirring of a hot wind that parched his lips and cracked his skin and carried no scent of life. He talked of despair, of collapsing and writhing on the harsh, hot surface, consumed by pain and terror.

"I couldn't take it," he said. "I lost it completely. This was my future and it wasn't going to last for a year or even a hundred years. This was forever.

"And I knew that good and evil didn't have a fucking thing to do with it. I wasn't in Hell. There isn't any Hell, or Heaven either. There's just the void, and it's the same for everybody. Death is nothingness and pain and loneliness, and it's eternity. Once you die, that's where you go."

"How do you know?" Kent asked.

Galen paused. "Because," he said, "that's what Seth teaches us."

Seth, Galen explained, was a rebel. "He rebelled against

death and the eternal void by restoring life to those who had died. For this sin he was cast out and made to wander the earth. He lives in two worlds, on earth and in the void, and with each soul he rescues he becomes stronger. He is our life and we are his!"

"Where was he cast out from?" Buzzy asked.

"What?" Galen said irritably.

"You said he was cast out, but you said there wasn't any Heaven, so where was he cast out from?"

"How the fuck should I know? Listen . . . I've been there! I've seen this place! It is not where you want to spend eternity, right? I've met Seth. He gave me my life back! He took a fucking pile of ashes and . . ." Galen thumped his chest. "Look! Believe the evidence of your own fucking eyes!"

Buzzy persevered.

"So everything they taught us is wrong," he said. "Everything about God and Jesus and Heaven and Hell and all that, it's all wrong."

Galen paced.

"Look," he said, trying to keep the anger and impatience out of his voice and coming up instead with an ominous monotone, "I'm telling you what happened. This isn't out of some book written by some guy a million years ago and handed down and translated and fucked up and sold to the masses to pump the plastic Jesus business. This is real!"

He closed on Buzzy, backing him against the fender of his Vega.

"Have I tried to sell you anything?" Galen asked. "Have I asked you for money? Am I getting something out of this? I'm trying to bring you the fucking truth and you're standing here telling me I'm full of shit! I came back from the dead, motherfucker!"

"I know! I was there!" Buzzy said. "It was freakin' weird,

man, and I'm having a little trouble getting my head around it, okay? I'm just trying to understand!"

"What is there to understand? I told you everything you need to know! Beyond that. . . ." Galen shrugged. "Beyond that, all you can do is experience it."

Darren and Kent exchanged looks that said He can't mean . . . and I think he does . . . and Holy shit, we're ass-deep in it this time.

Buzzy looked to Darren and Kent for assurance that Galen didn't mean what they all knew he meant.

"Yeah, you got it," Galen said, looking from one down-turned face to the next. "You've got to make the journey, my friends. You've got to make the farthest journey." He opened his arms and said, "It's the only way to fly."

"Forget it," Buzzy said, extricating himself from between Galen and the fender. He took a long draw on his beer and turned his back to the group.

"Fine," Galen said. "No skin off my ass. Enjoy the void, pal." And he went to work on Darren and Kent.

TWENTY

Maybe it was the beers. Maybe it was as simple as that.

The beers, and the flask of Jim Beam that had mysteriously appeared from Galen's back pocket after they'd polished off the twelve-pack.

They were plastered, for sure, and the needle on the Vega's speedometer blurred in and out of focus as Buzzy stared at it. Buzzy couldn't make out the numbers clearly but the needle was way over to the right and he could feel the wheel shake in his hands as the car barreled down the highway.

He looked over at Galen and Galen grinned back at him. How'd he let Galen talk him into this?

"Immortality," Galen had said to Darren and Kent. Buzzy stood apart from the group but he stayed within earshot. "Immortality, not just of the spirit, but of the body as well. That's what Seth offers, pure and simple. I am the living, walking, talking, drinking, belching, farting proof. I have cheated Death.

"All of those people out there," he'd said, gesturing toward town, "living their little lives, working their work . . . they're doomed. Doomed to the void. God won't save them. Jesus won't save them. Buddha and Mohammed won't save them. Only one person can save them from an eternity of night. Seth.

"Seth walks among us, right here in little ol' Anderson

U.S.A. He is here and he will save us from death, but we have to meet him halfway. He can't do it all. We have to show him that we believe in him and trust him to help us."

"How do we do that?" Darren had asked, and Galen had said, "Die." He opened his hands and strutted in front of the boys like a prosecuting attorney. "That's all. Just die. Doesn't matter how."

"How about old age?" Buzzy had said, wandering back to the others.

Galen glared at him. "Go ahead, make jokes about it. Laugh it off. Wuss out any way you want to. Be like Culler and run out of town with your tail between your legs."

The boys started, and Galen smiled at them. "Did you think I didn't notice? He wasn't at the service, he wasn't in school. I called his house, there was nobody there. It's okay. Some people can't handle it. They'll miss out. Too bad for them."

Galen wrapped an arm around Darren and another around Buzzy, drawing them close. It was more like a wrestling hold than an embrace.

"But you're my buds. I'm not going to let you miss it. We're all for one, right? Right?"

"I don't know," Buzzy said, extricating himself. "Suppose it doesn't work."

Galen looked at him in disbelief.

"Look at me," Galen commanded. He held up his arms, turned around in a full circle. "I was dead. Hell, I was fucking cremated, and I came back!" He leaned in close to Buzzy, intimidating. "Impossible, isn't it? Can't happen. But here I am. It fucking works!"

Galen calmed down and spoke confidentially, drawing the boys in. "Let me tell you something. There are forces in this world so powerful, we can't even comprehend. We're like an ant standing on the railroad track. Along comes a train and wham! He never knows what hit him. That train is so much more powerful, it isn't even funny.

"Seth is that train. And either you're on board, or you're that ant."

And that's how it had gone for the next hour. Galen had orated and proclaimed, he'd brow-beaten them, he'd pulled out the whiskey and gotten them drunk, and somehow he'd convinced them all, even Buzzy, that the best thing in the world they could do on that particular, deepening afternoon was to kill themselves.

Bringing them to this moment, in two cars racing down the highway with the pedal mashed to the floor, straddling the center line.

Galen was all smiles. Buzzy looked at him but couldn't bring him into focus. Galen reached over and steadied the wheel, keeping Buzzy on course. Darren and Kent hadn't come into view yet. Maybe they never would. Maybe, once they were away from Galen's spell, they'd drive off and just keep going.

No. There they were, coming over the rise. Darren's Satellite crested the hill, wheels on either side of the center line. It looked like a slot car, and Buzzy remembered how he and Darren had played with Buzzy's slot car set when they were kids, sticking two cars in the same slot, rear bumpers touching, and then they'd squeeze the throttle and watch the cars race around the track doomed to the inevitable collision.

They'd blown up a lot of stuff together. Half the fun of building a model airplane was the M80 they'd pack inside, fuse sticking out. Then they'd hang the airplane in a tree, dangling on strings, and light the fuse and run backwards so they'd be sure to see it when it blew. Model planes, model ships, model cars . . . all met the same fate through one means or another. Buzzy figured it was some kind of gene that the male of the species possessed, the "pyrotechnic gene" that gave them such delight in anything explosive. So common was that gene, it's a wonder every boy in America didn't grow up to be a demolition expert.

Now the game had become real. The cars sped along a real highway with real people inside who would die real deaths. So why did this veil of unreality hang over every moment? Why did the whole thing feel like a dream? Denial, probably, or Jim Beam.

I can always pull out, Buzzy thought. It was the comforting lie that kept his foot on the accelerator and the wheel pointed straight ahead. I can chicken out, swerve and miss, and they'll call me a coward all the time they're thanking their lucky stars that I did it. And I won't give a shit. Six months from now, this'll all be a memory, a story I'll tell my college friends.

Darren was flashing his lights at him. Buzzy fumbled for the switch and gave it a couple of yanks.

In the other car, Darren saw Buzzy's Vega toeing the line a half mile ahead. He flashed his lights and Buzzy flashed back. He'll wimp out, Darren thought. It wasn't like Buzzy to go through with something like this. Especially now, when he was going away and everything.

Darren glanced over at Kent. It looked like Kent was ready to climb out the window, he was so scared. They were all pretty fucked up but not so much that they didn't know what they were doing.

Darren was intrigued by Galen's story about death and the void and the man who promised them eternal life, but he didn't know if he believed it. Galen was living proof, but proof of what? That something incredible had happened. The rest could've been a dream or a hallucination, or maybe Galen wasn't Galen at all but some demon from Hell come back to lure them all to their deaths. Shit! That was a new thought!

He eased back on the accelerator to give himself a few

seconds to consider this. Problem was, his brain wasn't working too good right now. Neither were his eyes or his hands or his feet. He slowed down more than he meant to and the car lurched and Kent looked over and asked him what was wrong.

"Nothing," Darren said, and he mashed the pedal to the floor. Buzzy wouldn't go through with it. If Tom had been here, it never would've gotten this far. He'd have stood up to Galen and not been talked into anything. Where the hell was Tom, anyway?

The Vega was getting close. Darren's hands were slick with sweat. The wheel vibrated like crazy but Darren slipped one hand off and rubbed it on his jeans. Then he dried the other one. He wondered if Kent noticed his nervousness and looked over, but Kent wasn't noticing anything except the floor. He held his head in his hands.

Darren said, "Hey, if you're going to—" but the warning came too late. Vomit gushed out of Kent's mouth and soaked the floor mats.

"Shit!" Darren said as Kent continued to heave. He started to yell at Kent that he was the one who'd clean that mess up, and then he thought, Nobody's cleaning it up, not unless Buzzy comes through. Puke on the floor mats would be the least of Darren's worries if Buzzy didn't pull out. Still, he hated to die with the stink of Kent's vomit in his nose.

The front seat drama had distracted Darren for a few seconds and he'd let the Satellite wander. He looked up and was amazed at how close the Vega was, how the gap between them had narrowed so quickly. He made a fast course correction and was once more bound for glory. Or whatever.

Buzzy watched Darren's Satellite get closer and closer. The dreamlike veil disappeared and Buzzy's mind screamed at him: This is real! The onrushing car meant the end of everything, absolutely everything. No school, no girls, no cars. Images flashed through his mind of corpses and stainless steel tables and trocars and formaldehyde pumped through tubes, and he saw himself on the that table, slit open, organs scooped out, and Jed Grimm bending over him, applying rouge to his cheeks and paint to his lips, his parents looking down on his body in the coffin, his mother crying, and him lying there with barbed wire in his mouth and rubber forms under his skin, eyelids sewn shut, a look molded on his face of sweet repose, as if he were dreaming of angels.

You should be so lucky, his mind said. They'll wash you out of this wreck with a hose.

Darren watched Buzzy's Vega close in fast and couldn't believe that Buzzy hadn't pulled over. Kent watched out the windshield in helpless fascination, like a mouse hypnotized by a snake. He watched death bear down on him and he was as sure as he'd ever been about anything that he'd made the stupidest mistake of his life. How did he let himself get talked into this? His dad was right, he did have shit for brains. As the Vega ate up the road between them, all Kent could think was shit!

Buzzy glanced over at Galen. Galen knew what he was thinking, that he was thinking about swerving. Galen glared at him as if beaming strength of will into Buzzy's brain, freezing Buzzy's hands on the wheel, his foot to the floor. There was no way Buzzy was turning that wheel. He was in it to the end, to the ever-loving, ass-kicking end. He pulled his eyes away from Galen and focused on the Satellite, on the headlights Darren had left on, and he watched them get bigger and bigger as the highway between the two cars vanished.

Darren's mind screamed at Buzzy's to swerve. He was cutting it too close! Turn, damn it, turn! What in the fuck are you waiting for?

Kent couldn't take it anymore. He lunged at the wheel

and yanked it hard and it slid under Darren's sweaty fingers. The Satellite swerved hard to the right and there was the crying of tires and then the car was perpendicular to the road and going too fast and suddenly it was rolling, rolling, still on course, hugging the center line as metal crunched and glass shattered and it rolled toward the oncoming Vega.

Buzzy stared at the car rolling at him along the highway like the blades of a combine. The Satellite bounced and for one crazy instant Buzzy thought it might bounce right over the Vega's roof and on down the highway like a tumbleweed. Then the cars crashed in a terrible cry of metal and an explosion of glass, and death came so quickly that no one knew it.

And no one in either car saw the fireball shoot into the sky so gloriously and so vividly orange against the blue sky, roaring and tumbling, soaring into the heavens, rising on a column of black smoke that was visible for miles.

"Old Donny won't give you any trouble, Doctor," the orderly said. "The state cut him up pretty good before they sent him here."

"When was that?" Brant asked, amazed as always at how easy it was to claim credentials you didn't have. He and Tom and the orderly walked through the minimum security ward of the Greenhaven Convalescent Center. Few of the residents of Greenhaven were "convalescing" in the sense that they were getting better. "Greenhaven Storage Facility" would have been more accurate.

"Fifty years, give or take," replied the orderly. "Electric shock, lobotomy, drug therapy . . . Donny's been through it all. Every fad, every cure-all, Donny's been there. In the sixties they had him tripping out on LSD, can you believe that?"

Tom kept a wary eye on the inmates who stared at him

as he passed. One woman approached him and grabbed his arm and stroked it. "My boy," she said. She said it over and over while looking up at Tom's face. "My boy, my boy." At first glance Tom had thought she was a much older woman, but when he looked her in the eyes he realized that she was not much, if any, older than his own mother.

The orderly pulled her away gently but firmly.

"He's not your boy, Grace," he told her.

"My boy," Grace insisted forlornly, and Tom almost wished he was her son who, the orderly explained, had died in infancy fifteen years earlier.

"Grace is something else," the orderly said as they continued without incident down the corridor. "Usually if they've lost a child like that, they won't think about them getting older. If they lost, say, a three-year-old, they might develop a fascination with three-year-olds. Not Grace, though. She follows the years. Her boy keeps getting older. He really is alive in her mind. Here we are."

The orderly knocked on a closed door but didn't wait for a response. He opened the door without a key, revealing an old man inside on a hard wooden chair, rocking his body and humming a tune that neither Brant nor Tom could quite make out.

"Donald? You have visitors." The orderly turned to Brant and said, "Give him a little while to get used to you. Nobody visits old Donny much anymore. He doesn't have any family. Well, a sister, but she ought to be here, too, from what I hear. I guess it runs in the family. He's okay, though. Like I said, they messed him up pretty good."

Brant noticed the scar left from a frontal lobotomy performed circa 1936.

"Donald?" Brant said. Donald Pritchett didn't respond. Brant and Tom moved closer. "My name is Brant Kettering. This is Tom Culler. We'd like to talk with you for a few minutes."

Donald Pritchett continued rocking and humming softly. Brant looked at the orderly standing in the doorway. "Can he answer questions?"

The orderly shrugged. "In his way. I think he understands more than he lets on."

Brant moved around to face Pritchett directly, bending down to try to make eye contact with the old man.

"Donald, this is very important to us. I need to ask you some questions. Do you understand me?"

There was no response. Brant put one knee on the floor to kneel in front of Pritchett and look into his eyes. They seemed to stare at some point miles, or perhaps decades, away. He hummed quietly, a tune that faded in and out.

"I came here from Anderson. Something very strange is happening there. It's something I think you know about." Brant glanced at the orderly leaning in the doorway. If he pushed Pritchett too far and he became upset, the orderly would order them out. He had to proceed cautiously, and yet, there was so little time. Who knew what might be going on in Anderson?

"It's like what happened in Eloise," Brant said.

If the name meant anything special to Pritchett, he gave no sign. Brant continued.

"Some people have died. But Donald . . ." he shot another quick glance at the orderly. "They didn't stay dead. They came back."

Donald Pritchett stopped rocking, stopped humming. His eyes remained focused on whatever distant sight they beheld, but Brant knew that he had the old man's attention.

"We think this is what happened in Eloise. There was a man who was struck by lightning. Everyone thought he was dead. But he came back, didn't he? Were there others, Donald? Others who came back?"

Pritchett's mouth tightened. His eyes narrowed.

Tom saw the orderly, who had been leaning against the door jamb, straighten and scowl.

"What is this?" the orderly began, and Tom stepped forward.

"Please," Tom said. "I know this sounds crazy, but it's very important."

"Is that what happened sixty years ago?" Brant asked Pritchett. "First, they come back. Then . . . what?"

Pritchett worked his lips and finally a single word came out. "Come," he whispered.

Brant leaned in closer.

"Come," Pritchett said, louder this time, and then he said the word again, drawing it out like a mantra: "Come."

"Come where, Donald?" Brant asked. He glanced over at the scowling orderly. He saw that Tom had placed himself between the orderly and himself. If Pritchett became agitated and the orderly tried to intervene, Tom could hold him off for a few precious seconds. Those seconds might provide the clue they needed.

Pritchett's lips moved slightly, mouthing words he seemed to hear in his head. Brant put his ear close to Pritchett's mouth. He could feel the old man's breath, and he realized that Pritchett was singing. The tempo was all wrong, drawn out like a record played too slowly, but Brant could make out the words.

". . . church in the wildwood. . . ." Pritchett sang.

Brant sat back.

"What is it?" Tom asked.

Brant stood, wincing at the stiffness in his ankles and knees.

"He's singing 'Little Brown Church,'" Brant said. "That's the hymn they were singing last Sunday. 'Come to the church in the wildwood, come to the church in the dale. . . .'"

"I remember," Tom said.

"I think you two should go now," the orderly said.

"Look, I know how this must appear," Brant said, "like we should be checking ourselves in at the front door. But the fact is—"

Tom interrupted. "We think this delusion Pritchett has about people returning from the grave is at the heart of his psychosis," he said.

Brant was impressed. He'd almost blown it by starting to level with the orderly about the goings-on in Anderson. If he had, of course, they'd have been hustled to the nearest exit. Tom had instinctively known better, and he'd come up with a plausible lie that would sit better with the orderly than anything as unbelievable as the truth. The kid had a future as a reporter.

"We're trying to develop rapport through a shared delusion," Brant said, lowering his voice to a conspiratorial level.

"You understand," Tom said confidently.

"Uh-huh," the orderly said.

"I must've sounded like a nut case!" said Brant.

"You probably thought we were crazy."

"Yeah, you had me going there for a minute," the orderly said.

"I just have a few more questions for Mr. Pritchett. Do you mind?"

The orderly shook his head. "I guess after all he's been through, a few crazy questions won't hurt."

Brant smiled and thanked him, then he sat on the bed opposite Pritchett. Pritchett's voice had gone silent and he was rocking again, slowly, in time to the tune in his head.

"Donald," Brant said. "There was a man. He lived in Eloise, but he wasn't like the others. Do you know the man I'm talking about?"

Pritchett appeared not to hear.

"He was different. Special. You . . . you buried him."

"Come, come, come, come," Pritchett intoned, "Come to the church in the wildwood. . . ."

"Do you know the man I'm talking about? You buried him, but they say he wasn't dead."

"Come to the church. . . ." Pritchett sang loudly.

"They say you buried him alive."

Louder: ". . . in the vale!"

The orderly stepped forward. Tom blocked his path, putting a hand on the man's chest.

"Wait! This is the breakthrough we were hoping for!"

The orderly glared, but he took a step back.

"He wasn't alive, was he, Donald? He was dead when you buried him. But he came back."

"No spot is so dear. . . ." Pritchett sang. His head trembled. Brant could see the pounding of Pritchett's heart in the veins of his neck, pulsing under the thin skin.

"Was he the one responsible for Eloise?"

". . . to my childhood. . . ."

"Was he responsible for the slaughter?"

Pritchett's eyes bored into the past and his voice cracked with emotion. The words poured out with anger, with a vehemence born of outrage and loathing.

". . . as the little brown church in the vale!" he sang, shouting the words, his sunken chest heaving, his voice hoarse with effort.

"Is that why you killed him, Donald," Brant persisted, "and then buried him so he couldn't come back?"

"That's it!" the orderly announced. He shoved his way past Tom and grabbed Brant by the arm. "You're out of here! Come on!"

Brant let himself be hauled to his feet but he didn't take his eyes off Donald Pritchett.

"It's happening again, Donald!" he said. "In Anderson! You have to help us! What do we do to stop it?"

"I said that's enough!"

The orderly dragged Brant toward the door. Tom rushed in to take his place in front of Donald Pritchett. He bent down and took the old man's hands. He spoke quietly but with urgency.

"Tell us, Donald! How do we stop it?"

Pritchett's eyes moved, locked onto Tom's. Tom saw that the pupils were dilated with . . . what? Fear?

"Seth!" Pritchett said with a sudden clarity that took Tom by surprise. "Kill Seth!"

"Who's Seth?" Tom asked frantically as his side vision registered the orderly's form closing on him.

Tom felt strong hands on his arm as he was yanked to his feet and propelled toward the door in a flurry of profanity. His last view of Donald Pritchett was over the orderly's shoulder as the orderly shoved him into Brant and forced both of them into the hallway, cursing steadily.

He saw that Pritchett had curled one bony hand into a fist. The tendons stood out on his thin forearm as he shook the fist, beat it against his leg.

"Kill Seth!" Pritchett shouted as loudly as his aging lungs could manage. "Kill Seth!"

"Where are we going?"

"Wildwood Cemetery."

The sun had been going down as the two security guards escorted Brant and Tom to the parking lot of the Greenhaven Convalescent Center. Now, as they raced back toward Anderson, the sky was on fire with a glorious sunset that spread all around the horizon from west to east. It was a spectacle so grand, it demanded a keen and profound appreciation. Though he'd witnessed such sunsets many times before, Tom couldn't take his eyes off the sky. Was this the last awe-inspiring sunset he would see? Did Risen appreciate such

things even more than the living, for having seen the other
side?

"Seth," Brant said, shattering Tom's reverie. "That's a
Biblical name?"

"I suppose." The overwrought synapses of his brain re-
connected. A memory leaped forward. "It's Egyptian," Tom
said. "Seth. Set. All the Egyptian gods had a dozen names."

"Who was Seth?"

"Bad news. I think he was the god of chaos or evil or
something. He tore out somebody's eye and got castrated
for it."

"So, we're looking for a ball-less ancient Egyptian
deity."

"Or somebody who gets his power from Seth, or someone who named himself after Seth, or maybe it doesn't
mean squat."

"Whoever Seth is," Brant said, "his powers are limited.
Donald Pritchett, at the age of eighteen, was able to kill
him, to stab him to death apparently."

"For what it was worth. Apparently he came back, probably at midnight. He couldn't get out of the coffin, and so
he suffocated to death."

"And without him, the Risen of Eloise lost their ability
to defy death. They dropped where they were, though
they'd been killed hours or days earlier."

"That would definitely baffle the police," Tom observed. "They'd look for murder weapons and signs of
struggle that could've been miles away and cleaned up by
then."

"But the wounds on the bodies would be fresh. The
murders would appear to have happened simultaneously
all over town, but they could've taken place days earlier.
The police would have been looking for one impossibly
active killer, or for an extremely sudden and widespread
outbreak of murderous mass hysteria."

"I wonder. . . ." Tom began, his voice trailing off.

"Yeah?"

"About Seth. When he woke up inside the coffin and wore his fingers to the bone scratching to get out, was it just that one time? Or did it happen over and over? Did he come back every midnight for sixty years until he finally wore through the coffin and dug his way up through the earth?"

"That's what we need to find out at Wildwood," Brant said.

"We should just go home."

"Cemetery's on the way."

The sun went down while Tom thought about waking every night to find yourself entombed. It was truly a fate worse than death. Did Donald Pritchett realize the hell he was sentencing Seth to when he buried him at Wildwood Cemetery? He must have. That thought alone was enough to drive anyone insane. The guilt. . . .

Brant asked Tom to check the map. "In the glove box," he said. "There's a little flashlight in there, too."

Tom dug out the map and unfolded it.

"What am I looking for?" he asked, refolding the map to their section of the highway and scrutinizing it under the flashlight's beam.

"There should be a road on our left that leads to the cemetery."

"Just ahead. Half a mile or so."

They drove the distance in silence. The road appeared and Brant slowed for the turn. As the headlights swung around they splashed a large, almost billboard-sized sign.

Brant backed up to toss the lights back on the sign.

Future Home of the Coyote Creek Power Facility read the headline, and there was an architectural drawing of a domed generating station, the nuke plant.

Brant drove on down the road until he encountered a

twelve-foot chain link fence and a security check point. They'd missed shift change for the construction workers and the guard had a moment to talk.

"The cemetery?" he said. "Shoot, they moved that when they cleared the site. Moved it over to Landon County."

Brant gave the guard his thanks and turned around. He drove back down the access road, shot a glance over at Tom and found the boy looking at him grimly.

"So Seth didn't have to dig himself out," Tom said. "The electric company did it for him."

"What about the people of Eloise?" Brant said. "Did they come back when he did?"

"If so, you'd think it would make the paper."

"You'd think."

"Maybe that's another limit on his abilities."

"Could be. My guess is, he left them for someplace new."

"Anderson."

"Anderson," Brant echoed, and there didn't seem to be anything more to say for the next several miles.

They'd discovered what they set out to find. Whatever was going on in Anderson had happened before, sixty years earlier in the tiny community of Eloise. It was the work of a man named "Seth," and to put an end to it, they had to find Seth and kill him . . . and worse. It could be done—Donald Pritchett had done it—but Seth would certainly have learned from experience. He wouldn't be so easy to catch this time. Maybe they shouldn't even try. Maybe they should grab Peg and Annie and run, get out of town and hope they found someone of authority they could tell their story to, someone who wouldn't write them off as a bunch of hysterical crazies who belonged in the Greenhaven Convalescent Center.

"Oh, Christ!" Brant said.

"What?"

"I just thought—remember what Madge Duffy said about John, about his bursitis being gone after his rise?"

"Yeah."

"The last time I saw Doc Milford, he wasn't limping. He's a damn Risen."

"Mom would need his okay to move Annie. She's talked to him."

"They know what we're planning to do."

Tom stared out the side window at the passing fields and turned these thoughts over in his head.

The sky was inky dark under the barest sliver of new moon as they approached the city limits. Brant slowed, then eased over to the shoulder and coasted to a halt.

"Shit," he said, and he cut the engine and the headlights.

Tom poked his head out of the side window to peer into the darkness. Ahead of them, across the turn-off, were flashing lights and a police barricade.

"They've sealed off the town," Brant said.

TWENTY-ONE

"I love you, Franz," Irma said.

She lay spread-eagled on the bed, her hands and feet tied to the bedposts. Franz had not gagged her, knowing she wouldn't scream. She didn't want to draw attention to herself any more than Franz did.

Franz hustled around the room, packing a bag, trying not to listen.

"That's the only thing that's stayed the same through it all," she continued. "When we were young, I thought you were the handsomest man I'd ever seen. You could call it infatuation, I suppose, but it felt like love to me. I couldn't believe you wanted to marry me. I was afraid of you on our wedding night, did you know that?

"I don't know what I expected. For you to hit me, I guess. If I'd had money, I'd think you were marrying me for it, but I was poor as a church mouse. I couldn't imagine. . . .

"But you were so gentle and patient, so kind. You are the kindest man, Franz. Oh, I've seen you bluster and I know you're stubborn as an old blind mule, but your heart is grand. Even when the sickness moved in and I felt so confused in my mind, I loved you. I couldn't say the words or show it in any way, but the feeling was always there. You made me feel safe.

"I love you now, Franz. You think I don't, you think I'm some kind of monster, but I'm not. I'm clear-headed for

the first time in ages. I've made the farthest journey, Franz.
I've been to infinity. Seth was there and he healed me, and
he sent me back to bring the joy of his love to you. I would
never hurt you, you have to believe that.

"Can't you believe me, Franz? I love you. I love you so
much."

Franz snapped the suitcase shut and headed for the door.
He glanced at Irma and saw the tears streaming down her
cheeks.

"Please don't leave me like this," she pleaded. "Don't let
someone find me like this. Untie me. I won't try to stop
you. You can't get away. They'll stop you. But don't leave
me like this. Please, Franz. Please."

Against the wall, a bedspread covered Elmer's body.
Blood stained the floor, the knife lay under the bed where
Franz had thrown it. His leg burned from the gash Irma had
made in his calf, and every breath he drew reminded him of
his cracked ribs, one of which had saved his life. He'd felt
battered and sore before his fight with Irma, and now he was
limping from the leg wound, imperfectly bandaged, and his
mind was in a fog. His body went through the motions of
packing while images assaulted him from the mist, appear-
ing before his eyes like hallucinations, too alien to be real.

Irma descending on him with the knife.

His fist knocking her unconscious.

His hands tying her to the bed.

Images of Irma screaming with the night terrors, of
Elmer spinning across the floor, of the Ganger boy's car
hurtling at him down the highway, of the boy's face at the
moment of impact, grinning like a madman.

He stood in the doorway with his suitcase in one hand,
the other hand on the knob, and felt the blood pound in his
temples. He had to get away and leave the madness behind.
He had lived with madness for too many years and he
could not take any more.

He closed the bedroom door behind him. Irma continued to plead with him to cut her free, her voice rising behind the closed door. Only after the door was shut did Franz remember the shotgun in the bedroom closet. "They'll stop you," she had said.

He didn't know if he could stand to go back into that room. He didn't know if he could stand looking at Irma again.

They'll stop you.

He twisted the door knob and saw Irma's face brighten with hope as he entered. Her mouth curled into a smile and she spoke his name with such warmth, such love, that it made a lump rise in his throat. He looked away from her and strode to the closet. He looked away, but not fast enough to miss the disappointment and the hurt in his wife's eyes.

He hated himself for what he was doing, as if he was walking out on her when she needed him the most. He had to remind himself that she'd try to kill him. She'd tried before, that Friday night when she rose with the night terrors and he'd found her in the kitchen, terrified out of her wits, and she'd come at him with the knife. It was madness then and it was madness now, but this new madness was worse. It was a quiet and seductive kind that would wrap itself around him and pull him in if he didn't fight it with every ounce of strength and will.

His hand closed around the barrel of the shotgun. He drew it out of the closet and reached up to the shelf for the box of shells.

He tried not to look at Irma as he walked back through the room. She had gone silent, perhaps in fear. She didn't say a word as he closed the door and marched out of the house he'd lived in for forty-seven years, leaving it, if need be, forever.

He threw his suitcase into the back of the pickup and limped around to the driver's side. He tossed the shotgun

on the seat and climbed in. It felt odd, not having Elmer
at his heels barking to go along. It felt wrong. Everything
felt wrong.

Pain shot through his leg as he depressed the clutch and
twisted the key in the ignition. He manipulated the choke
with sweaty fingers. The engine cranked and sputtered and
coughed to life. He let it warm up while he loaded the
shotgun, then he pulled onto the dirt road that led to the
highway.

The truck bounced along the road. Franz felt every
bump as a sharp rush of pain in his battered ribs. Tears
welled in his eyes. He wiped them on his sleeve and kept
driving.

He wasn't sure where he was going, but he had a cousin
who lived a couple hundred miles across state, maybe he
would go there. Maybe he would just hit the highway and
drive and keep driving until it got dark. His eyes didn't
work so well at night, so he'd stop at the first motel he came
to after the sun went down. It was mid-afternoon, which
gave him a good four hours of driving time. He thought
about stopping in town to draw some money out of the
bank, but there was no way he was going into Anderson,
not after what the reporter had told him. There are others,
he'd said. But he didn't know how many. Deputy Haws was
one. There could be dozens.

Irma had known what was going on. Deep in her madness, she knew that evil had come to Anderson. She heard
it tolling the bell at midnight, and she saw it in her dreams.
She saw it that night in the kitchen when she raised the
knife against Franz, but he himself had been blind to it. It
was his own fault that things had gone this far.

Franz crested a small rise that gave him a view of the
highway a quarter mile ahead. He saw red and blue flashing lights—a police car blocking the road where it met the
highway.

They'll stop you.

He reached over and picked up the shotgun and placed it on his lap.

Sheriff Clark was waiting at the end of the road. Ditches on either side kept Franz from driving around him at any speed faster than a crawl. He had to either bluff or shoot his way through. He moved the shotgun close to the door where Clark wouldn't see it.

"Afternoon, Franz," Clark said amiably.

"What's the problem, Sheriff?" asked Franz.

"Well, I might be asking you the same question. Everything okay?"

Franz nodded and tried to think of a reasonable lie. "Irma needs her medicine," he said.

"Medicine?" Clark seemed skeptical. "Pretty incredible about Irma. People coming back from the dead. Who'd have thought such a thing would happen right here in Anderson? It's a miracle."

"Call it what you will. Now are you going to let me by, or—"

Clark shook his head. "Can't do it, Franz. Tell you what, though. I'll have my deputy bring you that medicine. Just tell me what it is, and I'll have him bring it out to you. If you really need it."

"I didn't haul myself out of a sick bed to—"

"You're a terrible liar, Franz. That's what comes of sixty years of honest labor . . . you lose the ability to bullshit when you need it most."

Clark nodded toward the bed of the truck.

"You want to explain that suitcase?"

Franz fingered the shotgun at his side. Could he raise it and fire before the Sheriff drew his revolver? It would be awkward raising it and swinging it around, clearing the steering wheel, pointing it out the window. . . .

"I think you'd better get out, Franz," Sheriff Clark said,

and he yanked open the door. Clark saw the shotgun and immediately his hand slid to his hip, going for his pistol. Franz swung the shotgun around with his left hand and reached for the trigger with his right. Pain shot up through his chest as he twisted around, courtesy of his abused ribs. He winced and cried out, and his moment's hesitation gave Clark the fraction of a second he needed to get the drop on him.

Sheriff Clark's revolver shot twice and blood spattered the cab of Franz' truck. Franz fell back in the seat and lay there, one hand still curled around the shotgun, his eyes wide and his mouth hanging open as if in surprise.

Clark scowled at Franz Klempner's body and sighed. Converting Franz was supposed to be Irma's job. He was just there to keep out the curious and the well-wishers. He wondered what went wrong and decided he'd better drive up to the house and see, but he couldn't spend much more time out here. He had things to do.

They would be needing him at the roadblock.

Doc Milford knocked softly on the door to Annie's hospital room.

Peg looked up and smiled a sad, pretty smile. She was stroking Annie's hand, playing with the tiny fingers.

"I trimmed her nails this morning," Peg said. "Her hair is next." She brushed the bangs out of Annie's eyes. "I used to let my bangs grow when I was her age, and I'd scream bloody murder when my mother tried to cut them. She'd say, 'I want to see your pretty face.' Now I know how she felt. I could sit here for hours just looking at Annie's face."

"'A hundred years should go to praise thine eyes, and on thy forehead gaze,'" Doc quoted as he entered. "'Had we but world enough, and time.'"

"That's a poem of seduction. We studied it in school."

"Love is love, though, isn't it? There's a physicality to it that's part of being human. Cooing and cuddling, stroking, caressing. We've known for fifty years that babies fail to thrive without touch. But look at us now, what we've become. Grade school teachers afraid to hug a pupil. The old baby-on-a-bearskin-rug photo will land you in jail. I counseled a father the other week who felt guilty holding his four-year-old daughter in his lap."

"What did you tell him?"

Doc sighed as he pulled up a plastic chair. "Oh, some blather. No, it isn't child abuse to stroke your child's hair. You aren't a pervert for loving the scent of your baby or the feel of his skin when you rub lotion on his bottom. There are lines you don't cross. But intimacy is part of raising a child, isn't it? You would know better than I, Peg."

"You had a child once. A boy."

Doc nodded. "So briefly. These days they could've saved him, but back then . . . well. I guess in more ways than one, he was just born too soon."

"It's the hardest thing, losing a child," Peg said.

"Nothing harder," Doc agreed.

They watched Annie, asleep in her tangle of tubes and wires. Minutes ticked by in which neither of them spoke.

Finally Doc said, "You were at the service this morning."

"Uhm-hm."

"Quite something."

"Uhm."

"Peg—"

"Don't say it." Peg held up a hand. "I've been sitting here all day thinking about it. It's all I can think about. If John Duffy can rise, and Irma Klempner . . . Galen Ganger, for Chris'sakes . . . !"

"Then why not Annie? I know. I thought the same thing at church this morning."

"I want her back, Doc." A tear escaped down her cheek.

She brushed it away with a quick swipe of her hand, like someone shooing an insect. "These people who've come back . . . it isn't right. I don't care what Reverend Small says about miracles. I want to believe him but I don't. People are supposed to die and if there's something beyond death then they move on. They make the journey. They don't come back. That's how things are supposed to be."

"Isn't that Reverend Small's department? You and I turn to—"

Peg interrupted. "But that's just it, Doc, it doesn't matter to me. I don't care if it's right or wrong. I'd sell my soul to get my little girl back."

"You think these miracles are the work of the Devil?"

"I don't know! I don't know what they are! I don't know who's behind them, but don't you see? Nothing is more important to me than Annie, absolutely nothing. I'll do anything. It's just. . . ."

Peg took a deep breath and swallowed the lump in her throat. She raised her eyes to look at Doc and found him staring at her, not from his usual paternal distance but right there, hanging on her every word as if weighing each syllable for hidden portent. The intensity took her aback.

She looked away, shaking her head.

Doc leaned forward.

"It's just what?" he asked.

Peg wrapped her hands around Annie's. She leaned down and kissed Annie's hand, lifted it gently and brushed it against her cheek. "Before she can rise, she has to die," Peg said. "I have to withdraw the life support. I have to lose her. What if it doesn't happen for her? What if she doesn't come back? I'll have killed. . . ."

The tears were running freely as Peg turned to look at Doc Milford, her eyes pleading.

"What should I do, Doc?"

Doc took a deep breath and blew it out slowly through puffed-out cheeks. He shook his head.

"There are no guarantees, Peg. Do you want my promise that Annie will come back? I can't give it. I don't know any more about what's going on in Anderson than you do. But for whatever reason—divine intervention or the alignment of the planets and stars or God knows what—Death is on holiday in our little town. And holidays don't last forever. Maybe it's over already and Duffy and Irma and the Ganger boy were the last ones to come back. Maybe there will be more. But if it were my decision, I wouldn't wait. Whatever you decide, you should decide soon. Today."

Peg nodded. She snuffled and Doc handed her a tissue. She blew her nose and sat there with the wet tissue balled in her fist. She stared at Annie, at the tubes and wires, and listened to the rhythmic sigh of the respirator.

"Nobody told me it would be this hard," Peg said. "You imagine having a baby and think that once you get through childbirth, the pain is over. But it isn't."

"People shouldn't have to make decisions like this," Doc said. "Maybe some day they won't. If this miracle keeps up, if it spreads through the rest of the world, you might be the last mother who ever has to decide such a terrible thing."

After a few moments of silence Doc moved as if to leave. Peg said, "Wait," and leaned over and kissed him on the cheek.

"Thanks, Doc," she said, working up a faint smile. He smiled back at her, patted her hand and left.

As he walked down the hospital corridor, he wondered if his pitch had been too soft. Maybe he should have been more adamant. But then, Peg had a stubborn streak. If she thought she was being pushed too hard in one direction, she'd dig in her heels. No, he'd done what he could.

He wondered why it was so important to Seth that Peg

make the decision about Annie. Doc could convert them both this evening with no trouble at all. If Peg didn't terminate Annie before midnight, Doc would do it himself, and then he'd convert Peg.

Well, maybe it would come to that and maybe it wouldn't. It wasn't something Doc had to stew about. Seth's will be done, he thought, and he walked back to his office to feed the fish. It had come back, as he knew it would.

TWENTY-TWO

Brant's neck was so knotted, it felt like a piece of lumber. He swiveled it and listened to the crunch.

"What do you think?" Tom asked him.

They sat in the dark on the shoulder of the road and stared at the flashing lights. Shotgun wielding silhouettes milled around the roadblock. One of them was unmistakably Deputy Haws.

"We could try the county road on the other side of town," Brant offered, "but they probably have that blocked, too."

"What if we ditched the car and hiked in? We could enter from the woods, then cross Miller's field to the co-op. We could follow the railroad tracks . . . what?"

Brant's mouth was tight, he was shaking his head.

"Nobody walks anymore. We'd stick out like a sore thumb. We've got to figure that most of the people in town are Risen, otherwise they wouldn't be making such a blatant move. They'll be watching for us and anybody who isn't one of them. I'm guessing that once the town is secure, it'll be open season."

"We have to get Mom out of there!"

"Yeah, and we can't waste any more time doing it." Brant twisted the key and started the Toyota. He turned on the headlights and pulled slowly back onto the highway. "They'll give us some bullshit reason for the roadblock.

Pretend to swallow it and we'll try to bluff our way in. We'll find Peg and get the hell out of town."

"She won't leave Annie."

"If she's arranged to move her, we move her. Otherwise, we can't wait."

"Mom won't leave her behind. She just won't."

"She'll have to."

"What about Seth?"

"What about him?"

"Killing Seth is the only way to break the cycle. You heard Pritchett."

"Pritchett's a nut case. Maybe he's right about Seth and maybe he's had too many jolts to the brain. Even if it's true, Seth is somebody else's business. The police, the FBI. . . ."

"Like they'll believe us. We're the ones who know. If we don't do it. . . ."

"We don't even know who he is!"

"It's Small, it has to be! This whole thing started when he came to town. And right from the first he's been saying, 'Oh, it's a miracle . . . it's wonderful. . . .' Of course it's him!"

"He'll be surrounded ten-deep by his handiwork, too, you can bet on that. Jesus, Tom, this isn't a comic book. I'm no Batman and you aren't the goddamn Boy Wonder!"

Tom pounded his fist against the side window. "Shit!" he said.

Brant took a deep breath. Someone at the roadblock was waving a flashlight at them.

"Shit is right," Brant hissed. "We're up to our necks in it and I'm getting Peg out of town. If you want to run off and play Rambo, that's your choice, but I'd rather we stuck together."

"Brant, read my lips. Mom won't leave Annie," Tom said. "We can't run away from it because Mom won't go."

"We'll cross that bridge when we come to it. Right now, here comes Haws."

Haws sauntered into the Toyota's headlights. His revolver, normally holstered, was in his hand. He carried it casually, his arm hanging loose and swinging freely, but he carried it, and that bothered Tom.

"He's got his gun out," Tom said.

"I noticed."

Tom tried to peer into the glare of the revolving red and blue lights. John Duffy was there and he had a shotgun. He'd been hanging back, but now he moved slowly, easing himself around to the Toyota's flank.

"There's Duffy."

"Where?"

"On the right, moving like a cat stalking a wounded bird."

"Got him. Anybody else?"

Tom shielded his eyes and tried to discern faces on the shadowy figures.

"Merle Tippert. Oh, Christ! It's Carl Tompkins!"

"Shit. He sells shotguns, hunting rifles, even a few handguns. If he's opened up the store to the cause, he could supply a small army."

Haws was getting closer. He held up a hand to shield his eyes from the headlights and squinted in the glare.

Then he stopped.

"What's he doing? Why's he just standing there?" Tom asked.

Brant turned to look at Tom and saw John Duffy raising a shotgun to his shoulder.

"Get down!" Brant yelled and he mashed the accelerator to the floor. Tires squealed on the asphalt and the Toyota surged forward. The window glass behind Tom exploded, showering the back seat with glass and buckshot. Pellets of safety glass pelted the back of Tom's head and

lodged in his hair. He looked back to see Duffy running
behind the car, clutching his shotgun to his chest like a
commando, then looked up in time to see Deputy Haws
frozen in shock, eyes wide, while Brant bore down on him
with no thought of stopping or swerving to the side. There
was a crunch of bone as Brant's bumper met Haws' legs
just under the knees and then a thump as Haws jackknifed
onto the hood. He lay there until Brant smashed into the
police vehicle blocking the road, crushing Haws' legs between the cars and flopping his body upright like a figure
in a child's pop-up book.

Haws collapsed screaming to the ground as Brant
slammed the Toyota into reverse and pulled away. He
twisted the wheel, spinning the car ninety degrees to make
a short, fast, three-cornered turn on the narrow road. He
saw Duffy running up to them. Duffy paused and raised
the shotgun and Brant screamed for Tom to duck and then
ducked under the wheel himself, the Toyota aimed at John
Duffy and the accelerator pushed to the floor.

The windshield exploded over their heads and glass pellets rained down on them. Brant raised his head to peer
over the steering wheel. Duffy leaped out of the way and
Brant headed for the highway. There was another blast
from the shotgun and a back tire blew. Brant heard it flub-
bing on the asphalt. The car was in bad shape, the rear tire
ruined and the radiator leaking fluid from the collision
with Haws' police vehicle. All hope of driving anywhere
to get help died.

Brant made it to the highway and turned right. The
engine lasted long enough to get them beyond the reach
of the flashing lights and under the cover of darkness,
then it clattered and froze and the Toyota coasted to the
shoulder.

"Somebody's coming!" Tom yelled. Brant glanced
down the highway to see a pair of headlights float along

the access road and then turn right onto the highway,
heading their way.

"Come on!" he said. He yanked open the door and he
and Tom dashed for the cover of the woods. They hadn't
gone more than a few steps before Brant felt Tom's fingers
grab his arm. In a flash of panic he thought it was Haws or
Duffy and his heart nearly stopped in his chest.

"The other way!" Tom said. "They'll search the woods!"

The kid was right. The Toyota was pointed toward the
woods outside of town. It would be natural for anyone trying to reach Anderson to head that direction. By crossing
the highway and running the opposite way, they might
throw their pursuers off the track. Unless they had dogs, of
course, in which case Brant and Tom were royally screwed.

The headlights were closing fast as they dashed across
the highway and dived into the ditch between the shoulder
and a stretch of dusty wheat field. The headlights solidi-
fied into John Duffy's rattletrap Ford that skidded to a halt
in back of Brant's Toyota. Long moments passed.

"What's he doing?" Tom hissed, and Brant shushed him.
He was about to raise his head when a bright beam of light
passed over the ditch and the field behind them. Brant
raised his eyes above ground level. Duffy was busy inside
the car, doing who-knows-what, then the door flew open
and Duffy leaped out with a shotgun in one hand and a
flashlight in the other. The flashlight was new and heavy
with five D-cells fresh from Carl Tompkins's hardware
store. Its powerful beam cut through the darkness with a
cold, alien intensity.

Brant ducked as Duffy walked toward them. The light
played over the field, illuminating stubble and dirt. Brant
and Tom held their breaths, hearts pounding in their chests,
and Brant found himself praying to a God he didn't believe
in that Duffy continued to overlook the obvious.

Duffy's footsteps moved away from the ditch. Dark

seconds passed and Brant ventured another look. He saw
the light receding into the woods.

"He's searching the woods," Brant said.

Tom raised his head to look. He nodded toward Duffy's
Ford and said, "There's our ride."

"Suppose he took the keys."

"Who needs keys?" Tom said, and he heaved himself
out of the ditch and ran for the car. Brant followed.

Tom yanked open the door and said, "Shit." He jerked
his head toward the steering column. The Club jeered at
him like an upraised middle finger.

"Can you get it off?" Brant asked.

"If you've got the saw."

They looked toward the woods. Other lights were joining
John Duffy's, sparkling like fireflies among the trees. The
word was out—Brant and Tom were officially hunted men.

"We have to skirt the woods," Brant said. "Which means
we hug the ditches and work our way around town and
come in where they aren't expecting us."

"That'll take time."

"You've got a better idea?"

They both jumped as a rifle shot cracked in the distance.

Back at the roadblock, Carl Tompkins had just put
Deputy Haws out of his misery.

Under the new moon, away from the city lights, Tom
and Brant couldn't see squat. On the other hand, they were
themselves invisible as long as no cars were near. Most of
the headlights were passers-through with no interest in
Anderson or any of the small towns along the way, and
Tom considered trying to flag one of them down. He
wouldn't tell them the truth, of course, since they'd instantly write him off as a psycho, but if he and Brant could
get a lift to Isaac, they could. . . .

They couldn't do anything. Nobody would believe them, and his mom would still be trapped in Anderson.

They'd have to hijack the car, run the roadblock, pick up Peg and get out again. Of course, with no way to tell which cars held strangers—who were now, in this new bass-ack-wards world, more trustworthy than the people he'd grown up with—they couldn't risk being seen by anyone at all. At the first sight of headlights, he and Brant headed for the ditches.

"What we need is a truck," Brant said as they walked along in the darkness. "A semi. We'd know it didn't come from Anderson, and it'd plow through the roadblock like a son of a bitch."

"Trucks take the Interstate," Tom said.

"You never know. If one does come by, I'm going to wave it down."

"Fine by me."

No truck came.

The woods quickly gave way to more dry, autumn fields. Brant and Tom kept to the highway until they were out of flashlight range of anyone searching the woods, then climbed over the barbed wire fence and headed across the field. They picked their way over the wheat stubble, walked down the plowed rows, stumbling and cursing silently and taking, it seemed, forever to make any headway at all.

It was the perfect time for Tom to slip into the Black-lands. Instead, he realized, he was charged with energy, his mind racing a mile a minute. Peering into the darkness ahead, turning to regard the darkness behind, surrounded on every side by deep country dark, the Blacklands had come to Tom. They had become manifest, swallowing him physically as the horror radiated from its evil center and spread, ripple upon ripple, engulfing everything he knew and (he was only now, this very minute, realizing) all that he loved. Suddenly the little town that had constrained him, that pinched and chafed with his every movement, seemed precious beyond all belief, precious and lost and irrecoverable.

It would take everything he had to hang on to the vestiges that remained.

He had to cross the Blacklands and see what lay beyond.

For the first time in his life, Brant regretted his lack of military service. He could've used some basic training right now, or better yet, experience as a Green Beret stalking Charlie through the jungles of 'Nam.

The broken ground, invisible in the darkness, made every step a chore. Trying to walk in the furrows bent his ankles at an awkward angle. The wheat stubble scratched and poked and crackled underfoot. He couldn't get any rhythm going in his stride. It was frustrating. He felt time running out on him. He was worried sick about Peg.

He looked at his watch. The radium numbers glowed so brightly that he feared they would attract attention. He unfastened the strap and stuffed the watch in his pocket, and he hissed at Tom to do the same.

It was after nine o'clock.

At midnight, whatever victims the Risen had claimed would be back. The odds against him and Tom would double or triple or worse. And Peg . . .

If he didn't reach her before midnight, how would he know if she was still the woman he loved? How would he know that the Risen hadn't gotten to her first and made her one of their own?

He tried to walk faster. His foot slid into a rut and he felt his ankle twist and he fell to one knee. He was picking himself up when Tom stumbled into him and both of them tumbled to the ground, cursing.

Brant regained his feet and tested the ankle. It wasn't

sprained but it was sore. That's what he got for being in a hurry.

He had no idea how far they'd gone or how far they had yet to go. Not a light was visible except for the stars overhead, a brilliant swath across the black sky that dazzled the eyes and did nothing to illuminate the ground below. If he got turned around, he could walk for hours in the wrong direction and never know it. He tried to fix the town's location by the stars but couldn't. He didn't know how.

He felt Tom's hand on his shoulder.

"This way," Tom said.

Thank God, Brant thought, the kid knows where he's going.

He staggered on in the blackness. Somewhere not too far away a dog barked, then a gun, and then there was silence broken only by the pounding of blood in his ears and the crunch of dry wheat underfoot.

The Lunger house was haunted by the ghosts of children Old Man Lunger had caught in his peach orchard, fattened up in the cellar, and dismembered over a period of weeks while he feasted on their flesh.

Lunger had an understanding with the parents of Anderson that he would not prey on their children in their homes and yards or on the school grounds or anywhere in town except his orchard. This way the "bad children" who stole peaches were selected out of the population and the "good children" were allowed to thrive. Thus he got away with murder for several decades, until 1982, when he broke his vow and took a Girl Scout who'd come to the house selling cookies. He killed and ate her and, as God's punishment for breaking his promise, choked to death on her finger bone.

Lunger's ghost and those of the murdered children still

infested the ramshackle house. On windy nights you could hear Old Man Lunger's maniacal laugh as he stripped the flesh from his victims, and you could hear the shrieks of the tortured children carried on the wind.

Or so the story went when Tom was nine years old.

The Lunger house then sat in ruin on the edge of town, abandoned, boarded up, and given a wide berth by anyone with a lick of sense, which naturally excluded every boy in town, Tom among them. It was worth a Playboy centerfold to anyone with the guts to run up and pound on the front door at night.

Tom had done it once. He banged on the screen door with his fist and turned and ran full speed off the rotting porch, but a warped board snagged a dangling shoelace and down he went. He tried to jerk his foot free but he could feel that Old Man Lunger had a tight hold of it from his hiding place under the porch. Galen yelled at him from a safe fifty feet away. Tom looked back knowing that he would see Old Man Lunger's bony fingers wrapped around his foot and perhaps another hand rising up from below with a meat cleaver ready to whack his foot off at the ankle. Instead he saw the pinched shoelace and summoned enough courage to reach back and work it free, and then he sped off the Lungers' porch and he and Galen plunged into the orchard.

The orchard stank of rotten fruit. Their feet slid on peaches mashed underfoot, but Tom kept running and running until a stitch in his side forced him to slow down. Even then he staggered on, winded, his knees smarting, praying the breeze would dry the wet spot on the front of his shorts before Galen noticed.

Now he and Brant watched the house from behind one of the crooked peach trees in the surrounding orchard. Lights burned in some upstairs windows but no shadows moved inside.

A few years ago, a pair of Old Man Lunger's distant

relatives—his nephew Mark and his new wife, Carol—rescued the house from demolition and began the long process of remodeling. They let it be known that they would lease the orchard for one dollar a year and a small share of the profits to anyone who would pledge himself to the organic method of farming. Edgar Miller's son, Tony, said he'd give it a try and had done all right, better some years than others, but most years coming out in the black. His crop was smaller than some, but the fruit commanded a premium price from health nuts and Tony saved a mint on expensive pesticides and chemical fertilizers.

Mark Lunger quit his job in the big city and became a private investment counselor who published a monthly newsletter. He also contributed a bi-weekly column called "It's Your Dime" to the *Cooves County Times* which he hoped to organize into a book one of these days. Carol maintained her real estate license but devoted most of her time to raising their son, Joshua, and to gardening, various civic functions, and handling secretarial duties for Mark's business.

They were not the sort to have a gun in the house, which made breaking in a lot more attractive to Tom and Brant.

"If they were in bed, they'd have turned off those lights," Brant said. "I don't think they're home."

"What if they are?"

"Then we have to assume they're Risen. If they try to bluff us, play along, but watch your back. If they make any overt moves. . . ."

"What . . . stab them with my keys? We need some weapons."

"Okay, let's break in through the kitchen and grab a couple of knives. I'll try to phone Peg."

"I can't believe I'm breaking into the old Lunger house," Tom said, shaking his head and feeling suddenly nine years old again.

"I don't believe any of this," Brant replied. "Let's go."

The light from the windows was a relief after the nearly total darkness of the countryside. Tom and Brant hugged the shadows as they dashed from the orchard to the house and worked their way around toward the kitchen door. Brant nudged Tom and pointed to a white lump lying thirty feet from the house in the side yard. The Lungers' prize-winning Spitz. They remembered the barking and the gunshot heard earlier.

"They never would've shot that dog if they weren't Risen," Brant whispered.

"Maybe somebody else shot it."

That thought gave them pause. Very possibly, they were about to break into the scene of a mass murder. Images of blood-spattered walls leaped unbidden into their heads. Carol Lunger could be lying on that kitchen floor in a pool of her own blood. Mark and Josh could be in the living room, cut down in the middle of a video game. Their killer could be waiting inside.

The thought stilled their voices and slowed their footsteps to a stealthy creep. Brant opened the screen door slowly. The closing spring sang, the hinges creaked. The inside door was locked. Tom thought of Kent and his lock picks and how easy it would have been for him to get inside quietly. Instead, Brant elbowed a pane of glass and broke it. He picked out the shards of glass that hung in the molding and reached through, unlocked the deadbolt, and swung the door open on more creaking hinges.

They stepped into the dark kitchen. Their dark-adapted eyes picked out vague forms illumined by the blue glow of electronic clocks on the stove and microwave. They couldn't see a telephone, but Tom spotted a knife block on the counter and pulled out the two largest knives. He handed the smaller of the two to Brant.

An open doorway led to the dining room, pitch black.

Tom's foot encountered a chair leg that groaned as it skidded on the hardwood floor, startling Brant into dropping his knife. Tom thought that, with all the noise they were making, they might as well have rung the front bell.

"We have to get a light on," Brant whispered. He was thinking of all the breakables planted like booby traps in the average dining room. Glasses, pitchers, vases, plates sitting on edge . . . all waiting patiently to be bumped by a careless elbow as he and Tom felt around for a telephone.

Before Tom could answer, the darkness exploded with a blinding flash and the crack of a small caliber pistol. A bullet whizzed by Tom's right ear and Brant's left and there was a shattering of porcelain on the wall behind them. They hit the floor as another shot rang out. In the flash of light, frozen like a photograph, they saw seven-year-old Joshua Lunger in his Spider-Man pajamas, holding a mag-loaded .22 pistol in both hands, chest high, firing blindly into the room.

"It's Josh!" Tom yelled.

"Josh, it's all right!" Brant said. "We aren't going to hurt you!"

"Put down the gun!"

Josh pulled the trigger six more times while Tom and Brant put as much Ethan Allen as possible between them and their would-be killer. Bullets tore into the dining room table, splintered the wood off chairs, pierced the china cabinet and sent shards of glass whirling through the air. Tom and Brant sheltered their eyes against the flying glass. Their ears rang with the explosions. Josh's footsteps retreated deeper into the house and Tom yelled, "Come on, before he reloads!" and he and Brant were on their feet in a second, running over broken glass in the total darkness.

Brant's fumbling fingers discovered a light switch and flicked it on. The light was blinding over their shoulders but it spilled usefully into the living room where they caught sight of Josh Lunger running up the stairs, still clutching the pistol.

Brant called out to him and the boy paused and stared at them over the banister. His eyes were narrow and he chewed his upper lip nervously, but there was no hint of fear. He stared at Brant with a coldness that shot straight through Brant's brain like a bullet, then he turned and dashed up the stairs.

"Josh!" Tom yelled and started after him, but Brant grabbed his arm and held him back.

"There's the phone," Brant said, pointing. "Call your mom. Tell her we're on our way."

"Where are you going?"

"Upstairs."

"He's one of them, isn't he? One of the Risen."

Brant nodded. There had been a few moments of doubt when he first glimpsed Josh Lunger in the flash of the pistol. He could have been a scared little boy left home alone by irresponsible parents, confronting prowlers in the middle of the night. But Mark and Carol Lunger weren't irresponsible parents and they would never have left their boy alone with a loaded pistol. Unless it didn't matter. So what if he shot himself or someone else? All would be well again come midnight.

"Here," Tom said, and he handed Brant the big knife. Brant accepted the trade and headed up the stairs to find out just how mad his world had become.

Lights were on and he could see down the length of the hallway. Nothing seemed unusual, from the new carpet and wallpaper to the family photos lining the walls. Brant glanced at the pictures as he passed: baby Joshua in Carol's arms, Joshua in his Little League outfit, Joshua and the dog, Joshua and Mark proudly displaying a fish that should have been thrown back.

None of the photos were of the boy that had glared at

Brant from behind the banister. The body was the same, and the face. But the boy in the pictures was warm and lively and his eyes held the spark of benign deviltry that was the hallmark of boyhood. The eyes of the boy on the stairs were cold and dead, eyes that saw but did not feel, a killer's eyes.

The doors to all the upstairs rooms were shut. Josh would be behind one of them, calmly (as Brant imagined it) loading shells into the twenty-two. Behind one of them, perhaps, were the bodies of Mark and Carol Lunger, murdered in their sleep by their son.

Brant slowly twisted the knob on the first door he came to. The door opened silently into a darkened room. Brant reached up and found the switch and flipped it. There was the roar of an exhaust fan—the bathroom. He found the second switch and flooded the room with light, crouching as he swung the door wide.

This is insane, he thought, you don't have a plan, why are you doing this?

Because I have to know!

He had to confront the boy and find out what was going on. He had to know what in the hell were they up against.

The bathroom was empty. No one behind the door, no one behind the shower curtain.

Brant eased into the hallway. Three more doors to try, two with light spilling through the cracks, one dark. If he were lying in wait for someone, he would turn off the room lights. Josh was probably in the darkened room. Then again, maybe that's what Josh wanted him to think. Josh was only a kid, but kids these days knew more about shooting people than many adults. Between television and the computer games. . . .

Brant crept silently down the hallway and paused in front of the first lighted door. His sweating palm was twisting the knob when he heard a footstep on the stairs behind him. He whirled, gripping the butcher knife hard, and moved toward the stairs just as three shots rang out and bullets ripped through the hollow wooden door behind him.

Tom called out from the stairs as Brant flattened himself against the wall. It was Tom's footstep on the stair, and it had saved his life. Brant reached around and rattled the door knob and five more explosions sent five more bullets crashing through the door.

Brant threw the door open and saw Josh Lunger crouched beside his parents' bed frantically dropping spent shells from the .22. A box of live rounds sat on the floor beside him. He looked up at Brant as if he'd just been caught stealing quarters from his father's pockets. Josh reached for the box of ammunition but Brant crossed the room in a second and threw himself at the boy. He landed on him with all his weight, flattening him to the ground. Josh's legs kicked out and rounds of ammo skittered across the floor.

Josh beat on Brant's side with the empty pistol, cursing and screaming. In another moment Tom was in the room. He pried the gun out of Josh's hand and Brant rolled over and grabbed the boy's arms and pinned them behind his back. Josh kept screaming until Tom had had enough and slapped him hard across the mouth.

Josh glared at Tom with savage hatred.

"You can't win!" Josh cried. "They'll get you tonight and you'll be converted! You'll be sorry you hit me when Seth finds out!"

Seth. Brant and Tom locked eyes. So it was true. The demon of Eloise was back.

"What will Seth do, Josh?" Brant asked.

"He'll punish you! He'll let you die and stay dead if you don't do what he says!"

"How do you know that?"

"I know!"

"Did you meet Seth?" Tom asked.

Josh nodded.

Brant and Tom exchanged a quick look.

"Is it Reverend Small? Is he Seth?" Brant asked.

Josh clamped his mouth shut and stared back at Brant defiantly. He'd hit a nerve, something Josh had been warned against.

"Tell me, Josh!"

Tom shook Josh by the shoulders. "Tell him!" he insisted, and Josh shook his head. For one instant, something like terror flitted through his eyes, but fear of what? It certainly wasn't Tom.

Tom threatened to hit him again and Brant told him to leave the kid alone and for a few minutes they played good cop/bad cop. Still Josh resisted all efforts to intimidate or cajole him into betrayal of Seth. Maybe they could wear him down, in time, but time was running out. They could torture him, but then who would be the monster? Tom and Brant exchanged exasperated looks.

"We don't have time for this," Tom said.

"Just a minute."

Brant turned Josh around to speak to him face to face. He waited for their eyes to meet, and when they did, a chill went up Brant's spine at the deadness he saw there.

"Josh, tell me one thing. Just tell me why. Why does Seth want you to kill?"

"You have to die to know Seth," Josh said impatiently, as if trying to explain the obvious to the stupidest person on Earth.

"And everybody has to know Seth, is that it?"

"Yes!"

"Why?"

"Because!" Josh snapped. "That's how it is!"

"Why is that how it is? Because Seth says so?"

"Because, that's all!"

"Brant, forget it," Tom said. "He doesn't know. He's just a kid."

Something about those words made Brant shudder. No, he thought, he used to be a kid. Now I don't know what he is.

"Come on," Tom said. "We have to find Mom."

Brant stood, keeping a tight grip on Josh's shoulder.

"Did you get her on the phone?"

"No. There wasn't any answer at home. I could call the hospital. . . ."

"No! You'd have to go through the switchboard. So far they don't know where we're headed and I'd like to keep it that way."

Tom nodded toward Josh.

"So, what do we do with him?"

"We can't just leave him, that's for sure. He'll call the Sheriff."

"Technically. . . ." Tom said, and then his voice trailed off.

"Yeah?"

"Well, technically he's dead already. Somebody killed him, his parents probably." Tom played nervously with the pistol in his hand. "We could kill him again," he said.

"So what?" Josh said. "I don't care."

The horrifying thing was, the boy meant it.

They left Josh tied up with electrical cord and a gag in his mouth, though, here at the edge of town, all the screaming he could do wouldn't attract a soul. A quick check of the house turned up no bodies, living or dead or otherwise. The garage held a late model Saab and Brant found a spare set of keys hanging on a peg by the front door. The car was a blessing, meaning that the hospital was now only a few minutes away and they would attract far less attention than they would have on foot.

"Where do you suppose they are, the Lungers?" Tom asked.

"Church," Brant said, thinking of the gathering they'd seen that morning on their way out of town.

"And they left their kid home alone, with a loaded pistol."

"Why not? What could happen . . . he might shoot somebody?"

"Why didn't they take him with them?"

"Maybe it was past his bed time," Brant said dryly. The comment prompted Tom and Brant to check their watches.

"Ten-twenty," Tom said.

"Time enough. Did you find any more guns in the house?"

"No. Do you want the pistol?"

"You keep it. Open the garage door and let's get going."

Brant eased the Saab out of the garage and Tom closed the door behind them. Tom looked back at the Lunger house as they drove away, thinking about Old Man Lunger and the ghosts of murdered children, and he thought of Josh Lunger in an upstairs bedroom, tied to a bed post, whose last comment before they stuffed the sock in his mouth was that they would never get out of town alive.

The road through the Lungers' orchard became a street and soon Tom and Brant were gliding silently through Anderson proper.

At first glance the town seemed quiet, but, like a pornographic painting that reveals its obscenities under scrutiny, the quiet streets and familiar houses let slip their secrets by degrees.

Too many lights glowed in too many windows. The occasional gunshot popped and echoed like a Fourth of July firework and died unremarked. Dogs were silent in their yards, alleys were devoid of prowling cats.

As they drove, Brant and Tom became aware of the not-so-subtle evidence of Seth's influence.

Bob Walker knelt by the curb, vomiting from the death angel mushrooms his wife Julie had cooked in his morning omelet.

Night nurse Claudia White's father lay on the front yard where he'd fallen when the quinidine in his gin and tonic stopped his heart.

Matt and Gina Saunders sat slumped in their car in front of their house, suitcases in the trunk and clothes thrown any old way in the back seat. Each had been shot through the skull.

Jerry James carried his new wife, Amber, in his arms, taking her back home. She'd made it six blocks before Jerry was able to chase her down and finish crushing her throat.

Jerry nodded to Tom as he passed, and Tom nodded back.

"Jesus," he whispered to Brant. "The town's gone crazy."

"Just like Eloise."

Brant's voice was distant. He couldn't stop thinking about Josh Lunger's eyes and the evil he'd seen in their depths. Deputy Haws hadn't had that look, or John Duffy. But Haws and Duffy were grownups, and grownups were used to hiding their innermost selves. They smiled when their feet hurt and hid their amusement when someone else slipped on the ice. Kids were transparent. It's what made their joy so infectious and their hurt so intolerable. It's why Brant could peer into Josh Lunger's eyes and see straight through his empty soul and into the dark reaches beyond.

Brant thought about Josh Lunger and he thought about Annie Culler and he thought about Seth, and he began to think that leaving town was not enough for a man to do in the face of such ancient and deep-abiding evil.

Such were his thoughts when Hank Ellerby's Jeep Cherokee ran a stop sign and cut across his path, swerving from side to side as if the driver was drunk. Tom spotted Cindy Robertson in the passenger seat, her eyes wide. He gave a shout.

The Jeep bounced over a curb and flattened a speed limit sign and buried its nose in the trunk of an oak. Brant turned the corner and drove toward the accident. Cindy jumped out of the car and saw Brant and Tom heading her way. A splash of light from a street lamp caught her terrified face, and then she turned and ran.

TWENTY-THREE

When Tom saw Cindy leap out of Hank's Jeep and run into the alley, he had no choice but to go after her. He left the pistol with Brant, who was going to check on Hank.

The alley was dark but for the occasional security light that came on as Cindy ran past. Tom called to her once but she didn't even slow down. Obviously she'd learned not to trust anyone, and Tom wasn't going to win her confidence by yelling at her while chasing her down. He concentrated on overtaking her. Once she saw that he wasn't going to hurt her, maybe he could convince her to come with them.

He gained on her steadily. Cindy turned to look over her shoulder at him and her foot came down wrong. She cried out in pain and fell. She saw Tom gaining on her and hurried to her feet, but one step on her twisted ankle was all it took to bring her down again. She crawled away from Tom as he ran up. The terror in her eyes caused Tom to slow as he drew nearer.

"I'm not going to hurt you," he said. He tried to make his voice sound calm and reassuring but he was out of breath from all the running. To his own ears, he sounded like a telephone breather. He opted for a few moments of silence while he caught his breath and Cindy hauled herself to a more comfortable position against someone's board fence.

"We'd better get out of this light," Tom said, nodding toward the security light that had come on at their arrival.

"Come on." He moved to a shadowed space between the fence and a detached garage and motioned Cindy over. She looked up at the security light and scooted out of its beam and a few feet closer to Tom. He smiled what he hoped was an engaging, non-threatening sort of smile, then dropped it when she didn't smile back.

"Do you know Seth?" she asked.

Tom nodded. "I know what's going on, if that's what you mean."

"But you're not converted. You're not one of . . . them."

He shook his head. "Not yet," he said, "but it isn't for lack of some people trying."

Cindy's eyes darted about.

"I don't know who to trust," she said. "They have this code phrase, 'Do you know Seth?' They use it to identify one another. If you say 'yes' it means you've been converted. That's what they call it. Conversion."

"How do you know all this?"

"I overheard my parents talking."

So that was it. She was running from her parents. There was no telling how they'd died or who'd done the "converting," but something had set off her suspicions.

"What else do you know about Seth?"

"Nothing. I don't understand any of this. I know something strange is going on but I don't know what. I know people are coming back, and not just John Duffy and that old woman and Galen. There's more. Lots more. They're killing everybody who isn't converted already."

"What were you doing with Hank?"

"Trying to get out. He saw me running through the alley. He was avoiding the streets himself, he said. I thought he was trying to leave town, too, but he wasn't. He was looking for runaways like me. Cruising the alleys."

Tom consulted his watch. Eleven o'clock. They had to get moving.

"Tom," Cindy said, "I killed him. I killed Hank Ellerby. He grabbed me and I fought him, but I couldn't get loose. I had that knife, the one my brother bought in Tijuana. I stabbed him with it."

"People don't die of a single stab wound, not unless you hit a vital organ," Tom said. "You probably just surprised him into running into that tree."

"I'd like to think that."

"We don't have much time," Tom said, getting to his feet. "We have to put some miles between us and Anderson before all of these corpses start coming back."

Her eyes pleaded with him. "Take me with you," she said, and Tom replied, "Sure." He held out his hand to her, helped her up. She tested her twisted ankle and winced.

"I can't walk on it," she said.

"Lean on me. Come on. We have to hurry."

"Of course," she said, and she pulled him close and kissed him.

Brant kept Hank covered with the pistol until he was sure he was dead.

Hank's chest was wet with blood. The wound was low. If the angle was right, a knife blade could've entered at that spot and gone up under the ribs and straight into his heart.

A hunting rifle sat on the floor, canted up against the seat. It was Hank's new Winchester. Brant didn't know beans about rifles, but he knew from the Saturday morning talk at Ma's that Hank was fatherly proud of his new gun. Nobody went hunting at ten-thirty at night, not around these parts, anyway. Brant wondered if the new rifle had been drafted into service to Seth. Maybe Seth was on patrol for people like Brant and Tom and Cindy Robertson.

Then he noticed, lying on the floor at Hank's feet, dappled in blood, a bundle of envelopes held together by a fat rubber band. Brant pulled off the band and read the envelopes. All were addressed in a woman's hand and lacked a return address, but they were postmarked from Chicago where Hank went once or twice a year on business. Brant opened one letter and found what he expected. Hank's wife would not have been pleased with the content. The letter spoke of longing and understanding and "our situation," and it didn't take Brant long to realize that Hank Ellerby's life was torn between obligation to a wife and children on one hand and undeniable passion on the other.

Brant felt a sudden chill. A man does not take love letters on patrol duty. Hank Ellerby was running away, and someone had killed him, and that "someone" was Cindy Robertson.

Brant had to find Tom, and fast.

Cindy's lips against his felt so good. Tom wondered how he'd ever had the strength to break up with her. Maybe it wasn't strength at all, but sheer stupidity. She felt so right in his arms, he must have been seriously mixed up in the head to think he was better off without her.

The one impediment to their love had been removed, thanks to the Risen. Anderson held no sway over Cindy anymore. They were headed in the same direction, she and him, away from their little town and out into the real world.

Over Cindy's shoulder, Tom saw headlights appear at the end of the alley. Brant, probably. The car drove slowly, searching. The headlights winked off and on and then winked again. Brant was looking for him.

Tom gently eased himself out of Cindy's embrace.

"There's our ride," he said, and Cindy turned to look at the headlights. Tom said, "Not much time. We have to hurry."

"I want to show you something," Cindy said.

Tom stepped to the middle of the alley and waved his

arms to Brant, wondering as he did so if he'd just given them away to some Risen, maybe to Hank Ellerby who'd gotten the drop on Brant and come after them. But no, the headlights were too low to be Hank's Cherokee. It had to be Brant in the Saab.

"Look at this," Cindy said, cradling something against her stomach.

"What is it?"

"Just come look."

"Why don't you just tell me?" he began, drawing closer, but then the Tijuana switchblade went snik and the blade shot out to its full length and in one continuous movement it leaped forward headed for Tom's chest cavity. He jumped back instinctively.

Cindy lunged at him again with the knife. She moved frantically as the headlights approached from down the block.

"Hey!" Tom shouted, dodging the slashing blade. "It's okay! I'm not one of them!"

"Not yet," she said. She lunged again with the knife. She was awkward on the twisted ankle and Tom sidestepped easily. She swiped the knife through the air two more times and each time Tom leaped back, out of striking distance. She tried again and Tom grabbed her by the wrist. He twisted her hand, folded her arm behind her back, then pulled it up until it hurt enough for her to drop the blade. He caught it and held it to her throat.

"When did it happen?" he demanded.

"Last night, when I was sleeping."

"Who did it?"

"My father. But Tom, it's not a bad thing. Once you meet Seth you'll understand."

"You wouldn't care if I slit your throat right now."

"I'd welcome it. This ankle hurts like hell."

The Saab pulled up and Brant leaped out of the car.

"Looks like my warning comes too late," Brant said as he strode up. "Hank's dead, a knife through the ribs. He was trying to get away."

"Let me convert you, Tom," Cindy said. "You'll be glad once it happens. You're just afraid of change, but it's change for the better. Let Seth heal you. Whatever's wrong, Seth can fix it."

"I'm happy just as I am."

"Is that right?" she said flatly.

No, it wasn't. The truth was, Tom would have been hard pressed to name a single happy moment he'd had since he'd broken up with her . . . until a minute ago when their mouths were together and the empty ache he'd felt for the past few months was gone.

"What do we do with her?" Tom asked. He held the knife pressed close against Cindy's neck, on the jugular. He knew what he should do. He should press a little bit harder, break the skin, rupture the vein and let her die. She was dead already, despite the fact that she was warm and breathing and, even in this unseemly position, felt so damned good in his arms.

"Kill me," she said. "What's so hard about that? I'll be back before you know it. What's stopping you? Do I have to scream to make you do it?"

"She'll have the whole town down on us, Tom."

"So I should just slit her throat, is that it?"

"He's right, you know," Cindy said. "I'll have them running from their houses, chasing you through the streets, chasing you down like rabbits. Go ahead, cut my throat. I'm not afraid. Do you want me to struggle so you can tell yourself it was an accident?"

"Why are you doing this to me? Is it revenge, is that it?"

"I want you to know there's nothing to be afraid of. If you won't let me convert you, let someone else. Let Galen. Let Peg."

"What about Peg?" Brant said. He grabbed Cindy's shoulders and pinched them tight. She winced under his grip. "Is Peg one of them? Tell me!"

"Probably. Most everybody's converted. Join us. Join Seth and everything will be all right. What have you got to lose, anyway? Not much, from what I hear."

Brant raised the pistol to Cindy's face. He pressed the end of the barrel against her cheek, aimed it up toward her eye.

"You're telling me this doesn't frighten you, not even a bit?"

"It's annoying the hell out of me, is what it's doing. It hurts. I wish you'd pull the trigger and quit fucking around."

Cindy gasped and Brant saw red liquid spilling around the knife. Cindy's heart gave a beat and the blood spurted and Brant jumped back reflexively. Blood flowed over Tom's knife hand and down Cindy's front as Tom brought the blade around. Tom relaxed his grip and let her slide out of his arms. Her eyes rolled back in her head and her mouth curled into a smile as she collapsed to the ground.

Brant looked at Tom's face and saw the tears streaming over his cheeks. Tom threw the switchblade to the ground and shook the blood from his hand as best he could. He stood there looking down at the body. He wiped a clean sleeve across his face, destroying the tears.

"Shit," Tom said. His voice choked.

"Come on. We have to get to the hospital. We have to get Peg."

"It's too late."

"We don't know that. Come on. There's still a chance."

Brant pulled at Tom's arm and Tom moved reluctantly. He walked like a condemned man to the car. He stood looking at the door handle for long moments, trying to remember how it worked, what it was for, what he was doing in that spot at that time.

Finally Brant opened the door from inside and commanded Tom to get in. They were getting Peg, he said, and the Devil take anybody who got in their way.

Tom and Brant's thoughts were running deep. Neither spoke as the Saab navigated the dark streets. Occasionally Brant spotted another pair of headlights and casually turned the corner, then he watched the rear view mirror for any sign that they were being followed, his heart racing and his fingers drumming on Hank Ellerby's Winchester.

He kept thinking of Josh Lunger's eyes, mentally flipping back and forth between the dead, otherworldly boy he'd tied to a bedpost and the exuberant child of the hallway photographs. What Seth had done to Josh was worse than murder. Seth had taken a lovely and loving child and ripped out his soul and twisted what was left into an abomination. Josh was as dead as any corpse in Wildwood Cemetery. What walked the earth in his guise was a thing neither living nor dead, soulless as the devil and with a demon's taste for blood.

How many children lived in Anderson? How many had already received Seth's "blessing?" How many more would be murdered and resurrected if another midnight passed and Seth's crusade were allowed to continue unopposed?

Tom's thoughts were at least as black. He studied his hand, the one that had pressed the knife to Cindy's throat and parted her flesh. He'd felt her warm blood cascade over those fingers. The blood remained, dried under his fingernails, lodged in the crevices of his skin. Cindy's blood.

Only now, with her loss, did Tom realize how much she'd meant to him. What a fuckhead he was. He'd turned his back on the best thing that had ever happened to him. He'd shut her out of his life, not because of what she was, but because of what she stood for in his screwed up, twisted, bullshit-befuddled mind. Who knows what might have been if they'd gotten out of Anderson together, traveled, seen the world?

He tried to tell himself that the creature he'd killed was not Cindy, not really, but something that had taken her place. He'd killed . . . temporarily, for less than an hour, actually . . . a being that looked like Cindy and, Jesus, that kissed and felt like Cindy, but it wasn't her, not in any way that mattered. That's what he told himself over and over as the car glided between pools of light from the street lamps, as it moved with excruciating stealth toward the hospital. That's what he had to believe or the guilt would have been unbearable.

Tears welled in his eyes. The pressure in his chest demanded release, but he was not going to break down, damn it, he was not going to break down in front of Brant. He was going to see this thing through like a man. Whatever rewards life had in store for him, they lay beyond this terrible, black night. He had to muscle his way through it or die trying.

With the delays, the waiting with the headlights off while a car passed, with the circuitous route they were forced to take, it was past eleven-thirty by the time Brant and Tom reached the hospital. Peg's car was in the parking lot. Brant pulled into the empty space beside it but did not turn off the engine.

He swiveled in the seat to face Tom. "I'm not going with you," he said. "You'll have to convince her yourself. Tell her the truth, lie to her, do whatever you have to do but get it done before midnight in case. . . ." Brant knew what he had to do, had known it for the last half hour, but speaking the words aloud made it too real.

"In case what?"

"In case I don't get to Reverend Small in time. I have to go after him, Tom. I can't let this go on. Even if we get out of it for now, it'll catch up to us."

"Like ripples, getting wider and wider. I know. Maybe you should get Mom and I should go after Small."

"No, getting her away from Annie . . . I don't think a stranger could do that."

"You're not exactly a stranger."

"But I'm not family, either. You're her son. If she'll do it for anybody, it'll be for you."

"I don't know. We've been at each other's throats a lot lately."

"Tom, believe me. She loves you. She might not leave Annie for her own sake, but she'll do it for yours. Tell her you aren't leaving without her. Force her to choose."

"Suppose she chooses Annie."

"Then drag her out by the heels. Take her car, meet me at that diner in Junction City, the place across from the newspaper office."

Tom nodded. He opened the door and slid out. He stuffed the pistol in the small of his back and headed toward the hospital. He heard the Saab back out of the parking stall and he turned to watch Brant drive off.

If Brant didn't eliminate Small before midnight, the town would be crawling with Risen. Deputy Haws, Hank Ellerby, Cindy and who-knows-how-many others. He might be able to bluff his way out, but he wasn't going to count on it. He figured he had ten, maybe fifteen minutes to make his case and get him and his mom out of the hospital. They'd have to drive straight to the highway, maybe shoot their way through the roadblock. If they made it that far, they'd have a chance.

He walked into the hospital and felt Claudia White's hostile eyes on him as he passed the nurse's station. The net was closing around him. He'd waited too long.

Pulling this off would take a miracle.

* * *

Peg, too, was praying for a miracle.

The room was silent but for the rushing of blood in her ears, a side effect, probably, of the sedative Doc had given her. She hadn't wanted the shot at first, but as the minutes ticked ever slower toward midnight and then seemed to just stop and hang in the air, and as the panic rose in her throat until she thought she would scream, she'd asked for a little something to calm her nerves. Doc had said it would take the edge off and it certainly did that. It could have been the stress or the fact that she'd eaten dinner out of a vending machine, but the tranquilizer was hitting her harder than she'd expected. Had Doc miscalculated the dose? Her head was spinning.

She leaned forward and massaged her temples. It was strange not to hear the hiss of the respirator. She'd called for Doc around eleven and signed the forms consenting to withdrawal of Annie's life support, then watched the proceedings from a million miles away. Claudia White drew out Annie's breathing tube and wheeled the respirator away. Why remove the machine? Peg had wondered. So I can't change my mind? The remaining nurse worked quickly and precisely, removing the feeding tube and the IV. Soon, according to the monitors, it was done. Her little girl was gone.

Peg had broken down, then. She'd fallen into one of the plastic chairs and bawled like a child. Doc's hand on her shoulder did nothing to ease the pain. She wanted to punch him when he told her to "let it all out," as if she needed his permission. Annie was dead, for Chris'sakes, she had all the reason she needed to cry and wail and moan and carry on. She would pound the floor or throw one of these stupid plastic chairs out the window if she wanted to, she had the right.

Only when he told her that everything would be all right, that it would soon be midnight and she'd have Annie back again, did Peg begin to regain control. He sounded so sure. How could anyone confidently predict a miracle? But there was something in his voice that made her believe him, and by degrees the sobbing stopped and she quit filling tissues with her tears and she experienced a few moments of grace.

As the minutes passed, the fear set in. Panic welled in her chest and she asked Doc for something to calm her down, expecting a pill. Instead he'd come back with the syringe, saying that a pill would take too long to have any effect. She'd let him inject her and soon her head was swimming, but the body shakes had gone away and there was a pleasant mist over everything, muffling sight and sound and thought alike.

Tom's voice called to her. It floated to her from a distance, as if from across a lake, until his face was in front of hers, blurring in and out of focus. He spoke urgently to her, with an edge in his voice that cut through the fog and penetrated her drug-clouded brain.

"What's he done to you, Mom?" he was asking. His hands gripped her arms and shook her. His eyes sought hers, striving for connection. She tried to speak, to tell him that everything was going to be all right, but her mouth wouldn't form the words. If she could only lift her head, but it seemed to weigh a hundred pounds. . . .

He was pulling at her, trying to lift her to her feet. She held back and his hands unexpectedly let go and she fell back into the chair and there was a scuffle . . . shouting . . . a crash and Doc collapsed on the floor in front of her. Blood trickled from his mouth and for what seemed like minutes she watched the blood run between his lips and drip to the pristine hospital room floor. Then Tom's hands slipped under her arms and were lifting her from behind. His voice in her ear urged her to rise, to walk, to hurry, that time was short and they had to leave. She tried to tell him about Annie but he wouldn't listen. It was everything she could do to put one foot in front of the other as he hurried her into the corridor.

She tried to follow Tom's lead. Things were going on that she didn't understand. She didn't know who to trust. She'd trusted Doc but look at her now, drugged out of her mind. In her confused state, she had to put her faith in her son.

Sights came to her in stroboscopic flashes. Tom struggling with Claudia White. The cold, clear numbers of a clock. There was an explosion, then more, and then Tom was yelling at her, angry and impatient.

The minute hand of the clock jumped, and it was fifteen minutes to midnight.

The instant Tom stepped into Annie's hospital room, he knew that everything was wrong.

Equipment had been removed. Annie sat in bed like a doll, the covers neatly folded over her legs, stripped of her life-sustaining tubes. Peg sat beside the bed, head in her hands.

"Mom?" Tom said. When she didn't answer he marched into the room under Doc Milford's watchful gaze.

"Tom, your mother came to a decision—" Doc began, but Tom cut him off with an angry glance.

"Did she? Or did somebody decide for her?" Tom kneeled before his mother. "Mom? What's going on?"

"I have the forms with her signature. No one coerced her."

"Can you understand what I'm saying? Mom?" He put his hand under Peg's chin and lifted her face. Her eyes were wide and blank, but he could see she was trying to focus on him. "What's he done to you?" he asked.

"I gave her a tranquilizer. She was having a panic attack."

"She isn't tranquilized, she's stoned to the gills," Tom snapped.

He grabbed Peg's arms and shook. Her head lolled on her shoulders, a dead weight. Her lips moved soundlessly, trying to form words that wouldn't come.

"Think about it, Tom," Doc urged. "Think about all that's been happening. If Annie's to have any chance of recovery, any chance at all, it has to come now."

"How? Through Seth?" Tom took Peg's hands. "We're getting out of here, Mom. Come on. I'll help you up."

"I can't let you do that, Tom."

Tom looked over to see Doc rushing at him with something clutched in his upraised hand. A syringe. Tom let go of Peg and whirled and planted his fist into Doc's belly. Doc whuffed and stepped back, still clutching the syringe.

"You don't understand," Doc hissed through clenched teeth. He held his stomach, his breath came in labored gasps.

"I understand enough," Tom said.

"You don't understand anything because you don't know Seth! Seth is life, don't you see that?"

Tom replied with a blow to Doc's mouth that sent the older man reeling. Another one dropped him and his head impacted on the hard floor. Doc lay unmoving at Peg's feet, the object of her drugged fascination.

Tom stepped around behind Peg and lifted her from behind.

"We have to go," he said. "Come on. You need to stand up. That's it. That's good." He spied her purse on the floor, picked it up and forced it into her hands. "You have to walk now. Hurry. There isn't much time and we have to go."

"Annie. . . ."

"Annie's fine. Hurry. We have to leave."

Tom supported Peg as he ushered her into the corridor. He saw Nurse White marching toward them and too late noticed the scalpel in her hand. The scalpel shot forward and Tom deflected it with his hand. The blade sliced across his palm, cutting deep, but Tom grabbed Claudia's wrist and twisted. She cried out. The scalpel clattered to the floor. Tom shoved her aside and urged Peg on.

Claudia quickly retrieved the scalpel and rushed at Tom's back. He let go of Peg and whirled around in time to grab Claudia's wrist, already descending toward him with the scalpel. He held the wrist with both hands and kneed her hard in the stomach. She doubled over and Tom raised his knee to her face. He heard cartilage crunch and knew he'd broken her nose. Claudia moaned breathlessly and fell to the floor, hands cradling her face as blood streamed between her fingers.

Tom found Peg staring at something on the wall. A clock. It was a quarter to twelve.

The fight had attracted attention. Though the hospital was minimally staffed at this time of night, Curtis Waxler, the night orderly, rushed in their direction from down the hall. A voice called out, "Tom!" and Tom saw Doc striding toward them angrily. A smear of blood stained his chin where Doc had wiped at it with the back of his hand. Caked blood squatted in the corner of his mouth.

"Come on, Mom," Tom said. He tugged at her arm but she stood transfixed by the clock.

"Almost midnight," she said, slurring the words.

"Yes, we have to get away before midnight. Hurry, please."

He considered knocking her cold and dragging her to the car. It couldn't have been much harder than motivating her to walk. Curtis Waxler was almost of top of them when Tom decided to quit pussyfooting around. He reached under his t-shirt and pulled out the pistol he'd stuffed in his jeans, in the small of his back. He aimed at Curtis, gripping the pistol with both hands, and threatened to pull the trigger.

Curtis didn't slow and Tom realized that intimidation

was useless. Risen had no fear of death. Josh Lunger had looked him in the eye with Tom's pistol aimed straight at his head and said "So what?" Cindy had welcomed death as an alternative to a twisted ankle. It was useless to point a gun at the Risen unless you intended to use it.

Tom pulled the trigger. Peg jumped at the sound and Curtis Waxler staggered. A red splotch appeared in the center of his chest. Tom fired again and Curtis went down.

Tom swiveled the gun over to point at Doc. Doc looked at him wearily but did not break his stride.

"Oh, come now, Tom," Doc said, and then Tom pulled the trigger and a bullet whizzed by Doc's head and ripped a chunk from one ear. Doc cried out and grabbed the side of his head. Tom's second shot went wild but his third entered Doc's temple squarely and emerged on the opposite side in a shower of bone and brain and blood, tumbling end over end.

Tom grabbed Peg and dragged her toward the door. His patience was gone and his voice was angry as he ordered her to walk, damn it, they were getting the fuck out of there.

The parking lot was eerily quiet as Tom pushed, pulled, and bullied Peg toward her car. Tom heard the distant crack of a gun and knew there would be one more Risen come midnight. Then he heard more shots and realized that the massacre had begun in earnest. Anyone who was not Risen was being openly murdered as midnight approached. Gone was all subterfuge, what little was left. Outside interference was not likely in the next . . . what? Ten minutes? The Risen would be taking no chances. If they mistakenly killed one of their own, what difference would it make? All would be back come midnight.

A heavy form appeared from the shadows as they reached Peg's ancient Impala. Tom used his last bullet, not waiting to see who it was or to determine if they were friend or foe. It wasn't Brant, and that was all Tom needed to know. The form went down. Tom maneuvered Peg around the body as they passed. It was Clyde Dunwiddey, and he still held a new Beretta pistol in one hand.

Tom managed to get Peg into the car. He took a minute to reload and then started the car and pulled into the street. Peg turned in her seat to keep her eyes on the hospital as they pulled away. It occurred to Tom that she probably knew which lighted window was Annie's.

The car clock said eleven-thirty and for a moment Tom thought they had a chance. Then he remembered that it was later than that when he'd entered the hospital and that the clock in Peg's car had said eleven-thirty for the last three years. He checked his watch. They had twelve minutes to make it to the highway, and he could see that something was happening on the road ahead and he'd have to circle around.

They'd never make it.

It was all up to Brant, who had twelve minutes left to kill Reverend Small and put an end to the madness.

TWENTY-FOUR

Brant loaded three rounds into the Winchester, raised it to his shoulder a couple of times for practice, and decided he was ready to go to church.

He wished for the pistol. That gun held eight shots and would be better in close quarters. While he was at it, he wished for an Uzi or, better still, a few grenades he could lob through the stained glass windows. Instead, he had a hunting rifle and three shots with which to bring down an ancient, evil spirit that had fought this fight before. Brant tried to encourage himself with the thought that Donald Pritchett had brought Seth down sixty years ago, and he tried not to think of the price Donald had paid for his victory . . . a lifetime locked in a mental asylum. If it came to that, Brant wouldn't try to explain his actions to the authorities. Let them throw him in jail for murder.

There were only a few cars in the parking lot. Contrary to Brant's expectation, the Risen were not gathering at the church. They had spread themselves throughout the town, "converting" those who had not yet discovered Seth and turning Brant's drive through the city streets into a game of stealth and avoidance. Thanks to the prowling Risen, it had taken Brant longer than he'd anticipated to reach the church. Time was woefully short as he tried to figure some way to get inside and find and kill Reverend Small with his pitiful allotment of firepower.

Brant had parked the car a couple of blocks away and sneaked up on the church on foot. From his vantage point in the bushes across the street, he could discern two people on the front steps, standing under the incandescent glare of a single outdoor lamp. Brant shielded his eyes and determined that it was Jack and Dolores Frelich. Jack cradled a shotgun across his chest. Dolores held some kind of rifle, maybe a .22, it was hard to tell from this distance.

An experienced hunter could have picked them off easily, but Brant had no idea how accurate he'd be with Hank's Winchester. The noise might attract attention even on a night as gun-noisy as this one. If he'd had more time he might've scouted for an unlocked basement window and tried to sneak inside, but the clock was ticking and there weren't that many ticks left before midnight. No, it had to be a frontal assault, quick and clean.

He raised the rifle to his shoulder and took aim at Jack Frelich. Then he thought better of it. Even if he did drop Jack with one shot, it would alert Dolores and she'd have time to raise the alarm with anyone inside while Brant was crossing the street. He'd have to get closer to ensure a clean shot and get inside while he still had the advantage of surprise.

Jack and Dolores would be nearly blind under that light. They wouldn't know who he was until he reached the sidewalk in front of the church, even if some kind of general alert had gone out regarding him and Tom. He stepped out from behind the bushes and strode confidently toward the church. He let the rifle dangle at his side as if using it were the last thing on his mind.

Jack and Dolores were engaged in conversation, and Brant was nearly across the street before Dolores noticed him. She slapped Jack on the arm, pointed toward Brant, and Jack turned to look his direction. Brant held up a hand in a friendly greeting but said nothing. Jack did not seem alarmed. The shotgun lay in his arms like a sleeping baby, then it dropped to his side as Jack unfolded his arms and put one hand over his eyes to shield them from the overhead glare, scrutinizing Brant.

Suddenly Jack recognized Brant and stiffened. Brant raised the hunting rifle waist high, pointed it in Jack's direction and pulled the trigger. At that range he couldn't miss. The bullet plowed into Jack's stomach. Brant expended the cartridge and lifted the rifle higher and swung it over to point at Dolores. Her .22 was already on its way to her shoulder when Brant pulled the trigger again and planted a bullet in her chest.

Brant stepped over the bodies and glanced inside to see Jimmy Troost headed toward him at a full run, a few yards from the door. Brant fired again and put his third bullet into Jimmy's belly. Reverend Small looked up from the pulpit where he'd been practicing a sermon before an invisible audience.

Brant thought about reloading the Winchester but that would give Small a chance to run. Instead, he dropped the rifle to the floor and snatched up Jack Frelich's shotgun.

The sanctuary was empty but for himself and the preacher as Brant strode down the center aisle, eyes locked with Small's. With no threat imminent, he wanted to get good and close to his target.

"What are you doing, Brant?" Small asked with infuriating calm.

"I know who you are," Brant said. "I know about Eloise."

"You don't know what you're talking about. Put down the gun."

"What are you afraid of? Being buried alive for another sixty years?"

"You don't understand anything. You don't understand the miracle that's been visited upon this town. You should be joyful, and grateful to Seth for his blessing."

"Bullshit."

"Don't do something you'll regret for the rest of your life. Let me explain. Two minutes . . . that's all I ask."

Brant had reached the pulpit. He raised the shotgun to his shoulder and took aim. He wasn't giving the bastard two seconds.

Before he could pull the trigger the pulpit exploded at him, blinding him with flying splinters of wood. He turned away instinctively as Small stepped to the side, a Smith & Wesson revolver heavy in his hand. Small fired two wild shots at Brant as he edged toward the sacristy door.

Brant's watering eyes reduced Small to a blurry figure in black. He pointed the shotgun at the blur and fired, pumped another cartridge into the chamber and fired again. He heard Small cry out. He wiped the tears from his eyes and for a moment thought that Small had escaped. His eyes followed the smear of blood on the sacristy door down to the body lying on the floor. Blood seeped from beneath Small's body and crept across the hardwood floor. The body twitched.

Brant approached it warily. The pistol lay near Small's twitching fingers. Brant kicked it away, then nudged Small with his foot. He kicked him hard in the ribs and watched his face for any reaction. None.

Seth was dead.

Brant pumped another cartridge into the chamber and pointed the barrel at Small's head. It was bare minutes before midnight. If Small came back, Brant was ready for him. After that came burial in a deep, unmarked grave, maybe in a field where he would lie, unsuspected and undisturbed, for decades. Or he would cremate the body and scatter the ashes on the wind. Even Seth's powers of resurrection must have some limit.

He heard a noise, the creak of hinges. The sacristy door was opening slowly. He aimed the shotgun at the door. With Seth dead, the other Risen should have died also.

Whoever was opening the door might be another survivor like Brant. Either that or something was horribly wrong.

The door opened to reveal Sheriff Clark, his hands raised shoulder high. He nudged the door open with his foot.

"I don't want trouble," Clark said. "You wouldn't kill a man in cold blood, would you? I just want to talk."

"Keep your distance," Brant warned. He would've pulled the trigger but he wasn't sure about his ammunition. He didn't want to spend all his shells on Risen and find he had none left for Seth if he came back. There was also the slight chance that Clark, like himself, had escaped the night's slaughter and wasn't Risen at all.

Footsteps behind him. Brant whirled to see Madge Duffy and Doris Gunnarsen enter the sanctuary. He swung the gun back around to cover the Sheriff. Clark had been joined by Frank Gunnarsen. Both men inched toward him from the sacristy, arms raised. Brant heard the murmur of voices on the stairs, coming up from the Sunday School rooms in the basement.

"Stay back," he warned. Risen seemed to be coming out of the woodwork.

He backed toward the side exit, pointing the gun first one way and then the other. Madge and Doris were joined by three other Anderson women, all dressed as if for church, who had been laying out refreshments downstairs. Bernice Tompkins wore a cotton apron and carried a paper cup of punch. They closed on Brant like gawkers surrounding an accident victim.

"Stay back," Brant said again, but they continued to advance. Brant was baffled. They were Risen, they had to be. So why did they fear the gun? Did they know that, with Seth dead, this life was their last? Without Seth to sustain them, would they expire at midnight? It frustrated him that didn't understand what was going on. He was sweating harder now than when he'd shot Small.

Suddenly strong arms closed around him from behind and pinned his arms to his side. The Risen surged forward. Brant closed his finger on the trigger and blasted a hole in Sheriff Clark's gut. Clark went down. The other Risen stepped over his body without a thought.

Frank Gunnarsen grabbed the shotgun and wrested it from Brant's hand. Madge Duffy clawed at his face. Frank drove the butt of the shotgun into Brant's stomach. The air whooshed from Brant's lungs and he fell limp. The arms holding him let him slide to the floor. He looked up to see Jed Grimm. Behind Grimm, the side exit door closed automatically and clicked shut. The others had been a distraction that allowed Jed to slip up on Brant from behind. They didn't fear the gun. They didn't fear death. They were sustained by the power of Seth. The undiminished power of Seth.

"Looks like you shot the wrong man," Jed said, bending down.

The Risen clutched Brant's arms and pinned his legs. They lifted him to a sitting position, twisting his arms until he thought they would pop from their sockets.

Grimm's huge fingers reached for Brant's face, closed over it, gripped it tight. Grimm's other hand grabbed the back of Brant's head.

"How's that stiff neck, Brant?" Grimm asked. "You've been under a lot of pressure lately. It feels tight. I think it wants a twist."

Grimm twisted Brant's head like an oil field worker closing a wellhead. The neck cracked, bones broke, tendons snapped. Brant saw the room spin and go sideways. Then he was looking up at his own shoulder, his head resting loosely against his chest. Behind him he saw Madge Duffy's upside down face smiling at him. Next to Madge, crowding in for a better look, Bernice Tompkins took a loud sip of punch.

* * *

With every corner he turned, fate seemed to move Tom further away from the access road to the highway. Peg sat beside him and stared out the window. Did she notice the two dead bodies inside the car with the shattered windows, or the corpse slung over the Optimists' cannon in the Square? Did she realize how warped the world had become, how tranquil little Anderson had been transformed in the space of a few days into a deadly caricature of itself, an image in a strange and malevolent mirror?

If so, she showed no sign of comprehension. Gunshots peppered the stillness, some in the distance, some alarmingly near. Every pair of headlights he glimpsed convinced Tom to duck the car into the next alley or to douse his own lights and cruise invisibly down another dark street.

He became aware of a pair of lights in the rear view mirror. He watched as the car passed under a street lamp. He recognized it as Carl Tompkins's Acura, an import that had foreshadowed Carl's stocking of Japanese power tools at the hardware store. It was a four-banger and Tom could have left it on a straight-away, but this was no time for a race. Tom was trying to remain inconspicuous. Tom turned the corner and the other car followed.

Tom turned into an alley and the Acura dogged his heels. It was on his tail, all right. He had to lose it. He glanced over at Peg. He'd strapped her in earlier, when he'd turned off the lights and cut the engine and fought the sudden loss of power steering to muscle the Impala into a shadowed driveway and wait for a car to pass. If the cat-and-mouse with Carl turned into a Hollywood car chase of screaming tires and battered steel, at least she wouldn't go flying around the passenger compartment.

He barreled straight through the alley, shot out the other end, bounced on worn-out shocks over the street and plunged into the alley on the opposite side. Carl did the same. He must have had the accelerator pushed to the floor as the Acura closed the space between them.

The Impala was doing sixty down the second alley with the Acura biting at its tail when Tom hit the brakes. The Impala skidded to a halt, kicking up a cloud of dirt, and Tom fought to keep its nose pointed straight ahead. If the car went into a spin, his plan would go bust.

Carl hit his brakes too late. The Acura rear-ended the Impala with a crunch of metal and a loud pop and the swelling air bag smashed Carl back into his seat. He fought it down, cursing. He opened the door and stepped out to face Tom and stare into the barrel of the brand new .22 he'd loaned to Mark Lunger.

Tom put a bullet squarely into Carl Tompkins's forehead. He watched the body fall to the ground, then he rolled it over on its back. Carl's eyes were wide and unseeing. Tom examined the rear end of the Impala. It was damaged but driveable.

He returned to Carl's body, the .22 in hand. Across town, the church bell tolled. Carl's body went into the spastic dance, drew in air to fill empty lungs. Tom watched in fascination, unable to tear his eyes away from the spectacle. He watched the hole he'd put in Carl's head close. He watched as new skin grew to cover the exposed skull. He watched as Carl opened his eyes and registered the gun pointed at his head.

"Shit," Tom said, pulling the trigger. Brant had failed. Anderson belonged to the Risen.

Tom checked Carl's car for weapons. He found a shotgun and a 9mm pistol. He took both and hurried back to the Impala.

Peg stared at him as he climbed in. The fog over her brain seemed to be lifting ever so slightly. She was fighting it hard, forcing herself to focus her eyes and her mind.

"Tom?" she said, puzzled.

"It's all right, Mom," he said as he started the engine. "Everything's going to be all right."

Even in her drugged state, Peg could tell when her boy was lying.

DAY FIVE, TUESDAY

TWENTY-FIVE

Risen walked the streets as if someone had declared a holiday, and maybe someone had.

Tom drove through the city-wide come-as-you-are party as if he had all the time in the world. He saw Toby Morris who worked at the gas station comparing bloodstains with Pete Klassen, one of the nation's few surviving milkmen. Someone had put a bullet straight through the embroidered name patch on Toby's gas station shirt, and Pete proudly displayed the entry and exit holes in his blood encrusted milkman's cap.

Tom saw Lucy Haws, the deputy's depressive sister, strolling down the street in her night clothes, greeting everyone she met with a smile and a wave. He saw Ma from the diner and Merle Tippert from the movie theater and Nathan Smart who played the accordion and his wife Opal who could not be beaten at bridge. Tom wondered if Nathan had squeezed the life from his wife as he squeezed music from his instrument, or if Opal had poisoned the hors d'oeuvres at their weekly bridge game with Opal's sister and her husband.

He saw Bernice Tompkins in a car full of agitated cats, driving slowly and looking from side to side, searching for her husband Carl whose thrice-killed body lay cooling in an alley five blocks away, the only true corpse in a town populated by the dead.

He saw Ira who delivered the mail and Franco who cut his hair. He saw his teachers, his classmates, the people he'd known since he was a child, the people he now recognized as the touchstones of his life.

He knew them all from the schoolyard, the neighborhood, the stores, the softball games, the picnics and county fairs. He knew them as the men who populated Carl Tompkins's hardware store and talked about feed and tools and harvests and wives. He knew them as the women who gathered in twos and threes to gossip and laugh and brag on the children who, at other times, would surely drive them to drink. He knew these people as he knew every lamp post on Main Street, every storefront, every common and boring and steadfast thing in his life, only he no longer knew them at all. With the turning of the earth and the tolling of a bell, they had become something alien, something deadly strange.

They would kill him if they knew he wasn't one of them. So Tom drove slowly, as if he, too, had been invited to the party. When they waved, he waved back, smiling, shooting worried looks at Peg in the passenger's seat.

She stared out the window, her left hand nervously massaging her right. The veil was lifting. She registered the bloodstains and the ripped clothing. She recognized the perversity behind the teeming midnight streets. But the underlying sense of it eluded her. She did not comprehend the why or how. She did not know—or could not summon the concentration—to force onto her face an answering smile or lift her hand in a mock-friendly wave.

It was only a matter of time before someone noticed her detachment. The lethal accusation would sear through the air and ignite the crowd. Risen would swarm the car like locusts, clawing at the windows, tugging at the doors. Someone would have a gun. . . .

"We have to lay low," Tom said. "You need time to clear your head. We'll get a chance to make a break for it soon

They have to sleep sometime. They're still just people, despite everything. They have to sleep."

"Annie," Peg said.

"We'll find Annie when your head's clear," Tom said.

He pulled in behind Ma's Diner and dug through Peg's purse until he found her keys. One of them opened the back door and they slipped inside. He sat Peg in the kitchen and went around to the front and snagged several packets of the No-Doz they kept by the cash register. He poured Peg a glass of water and fed her four of the caffeine pills, then decided what-the-hell and gave her four more. They sat in the darkness of the kitchen and, through the service window, watched the parade of townsfolk march by. Tom heard the church bell ringing, drawing Risen from all corners of the town, luring them out with its Pied Piper tones. It seemed that half the town passed by the diner window. The Meyerses, the Verheidens, the Coles, the Hogans, the Nowlans, the Cardenases. All the familiar faces, the children and grandparents, the high and mighty, the lowly, the pleasant and the mean of heart. All passed by, happy and sinister and murderous as crows. They didn't look in the diner window to see Tom and his mother hunkered in the dark, afraid, wondering if they were the last doomed souls in a town gone mad with life.

Time and caffeine were having their effect on Peg. She sat attentively as Tom told her about his and Brant's research in Junction City, about Eloise and Seth and Donald Pritchett, about their encounters at the roadblock and with Josh Lunger and Cindy Robertson. The flood of reanimated souls outside the diner window slowed to a trickle. Tom started to tell Peg about Reverend Small, but he stopped when she shook her head.

"It isn't Small," she said. "Seth is no stranger."

"But everything started happening when Small moved to town. Before that—"

Peg interrupted with a voice flat with resignation. "They moved the cemetery more than two years ago, before construction ever began on the nuclear plant."

Tom's stomach did a flip-flop.

"Jesus," he said, turning the new fact over in his head. Seth had been loose for two years. He'd been biding his time, studying the town, planning this night for two years. For one wild moment Tom suspected Brant. He'd shown up in Anderson two years ago. Who better to study a town than a reporter? But no, it didn't make any sense. If Brant were Seth, he'd have killed Tom long ago, when Tom first came to him with his fears. He tried to think of other new-comers, but Tom was sixteen years old two years ago, more keenly aware of the comings and goings of baseball players, rock musicians and super-heroes than of the adult population of his home town.

"Who else could it be?" he asked.

"It doesn't matter," Peg replied.

Tom stared at her incredulously, thinking that the tranquilizer hadn't worn off completely. She still wasn't thinking straight, didn't understand any of what he'd told her.

"Mom, listen to me. Seth is the key to everything. We have to kill Seth to put an end to this nightmare!"

"There's no end. One nightmare or another, that's all. Take your choice."

"You're not making sense."

"I don't think you and I would choose the same nightmare."

"It's the drugs. They're still messing you up."

"What was that?"

Peg turned, alert. Tom froze, listening hard.

"Something at the back door," Peg whispered.

Tom went to investigate. He put his ear to the door for long seconds but heard nothing.

"Probably just a cat," he said to the darkness. Then a

bell tinkled and Tom turned to see Peg throwing the front door of the diner wide. He called after her as she ran for the street, toward two figures standing silently in the middle of the road. Brant and Annie. Tom spat an oath and gave chase, the shotgun in his hand.

Annie ran to her mother and launched herself into Peg's arms. Mother and daughter held each other tight. Peg peppered Annie with kisses and murmured her name over and over. Tears from Peg's eyes dampened Annie's face and Annie said, "You're getting me all wet!" and Peg laughed and said she couldn't help it, she was just so glad to have her back.

Tom glared at Brant and ordered him to step away, aiming the shotgun at his head. Brant only smiled and shook his head.

"You know the gun doesn't intimidate me," Brant said. "Besides, I'm not here to convert anyone. Not you, not even Peg. If Seth had wanted to convert your mom, he could have done it long ago."

"So you're one of them."

"They converted me before I could reach Reverend Small, and now I'm glad they did. But none of that matters anymore, Tom. I'm not here as an enemy." Brant put his arm around Peg. He drew her and Annie to his side.

"I want to heal, not destroy," Brant continued. "Your family is broken. You know how nothing's been the same since the accident. Your father's dead and, unfortunately, there's nothing I or Seth or anyone can do about that. I know that I can't take his place, not completely. But I can be here for you and for Peg and Annie. We can be a family, Tom, whole and strong again, living in a wonderful little town. You don't even have to be converted, not if you don't want to."

"Bullshit. Seth is a cancer. Cancer doesn't make deals."

"Come with us to the church. Come and see for yourself. There's no evil at work here. The church is overflowing.

Everybody's there. They're singing hymns . . . you can almost hear them from here. The town's come together like never before. Anderson will be a better place to live than ever, because we're united in our devotion to Seth. We're of one mind."

"Everybody thinking the same, believing the same."

"Exactly!"

"Sounds like hell to me," Tom stated. "I'll keep my own mind, thank you."

Brant sighed.

"I know," he said. "I know how strange it sounds. I was skeptical myself, you'll remember. I fought against Seth, but I'm glad I lost. Seth is the way, Tom. Seth is the answer."

Tom stepped forward, keeping the shotgun trained on Brant's chest.

"Let go of my mom. She and Annie are coming with me."

Annie squeezed Peg tighter.

"No," Annie said, defiant and afraid.

Peg shot a reproving look at Tom and said, "You're scaring Annie."

Annie scares me, Tom thought, and he said, "She isn't Annie, Mom. She's a thing back from the grave. She's a walking corpse."

Peg shook her head angrily as Annie started to cry.

"I won't let you ruin things for us, Tom! Annie's back! I don't care how or why!" Tom started to protest but Peg cut him off. "I said I don't care!"

Brant took a step forward.

"If you won't listen to us," he said, "maybe you'll listen to your friends."

Tom heard a footstep behind him. He whirled to see Galen Ganger's fist fly toward his face. The punch connected and Tom staggered back. He tried to raise the shotgun but Galen's hand clamped over the barrel as his knee dug into Tom's diaphragm, knocking the wind out of him. Galen yanked the gun from Tom's hands. He swung the stock around and connected with the side of Tom's head.

Tom stumbled dizzily. He lifted his eyes to see his other friends circling around him. Darren, Kent, Buzzy . . . they closed in, hands hardened into fists. Shock dulled the feeling of the blows they hammered on his body and head. He was aware of Galen shoving the others aside to pummel him with short, hard jabs to the stomach, to raise a knee into Tom's groin. Tom tried to fight back but his arms refused to lift. He had gone numb, unable to fend off the punches that came at him from every side.

His knees buckled and Tom fell to the ground. Through swelling eyelids he glimpsed his mom and Annie, Peg turning away, Annie watching his beating with emotionless fascination. He saw Brant lead them off.

As darkness deep as the Blacklands closed around him, Tom knew where they were going.

They were going to church.

He was neither dead nor undead, and he felt like hell. The pain when he tried to open his eyes was excruciating, so he left them closed. His arms and legs did not want to move, so he quit trying. He lay on a cold floor with the smell of linoleum and sanctity in his nose and knew where they'd taken him, that they hadn't killed him yet, that something special and terrible lay in store.

A voice whispered into Tom's ear, a snakelike hiss.

"I know you can hear me. You know my name and you know my work. You nearly found me out, you and Brant. You got so close, thanks to your visit to the madhouse. I should've taken care of Donald Pritchett when I had the chance, but I didn't want to do him the favor. I wanted him to suffer for what he did to me."

Tom did not, could not answer. His brain couldn't deal

with the onslaught of sensation and thought and fear and confusion and outrage flooding through it. Maybe Doc Milford had given him a shot. It was all Tom could do to listen and try to understand the words. He could not identify the hiss of a voice, was not even sure whether it came from outside his head or in. He felt the world spinning beneath his prone body on the cool, cool tile.

"Can you imagine what it was like, waking every midnight in that too-short box? Imagine your legs healing and breaking, shattered by confinement, your lungs aching for air that had staled ages before. Every night you wake to the darkness and the damp, to the encroaching earth, your eyes and ears and mouth filled with vermin and decay. Every night the same suffocating death and a moment's respite, then another terrible wakening as the nights and years course by in breathless succession. Can you imagine the never-ending pain, the horror?

"That's what Donald Pritchett did to me, and that's why I let him live. I'll never admit him to my congregation, never. Never."

The world continued to spin, swirling the whispered words around inside Tom's head.

"I've had fun in your little town," the voice continued. "Madge Duffy, the long-suffering murderess, driven to follow in her mother's footsteps. Bernice Tompkins's hands around the throats of her beloved felines. Your own mother, pulling the plug on the object of her obsession. I love women, I honestly do. Men are so easy and uncomplicated and dull. It's the women who give life its color and texture, who make it all worthwhile.

"You and your mother are the last. Your time will come soon, and hers will follow. You're my last indulgence before the next campaign.

"Listen. The congregation is singing. Do you recognize

the hymn? I love the way it sounds, issuing from so many solemn throats, like a dirge."

The voice sang huskily into Tom's ear.

"Come, come, come, come. . . ."

A wave washed through Tom from his toes to his head and deluged his brain. The voice was drowned in the crashing surf. Tom fell into the darkness, fearing where he would emerge.

Brant took Peg's hands in his and told her what to expect.

"He'll be sedated. He won't feel anything. Reverend Small will call you forward and place the knife in your hands. One thrust, right here, up into the heart, and it'll be over."

Peg shook her head.

"I can't do it. I won't."

"You have to. They need this. Seth needs it. It's an act of faith. It demonstrates your good will."

"I can't kill my own son, Brant!"

"You aren't killing anyone. Seth will bring him back. Tom has to be converted, as I was, as Annie was, as we all were except you. How can Seth trust you if you don't trust Seth?"

"It's impossible. I can't."

"You have to stop thinking of it as killing. It's like when you were a kid and you became blood brothers with someone. You pricked your fingers to let blood. It's a ritual, nothing more. Seth will watch over Tom. Seth will restore him. He won't feel a thing, I promise. Doc's seen to that. We can't trust Tom. He isn't one of us. He will be converted, Peg, with or without you."

"Why doesn't Seth just kill me, too, and get it over with?"

"It isn't our place to question Seth's will. He has reasons that we can't comprehend. Fulfillment lies in doing his bidding, and this is what he has commanded. I don't understand it, I don't pretend to. But I don't have to understand to know that it's the right thing to do."

"Do it, Mommy."

Annie had sidled up. She stood on the chair next to Peg's and put her arm around Peg's shoulder.

"You have to do what Seth says," Annie said.

Peg felt the tiny fingers on the back of her neck, stroking her gently. Seth had worked this miracle. What further proof could she need? Her little girl was standing beside her as big as life, playing with her hair the way she always did. Her skin was pale from her long convalescence. It made her eyes seem so dark.

"I believe what you tell me," Peg said, "that Seth will bring him back. I just don't think I can do it. He's my son. Even if he weren't, the thought of taking a knife and . . . and. . . ."

A door opened and the voices of the congregation, joined in a hymn, flowed in. Peg looked up. Reverend Small had entered, walked over to her. He picked up Annie and sat beside Peg, Annie on his lap.

"She doesn't think she can go through with it, Reverend," Brant said.

"But you must," Small said to Peg. "I know it's difficult. It's almost too much to ask. But Seth never asks more of his followers than they are able to give. You'll find the strength."

"But why? I don't understand!"

"Nor did Abraham when God required him to sacrifice a son. Seth asks far less. Tom will be returned to you. It's just a ritual, a step in a passage from one state of being to a higher state. You're helping Tom, actually. He's in pain now. He suffers from many inner demons. It's within your power to banish those demons, Peg. I know it feels strange. I myself converted many of the people who sit outside this room, and every one has thanked me for it. You have to trust Seth implicitly. Trust him with your life, with your children's lives."

He looked at Annie, smiled, and she smiled back. The sight brought grateful tears to Peg's eyes.

Peg and Brant and Reverend Small spoke for several minutes while the congregation intoned their hymn, concluded it and began another.

There's a church in the valley by the wildwood. . . .

"Come," Small said. He stood and extended his hands. Peg reached out for them, and Small gently lifted her to her feet.

The voices behind the door chanted.

Come, come, come, come. . . .

Tom floated over the heads of the congregation on a sea of hands. He stared up at open beams and stained glass windows dark with the night, his head spinning, while many hands conveyed his body like a slab of meat down the length of the sanctuary.

Voices droned in his ears along with an industrial pounding like a great machine, but it was only blood pumping through damaged vessels to a brain knocked senseless and slowly, by painful degrees, groaning back to life. The smell of too many bodies in too small a space was suffocating. His stomach churned and sent bile traveling up his throat to burn bitterly on his tongue. He swallowed, fought down the nausea.

He arrived at the back of the sanctuary. A chorus of voices from outside rose like the roar of hungry animals. He thought for a moment that he would be tossed outside, thrown to the lions and devoured, but the hands spun him around. They grabbed his shirt, tore at it as he passed, ripped it off his body as they propelled him toward the pulpit where Reverend Small shouted and gestured and banged his fist and called for blood.

His head lolled and he saw, upside down, the faces watching his nightmare journey. Galen and Brant waited for him. They grabbed his arms as he came to them over the sea of hands. They held him tight, arms twisted behind his back, kept him on his feet as the swelter and the voices and—he was sure of it now—the drugs dizzied his head and weakened his knees.

With great effort Tom lifted his chin and gazed out over the assemblage. His eyes swam in and out of focus. By ones and twos the faces came and went in the hallucinatory fog. Doc Milford. Deputy Haws. Old Merle Tippert. Clyde Dunwiddey, alarmingly sober. Franz and Irma Klempner, holding hands. Josh Lunger, who had tried to kill him, standing between his parents. Darren and Kent and Buzzy. Cindy, who gave him a reassuring nod and mouthed the words, "I love you."

He scanned the less familiar faces. One of them had hovered behind him and whispered into his ear a story of premature burial and lives corrupted and souls destroyed. Which one was the whisperer from behind? Which one was Seth, the resurrector? Which one had infiltrated and murdered his town?

The preacher's voice thundered and the congregation echoed its response. Isolated words penetrated Tom's consciousness.

Glory.

Dominion.

Seth.

Blood.

Flesh.

Sacrifice.

Blood.

Seth.

Blood.

Blood.

Blood.

A knife appeared in the preacher's hand. It gleamed in the spotlight. A name was called and a figure pulled itself from the mass and stepped forward. Tom focused on the figure as the knife passed from hand to hand.

Peg.

She turned her head to look at him, tears streaming from her eyes. She looked over her shoulder and the gathered mass shouted its encouragement. Her eyes remained long on a single face. Tom followed her gaze and discovered Annie. Sweet Annie, standing on the pew at the front of the sanctuary, her voice joined with the chorus, chanting, calling for Tom's blood.

The world shifted and Tom closed his eyes to the swirl of faces. He opened them again to see Peg approaching with the knife clutched in her hand, borne on a wave of chanting voices. He saw Annie in the front pew, and beside her was Doc Milford, and on the other side, moving closer to fill the space left by Peg, was Jed Grimm.

Grimm smiled at him.

Grimm. Grimm had come to town . . . when?

Two years ago, give or take.

Two years.

"You," Tom said too softly to be heard, his eyes locked onto Grimm's.

Grimm winked.

Then Peg was standing in front of him, blocking his view. Her breath was on his face, her lips brushed his cheek.

"Mom," Tom said, "Don't." He looked deeply into her eyes and she into his, soul searching for soul.

The smallest of motions—Peg shook her head.

The knife glistened, flashed, and struck like a snake.

* * *

"For the common person, nothing is more terrifying than death."

Reverend Small spoke to a standing room only crowd in the sanctuary. His voice was translated over wires to loud-speakers outside the church where believers had gathered on the lawn. Peg, as guest of honor, sat in the front row of pews with Annie and Doc Milford.

"For those of us who have made the farthest journey," Small continued, "death is a viper without fangs. Death holds no terror for the children of Seth.

"For we have seen the terrible dark plain. We have heard the shuffle of the great beasts. We have endured the cries of the damned.

"And we have been delivered by the power and the blessing of Seth back into the world of light and warmth, back into the world of life!

"Seth is our savior! Praise his glory and his name! Hallelujah!"

"Hallelujah!" the congregation replied.

"Hal'lujah!" Annie cried. Peg started at the enthusiasm behind Annie's cry. Annie had always been such a wig-gle-worm in church.

"What are we to do with this blessing? Is it ours to keep secret, to withhold from those unblessed and unknowing of Seth's love?

"No!" Small banged his fist on the pulpit. "No! It is not a treasure to be hoarded by the few! It is a treasure to be shared with all, for the more who share in Seth's blessing, the greater it becomes!"

There was a collective gasp. Peg's heart stopped in her chest as Tom was led out, supported on one side by Brant, on the other by the Ganger boy. He showed the marks of his beating, and he looked drugged.

"Behold, the infidel!" Small announced. He gestured to-ward Tom. "Behold one who would reject Seth's glory!

One who would thwart the dominion of Seth! Behold one who would consign you to death everlasting!"

Peg wished she could seal her ears against the chorus of jeers that issued from the congregation. They leaped to their feet, booing and hissing, reaching for Tom. They don't know I'm not one of them! Peg thought. A reptilian hiss sounded in her ear, and she realized that it was Annie. The voice and the empty eyes were parts of the same dark creature. Peg was less sure, studying the fresh, hissing face, that this creature was her daughter.

Peg closed her eyes. The heat, the sweat, the lack of oxygen made everything seem so unreal.

Of course the creature was Annie. It was the flesh of her flesh. It was. . . .

When did she stop thinking of Annie as "she," and start thinking of her as "it?"

Peg opened her eyes to find Tom gone. No, there he was, floating over the congregation like a supine Christ. Reverend Small was preaching about blood. The blood of the lamb. The weakness of flesh. The need for sacrifice. He read from the Bible. Ezekiel.

"I will drench the land even to the mountains with your flowing blood!" he proclaimed. He seized the Bible in one hand and waved it aloft. "So spake God to Pharaoh! But Seth is not a vengeful God! His bloodletting is not an act of retribution, but an act of love! To spill the blood of the infidel is to embrace him! It is to open our hearts to him and say to him, Welcome, brother! Through your blood shall you know Seth and taste his glory and his greatness!

"Open wide the mortal vein! Rend the impermanent flesh! Let flow the blood that numbers our days and condemns our souls to the eternal void! Cast out the life that fails and admit life everlasting through the blessing of Seth!"

The words struck Peg like stones. She knew what was required of her, and she did have faith in Seth. Tom would

be restored as all the others had been. She was surrounded
by the proof of Seth's power. Reverend Small's speech had
her heart pounding, but had it given her the strength she
needed to carry out his will?

The millipede hands of the congregation transported
Tom in her direction. She watched him approach, arms
spread, head drooping, his eyes black with delirium. He
didn't know what was going on, he couldn't or he would
have fought it. Tom would never go gently. Seth could convert the entire town but Tom would resist to his last breath
if he thought Seth was wrong. Peg herself had taught him
that a hundred people doing something wrong didn't make
it right.

But Seth was right. Annie was the living proof.

Peg rose as Tom approached. She stretched out her
hands to support him. His eyes did not meet hers, and she
wondered if he would recognize her touch. Of course not,
not in a mass like this. It was pure romanticism to think
otherwise.

Brant and the Ganger boy stepped forward to receive
Tom. They stood him on his feet and held him there. Peg
started as hands wrapped around her neck, but it was only
Annie, beaming, her mouth stretched into a wide grin. She
gave Peg a hug.

Peg turned and buried her face in Annie's hair. She'd always loved the way Annie smelled, even when she'd been
playing hard. It was an intimate scent, a blood scent that
united mother and daughter on the most primitive level.
Peg drew on that scent now to give her strength.

But the scent was wrong. It was cool and distant, and
sterile somehow, not antiseptic like the hospital, but life-
less the way Peg imagined the North Pole must smell, or
the peak of Mt. Everest or the sands of Mars.

Peg drew back and Annie asked her what was wrong.
Peg forced a smile and said, "Nothing, sweetie." She heard

Reverend Small mention her name but she couldn't take her eyes off Annie's face, that perfect little-girl face, suddenly grown-up solemn and concerned. Annie looked over Peg's shoulder, toward the pulpit, and her eyes widened with delight.

"Look, Mommy!" Annie exclaimed, pointing. Peg turned around and lifted her eyes to see Reverend Small holding a long, thin knife, the blade ceremonially curved, inscribed with symbols Peg could not decipher.

She had not been listening to the words, but she knew what was expected. Doc Milford nudged her, and the voices of the congregation lifted her to her feet and moved her toward the pulpit. She glanced at Tom. He seemed to be struggling to comprehend what was going on. The knife caught a beam of light and reflected it onto his face. He winced but did not look away. He focused on the knife and the curved blade and the hands that offered and received it. Then his eyes met Peg's and Peg felt the tears pouring out and streaming down her cheeks.

She gripped the knife hard. She looked over her shoulder at the congregation, then to Annie. Dear Annie. Angel. She stood on the pew between the doctor and the mortician, chanting along with the crowd a single word that, through repetition, had become a thought-paralyzing mantra.

"Blood, blood, blood. . . ."

Peg stepped toward Tom, sustained and propelled by the chanting. Tom's eyes were closed as she approached, for which blessing she was thankful. They opened lazily as she drew near, but their gaze washed over her like a searchlight on an empty yard. When they stopped, Peg knew he was looking at Annie. She wondered what he saw—his little sister, or the thing she had become? Tom opened his mouth to speak. His lips formed a word that emerged almost soundlessly.

"You," he said, but not to Peg. To the person behind her shoulder. To Annie?

Peg planted her feet directly before Tom and leaned close and kissed him on the cheek. She fastened her eyes on his, waiting for the moment of contact, resolving on the spot that there must be connection. She would not insulate herself from his shock or his pain or his terror. She would spare herself nothing.

She tried to tell herself that it would be fine once he came back, but then she thought of Annie. Her newly-born doubts crept in and nibbled at her resolve. Annie was changed, she was, there was no denying it. Tom would be changed, too.

The moment came and Tom's eyes locked with Peg's. She gripped the knife harder and let the crowd's voice flow into her arm for strength. She pressed the knife against Tom's skin, aimed the point at his heart.

"Mom, don't," he whispered. The words shattered Peg's determination. Cracked and weakened by doubt, it flew into a thousand pieces. She shook her head.

No.

No, she wouldn't.

Fuck Seth.

The knife flashed and bit deeply into the Ganger boy's side. The boy cried out and let go of Tom and staggered toward the pulpit. Peg felt the knife slip from her fingers but she did not hear it hit the floor. A man screamed and she saw that it was Brant and he was bleeding and Tom held onto the knife that dripped blood. Then Tom knocked her aside and she fell to the floor. When she looked up, she saw Tom sinking under an onslaught of bodies, the center of a whirlpool of screaming faces and pummeling fists.

Then the horror began.

* * *

The instant that Galen's grip on his arm relaxed, Tom saw as if in a vision what he needed to do.

He caught the knife as it fell from Peg's hand and twisted sharply, muscling into Brant. Brant's half-nelson hold on Tom's arm tightened but Tom reached around with the knife and cut a gash into Brant's forearm. Brant yelled and Tom squirmed free. He shoved Peg aside and dove into the pews, squarely at the disbelieving face of Jed Grimm.

Tom buried the knife deep, up to the hilt in the mortician's throat. Grimm bellowed. The voice that emerged gurgled with blood. It was an ancient, animal cry of rage and pain.

Grimm threw out his arms and Tom felt himself lifted off his feet and flying backwards through the air. He landed hard. Immediately Risen swarmed over him, pounding him with their fists, biting and scratching and screaming his name. Suddenly Annie's face was an inch from his, contorted with rage. Her tiny hands clawed at his face.

Tom placed a hand on her chest and shoved her away. His fists lashed out at the twisted faces, connected with the satisfying crunch of cartilage. He bit at the finger pulling at his mouth and tasted blood on his tongue.

He caught a glimpse of Jed Grimm writhing on the floor, blood spewing from his ravaged throat, choking to death as his lungs pulled in blood and expelled it in great, heaving gasps. Doc Milford flung himself on top of Grimm's convulsing body, stuck two fingers into the wound and tried to hold open the airway, but too much blood had already filled Grimm's lungs, too much blood continued to pour into the gash.

Tom rolled into a fetal position, hands curled over his head, and accepted the blows that rained on his body. Fists pounded and feet kicked and he heard a rib crack but he stopped trying to defend himself. He couldn't beat them all. His only hope was to wait it out.

A woman's shriek sounded above all the rest. Moments later the blows ceased and Tom dared to lift his head.

The shrieking woman was Madge Duffy. Her husband John stood with his hands at his throat, desperately clutching parted flesh that had split from one side of his neck to the other. Blood gushed between his fingers. His face wore a look of disbelief and terror as his legs gave way and he toppled to the floor.

Madge fell silent as the back of her head simply disappeared, and she crumbled to the ground.

Cries and moans rose around Tom like tormented ghosts rising from the grave. Everywhere he looked he saw ripped flesh and blood oozing from resurrected wounds.

Deputy Haws clutched his stomach over the neatly patched hole in his shirt. A wet puddle of blood soaked through from the gunshot wound in his belly. Beside him, his sister Lucy gasped for breath that would not come.

Clyde Dunwiddey collapsed with a hole in his forehead and the back of his skull missing.

Frank Gunnarsen's head was a bloody, pulpy mess as he fell.

Cindy Robertson sat upright in a pew and looked at Tom with eyes burning with the sting of betrayal. Blood issued freely from her slashed throat. She did not try to staunch its flow. Her lips formed the question "why," then her eyes died and her head lolled quizzically to one side.

Reverend Small's hands clung to the pulpit as he slipped to the floor.

Doc Milford clutched his gut and fell to his knees, then pitched face first onto the hardwood.

Galen and Darren and Buzzy and Kent screamed in agony as their bodies burnt themselves black. Fat crackled and skin crisped from an invisible heat. Tom turned away, but not before he saw Galen's eyeballs explode in their sockets.

He saw his mother sitting on the floor beside the pulpit. Brant lay beside her, his head cocked at an impossible angle. In her arms, Peg held Annie, cradling her head with one hand. She rocked back and forth and sang in a sweet voice that propelled Tom back to his own childhood, when he was the one she'd cradled and rocked and sung to sleep.

The floor heaved and swayed beneath him as he staggered over to her. His head throbbed and he ached everywhere he could imagine. The stench of the burning bodies tightened his throat so that, when he spoke, his voice was weak, barely more than a whisper. He held out his hand to Peg, but she didn't seem to see it. Her eyes were blank. Tom knew the dark dimension that had claimed her mind. She had taken up residence in the Blacklands.

"Come on," he said. Peg continued to rock the child in her arms, singing sweetly. Tom moved to her side and helped her to her feet.

"We have to go," Tom said. He guided her down the aisle between the pews and the stained glass windows, past Franz Klempner lying on the floor, the charred body of his wife clutched to his bloody chest, past Merle Tippert and Jack and Dolores Frelich, past Mark and Carol Lunger and their son Josh in his Spider-Man pajamas soaked with blood, past all the bodies in all the many contortions of death.

They picked their way across the lawn in front of the church, threading a path among the corpses that had gathered for the midnight service. He found a car with keys in the ignition and drove his mother and sister home.

He left them in the living room. Peg sat in the easy chair and sang to Annie as Tom picked up a few items and headed back to the church. It was the last place he wanted to go, but his work for that night was not yet finished.

He still had to send a man to Hell.

TWENTY-SIX

It was hard to say which swarmed thicker around the corpses, the flies or the reporters.

True to Carl Tompkins's prediction, it was the biggest thing to ever hit Anderson. The networks showed up in force. Police were called in from all corners of Cooves County to barricade the area and seal off the town from curiosity-seekers. The pounding roar of helicopters seemed never to cease.

Because all the bodies were discovered at the church, the comparisons to Jonestown came easily. Phrases like "Satanic cult" and "religious fanatics" were tossed out over the airwaves. As closer examination of the corpses revealed bullet holes with no slugs and murders with no evidence of murderers or weapons, the case took on more mysterious overtones.

Peg screamed and fought and bit and had to be restrained physically and chemically when they took Annie away from her. She was hospitalized in Junction City until arrangements could be made to transfer her to the Greenhaven Convalescent Center.

Tom peacefully accompanied the officers who took him into custody but refused to answer questions until a lawyer could be found to represent him. He was flooded with offers of pro bono representation from attorneys in need of a high-profile case to clinch their book deal, but he accepted the attorney appointed by the court, who advised him to say nothing.

He was placed under twenty-four hour guard at the Junction City Hospital where he was confined for observation, and from which he escaped at eleven o'clock on Tuesday night.

He rode his Honda out to the Cooves County Reservoir and looked out over the still water to the center of the lake. The boat he'd borrowed the night before was still tied to the dock. The chain that had once blocked the access road and the concrete chunk fastened to it were hidden from view. They were wrapped and padlocked around the body of Jed Grimm, which now floated near the bottom of the reservoir.

Tom recalled all too clearly dragging Grimm's body out of the church and loading it into the car. He remembered staring at the nearly bald head as he dragged the body across the grass, weaving around the corpses, and thinking how ironic it was that Seth, who could raise the dead, couldn't resurrect the follicles of his own scalp.

He'd brought the padlocks from home. He'd wrapped Grimm securely with the chains and fastened them tight in two places. If the water rusted them shut, so much the better. Then he'd paddled the body out to the center of the reservoir and dumped it over the side and watched it sink.

He looked at his watch.

Five to midnight.

Five minutes to think about Anderson and all the people he'd grown up with, now dead, sealed in zippered bags awaiting the inquisitive scalpel of the coroner.

To remember Brant, too late and too briefly his mentor.

To remember Merle Tippert's movie house and Carl Tompkins's hardware store, and school, and Galen and Darren and Buzzy and Kent.

To remember Annie as she was in life.

To remember his mom before Seth and her own obsession led her into lunacy.

To remember Cindy Robertson and to imagine everything that might have been.

To remember his past life, which was as distinct from his future and as separate as if a surgeon had parted them with a knife.

His past was everything before midnight. Come twelve, it all would change. He knew that he should return to the hospital. He should face the police and tell his story and let the chips fall where they may. But the call to vanish was strong. He could ride off and never return, hole up in some other no-account town, or disappear in the streets of New York or Los Angeles.

Wherever he ended up, he would never view the world in the same way again. He had discovered the existence behind existence, and he would never be able to put it out of his mind. It would wait in every shadow and lurk in every mystery. It would drive him crazy if he let it.

Twelve o'clock.

Tom watched the crescent moon reflected in the lake. The image shivered and broke as bubbles erupted to the surface. Ripples spread across the water as it boiled. Long, turbulent moments passed.

Eventually the water grew still. The shattered moon restored itself. The ripples died before reaching any shore.

Satisfied, Tom kick-started the Honda and headed for the highway. When he reached it, he would decide which way to turn.

ABOUT THE AUTHOR

Jaroslav Knight has spent most of his life sitting in a small room writing stories. It's what he did in his home town of Wichita, Kansas, and it's what he did after he moved to Los Angeles with his wife, Julie.

He's written comic books, cartoons, screenplays and teleplays. He's worked for Disney, Fox, MGM, Sony/Columbia, Universal and other studios. His work has appeared on ABC, CBS, Fox, the WB and HBO. *Risen* is his first published novel.

Knight maintains a web site at www.AtomBrain.com featuring essays, short fiction and contents that defy categorization.